Boss in the Bedsheets

KATE CANTERBARY

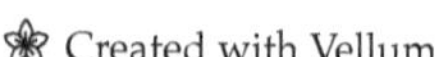 Created with Vellum

ABOUT BOSS IN THE BEDSHEETS

Mr. Santillian,

Despite the fact I'm currently living out of your guest room and sleeping with you most nights, I am writing to announce my resignation effective two weeks from today.

In other words, I'll locate someone who is both obscenely overqualified and willing to devote their days to the handful of tasks you are able to wrench from your perfectionist, micro-managing grip. It may be difficult to find a Nobel laureate genius looking for basic filing work on such short notice, but I'll do my best.

Don't worry about your sister's wedding this weekend. I still plan to attend as your date, assuming you've finished hating me by then.

Thank you in advance for your understanding.

Zelda

Ms. Besh,

Resignation *not* accepted.

I'll see you at home.

Ash

ONE
ASH

Today wasn't off to a good start.

I made a point of arriving at the airport two hours before my flight. That was my way and I didn't care whether it was excessive. Two hours meant plenty of time to unpack my entire life at the security checkpoint and then put it all back together, a leisurely stroll to my gate, and a coffee and snack before takeoff.

That was my way.

I wasn't getting my way today. Not after a morning of hellish Denver traffic, a shitshow at the rental car return lot, and now—apparently—major staffing issues at the baggage check counters. As far as I could tell, the airline had one agent processing a line of passengers that now extended out the terminal door and onto the curb.

I checked my smartwatch again. I had an hour before boarding my flight to Boston and I knew that was enough time to get me from here to the gate but that didn't stop me from scowling at my wrist. Rather than waiting for the pot to boil, I banded my arm over my chest and tucked my hand under my arm.

But sweating over time would've been easier than watching the family of four in front of me. I'd stopped counting but it seemed like a solid estimate to say they had a million pieces of luggage between them as well as a complete inability to gather their boarding passes and passports.

It took everything in me to keep myself from jumping in and organizing them. I blinked, rocked back on my heels, tapped my fist against my lips. And then I checked my watch again. Only two minutes had passed but I lived my life in six-minute billable hour increments. Those two minutes mattered.

The family shuffled away from the counter—not all the way because chaotic messes never cleared out efficiently—and I stepped up, documents in hand. My luggage was on the scale before the agent could ask whether I was checking any bags today.

"One bag checked through to Boston Logan, Mr. Santillian," the agent announced, her gaze glued to her screen. I didn't correct her pronunciation. Not worth the effort to explain it was Sahn-tee-yawn and not San-till-ee-an. Not worth the time. "You'll be departing from gate A35 and your flight is on time."

I shot another glimpse at my watch as I slipped my boarding pass and ID into my pocket. While I had a long, successful history of simultaneously walking and telling time, today just wasn't my day. I knew it while suffering through gridlocked traffic and car rental hassles and the luggage check queue from hell, and I knew it the minute my wingtip connected with child-shaped soft tissue.

Though time slowed to stillness, my body was moving, flying through the air at a speed I couldn't harness. There was a yelp, a scream, the clatter of bags hitting the ground and shoes slapping against linoleum tile, and then a crack, a crunch, a grunt.

The grunt was all mine. The crack and crunch too. The remainder of the noise belonged to everyone else. I knew that as well as I knew this day was well and fully fucked.

From the unpleasant heap in which I'd landed on this unforgiving floor, I blinked up at the terminal's blinding fluorescent lights. I lifted my arm, pouted at my cracked smartwatch. The movement sent pain pulsing through my shoulder, down to my hip. I tasted blood on my tongue.

I gathered myself up, brushed my hands down my trousers. My suit coat sat crumpled against the wall of a vacant counter, my laptop bag beside it. Then I heard a shout in my direction. "Watch where you're going next time, man!"

Glancing back at the source of my stumble, I found several people kneeling beside a child. Tears streaked his cheeks though he appeared intact. "Sorry," I replied. As much as I wanted to suggest the kid—who was anywhere between four and fourteen years old, for all I knew about children—not crouch down in the middle of busy airports, I wasn't dying on that hill. Especially when the clock was ticking and I needed to exchange that preflight coffee for a whiskey sour to ease the throb in my shoulder. Hell, the throb on the entire right side of my body. "Is everyone all right?"

"Fine, no thanks to you," a woman answered. She thumbed away the child's tears.

Out of habit, I consulted my watch. The dead-eyed gaze of the black screen sent a bolt of cool anxiety down my neck, through my belly. I didn't have time to not have the time. Not today. Not after sealing a new deal that would either bring my father around to my vision for our accounting partnership or kill that partnership altogether.

"Again," I started, glancing around the terminal for a clock, "I'm sorry." This fiasco had me four minutes behind schedule and that schedule was already compressed due to the other failings of this day. I bent down to collect my suit coat and laptop bag. Later, I'd thank my good sense for investing in a satchel meant for war zones because I couldn't survive losing my laptop *and* my smartwatch in one shot. "I hope you have a good flight."

I didn't wait for a response, instead marching toward the security checkpoint. All I had to do was disembowel my carry-on, walk barefoot and unbelted through a body scanner, and reassemble myself well enough to order some liquor.

It didn't matter that it was seven thirty in the morning, right?

No, that didn't matter. For as horrible as this day was turning out to be, the week ahead would be worse. I was flat-out slammed, completely overcommitted right now. I still hadn't found a decent auditing assistant to replace the one I'd lost to KMPG. My father and I were long overdue for a serious conversation about the future of our firm. Add to that my broken watch and certainly bruised body, and my plate was overflowing.

But that wasn't all of it.

My sister was getting married next weekend.

But my sister, the one born three and a half minutes after me, wasn't just exchanging vows and then eating some cake. No, that would be asking far too much. My sister and her fiancé were having a wedding rehearsal and a party to welcome their out-of-town guests. All of that was before the actual wedding ceremony and reception but it didn't end there. No, the marital mania extended into brunch the next morning.

Motherfucking brunch.

For reasons I could not comprehend, I was obligated to attend all of these events. I wasn't an out-of-town guest but my mother had verbally backhanded me when I'd questioned whether I could pass on that shindig. And I loved an omelet as much as the next guy but I preferred them without the associated marshmallow fluff of weddings.

That was my plate. Work and work and disapproving dad drama and work with a side of three-day wedding weekend.

Not on my plate was Millie, my on-again, off-again (mostly off) girlfriend. She wasn't on the plate because she woke me up with a text announcing her desire to skip the wedding...and while she was at it, she wanted to explain she was skipping me too.

If I believed in signs, I would've seen that message as a big one. I would've yanked the blankets over my head, changed my flight, and spent the morning eating an omelet unaffiliated with nuptial events. Not because I loved Millie or felt the sting of her rejection but because now I had to explain this shit to my mother, the self-appointed ruler of the seating chart.

But I didn't believe in signs unless they were in a mathematical equation.

———

GETTING DRUNK FIRST THING IN THE MORNING WASN'T PART OF MY standard air travel procedure.

It wasn't part of any procedure of mine. I didn't get drunk. On occasion, I enjoyed a beer or two, a glass of wine if it was offered, maybe a cocktail, but I rarely drank to the point of feeling it the next day. There was no space in my life for hauntings by ghosts of decisions past.

But I was well on my way to drunk this morning.

I had coffee topped with a hearty dose of whiskey and the ache in my shoulder had quieted to a low throb. While I waited for the rest of the passengers to board, I amused myself by scrolling through résumés. I'd never screened applicants while under the influence but I was enjoying it. There was no reason to stress over the complete shortage of qualified candidates. Not when I had a whiskey latte to dull it down to a mild irritation.

That was all it was to everyone else. An irritation. My father couldn't find it in him to get worked up over our glaring need for more support staff, better systems, new revenue sources. He didn't get worked up over anything, not even fiscal year-ends or tax season. I was busy pulling late nights and weekends while he shrugged off the mountains of extensions and corporate filings waiting to be reviewed with little more than, "It will get done."

"Yeah," I muttered to myself. "It gets done because I do it."

Millie wasn't fond of my urgency either. She worked at one of the high-profile management consulting firms in Boston and couldn't conceive of anyone leaving an international financial services giant for a small accounting shop as I had a few years ago. She couldn't understand that shop having enough business to require anything more than nine-to-five either.

"You can go fuck yourself, Millie."

I washed that thought down with another sip and toggled to the next résumé. A quick scan had me copying and pasting my standard "thanks but no thanks" response but I stopped short of sending it when a man edged into my row.

"Hi there." He flashed an amiable smile and gestured toward

me in a way that announced we'd be discussing something rather than sitting beside each other in relative anonymity for five hours. "There was a mix-up with seat assignments. My wife is in the back"—he gestured toward the tail end of the plane —"with our sixteen-month-old."

I bobbed my head as if I understood but I was stuck on the age-in-months thing. When did months stop being the unit of denomination? How many months old was I? Four hundred and…and twenty-five. Shit.

"That's a lot of months," I murmured.

He shrugged, shoved his hands in his pockets. "Yeah, the time really flies." We nodded as if we were talking about the same thing before he continued, "Would you mind switching seats with my wife?"

I blinked down at my watch, once again disappointed to find the lifeless screen. I didn't want to be the prick who wouldn't move to make things easier on a family but *I had a routine.* This day hadn't allowed me to maintain much of it but this was my seat. This seat. 5A. I didn't mind bumping back or forward by a row or two so long as I stayed in the right-hand window seat.

The one time we'd traveled together, Millie had railed against my preferences too. Real business travelers didn't get hung up on that kind of nonsense, I was told. She could go fuck herself. Truly.

It seemed there were multiple benefits to morning drunkenness, one of which being that I required six days to answer simple questions. When I struggled to respond, he waved at the tray table where I'd spread out my laptop, phone, and earbuds. "You've settled in here. No worries. I'll ask the person seated with my wife if she'll move."

I bobbed my head as he stepped into the aisle. "Yeah. Okay."

With that crisis averted, I returned to my email, quickly sending the rejection message before toggling to the next. My approach was simple: scope out recent experience, check it against education, and then scan for finance or accounting keywords. Anything involving revenue, audits, P&L, budgets, margins, expenditures, financial analysis. I could manage this task asleep, or—as this day would have it—drunk.

There was no mention of profit or loss on this résumé, no keywords worth clinging to, no connection to money math whatsoever. It was a dog's breakfast of scattershot jobs and schooling. I found myself shaking my head in dismay as I skimmed the document. How did anyone live a life marked by this much incongruence?

I understood that much of the world didn't operate like me. Most people didn't live by the billable hour and they didn't keep their lives as ordered as a cash flow statement. There was no greater proof than my siblings Linden and Magnolia. We were triplets, for fuck's sake, but we couldn't be more different.

Linden was an arborist and—god help him—only earned a living because I processed invoices, deposited payments, and managed his personal bills. Otherwise, he'd be a thirty-five-year-old man who performed actual tree surgery but had no money and lived with his parents because he never remembered to cash his checks.

My sister had a better handle on business administration but she'd invested a solid portion of her twenties waiting for lightning to strike. Lightning, divine intervention, the arrival of her fairy godmother, whatever. Something *had* hit her because she owned a sought-after landscape architecture firm but I'd survived years of sitting on my hands to keep from shaking sense into her.

They were my only siblings and—without a doubt—my favorite people in the entire world but our brains functioned in radically distinct ways. It'd worked in our favor when we were kids. Magnolia had always been the spirited one, Linden had all the imagination, and I'd kept us fed and watered and out of oncoming traffic.

The beautiful part of being a trio was never leaving anyone behind. From my earliest memories to the baseball game at Fenway two weeks ago, it was the three of us. Even as we'd grown into our separate identities, we'd made a point of sticking together.

But it wasn't just the three of us anymore. Magnolia was getting married and it was a matter of time until a forest nymph claimed Linden as her own. Until this morning, I'd been chugging along with a private promise to make time to live, once I bested this eleven-years-long busy season, and occasionally dating a woman who actively disliked me.

I washed down the melancholy with my boozy latte and blinked at the résumé again. "Hard pass," I said, control-arrowing to my email.

From somewhere behind me, I heard a brittle laugh and, "Hard pass, huh?"

Before my liquor-softened reflexes could find the source of those words, a woman-shaped flash of hot, glowing chaos dropped into the aisle seat beside me.

TWO
ZELDA

Okay, so, things weren't great. But they would be. I just knew it.

Airports were wild and crazy on an average day but forgetting my purse at the bottom of the X-ray machine's conveyor belt and accidentally triggering a terminal-wide lockdown on account of my unintentionally suspicious bag was more than the routine wild and crazy.

What could I say? I got discombobulated with shoving my things back into my backpack while also jamming my feet into shoes. Just like I'd told the grumpy government agents who pointed an excessive number of guns at me in the women's restroom, if I was going to bomb an airport, I would've done it with something spiffier than a beat-up crossbody bag. The most dangerous thing I had in there was a half-eaten bacon, egg, and cheese sandwich but they didn't want to hear that.

Apparently, hypothesizing about airport bombings was ill-advised. If they'd asked my opinion, I would've told them it was also ill-advised to sneak up on someone while they used a public toilet. Yes, sure, I hadn't heard them on account of the podcast blasting through my headphones but wasn't a team of twelve agents a bit much when it came to apprehending one occasionally absentminded woman? It wasn't like I was going to portkey through the plumbing.

I'd hoped for a smoother getaway from Denver. As a matter of course, I always hoped for smooth exits. Graceful like a swan. Hell, I was fine with graceful like migratory geese. Whatever it was that got me the fuck out of here without breaking anything —else.

But shutting down an airport didn't count. That was what I was telling myself. It was a temporary thing and then—lickety-split—back in business.

As I shuffled down the jetway with the rest of the passengers, I mentally picked up the morning's dramas, set them on fire, and sent them out to sea. I couldn't imagine Viking funerals were the norm as far as coping mechanisms went but it worked for me. There was nothing I could do about tripping the terrorist alarm and there was no reason for me to dedicate brain cells to that unfortunate series of events now that it was over.

No brain cells dedicated but you can bet I kept my fingers curled around my purse's strap where it bisected my breasts. It was one thing to toss up my hands in the face of tiny catastrophes of my own creation and proclaim, "This is how I am!"

It was one thing and I'd stuck with that one thing for ages.

I did mean *ages* because this was the way my brain worked and why the hell should I override my brain for the sake of anyone else's preferences? But it was another thing for all of my me-ishness to hit me in the face like a lemon meringue pie.

That was how it was. A pie to the face without the punch line.

I wasn't fun or cute or fascinating or unique or charming or any of the things I'd imagined myself to be. I didn't fit and I didn't fit *in*. Not here in Denver. Probably not anywhere.

I stared at my boarding pass as I stepped onto the airplane anyway. Perhaps my me-ishness didn't fit here and it wouldn't fit anywhere but if I was meant to spend a lifetime gathering up my odds and ends and tucking myself into smaller, quieter, more acceptable shapes, I didn't want to do it while Denver and all its extremities watched.

The recycled oxygen and rhythmic slam of overhead compartments assaulted me as I moved down the aisle, each step an emotional mile from everything I'd left behind. When I spotted my seat, I realized I wasn't leaving. I was already gone.

And maybe—I wasn't sure, but *maybe*—I'd left a long, *long* time ago. My body might've been here in Denver but I'd let go months, perhaps even years ago. If I'd ever been holding on at all.

I dropped into my seat, hugged my backpack to my chest, rested my forehead on the bag's top handle. Doing this felt good and right but that didn't cancel out the whispers of doubt in my mind. Save for a few couches offered for short-term crashing, I had no plans to speak of, no vision. I had money but not *girl living in one of the country's most expensive cities without a job* money.

This is what you do, I heard in my head, a voice all too familiar and disparaging. *You leap and then you look, and that's why your whole life goes to shit. You're a series of mistakes.*

"No, I am not," I whispered. "I sent a million résumés last night and I have places to stay for a month. I looked. *I looked.*"

"Excuse me? Excuse me, miss?"

Dammit. I was the miss. I was always the miss. *Excuse me, miss, your skirt is tucked into your underwear* and *Excuse me, miss, you left your headlights on* and *Excuse me, miss, your credit card was declined* and *Excuse me, miss, that's wet paint.*

I lifted my head and found a man staring down at me, his expression pinched like an apricot past the point of freshness. If he was an air marshal telling me I wasn't cleared for flight after the security checkpoint dramatics, I was going full *Bridesmaids* and making him carry me off this tin can. "Uh, yeah?"

To my surprise, the wilted apricot perked up. "There was a mix-up and my wife and I were seated separately. Would you be willing to take my seat? It's in the front, row five. Business class." He gestured to the woman with a small child on her lap beside me, the one I hadn't noticed during my *what am I doing with my life?* spinout. "No teething kiddos up there."

Pushing to my feet, I replied, "You got it, my friend. Show me the way."

See, this was how I knew everything would work out. I knew it because it always did. The universe had a way of smoothing out the wrinkles in good time and all I had to do was pay my karmic dues and wait for it. And I'd *waited.* Now my karmic dues were giving me a free upgrade to the open bar in business class and I was taking that as a sign I was on my way to the places I needed to go—wherever they were.

But the universe didn't smooth out those wrinkles with an iron. The universe smoothed much in the way retreating glaciers smoothed the Finger Lakes into existence—by dragging massive boulders over the earth and carving up the mantle as it went.

Slow and a bit violent.

And now, this universe had smoothed my path by getting me out of Denver, onto this flight, into business class, and…an arm's length away from a man who was muttering "Hard pass" as he scrolled through—

Oh my god, that was my résumé.

There was a boom in my brain, an explosion that'd waited decades to detonate, and I dropped my backpack into the wide expanse of legroom in front of the vacant seat. "Hard pass, huh?"

This was going to be fast and violent.

"Tell me, friend," I started, gesturing toward his screen, "what's the problem here?"

Instead of responding or—oh, I didn't know, blinking—he stared at me with the type of secondhand shame I'd encountered my entire life. As if he was mortified on my behalf but he couldn't begin to summarize the reasons why. They never knew why they were so damn embarrassed for me and that was because they were embarrassed *with me*. The shame, the mortification—it was always about them. It was how I made them feel, not how I, myself, was feeling.

And yes, of course, there were moments in my life that lived in the shame box. Others in mortification. A great handful in embarrassment. But I wasn't sitting here and beating myself up over it. Not long ago, I'd had a twenty-one-gun salute pointed at me in a public bathroom because I'd spaced out. That was some kind of embarrassment.

But this wasn't that. It was a quick, dam-bursting break from the old normal.

"No, really," I continued. "What's the problem? Why is it a— what did you call it? A *hard pass*?" I forced a snicker. Snickering didn't come naturally to me, probably because I didn't dedicate much time to condescending to others or mocking people. But this guy? The one in the trousers pressed within an inch of their fancy-fiber-loving life? The one with the artfully tousled golden brown hair and the eyebrow arched as if speaking words was too great a request for him? He did more than enough condescending. He could take some coming back in his direction. "It sounds like you're dealing with a kidney stone, not scanning a résumé."

He bobbed his head, his gaze locked on the stripe of blue hair tucked behind my ear. The stripe I'd been told was childish. "Okay."

"No, no, friend. I asked you a question." I tipped my head toward his screen, the one with *Zelda Besh* screaming across the top line. "What's the disqualifier here?"

"I'm sorry but," he started, his infuriatingly beautiful hazel eyes crinkling as he spoke, "what are we talking about?"

I leaned back, crossed my legs, folded my arms over my chest. Stared at him for a beat. "That's my résumé."

"That's not possible." He laughed, but it sounded like a sticky grocery cart wheel. He glowered between me and his screen. "That's…that's just not possible."

"I'm not sure why you're saying that," I replied. "I know what my résumé looks like. I know I sent gobs and gobs of them last night and this morning. When you think about the odds, it's not so impossible."

Another sticky-wheel laugh from Mr. Fancy Pants. "Tell me about the odds, uh"—he glimpsed back at the document on his screen—"Zelda."

He said my name the way most people did at first. *Zellllllda.* As if it wasn't a name so much as a curiosity. If I had a dollar for every time someone asked if it was my real name, I wouldn't be praying my friends didn't mind me squatting in their apartments for more than a few weeks.

"All right, well, this is a flight to Boston," I started, waving both hands at the cabin around us, "and I'd estimate one-quarter to one-third of the passengers live in or around Boston. Given the early morning flight time and day of the week, half of these folks are business travelers." I shot a pointed stare at the trousers-and-dress-shirts dudes across the aisle, the ones with their Bose headphones around their neck and slim laptops on their tray tables. "Even by the most conservative estimates, that means twelve percent of the passengers are Boston-based business travelers. Are you with me so far?"

He blinked but I could tell he wasn't happy about it. Either the blinking or my reasoning. Could've been both. "I'm with you."

I shifted, leaning out into the aisle for a second. "On the low end, it looks like there are two hundred and twenty seats filled, meaning a little more than twenty-seven of them are business-people going home to Boston. Even if we eliminate ninety percent of those twenty-seven on the basis of whatever, the probability of one of those remaining twenty-three having the résumé I blasted all over internet job sites and to all of my friends between Newington and New York is greater than zero."

He stared at me for a long moment. Long enough for one of the flight attendants to march down the aisle, snapping overhead compartments shut as she went, and make her way back to the front. Stared and stared and stared as if he was trying to determine whether I was playing an enormous joke on him or this was a complete hallucination because there was no way in hell I was real. I knew this because I got that question about as frequently as the one about my name—*Are you for real?*

The pilot came over the speaker, drawling on about flight times and headwinds and the current weather at Logan International. The flight attendants yanked the doors shut and briskly paced the aisle. The plane pushed back from the gate with a jerk, and still, he stared at me.

If he could've done it without blinking, I was certain he would've.

The flight attendant stopped at our row and gifted my seatmate with a stern stare. "It's time to stow your tray table and power down all electronic devices, sir."

I smiled up at her while Mr. Fancy Pants complied with the request.

When we were alone again, he lifted his paper coffee cup to his lips and gulped the liquid down, never once breaking his gaze. Then, "How did you do that?"

THREE
ASH

The whiskey, it wasn't a good idea. Not a good idea at all.

I knocked back the rest of it anyway.

I peered at the woman beside me, the one who'd played a probability parlor trick while I tried to figure out whether her eyes were both the same color. All that staring and I still didn't know whether they were dark blue or dark green, or whether the cabin lighting was tricking my mind into believing one was blue and the other green. It was annoying. There was no need for complications in eye color. Nor was there need for staring. I never would've stared at someone the way I was staring at her if whiskey hadn't been involved. "How did you do that?"

The aircraft rolled away from the terminal. Her lips quirked up. "Which part?"

I leaned back, resting my head against the seat. "Start from the beginning. How do you know half of this flight is business travelers? Where are you sourcing that data?"

She stifled a laugh as she unzipped the purse slung across her chest. "Where am I sourcing my data," she murmured, now busy rifling through her bag. "Come on, man. Do I look like

LexisNexis? I'll solve that problem for you too. No, I don't look like LexisNexis but I do know that business travelers account for something like fifteen percent of all air passengers. When taking into consideration the time of day, day of the week, and day relative to holidays and other travel-ish events, it's reasonable to conclude this flight has a much higher concentration of business travelers than the fifteen percent, even if I can't remember where I saw that statistic. It was probably one of those graphs on the bottom corner of the *USA Today* cover."

"That's reliable science," I quipped. The pilot broke in with a muffled update about our position in the takeoff line. I heard but I didn't process. My shoulder fucking hurt and her eyes were annoying. "And the ratio of locals to visitors? Was that an infographic on Facebook?"

She—Zelda, her name was Zelda like legends and Fitzgeralds—leveled me with a glare. "What's the real reason I'm a hard pass? Because it doesn't matter whether I find a pen and show my work all over the back of an arm-long CVS receipt right now. It doesn't matter whether I can remember where my stats come from. It only matters that you passed before I logic'd through the odds of us sitting next to each other on this flight."

I still had my coffee cup tucked against my chest like a shield...or a security blanket. I wasn't sure there was a substantive difference between the two, not in my current predicament. "While that was—uh—bizarre, I'm looking for a specific skill set."

Zelda's brows creased as a flash of understanding crossed her eyes. "Yeah, about that. Which job did I apply for?"

She had a streak of blue hair right behind her ear. I noticed it only when she tucked her hair back. I'd noticed it sixteen times. "Auditing assistant."

Her eyes widened but she chased that reaction away with a shrug. "All right, well, you tell me what the job involves and I'll tell you why I'm perfect."

"That's not really how—no. No." We weren't doing this. It was a bad idea and I was far too distracted by blue hair and mismatched eyes and my fucking shoulder to deal with this. "Look, I'm sorry you heard what I said. It was—it wasn't professional. But this isn't a good fit."

I shifted my attention out the window just as her fingers slipped through her hair, dragging it over her ear a seventeenth time. The terminal faded from view as the plane taxied down the runway. Denver faded as we took off. I studied the sky, the clouds, the mountains until hearing the loudspeaker's chime. I had my laptop out of the seat-back pocket and open on my tray table before the flight attendant spoke.

And I found myself staring at Zelda's résumé once again. *Motherfuck.*

"Let me see if I can get this too," she said, both hands held up in front of her as if she was about to conjure magic. And she could. I hated to admit it but I knew she could. "You prefer things to be"—she held her thumbs and forefingers an inch apart—"just so. You need someone who can organize your things and prepare it all such that you're able to go ahead and do everything because you don't trust anyone to do anything correctly. I am wonderful when it comes to handling egomaniac micromanagers. I have lots of experience in that arena and I don't notice the toxic air quality of being treated like I'm incompetent anymore. I adapt to shit situations shockingly well."

"Excuse me" was all I could manage. And then, "I am not an egomaniac micromanager."

She dropped her hands to her lap and gave me a patient

smile. It was the kind of smile reserved for small, feeble, clueless things. "It's okay, honey. I understand. We don't have to use those words."

"The words are fine," I snapped. "They are fine and they don't describe my management style." I pointed to my screen. "Since you've pushed the issue, Miss Besh, I'd love to hear how your recent experience"—I blinked at the screen, forcing myself to reread the bullet several times for fear the whiskey was playing games on me—"managing a spirituality shop, whatever that is, would meaningfully contribute to my accounting practice."

"Let's start with the spirituality shop piece of this puzzle. It's Denver, my friend. People love their crystals and smudge sticks and tarot readings. Just because you're not pulling cards every day doesn't mean it's not a worthwhile business."

She tucked her hair over her ear again—eighteen—and this was the first time I noticed the tattoo on her inner forearm. The phases of the moon, of course.

"The worthiness of the business isn't my concern at the moment," I replied.

"But it is," she countered. "You said, 'a spirituality shop, whatever that is.' The implication was clear—my job was at a non-mainstream business and thus my experience is equally non-mainstream. You're discounting the possibility that I'm capable of managing a retail store and a staff of part-time clerks as well as tarot readers—who, by the way, are paid as indepen-dent contractors. You're skipping over the part where I handled scheduling and ordering and made sense of daily receipts such that the lights stayed on the entire time I worked there. I kept all of the cats alive too."

I wanted nothing more than to glance at my watch. I wanted to know which segment of this billable hour I was losing to a lecture on the goods and services of some new-age witchcraft emporium.

"While that is fascinating, none of it points to experience with SAP or Oracle," I said, taking another scan of her résumé. "I'm not seeing anything in here that gets at Sarbanes-Oxley or even an entry-level understanding of GAAP."

Nineteen.

"I know you believe those things are essential but I stand behind what I said about you doing all the work," she answered. "And I say that with love so don't get all offended on me now, uh"—she paused, frowned—"I don't know your name. You're elbow-deep in my life history and I don't know your name."

"Ash," I replied. "Ash Santillian." I tapped my keyboard to view the bottom portion of the résumé. "Tell me how your degree in"—I smothered a laugh—"*archaeology* will inform work on financial audits."

"You and your little snicker tell me you don't know much about archaeology." Zelda ran her hands over her denim-clad thighs. "It's not all Indiana Jones and raiding Egyptian tombs."

"Maybe not," I conceded. "But your primary research involves ancient death rituals and something called NAGPRA—"

"The Native American Graves Protection and Repatriation Act of 1990."

"Right. Of course." I nodded because everyone knew that. "And why is it you aren't looking for a role more closely aligned with that study?"

"That's a long story and we don't know each other well enough for long stories."

Before I could argue with Zelda, the flight attendant stopped at our row to take drink orders. When I had a bottle of water on my tray table—no more whiskey for me, thank you—I asked, "What's the short version?"

She made a sour face at her can of Coke. "Most archaeology jobs are in academia. That direction wasn't on the horizon for me."

"And that's why you"—I scrolled the document again—"have spent the past ten years in graduate assistantships and retail and…summer camps?"

She hit me with a severe scowl. "Do not come for summer camp. You won't make it out alive if you think you can condescend to summer camp in my presence."

"All right," I drawled. "But the reality is I need someone who can build spreadsheets—"

"You don't let anyone build your spreadsheets and you know it," she said under her breath.

"—and analyze financial documents for the purpose of providing me a high-level overview—"

"You don't trust anyone else's high-level overviews."

"—and push huge amounts of transactions through data-mining programs to identify trends and anomalies." I stared at her, waiting for another murmur. It didn't come but—twenty. "How is this even interesting to you, Zelda? That's what I don't understand. Even if your background and experience had the slightest bit of overlap with the role, I still don't understand how this job would interest you for more than ten minutes."

She scanned the document on my screen, touched her fingertips to her lips. She was quiet a moment. I had to believe she was searching for a way to agree with me while maintaining she was the ideal candidate. I'd let her have that. I could be right without being a jackass about it. I did it all the time.

But then she grinned. "I'll build you a spreadsheet right now. Tell me what you want it to do for you."

I gulped. Twenty-one.

"What? No. Don't—don't do that." I lifted a hand to wave away her reach for the zipper of her backpack but that sent a snap of pain through my shoulder. A snarl rasped in my throat as I eased back. "You don't have to do that. Okay? I believe you. You're an Excel ninja."

Bent at the waist with her hands frozen on her bag, she frowned at me. "I'm sorry. I didn't hear anything you just said because I think you growled. Like, a second ago. A growly-soundy thing. That came from you. Right? That happened?"

"Not intentionally," I replied.

Still in that awkward, folded-over position, she asked, "Does that happen a lot? That you unintentionally growl at people?"

Her t-shirt was riding up in the back. I didn't want to look but it felt as though every cell in my body was pulling my gaze toward this newly exposed swath of olive skin. I wouldn't let myself peek, not even for a second, but that left me boring a glare straight through her skull. Even as I glared at her, I was aware of the tattoo low on her back, something I couldn't decipher with peripheral vision alone and—god help me—I was working my ass off to keep the words *tramp stamp* out of my mind and mouth.

No need for pejorative comments like that with several hours of confinement ahead of us. Or…ever.

"I didn't growl *at* you," I replied.

She sat back and took her tattoo with her, thank fucking god, but she crossed her arms under her breasts and—and that was not an improvement on this situation. A glance downward would've been worse by orders of magnitude. I knew this. Yet I couldn't climb past the overwhelming urge to *look* at her.

Instead, I looked at my watch. It couldn't tell me the time or the steps I'd walked or how many new emails I had waiting for me though it saved me from something I didn't understand. And I didn't understand it, not at all. Rarely did I find myself with the desire to check someone out or gather more than the most basic information about them. As a point of fact, physical appearance did little for me. I wasn't much attracted to bodies. My dick even less.

Once, Millie and I'd planned to meet downtown for drinks after work. According to her, I walked past her twice before she called my name to get my attention. And now that I was thinking about it, I wasn't positive I'd ever intentionally looked at Millie with the purpose of drinking her in.

I definitely couldn't describe the small of her back.

"It sounded like a growl."

"*I said* I didn't growl at you," I snapped. "There's a difference."

She arched an eyebrow and drew in a breath, somehow aggravated and resigned at the same time. "And you don't want me to build a spreadsheet for you."

"It's not going to change anything, Zelda."

It wasn't. I could not hire this woman. Plenty of people knew how to churn data in Excel. That didn't mean she understood anything about my business. I needed someone with a background in financial accounting, not archaeology. The last thing I had was time to educate someone on the basics of this work. The ideal candidate was someone who could jump right in and knew what I was—

Oh, fuck.

I wanted someone who knew what I was thinking before I thought it.

"Well…" She tipped her head to the side, her eyes wide. I still couldn't make out the colors with certainty and I wasn't about to ask. "No, Ash, it's not going to change the fact you're a bit of a micromanaging tyrant. I could've invented pivot tables and you'd insist on hoarding the work."

She looked away and that was a blessing. I went through life without anyone dismantling my entire existence piece by piece. Sitting here with my head soft on whiskey and my skin tight and sensitive under her gaze wasn't an experience I relished.

"I might be a micromanaging tyrant," I muttered.

"With a hoarding problem," she muttered back.

"And yet somehow, you still want to work for me."

Zelda unzipped the small bag she wore across her chest and set to unpacking the items inside. Wallet, gum, lip balm, rubber bands, keys, woven coin purse, and a napkin-wrapped breakfast sandwich. She piled everything back into the bag, save for the sandwich.

"What the…" My voice trailed off as she lifted the sandwich to her mouth. I reached out, closed my hand around her wrist. "Where did you get that? Better yet, *when* did you get that?"

She glanced at the sandwich, then back at me. "Of course. Mmhmm. You're also a food tyrant. Should've seen that coming. Is it all food or just purse food?"

"I don't even know what purse food *is* but I don't think it's unreasonable to be concerned about how long you've been carrying around scrambled eggs and bacon."

"Unreasonable? No." She considered my hold on her wrist. "On brand? Absolutely."

"Are you really going to eat that?"

Shrugging, she said, "I mean, I'm not building a spreadsheet so…what else am I going to do?"

A slow, distant part of my brain registered the beat of her pulse under my fingertips. I forced myself to release her. "Do you know how to read a cash flow statement? What about a general ledger? P-and-L?"

She set the sandwich down on its grease-spotted napkin. "Give me one and find out."

Since a few companies still reveled in killing trees, I had two glossy annual statements in my bag. I dropped both in her lap. "Find the cash flow statement. Then, talk to me about it."

She laced her fingers together over the reports. "Allow me to save you the suspense and tell you what is going to happen, Ash."

As she spoke, that desire to look at Zelda—to drink in her olive skin, her mermaid tail eyes, her shoulder-length black and blue hair—condensed itself down to a better-but-so-much-worse solution as I found myself gazing at her lips. This was far more acceptable than studying the way her t-shirt stretched across her breasts or the exact specifications of the tattoo at her waist but it was like falling through the devil's trapdoor because now I was thinking about her lips, her mouth. Her taste.

And that was unacceptable. I didn't know whether her heart-shaped lips were naturally that shade of soft, pale pink, but I knew this wasn't normal *for me*. I was more intoxicated than I'd been in years, slowly dying from the pain in my shoulder, and busy resenting seventeen different things. She was nothing more than a novelty and I was nothing more than preoccupied with her.

"And furthermore," she continued, "I think we both know you're going to hate anyone with all the knowledge and experience you claim to want. Since they'll arrive on your door with an armload of competence, they'll labor under the belief that you'll allow them to perform competently. Since we both know what you want—"

"You have no clue what I want, Miss Besh," I interrupted.

She gave me another one of those *you're an idiot* nods. "You keep on thinking that, sweetie. It's nice to believe your moods don't precede you." Another nod. "Anyway. We both know you want someone who is competent enough to stand back and allow you to do everything. I believe it's clear you're not looking for someone with all this experience and education and whatever. You'll struggle to tolerate them. You'll drive them away because you'll keep them on the bench." She paused, squinted at me. "That's why you have this opening, right? Someone left because you wouldn't put them in the game."

It happened again. The growling. This time, Zelda grinned.

"There were a number of factors," I replied. "Small firms don't offer much in the way of upward mobility so—"

"Okay, sweetie. We don't have to talk about that either. We'll file it away with your egomaniacal management style and your aversion to purse sandwiches."

"You can't just walk around with scrambled eggs in your pocket, Zelda," I cried. "It's not—it's not how one transports scrambled eggs."

She reached over, patted my forearm. I tipped my chin down to match the sensation of her hand on my body to its physical form. It didn't make sense to me that it felt this way while looking like an ordinary hand. Her fingernails were painted mint green and, by my estimation, she wore at least twelve tiny rings, and she was going to melt my skin off.

"It's okay," she said, nodding. "We won't talk about it

anymore." She removed her hand. I frowned at my arm because, for the first time in forever, I wanted to find out how it felt for my skin to melt off. I wanted to know the beginning and end of that sensation. "*You* tell *me* about these statements. That way, I can agree with you and you can have a single moment of happiness in your otherwise tyrannical and obsessively pessimistic day."

Well...fuck me.

FOUR
ZELDA

And...there it was. The line. The one I'd long-jumped past because why merely cross a line when you could medal in an Olympic decathlon of awkward?

Because that was what I did. I made it awkward in ten different ways.

This time, I went there with some funny-mean. The entirety of my conversation with Mr. Yes-I-Am-Very-Posh-and-Proper was rooted in funny-mean, but that last comment, the one about him being happy for a hot second, wasn't funny. It was just mean.

It would've been funny if his frown hadn't straightened into a flat, bloodless line and his gaze cooled by a thousand degrees. It would've been funny if it hadn't been the exact button I wasn't meant to push.

Yet that was my gift. My great talent in a life marked by useless gifts and talents. I was direct and honest, and I saw through the bullshit...though *direct*, *honest*, and *no bullshit* were gifts best handled like sweating dynamite. I handled them like a sack of soccer balls. I said quick, snappy things that were horribly inappropriate. I made jokes about myself that were unnecessary. I was quippy in a superbly off-putting way.

Once upon a time, in a faraway land, I was giving a presentation to a big group on ancient burial practices in the Hopewell culture. That was my sweet spot—analyzing archaeological evidence of ancient death customs in the indigenous peoples of North America. One woman kept raising her hand with questions that not-so-gently attacked every shred of research in my slide deck. When she raised her hand toward the end of the session and said, "I'm sorry, can I ask one more thing?" I'd replied with "You're not sorry but go ahead, ask anyway."

So, that was great. Almost as great as informing Ash he only knew how to be happy in tiny increments when spoon-fed righteousness.

And now, with my seatmate blinking at the clouds on the other side of his porthole window, I'd well and truly fucked up. Not only did I turn the screws on his soft spot, but I probably cost myself this job. The one I'd nearly landed. Ash probably wouldn't cop to it but he was warming up to me. If I hadn't stomped all over his tender soul, he might've hired me as an interim helper while he searched for someone with the alphabet soup skill set he thought he wanted. I would've been good at it too. When it came to creating lists and plans, organizing things, and making it easier for smart people to do their work, I was the tits. Sixty years ago, I would've been the top student in my secretarial school class, I would've rocked a beehive and cat's-eye glasses, and my shorthand would've been on point.

But, no. No circle skirt, no retro glasses, no wicked typewriter skills. Not for me.

Because not only did I make it awkward on the regular, I was also fully incapable of reversing course. If I tried to clean up my mess, I only succeeded in leaning into the mess. Case in point, the you're-not-sorry incident. An uncomfortable giggle sounded after I'd said it and the woman announced she'd hold her question. That meant I had to push through the remainder of the presentation knowing I had a one-on-one conversation waiting for me after. Since I wanted the whole damn world to know I wasn't a bitch—because the worst thing for a woman to be was *not nice*—I spent that time responding with uncomfortably kind, sugarcoated answers to everyone else asking questions.

It was like, *Hey, guys! I am* not *that miserable dragon woman who accidentally burned that lady's head off because she was making Swiss cheese out of my work! I am nice, and nice is good even though it's really bullshit, so please like me and all my niceness!*

In the end, I was left with that one-on-one convo from hell. Not unlike this moment right now.

I glanced over at him. Given the way I'd launched myself into this situation, I'd viewed him as the opponent and avoided taking in any of his features. Not a strategic use of time. I'd noticed his hair because it was the stuff of shampoo commercials, and I'd noticed his severely pressed trousers because that crease could slice bread. I'd picked up the basics. Enough to know he was the kind of guy who required things a certain way and that way was both precise and expensive. Now that he was busy blinking at the clouds and resenting my existence, I had an opportunity to look him over.

He was a pretty one. That hair was a good chunk of it. Thick, dark, shot through with natural gold and copper highlights. They had to be natural. That kind of coloring took some coin, and I couldn't see him spending money on highlights when he could invest in aggressive trouser ironing services.

He was a big guy though not so big that he seemed shoehorned into his seat. Broad shoulders, strong arms, trim waist. He wasn't about to Hulk out of his button-down shirt and I appreciated that. There was nothing that stopped me in my tracks faster than spotting man nipples through a dress shirt. Nothing against man nipples but I didn't care to see them poking out at me in the regular course of business.

I shifted my gaze down his body, taking in the long, long lines of his legs. He was a tall one too. I glanced at his shoes, an expensive-looking pair I could only categorize as Fancy Man. But it wasn't the type of shoe that held my attention. It was the old adage about shoes of a *certain size*.

So, naturally, I choked on my own saliva.

Ash whipped his gaze toward me as I coughed. "Do you need the Heimlich or something?"

I shook my head, still coughing and now flapping my hands in front of my face as if that would help anything.

"This is what you get for eating pocket eggs, Zelda."

I tried to wave him off while wiping tears from my cheeks, which turned into slapping my face and patting his arm. Perfect. Just perfect.

He pushed his bottle of water into my palm. "Drink," he ordered.

I complied, chugging while he regarded me with a wary stare. When I'd drained the bottle and coughed myself back into order, I murmured, "Thanks. Sorry for the—you know—this."

He went on staring. "You're wackier than a bag of hammers."

I laughed at that but covered my mouth because it was a rusty, phlegmy laugh that really tested the limits of tolerable behavior among seatmates. "That doesn't sound like something you'd say."

His brows furrowed a bit. "And why not?"

I tugged my lower lip between my teeth, squinted away from him. Glancing away meant I was looking at his enormous shoes again. What was the rule about the foot-penis ratio? Was it one to one? Or was it simply a matter of the sock fitting either way?

"Zelda," he prompted. "Was your brain deprived of oxygen too long?"

I jerked up, forcing myself to meet his eyes and stop thinking about his dick. *Oh my god, I was thinking about his dick!* After I'd called him joyless and tyrannical—oh my god, again! What was wrong with me? Why did I do this? Me and my me-ishness, yes, but I wasn't supposed to invite anyone's dick into that riot. Oh my *god*. "Nope. I'm all right here. All good," I replied. "It just doesn't sound like you. The wacky hammers. You're not a metaphor guy. You're finite, specific, tangible."

He shrugged. "My mom says it a lot. I think I picked it up from her."

I crossed my arms over my torso and grinned. "Ah. I see."

"You need not gloat about it," he replied.

"I'm not gloating." I gave him a dramatic headshake. "I'm pleased that my instinct was correct."

"You delight in that correctness," he said. "You're not going to say 'I told you so,' but you'll feel that. Won't you?"

"And why do you say that? Why wouldn't I hit you with the 'I told you so'?"

His gaze skated over me, taking in my Zion National Forest t-shirt, old as hell jeans, and hot pink low-top Converse as if he was sorting out the pieces of my puzzle. He was gathering the edges and corners, flipping over the upside-down pieces, planning his path through.

"You'd rather be right and bask in your sanctimonious rightness than announce it," he replied.

"Sanctimonious?" I barked. "I'm the sanctimonious one here? Really? That's a special way of looking at it."

He had the balls—god, those were probably big too—to look smug. Maybe it was the dick. And balls. Oh, shit, I had to stop thinking about his serving of fruit and vegetables. It was not the place for my mind to wander. Aside from the fact he abhorred everything about me, I wanted to get a job with him. I wasn't looking to give him one, not…really. I snickered at that thought, covering my face with my hands to hide it from him.

"Please tell me you're not choking again," he said. "I'm out of water."

"Not choking," I replied, still behind my hands. "Just clearing my head. Finding my center. Spot meditating. It's a Colorado thing. You wouldn't understand."

Ash didn't say anything and after a moment I peeked at him. He was staring at his smartwatch though the screen was blank. I wanted to run my fingers through his ridiculously beautiful hair and trace his eyebrows and fold him into a hug, and I didn't know where the fuck any of it came from. Something about the way he turned that sorrowful gaze toward his watch, his brows pinched and his shoulders slumped, made me want to fix everything for him.

That was another one of my gifts and talents: adopting problems that didn't belong to me. It sat alongside quippy comments and creating order from the most irrational patterns. In the right situations, it made me indispensable. I could be the Girl Friday of whatever the fuck you needed. In the wrong situations, it grew toxic relationships like mushrooms in a shady patch of grass. Some of those mushrooms were innocuous but a few would kill you dead if you ate enough. Some could even kill you with the barest of touches.

I was a hot, messy mess with more problems than solutions. I didn't know where I was going or how I'd get there but a messy life was better than one hundred tidy deaths from that same old patch of toxic mushrooms back in Denver.

"I'm going to assist the shit out of you," I announced. "I hope you're ready for the full force of me and my sanctimonious assisting."

He gave his watch another baleful stare before glancing over at me. "I'm not sure how I could possibly prepare for something like that."

I nodded. "Fair point."

———

AFTER I ANNOUNCED TO ASH THAT I WOULD BE HIS ASSISTANT— carpe that fucking diem, right?—things in row five went from weird to strange.

First, when I asked if he wanted me to start tomorrow, he replied, "Yes."

Just "yes." He didn't even try to dismiss the question. Didn't revisit his original argument that I wasn't qualified to reload the toner in his copy machine or whichever tiny tasks he allowed others to complete.

After that bizarre response, I asked if he was placating me. He shook his head and said, "No."

Then, when the flight attendant stopped at our row with breakfast offerings—served on real plates, no less—he accepted the assortment of fruit, bread, and yogurt, and asked, "Do you have any cookies?"

Cookies. The last thing I'd expected from Fancy-Man Shoes was cookies for breakfast.

Of course, the flight attendant accommodated him. I wasn't sure anyone could look at him with his Please Touch Me hair and I'm Never Satisfied pout and deny him anything. It was second nature to argue with him but denying him cookies was another matter.

I only half liked the guy and I already knew I'd give him the cookies. Every damn time.

The final bridge to strange materialized while Ash housed two saucer-sized chocolate chip cookies in the time it took me to unfold my napkin. He wolfed them down like they were the last cookies he'd ever see and we were there, firmly in the land of strange.

"Okay, so," I started, wagging my spoon in his direction, "let's talk about something. Anything. What's going on with you right now? What do you have on deck for projects or clients or enemy targets?" When he responded with a shrug I could only interpret as irritated indifference, I continued. "Am I interrupting your private cookie time?"

"A little bit, yeah." He tipped his head toward my breakfast tray but didn't meet my eyes. "Better than pocket eggs?"

"Hardly," I answered. "I like finely sliced melon as much as the next upper-crusty lady but there is something profoundly American about the breakfast sandwich."

That did the trick. He shifted, blinked over at me. Ogled me as if he expected me to shape-shift into a Fourth of July fire-cracker. And...I wanted that. I wanted his attention and I didn't care if I had to dig in my usual bag of crazy to get it. My me-ishness came in handy once in a while.

"You derive nationalist pride from a sandwich? One I believe you had encased in an *English* muffin?"

"Hell no. But you have to agree that breakfast sandwiches are a homegrown construct," I argued. "Mindless consumption with the purpose of checking off a box and getting another one of the day's tasks done is an American right. In our gilded, antiquated view of people in other parts of the world, breakfast still exists as a seated, plated experience with someone's little old grandmother toiling over a pot of porridge at the hearth."

Ash snatched a strawberry from my plate, popped it in his mouth while he stared at me. Then another.

Strange, population: the two of us.

He blinked and I was forced to admire his long, thick eyelashes. This prickly, discontented man had all the best things. Then he said, "She probably chops her own wood too. Right?"

"No, she does not," I cried. "She's the little old grandmother. She's not chopping wood. Her ass-kicking granddaughter does it or maybe the nice widower from down the road. He always has fresh wood for Grandma."

Ash's eyes widened and then—then he burst out laughing. It wasn't a *ha ha, that was funny* moment. It was one of those *I might die laughing* moments. And I couldn't help it, I started laughing too. We laughed and snorted and cried in the most raucous ways.

I didn't have to look around to know we'd attracted a significant amount of attention from our fellow passengers. I knew how it felt for others to stare but I had no interest in staring back at them. Not when I could stare at Ash while he seemed light and happy for the first time.

"That wasn't what I meant, you know." I brushed the tears from my lashes. "You were the one who heard it that way."

Ash rubbed the back of his neck. "There was only one way to hear it, Zelda." A quiet laugh moved through him as he spared me a quick glance. He was frowning but it was still a smile. I kind of loved that smile from him. "I can't believe you said that. My god. 'Fresh wood for Grandma.'"

"We were talking about breakfast," I said, my tone tart.

"Yeah, that widower down the road eats well at breakfast," Ash replied.

With a gasp, I slapped a hand over my mouth. "Ash Santillian, you filthy bird."

"That wasn't what I meant. You heard it that way," he replied, feeding my words back to me.

I stole the chocolate croissant off his tray since we were now in the business of sharing snacks and innuendos. "I heard it exactly the way you meant it."

I tore the croissant in half and something about that action snapped Ash out of the iridescent bubble of strange we'd wandered into because he scrambled to shake out his napkin and drop it on my lap. "Fuck, Zelda. You have crumbs all over you."

Not breaking my gaze on him, I brushed a hand down my t-shirt to dislodge the crumbs threatening his sanity. "All better."

I took a bite and knew from the flare of his eyes that a new wave of croissant confetti littered my shirt.

"Actually, it's not," he murmured, shaking his head. "Let me."

He reached over but stopped with his fingers poised a breath away from my breasts. His lips parted and I heard a pained noise rattling in the back of his throat. It hadn't occurred to him until right now that he was going to feel me up in the pursuit of crumb control.

"Mmhmm," I murmured, tipping my head to catch his gaze. "Let you do…what, exactly?"

"I—um. Hmm." He snapped back, folding his arms over his chest and staring straight ahead. "Sorry."

"About giving me the *well, actually* treatment over a flaky croissant or nearly fondling me?"

He didn't look at me when he asked, "Which would you prefer?"

I…I didn't know.

And I didn't like that at all.

FIVE
ASH

Not long ago, I'd thought this day was off to a rough start.

I'd considered traffic and text message breakups and airport lines and smashing my shoulder into hard flooring to be rough.

That was before I reached for a woman's breast without her enthusiastic interest and then had to sit next to her for three more hours.

I was certain I could stare out the window that long. That was my only option as I saw it. I couldn't open my laptop and bang out a few reports while we pretended my hand hadn't been close enough to the underside of her breast to feel the heat of her. I couldn't pick up the mess I kept creating with Zelda and go back to business as usual. And I wanted business as usual but the inertia was all wrong.

Instead of working or staring out the window, I chose the next worst option: I fell asleep.

Now, I considered myself an experienced business traveler. I was in the air several days each month. That was all to say I knew how to nap on an airplane. I knew how to nod off without incident or neck injury.

All that business traveler's experience died with my watch today because I didn't simply fall asleep. I fell asleep on Zelda's shoulder and I slept there for the duration of the flight. This wasn't an innocent case of resting my head on her shoulder. No, it wasn't that at all. I'd shifted my entire body toward her and nestled myself into the cove of her shoulder. I was breathing—and I couldn't stress this enough—*on her neck.*

I woke up only when she patted my hand—the one I'd dropped onto her thigh—and whispered, "Ash, we're landing."

It took several seconds for those words to mean anything to me and I spent that time stroking my thumb along the inseam of her jeans. Then, the wheels hit the runway and I realized what I was doing.

"Oh—oh fuck." I jolted away from Zelda with enough force to knock me back against the window. "Oh, fuck," I said, groaning at the pain radiating through my shoulder. "That fucking hurt."

"Are you all right?" She reached for me but I kept myself plastered against the solid safety of the aircraft's wall.

I waved her off. "Fine, fine," I replied, flattening my hand against the offending shoulder. "I can't believe I, you know, I did that. I'm sorry." I glanced at her, too deep in my embarrassment to meet her eyes for long. "You should've pushed me away."

"So now it's my fault?"

We stared at each other while the pilot and flight attendants made announcements about baggage claim and items in over-head compartments shifting during flight. When quiet settled between us, I said, "It's not your fault. I was, um, no. Not your fault. I was only attempting to indicate that you were well within your rights to elbow me in the throat."

"Yeah." Her lips pursed in a pout as she nodded. "I know."

Her gaze darted to my shoulder as I doubled down on my attempts to ease the pain there. "Are you all right?"

I bobbed my head. "Completely fine. There was an incident in the terminal this morning and I clipped it at a strange angle."

Zelda unbuckled her seat belt and shifted to her knees. She reached for my collar, loosened the top three buttons, and slipped her hand under my shirt.

I yelped when her fingers connected with the most tender spot. "Sorry," I murmured. "Like I said, it's completely fine. Just a little sore."

A quiet laugh slipped past her lips before she gazed up at me. "Listen, my friend. I think your shoulder is dislocated. I don't know for sure but after enough years as a camp counselor, you learn how to spot these things."

Her hand traveled down my chest, over my collarbone, and along the back side of my shoulder, and my body was so confused. Her touch wasn't meant to be intimate, I knew that, but my skin hadn't received the same message.

I was a sucker for little touches like that. I didn't need to paw at someone in public—contrary to my behavior this morning—but I loved the little touches. And right now, my skin was under the impression we were adoring these little touches.

"In my first act as your assistant, I'm telling you this needs to be examined by a medical professional," she said, her palm still pressed to my back. "Why don't you tell me your doctor's name and I'll make you an appointment. All assistant-y and everything."

I blinked at her because—holy fucking shit—I'd tacitly hired her, and then—then all of this happened. "I'm sure it's fine but thank you for your concern."

"Okay. I see how it's going to be. I have to convince you to do things even though we both know they're the best course of action. That's cool. I can do that." She buttoned my shirt and gave the placket a quick pat when she was finished. "Ash, your shoulder is probably dislocated and if you allow it to stay in that condition, you'll have long-term damage. I could be wrong but I think you like being able to pull shirts over your head and wash your hair and, I don't know, play squash."

"You think I play *squash*?"

She held up both hands, shrugging. "Let's just say I'd believe it if you did."

Another one of those growl sounded in my throat. "I don't play squash."

"Well, you're doing something to maintain"—she zigzagged a finger at me—"all of this. I'm sure you'll want to be able to kick the golf ball and swing for the field goal and long jump to home plate."

"Now you're just being ridiculous," I said.

"Maybe," she conceded. "But don't forget you won't be able to type real fast on your laptop if one of your arms is fucked-up." Her eyes widened in amusement as I considered this. "Yeah. That's a big one, huh? Bigger than giving up pickleball or cornhole."

"Giving up what?" I asked, laughing.

"Oh, come on. You know, pickleball. The game you get when you screw with the genetic code of tennis, ping-pong, and badminton." She nodded as if this should make sense to me. "And cornhole is the hipster cousin of horseshoes, quite frankly. If I had a slab of plywood, I would definitely drill a hole in it and then ritualistically toss some beanbags into that hole. For sure. That is good, old-fashioned entertainment right there."

"I think I heard my sister saying she's having some cornhole games set up at her wedding reception next weekend." I glanced out the window, hoping I'd find an explanation as to why we were still trapped in the airplane despite being parked at the gate.

"See? You'll need to be in top cornholing shape," Zelda replied. "And I don't know your sister but I'm positive she wouldn't want you and your jacked-up shoulder situation ruining her photos. By next weekend, you're going to have a teeter-totter thing going on, one shoulder higher than the other. Sorry, Lurch, but your sister isn't allowing that." She shook her head. "What do you say? Why don't we call that doctor now?"

Finally, the aircraft doors gusted open and the passengers around us surged to their feet. Zelda shrugged her backpack on and waited in the aisle for me to join her. I followed but made the error of trying to swing my laptop bag over my injured shoulder. The pain nearly buckled my knees. Zelda observed all of this and tried to take the bag from me but I brushed off her advances and shifted it to the other arm as if I wasn't choking back a horrible cocktail of vomit, tears, and wounded animal whimpers.

We walked up the jetway and through the busy terminal in silence. When we reached the escalator to the baggage claim, I gestured for her to go ahead of me.

"It's funny that this is your chivalry," she said, paused at the entrance. "Of all the ways for you to show any gendered deference, you choose the ladies-first route here."

I had fifteen different things to say to her. Most of them contradictory and too opaque to form into clear thoughts. Most of them lurked around the reality that I didn't know how to interact with Zelda. She didn't fit into a tidy LinkedIn headline. She wasn't the standard formula of adjective, job title, career goal. And she was unlike anyone else in my life. I didn't know anyone who existed the way she did, all blue-streaked hair and moon tattoos and math tricks. And the rest of it too—her willingness to let me get away with shit as long as she could point it out in the process. Her refusal to take no for an answer. Her addictive warmth. I didn't know what to do with her.

All I could say was, "Zelda, people are waiting behind you."

She stepped onto the escalator. I followed.

IF I WAS THE KIND OF MAN WHO MEASURED MASCULINITY BY SHOWS of strength, that masculinity would've been shredded after a visit to the nearest urgent care clinic with Zelda.

It'd started long before this point but it went downhill when I tried to grab my luggage from baggage claim. I was certain I'd heard bone scraping against bone when reaching for the handle and pulling the suitcase off the belt. It sounded awful and felt a thousand times worse, but I didn't have to tell Zelda any of that. No, crying out and dropping the item on my foot was plenty of an announcement.

She was good enough to gather me up, busted shoulder, sore foot, nasty mood and all, and cart us and the sum of our luggage out of the terminal. She poured me into a car and pointed the driver in the direction of the clinic while I grumbled about my terrible day.

Then, I hadn't objected when she followed me into the exam room. I should have. I should've instructed her to stay in the waiting room but I didn't. I told myself I allowed her to join because I wasn't thinking clearly. I wasn't myself. The whiskey—

what a terrible idea—and my shoulder and the entirety of this day. And I let myself believe that.

I believed it when Zelda helped me out of my shirt and while she chattered on about nonsensical things between the doctor's exam and X-ray. She only stopped talking about whatever it was for brief moments. There was never enough silence for me to take stock of these events. It was probably better that way. I'd experienced enough reality for one day.

"Oh, this is going to be fine," Zelda said as the door closed behind the doctor. He'd gone to collect the supplies necessary to reduce my shoulder without worsening the hairline fracture to my collarbone, which was a technical way of saying he intended to manipulate my bones back into their proper places in a manner that sounded remarkably medieval.

"We must've heard different things because I heard 'intense pain and pressure,'" I replied.

"'Intense but *brief* pressure and pain.'"

"Yeah. That makes it so much better," I answered. "The only way this could be more intense would be if this guy rips my fucking arm off."

Zelda sat back in the chair beside the exam table, crossed her legs and folded her arms over her torso. "Riddle me this, boss. How did you sit through that entire flight with a bone halfway out of the socket? Because you were as pleasant as a peach, or, you know, as pleasant as you get. Not until we landed did I realize things were amiss in Ashville."

I ran my palm over my chest, suddenly aware I was half naked with a relative stranger by my side. The morning was a distant, misshapen memory. I couldn't remember where I was supposed to be this evening or what I'd meant to accomplish today. It wasn't this. It wasn't hiring an archaeologist as an auditing assistant and it wasn't dislocating bones. And I was annoyed about all that, annoyed about losing the day—and my watch. Annoyed about reverting back to some helpless infant version of myself. Annoyed about the entire disaster. "Whiskey," I answered. "A large volume of it."

She hummed in response, bounced her leg, and then, "Does that happen often?"

I glanced over at Zelda and found her worrying a spot on her jeans with her fingernail. "Which part?"

She didn't look away from her jeans. "All of it. Any of it. Whatever."

I continued watching as she worked her nail against the fabric. As far as I could tell, there was nothing there but she had a way of seeing things everyone else missed. Maybe it was that she saw the things no one wanted seen. Or some of both.

"No. Not often," I said.

Zelda bobbed her head a bit. "What does often mean to you?"

"It means there's usually only beer in my fridge when my brother buys it," I answered. "It means an expensive bottle of Scotch has been in my office for at least two years, since whenever I wrapped up the Hudson-Bolton audit, and it's only half empty."

"No more self-medicating, okay? I don't like being around that kind of behavior and it's not how I'm going to run this office. I won't have any of the Don Draper routine from you."

I leaned back on my good arm, peered at her. "Why do I have the impression I've hired the Mary Poppins of tax and audit?"

Zelda hit me with a slight smirk. "Not sure if I'm practically perfect in every way but it's possible."

I almost responded, insisting it was more than a possibility, but the doctor returned with several assistants and a large syringe.

"What the—is that for me?" I pointed at the syringe. It looked like a drill bit. "That doesn't seem necessary."

The doctor had the audacity to laugh. *Laugh.* "You'll barely feel this thing and you'll appreciate the muscle relaxant when it's on board. There's an anti-nausea drug mixed in and that stuff stings but I promise the sting will be worth it."

Zelda pushed to her feet and closed her hand around mine. "We're not going to look. Let's talk about something else," she said. "Tell me what's going on at the office. What are your issues and priorities right now?"

I stared at Zelda while a medical assistant rubbed an alcohol swab over my bicep. For the first time, I noticed a constellation of studs and hoops dancing up her left earlobe. A thin bar extended across the upper shell.

"How long have you had all those earrings?" The doctor was right about not feeling the needle. He was also right about the sting. I snapped my eyes shut as the medicine burned into my blood. "How many do you have there? Six, seven?"

"Two lobe, two snug, one helix, one industrial," she answered. "So, six. I've been adding to my collection since I was nine, although to be fair, I went ten years between my first and second piercings. It's picked up a bit since then." She paused, glanced at the squad of healthcare providers on the other side of the room. I didn't look away from her ear. "I've been thinking about a daith, but I haven't gotten around to it."

"You've been very busy," I replied with a grave nod. I didn't know what half of those words meant. I wasn't going to ruin it by asking. "By virtue of the pocket eggs alone, I have to believe you don't have a free moment to enjoy breakfast."

"That's where you're wrong. I enjoy the shit out of breakfast," she said. "Give me blueberry pancakes and crispy bacon and a nice, cheesy omelet and I'm a happy girl. But since I don't have a household staff to flip those pancakes and fry that bacon, I'm left to my own devices. Sadly, I must confess my devices aren't great."

"I don't believe that." My gaze slipped from her ear to her lips. They were full and pale and bare. No tint or shine to be seen. "Your devices are amazing."

She laughed and I was certain I felt the sound in my vital organs. It was then I registered the warm looseness melting my muscles. I felt like a marshmallow.

"It's my one deficit," she said. "That's why I stick with the pocket eggs."

One of the medical assistants eased me down, onto my side. If I cared about being the right kind of masculine, I wouldn't have twined my good arm around Zelda's or laced her fingers with mine. I would've whipped my belt off and gnashed my teeth into the leather and promised her a demonstration of high pain thresholds. But I didn't care. As I stared into her dark eyes, our noses nearly touching, I couldn't imagine a reason why I'd want to be anything other than my true self with her.

"I can't deal with that," I said. "Eggs don't belong in your pocketbook."

"No one calls it that, sweetie," she replied. "It's been a good twenty or thirty years since anyone carried a pocketbook."

"My mother carries one," I said. "That's exactly what she calls it. She keeps a little calendar in there too. The kind with a plastic cover and three years' worth of dates."

"Your mother sounds like a busy woman." Zelda held my gaze while the doctor moved my arm and drove his fingers into my tissue. I gave her hand a squeeze. "She's gotta keep her affairs in order."

"She's always on the hunt," I said. Zelda laughed, big and bright and close enough for me to feel it. Really feel it. "This is a very unusual first day on the job."

She shrugged. "Are most days like this?"

The doctor said something about the next part being quick and advising me to take a deep breath and breathe through it, but I asked, "Is it wrong for me to want them all to be like this?"

SIX

ZELDA

WHEN I PACKED MY THINGS AND LEFT HOME THIS MORNING, I hadn't started with a detailed idea of how this day would shake out. I wasn't a detailed idea kind of girl. I jumped first and worked my ass off to build the parachute before I hit the ground.

But even if I'd plotted this day down to the second, learning the sound bones and joints made when they popped into place wouldn't have hit the list. Breaking into Ash's apartment because he was too drugged to find his keys wouldn't have been on there either. Realistically, we could've asked one of his neighbors to call the property manager or returned to the lobby to find a security guard, but this guy was looped off his ass and I needed the bathroom, ASAP. Busting our way in was the fastest solution.

Once the lock disengaged, I wedged the door open with our luggage. If I'd learned anything from ushering him out of the urgent care clinic with his shoulder freshly set and cinched in a sling, it was that I'd end up supporting some of his weight and I couldn't do that while moving luggage or holding doors.

"This is where I live," Ash bellowed to the empty hallway. "And you're here too, Zelda."

I swung my arm around his waist and urged him away from the wall. "No lies detected."

"How did you know where I lived?" I deposited him on a bench just inside the door, grabbed our bags, and locked the door behind me. His head thunked against the wall and he huffed out a quiet, "Fucking ouch."

"Your address is on your luggage. Also your license, which I needed for the insurance paperwork," I called as I went in search of a bathroom. "Stay right there. Do not move."

I breathed a giant sigh of relief when I pushed open a door and found a sleek bathroom on the other side. I should've drawn some inferences about Ash or his apartment from the elegant fixtures and wallpaper that looked like real grass cloth but my bladder was too full for that kind of thinking.

Once I was finished, I washed my hands under the motion-activated faucet. Now, that required no inference. I was drying my hands on a dark green towel when the door burst open and Ash stumbled in, his feet bare.

"Do I want to know what happened to your shoes and socks?" I asked.

"Zelda, when did you get here?"

"You've been alone less than two minutes. How did you forget everything and lose your shoes in that time?" With his only free hand, he wrestled his belt open, worked his zipper down, reached into his trousers. "What—what are you doing?" I whirled around before seeing anything but I couldn't help but overhear what came next. "I don't know what you're paying me but I'd like a raise."

The toilet flushed behind me and the faucet switched on. "Name your price, Zelda. Whatever it is, I'll double it."

I peeked over my shoulder, found his trousers gaping open but the essentials stowed away. "That seems fair," I said. "Let's get you into bed, okay? You should sleep while you can't feel anything."

Ash reached for my hand, his still dripping wet, and brought it to his jaw. He was scruffy, the day's stubble thicker and darker than it was when I first sat down beside him.

"I can feel this." He dragged my palm up the carved granite of his jaw, rasping over his whiskers. He was rough and hard, and watching me. I held my breath, watched him watching me. He lifted his other hand to my face, cupped my jaw. "I can feel this too." His gaze dropped to my lips and lingered there. When he blinked up at me, he sifted his fingers through my hair. "I can feel you."

This wasn't on my list either.

"Yeah, it seems like you can but you'll be feeling something different in the morning. Something in your shoulder, that is. Not—not anywhere else." I pivoted out of this near embrace and herded him out of the bathroom, into the hall. "Where's your bedroom?"

He paused, flattened his hand on the wall, glanced around. "It's in my apartment."

"Yeah, that's a big help." As we shuffled down the hall, I spotted his shoes and socks, one of each abandoned every few steps. I almost laughed but shouldering the weight of a two-hundred-and-something-pound man required all my energy. "Here's the deal, Ashville. When we find your bed, you're going to snuggle up and go to sleep. Agreed?"

"Have you met Kirby yet? He's my pet."

"You…what?" I glanced around, half expecting to be attacked by a creature befitting my new boss. Something like a tarantula or, I didn't know, a ferret. "You have a pet?"

"Yeah. Kirby. He's my three-headed cactus. He stands guard and keeps watch over the kingdom." Ash pointed to the kitchen and yeah, a round cactus with three 'heads' extending from the body sat in a ceramic pot on the countertop. "Do we have any ice cream?"

We crossed a living room straight out of a home décor magazine and traveled down another hallway. "Not sure, sweetie. I can't imagine you keeping ice cream in the freezer. Seems about as off-vibe as you eating cookies for breakfast," I replied, kicking open a door. "Oh, thank god, it's a bedroom."

Ash leaned into me for a long, heavy moment where I let myself welcome that contact. It was new and foreign and amazing. And it'd been so long. Years and years without a touch like this had been almost enough to convince me I didn't need it the way I needed light and air. I needed it more than anything.

Then, he rasped, "I have missed my bed so much." He stumbled away from me, his limbs slow and uncoordinated as he weaved toward the bed. Before I could stop him, he flopped onto his back and promptly shouted, "Fuuuuuuucking ouch."

"Okay, okay. Easy there," I whispered, rushing to his side. "Let's get you situated."

Putting a grown man to bed was about as simple as swaddling a bullfrog. He wiggled and rolled, and struggled to find a comfortable position. I almost had him there when he said, "Can you take my pants off?"

A shocked laugh burst out of me because yes, a portion of me was extremely interested in more information on that topic but also no, not today, Satan.

He pushed to his feet, wobbled, plopped back on the bed like a baby fawn learning its legs. "Have I mentioned auditing is highly varied work?"

"I don't even know what to say to that, sweetie." I stood between his legs, beckoned him toward me. "Stand up, hold on to me, and then you'll step out. Got it?"

"I need you to get my shirt off too," he said as he followed my orders. His trousers dropped, the belt clattering as it hit the floor. That left him in boxers—or briefs. I wasn't about to look. A thin bit of fabric separated me from confirming the big feet hypothesis and that knowledge was more responsibility than I could manage tonight. "It's strangling me."

"Do you know how dramatic you are when you're drugged?"

"My mother says I'm moody," he said with a perfectly adorable pout. Yes, he was moody.

Before I could get him out of the shirt, I had to free him from the sling and the straps crossing his chest and circling his torso. That meant navigating tender, swollen skin and proceeding despite his groans and grimaces. It hurt my heart to put him through this. "Are you sure you can't deal with the shirt for one night?"

"I don't know how to sleep with clothes on."

"Mmhmm." I nodded, murmured to myself again. "Mmhmm. This is perfectly reasonable information. Nothing about this is unusual, not when compared with the rest of this day."

Once the straitjacket sling was off, I started working the buttons loose at his collar, my touch professional as hell. I refused to let my fingers brush his heated skin or my mind wander to the fact he was nearly naked, in his bedroom, at night, with me.

When I pulled the shirt off his arms, he blew out a sigh of relief, saying, "This is much better."

And then he shoved a hand into his boxers—this time, I looked—and fondled himself for the longest minute of my life. I was too surprised by that move to stop myself from watching.

Yeah, my hypothesis was spot-on. Big feet, big…moods.

"We need to get you into that sling, Ash," I said when he finished reorganizing his man business. "Sit down on the bed so I can reach you. Okay?"

He let out a deep, rattling grandpa yawn as he sat down. "I'm so tired, Zelda."

Grabbing the sling, I tried to remember the proper way to get it on. "I'm sure you are. You have enough drugs in you to take down an elephant."

"I'm not tired from the drugs," he argued. "I'm tired from this whole fucking day. Do you know how it started? Do you know what I got this morning? A text message. Can you even believe that shit?"

"Nope, I cannot believe it." I glanced up from the sling and found Ash tucked into bed, the blankets pooled at his waist. "How am I supposed to reach you over there?" He patted the mattress beside him and I snort-laughed. "Oh, no, no, no, no. No."

He dropped his head back against the pillows. "I'm gonna go to sleep now, Zelda."

"Not without this damn sling," I said. "Don't you remember what the doctor told you? It's important to keep everything steady and immobilized."

He closed his eyes, patted the bed again. "Come here and do it."

And—dammit—I did.

I climbed onto the bed and wedged myself between Ash and the wall of pillows at his back. It only took me two attempts to get the sling in place and he only howled a string of curses once. But when I was finished, he shifted, scooping his good arm around my waist and resting his head right between my breasts, and trapped me under the solid mass of his body.

He mumbled a drowsy, "Thank you for everything, Zelda. You saved me today," and that was it. I was in bed with my boss.

I never planned on knowing the sound of bones sliding into place. Never imagined I'd share a bathroom with a man I'd met a handful of hours ago. I never anticipated I'd fall asleep with his head on my chest and his arm wrapped around my waist.

And I never dreamed of waking up to find a woman in the middle of Ash's bedroom, smirking as she said, "You're not Millie."

It seemed this was the one time I couldn't build the parachute before splattering on the ground.

SEVEN
ZELDA

"You're not Millie."

Wait. Where the hell am I?

Blinking the sleep from my eyes, I asked, "Is that a compliment?" I peered down at Ash, his body sprawled over mine, and it all came rushing back. Leaving Denver, the airport, the résumé, the urgent care clinic, the new boss currently using my belly as a pillow. What a day. I couldn't go home so I had to go big. And now, the woman standing in the doorway to Ash's bedroom was certain to keep the crazy streak alive. There was no other way for women who appeared in bedrooms like this. "Or an accusation?"

Who was she? Too calm about this to be his girlfriend. Too dressed up to be his personal trainer. Too *in his apartment on a Saturday morning* to be a colleague or business partner. I knew he didn't have a Pepper Potts-inspired personal assistant to rouse him from bed and manage his days because that was *my* new gig.

Maybe she was a friend. An extremely familiar friend who

had a key to his apartment and free rein to visit as she pleased. I'd assumed that only happened in the land of sitcoms but the world was in the process of proving me wrong about everything.

The woman considered my questions, the corner of her mouth pulling up as she pointed at Ash. "How is he still asleep? And what the hell happened to him?" Not waiting for a response, she pressed two fingers to her lips and whistled. "Ash Indigo. Time to get up."

He groaned against my belly and the sound vibrated through my skin and bones and organs. Not moving from his tangled-around-me spot, he said, "Oh my fucking god, Magnolia. Shut up and go away."

"Your…your name is Ash *Indigo*?" I asked, running my palm over his good shoulder. The other was a mottled mess of purple, red, and yellow.

"You are not Millie," she repeated, a laugh ringing in her words. She dropped her hands to her waist, tapped her pale pink polished fingers there. "Not even a little bit."

Still rubbing his shoulder, I continued, "Is that your two-name first name? Like Mary Anne?" As uncomfortable as this wake-up call was, I couldn't stop touching him. "Or is it your middle name? Or a stage name? That seems unlikely but…Indigo."

Ash groaned again and whatever the arousal version of a contact high was, I had it. I was already hooked on his growls and grumbles and groans.

The woman—Magnolia—tilted her head, smiling at me. "It's his middle name," she said. "Ash, you need to get your precious mood-ring ass out of bed. Mom is going to be here any minute and I know she would *fucking love* this entire situation but I'm trying to do you a favor."

Mom. That explained so much.

"Why are you here?" he rumbled, his arms still fixed around my waist and his face pressed to the skin exposed by my rucked-up t-shirt.

Magnolia glanced at me, her brows furrowed and forehead creased as if she couldn't believe his question. "Why am I here, Ash? Is that what you're saying to Not Millie's belly? I wasn't sure. I can't hear you on account of the belly mumbling."

"Her name is Zelda and you're being a pain in the fucking ass right now, Magnolia," he replied. All rumbles, all grumbles.

"Right, yeah, you're also being a pain in *my* fucking ass," she said. "You're getting fitted for your suit today. Remember? Remember how this was the only day in your extremely busy schedule and it's the absolute last minute the tailor could squeeze you in and guarantee the alterations for the wedding? And Mom and I said we'd pick you up and take you there ourselves because we didn't trust you wouldn't fall down a work hole and forget. Because you tend to forget things when they don't involve your primary interests of work and more work, Ash."

One more groan. One more grumble. And then— "*Fuck.*"

He rolled away from me, hissing with pain as the injured side of his body met the mattress. "Don't do that," I warned, slipping my arm around his shoulders. "Here. Let me help you up."

"Not to be annoying or anything but is anyone going to explain to me what happened?" Magnolia asked. "What's the sling all about?"

I scrambled to my knees to support Ash's exit from the bed. When his feet hit the floor, he turned to face me. I'd noticed the erection against my leg. *Of course I did*. One couldn't ignore that sort of thing. But seeing it barely restrained behind a thin pair of boxers was an entirely different experience.

"Oh my god. Put the wood away, dude," Magnolia said, sighing. She pressed her hand to her forehead, shielding her eyes. "You're scaring Not Millie."

He patted my head like I was a puppy and turned away, crossing the room. Over his shoulder he called, "I told you, Magnolia. Enough with that Not Millie shit. It's Zelda. Get it right or get the fuck out."

Not bothering to close the door when he entered the adjoining bathroom, Ash started and stopped the taps, brushed his teeth, and flipped the toilet lid open. Magnolia and I stared at each other while Ash relieved himself. How fortunate was I to witness that event twice in a matter of hours?

"Hi," she said with a wave. "I'm Magnolia."

"Zelda," I replied, still kneeling on the bed. "But I think you heard that already."

"Oh, I did." Her dark eyes glittered. "My brother never once snapped at me about Millie."

The toilet flushed and Ash called, "Stop. Talking. Now."

I pointed toward the bathroom. "He had a rough day. Yesterday."

She gave me an incredulous look. "You think? His arm is in a sling, he's bruised to shit, and—while you seem *delightful*—you are not the woman I expected to find in my brother's bed on a Saturday morning."

The door banged shut behind him and Ash said, "Magnolia, I told you—"

"What on earth? Why on *earth* is there luggage in the foyer like this?"

All heads swiveled in the direction of the hallway.

"I told you she was coming," Magnolia whispered.

Ash pressed his hand to his forehead, kneaded his temple. "And I told you to stop talking," he said. "I have the worst fucking headache and I swear to god, I'm going to stab myself in the arm."

"Don't stab yourself. I'm not taking you back to urgent care today. They'll think I'm abusing you." I crawled out of bed and fumbled for the prescription bottle on the bedside table. I dropped a tablet into my palm and held it out to him. "Take this."

He downed the tablet and leaned against me, his good arm around my shoulders. If I lived to be three hundred years old, I'd never understand how anyone could swallow pills dry. "I'd tell them you're not beating me," he said, resting his forehead against the crown of my head.

"I'd appreciate that," I replied, more than aware Ash's sister was watching us with rapt attention and his mother was a moment or two away. "Any chance you could tell me who Millie is?"

"No one," he whispered.

It seemed like an answer with too much simplicity, considering his sister was dead set on the belief Millie would be the woman in his bed. Yet I replied, "Okay."

"Any chance there are some over-easy eggs and home fries in my future? Can you make that happen too?"

"Is that what it's going to take to get you ready to roll for this suit fitting?"

"Don't make me go," he mumbled. "I swear, I will stab myself if I have to put a suit coat on today."

"One step at a time, all right? How about something more

than underwear?"

"I'll consider it," he said.

I wasn't sure but it felt like he might've kissed my hair then —right when his mother walked into the bedroom and said, "That's not Millie."

EIGHT
ASH

MY MOTHER WAS KIND ENOUGH TO SOUND RELIEVED AS SHE SAID, "That's not Millie."

I appreciated that as much as I could appreciate anything that invited my mother and sister into my bedroom at this unholy hour.

I didn't bother separating my lips from Zelda's hair or loosening my hold on her shoulders as I fired an irritable look at them. I'd hoped it would keep my mother in the doorway, one hand flat on her chest and the other gripping the doorjamb as if she needed its support during this difficult time.

My sister blinked away, her lips folded together and her cheeks pink with amusement as she said, "Nope. It's not."

And that was the final push my mother required to march across the room and introduce herself to my—my—

What the fuck was Zelda?

Oh. Right. She was my assistant.

The one who let me use her as a pillow last night. The one who held my hand while doctors manipulated my bones. The one who produced an egg sandwich from her purse and insisted I hire her at thirty thousand feet.

"Ash," my mother prompted with that wide-eyed, unblinking falcon glare. The special edition mother glare known to beat the truth out of children—even the grown ones—without lifting a finger. "Please explain to me how you came to be bruised up and down and in a sling, right after introducing me to your lovely *friend*."

"We're not friends." I said this with my cheek on her head. I said this with my arm around her shoulders like she was my life preserver. I said this with a sharp edge in my voice as if I found the suggestion more offensive than the truth. As for the truth, I didn't know what the fuck that was. "We're—I mean, we're—"

"Zelda," she said, meeting my mother's outstretched hand. "I'm Zelda and it's very nice to meet you, Mrs. Santillian."

"Please call me Diana," she replied. My mother met my eyes with a smile that could power the entire city of Boston for a week.

I held Zelda closer. I didn't want to share her. Which was ridiculous. *Fucking ridiculous.* It was probably a result of the pills. And Jesus Christ, the whiskey. Pills and whiskey and had I eaten in the past twenty-four hours? Probably not.

"Now, Zelda," my mother continued, her glee as restrained as my rising panic, "tell me your last name. I need to get it over to the calligrapher. They're working on place cards this week and—"

"Everybody get out," I yelled. I could not deal with calligraphers and place cards right now. "*Out.* Now."

My sister laughed as she stepped into the hall. "This lasted significantly longer than I'd expected."

My mother backed away but continued lavishing Zelda with

her adoring gaze. "We'll wait for you to get dressed, honey. I'm still waiting to hear about your injuries though it does seem Zelda has you well in hand."

If you only knew.

I was too busy scowling at my mother and begging her with my eyes to shut the hell up to realize Zelda was sliding out of my hold. "I should really"—she waved at her wrinkled clothes and ran a hand through her dark hair—"yeah, Ashville. I should really."

With more audience than I wanted for anything in my life, I reached out and twisted her t-shirt around my hand, yanking her back where I wanted her. "No, you shouldn't."

"She definitely isn't Millie," my mother loud-whispered to Magnolia.

Zelda cut a glance to the side, at my family. "Who is Millie?"

"No, not at all," my sister agreed.

"I told you," I replied, my knuckles brushing Zelda's belly, "no one."

"So happy to be rid of her," my mother said, no longer troubling herself to lower her voice. "She was such a *cold* girl."

"Someone," Zelda countered, tipping her head toward the onlookers.

"Oh, yeah, very cold," Magnolia replied. "Pretty sure her vagina doubles as an icebox. There's a half-empty pint of Phish Food in there. Some freezer-burned chicken breasts and a sack of peas too."

"Not anymore. Not to me," I promised, shifting us to block the commentary with my back. "Ignore them."

"Okay," she conceded, glancing down at my grip on her shirt. "If she's no one, then who am I?"

I opened my mouth to respond but I didn't have the words.

They weren't there. All I had was her shirt in my fist and my fingers on her skin and this moment where she was here with me and I didn't have to quantify anything.

And how irrational was that? All I wanted in this world was to assign values to every second, every little thing, but if I did that right now—if I made a definitive statement about who and what Zelda was—this would end. It would have to end.

It would end because the other option was irrational, intangible, subjective. None of the things I understood. Nothing I could control.

"I thought it was going to be Linden," my mother said to Magnolia. "I thought he was next."

I couldn't let myself fall for a woman right now, regardless of whether she'd nursed me through the worst day ever or we'd argued about statistics and pocket eggs in the most spectacular ways.

I wanted to. I really fucking wanted to. But I couldn't.

"Mom, Lin is literally lost in a forest every day of his life," Magnolia replied. "He's not next."

I needed Zelda. I needed the woman who knew how to handle me. The one who understood my tics better than I did. The one who sparred with math.

"That is an exaggeration," my mother said. "He's not *lost*."

I needed her in my office. I wanted her in my bed, even if only to sleep beside her, but I needed her organizing my work and running my office. I'd spent more nights alone than with someone and I knew I could do that again. But I sincerely doubted I could keep my career—and sanity—alive without a serious infusion of support.

"It's not an exaggeration at all," my sister argued. "He's gonna need to stumble upon an actual Snow White for that to occur and she's gonna need to be a boss bitch Snow White too. No one who waits for the huntsman to take charge because that's not his gig."

"You're both wrong. Lin sees more tail than a dogwalker. Now, leave. Out you go," I yelled, still staring into Zelda's eyes. Still fisting her shirt. "Both of you."

When the door snicked shut behind them, Zelda repeated, "Who am I, Ash?"

My gaze dropped to her lips and I was gone. I was done. This was over, just fucking over. I moved my fist up, between her breasts. I allowed myself that moment, that fleeting, final moment before releasing her shirt. And then, "You're my assistant, Zelda."

She glanced down, nodding as she ran her tongue over her teeth. "Do all of your assistants help you out of your clothes?"

"I believe the job description said something along the lines of 'other duties as assigned.'"

She tipped her head back, grinning at me. "Taking your clothes off, finding eggs and home fries, getting you out of a suit fitting," she said. "Those are the other duties you have in mind? That's what you *want*, Ashville?"

Fuck no.

"Yes," I replied.

Here I was, thinking this was irrational when it was prime all along.

———

The home fries did it. If not them, the eggs. Or the coffee.

Yeah, the coffee. That'd had a hand in this, I was certain.

Regardless of remedy, I came to my senses on Berkeley

Street, somewhere between Stuart Street and St. James Avenue, while Zelda and I walked several paces behind my mother and sister.

Right there, in the middle of the Back Bay, everything caught up with me like an overextended rubber band finally snapping back and whapping the shit out of me.

First, there was shock. What the fuck had I done? No, really, what the *fuck* had I done? If hazy memories served, I'd yelled at Zelda about her résumé, among other things, fallen asleep on her shoulder, and then hired her as my assistant. And that was only the start. I mean, for fuck's sake, I'd slept with her.

What. The. Fuck. Had. I. Done.

After the shock came embarrassment like I hadn't felt in years. The truth was, I fell the fuck apart yesterday. I was human roadkill, the kind too insolent to notice my state but not wise enough to stop myself from making that state someone else's problem. And not just someone else but a woman I didn't know and whose life I didn't have any business invading. I'd monopolized her time and damn near held her captive last night. Now, I was dragging her to this fitting when I had two perfectly good someone elses to stitch me back together.

But…I didn't want her to leave. Not yet.

Right behind the embarrassment that stuck to me like honey on my fingers was worry. As we walked down the busy street, my mother hooking glances over her shoulder every few minutes and Zelda's body brushing against mine as we weaved through crowds, I found myself spiraling into all-out anxiety. I'd crossed every line in the book, then found the sequel and crossed those lines too.

What did I do and how do I fix it?

The itchy reality was I couldn't run the office on my own

anymore and if Zelda was even half as proficient at management as she was at riding herd on me, I'd survive until I could get someone with an accounting background in there.

And then, maybe we could… No, probably not. Anything I might've interpreted as attraction was an illusion. Chemistry was a product of whiskey for breakfast and muscle relaxers for supper. This wasn't real. Zelda was a kind, affectionate woman who needed to get better at establishing boundaries.

Actually, yes—*that* was the issue. Zelda should not have done any of this. Just because I was a mess didn't require her to clean me up. She wasn't my mother or my siblings. There was no earthly reason for her to take me to the doctor, bring me home, and then get into bed with me. Jesus, no. That was on her. That was her inserting herself into my problems and it was completely unnecessary.

I wouldn't have woken up with a lead pipe for a dick if she hadn't been in my bed, all soft and warm and sweet enough to eat. She shouldn't have done that. Shouldn't have made me feel all…*this*.

Her hand brushed down my spine as she turned toward me and edged closer, out of the way of a large group incapable of modulating themselves to keep from mowing down other pedestrians. With my arm—the one not lashed to my body in this circus act sling—I tucked her against me.

It took me a full minute to realize what I'd done.

Zelda made one move and I checkmated the shit out of it, regardless of the arguments I'd patchworked together.

"You don't have to do this." I spoke these words with my lips pressed to her temple and my arm locking her body against mine, but I still said them. "You can skip this fitting. It's not a big deal."

She gazed up at me, a curious bend to her eyebrows. "Is that so? Not long ago you were singing a different tune, my friend."

I shook my head as I put space between us. "I did but this isn't mission critical."

"Yeah, that's not how your sister would describe this," Zelda replied, laughing.

My mother glanced back at us, a delighted grin splitting her face all over again.

"It's not critical to my accounting practice and that's the only kind of critical you need to care about," I said, and I sounded like a jackass saying it. "I have it under control, Zelda. You don't have to tag along for this."

She stopped walking. I did the same.

She crossed her arms over her chest as she peered up at me. "This is what you do, right? This is part of it."

I ran my hand through my hair. "Part of what, Zelda?"

"Part of you and your moods," she replied simply. "When you're not busy being serious and seriouser, you wiggle between hot and cold. It's okay. I get it. You've spent all this time learning how to be super good at your job—probably because you got it in your head you have something to prove—and when you're not doing your job, you don't know who you are."

"That—that's not the case," I argued. "I can understand how you might think that but—"

"But you only know two ways to be when you're not being the boss man: hot and cold," she continued. "You had some hot last night and this morning"—she sent a wide-eyed, brows-raised, tight-lipped grin at the sidewalk—"and now you remember how uncomfortable the heat makes you. Cold is so much easier, right?"

She stared at me, bobbing her head as she waited on my reply. I didn't say anything.

"See? It's easier like this. Just standing on a sidewalk, looking grumpy and inconvenienced. It's your thing, Ashville. You're much more comfortable in the chill because it's closer to your boss man vibe. It's okay, Ash. *I get it.*"

"You—I'm sorry, what?" No boundaries. Not a single one with this woman. "You get…what, exactly?"

With an indulgent sigh, she wrapped her hand around my forearm. "You. I get you."

"Charming," I said with a bitter laugh. "Pick that skill up at the voodoo shop, did you?"

After another indulgent sigh, Zelda said, "It would be so cool if you could tell me what's really bothering you. I could guess but we're already behind schedule because you needed an entire hen-house-worth of eggs and I don't think your sister is loving the delay." She tipped her head down the street, where my mother and Magnolia were watching us. "While it's not your norm, you could take this moment to be real with me about your feelings."

"I *know* I'm not paying you to watch me try on suits," I snapped. "I don't rely on feelings to make decisions, Miss Besh."

"Wow," she breathed, rocking back on her heels. "Wow. Whatever is happening in there"—she glanced to my forehead—"it's big stuff. It's real heavy if we're all the way back at Miss Besh."

"Ash!" Magnolia shouted, furiously gesturing to her wrist. "Let's *go*, dude."

Zelda set off toward my mother and sister, leaving me gazing after her.

"Come on," she called, not looking back in my direction. "We'll unpack this later."

I shuffled after her, not caring whether I was being petulant. "Nothing to unpack," I muttered.

She waited for me at the door to the tailor's shop, her hand covering the handle and her gaze clear, all the heat and joy and amusement I'd come to expect from her absent. "Let's straighten a few things out before we go in there," she said, jerking her chin toward the shop. "Most importantly, you need to fight fair. I'll fight with you all day long but only when you do it fair. Don't throw my so-called voodoo shop experience back at me because I recognize you and your eccentricities and all the little mood hurricanes swirling around inside your head. Don't do that shit."

I nodded. "Fine but I'd like you to stop unpacking me. I don't like it."

"Okay," she said. "I'll mention that I'm only telling you what I see but hey, it's cool. You don't want to be seen. You want to distract everyone by being above reproach. No problem."

"You're doing it right now," I said. "This. What you're doing. I don't like it. I never asked you to know me and my eccentricities. Okay? That's not part of the gig. I need someone who can handle my schedule and clean up spreadsheets, not a fucking life coach."

Zelda paused for a second, studying the passing cars and people before saying, "Your mother thinks we're going to get married and give her a fleet of grandbabies. As there is nothing further from the truth and she's your mother, you need to fix that."

"All right. I will," I replied. "What else do we need to discuss?"

"Nothing." Still focused on the street, she said, "You go inside. I'm going to stay here and make some calls."

Because I was a goddamn fool who felt entitled to everything about this woman and didn't want her out of my sight for a minute, I asked, "What calls do you need to make on a Saturday morning?"

"I need to find a place to stay tonight," she replied. "And… the rest of the week."

I stared at her for a moment, searching her face as she eyed the swarm of Lyfts and Ubers. "If you hadn't—um—if last night hadn't been what it was, where would you have stayed?"

Her shoulders lifted, fell. "Not sure. I was going to figure that out when the flight landed. See if any friends had a free couch." Another shrug. "That's the beauty of having friends from college and grad school. Everyone knows someone and someone always has a free couch." She shot me a quick, hollow grin before turning a gorgeous, glowing smile on a couple walking a pair of chocolate Labs. After they passed, she said, "I'll figure it out. It's what I do best."

I was a goddamn fool and I was entitled, and I didn't fight fair and I was an eccentric, moody hurricane. And I didn't understand the first thing about my reactions to Zelda. I didn't know why my stomach dropped to my toes at the thought of her not knowing where she'd spend the night. I couldn't explain why my skin prickled cold when she insisted she always figured it out.

And there was no justifying my decision to announce, "I have an extra room. You'll stay with me."

NINE
ZELDA

I should've known better.

I should've known.

After all these years of being me with all of my me-ishness, I should've known the fundamental truths of Zelda Besh.

Fun fact: truth number seven read something like "Zelda is heretofore unaware of truths numbers one through six. She knows only that she doesn't know anything."

Perhaps that was the only truth I needed to know. If I accepted this bedrock reality, then I could stop beating myself up about all the things I should've known.

Yeah, that was unlikely.

Why stop now when I could sit wedged between Ash's mother and sister while he did a poor job at pretending he wasn't studying me in the mirror? While my phone burned a hole in my back pocket—and the pit of my stomach—despite being switched off since yesterday morning. While I sewed that parachute together as I hurtled through the clouds toward the hard earth.

There was always a parachute in pieces. With all things, my

hands were filled with scraps and I was left to patch them together. I knew what would happen if I didn't and every time, I went on diving out of that plane only to get it together at the last minute. I'd come close enough to hitting the ground enough to know I didn't want to become paint on the earth but I couldn't stop myself from rushing toward it time and time again, as if I was trying to run all the way through disaster.

When Ash flicked a glance at my shoes—hot pink low-tops—and frowned, I responded with a smile. He didn't want to smile back, that much was clear, but his gaze softened. Warmed. Just as I had every single time he'd given me his hard and tough and followed it up with a glimpse at his ooey gooey center.

By now, he'd accumulated a full page of tallies in the "like" column. Even with his scowling and frowning, his growls, his moods, his unnecessary jabs. He was precious under all that grump and I lived for the prize of an ooey gooey center because I knew it wasn't won by many.

Hell, I hadn't expected to win it in the first place. It'd made sense to stay last night as that was a full-on emergency contact type of situation. I'd planned on climbing out of his bed once he was fast asleep and relocating myself to the sofa, far away from the awkward-but-admirable erection he'd pressed against my thigh. Far away from his hungry snuggles.

I'd expected I'd find him in fits of fury this morning, cursing everything and everyone for the disruptions his schedule had incurred. I'd expected he'd pretend all of yesterday's ooey gooey goodness hadn't happened. He hadn't napped on my shoulder or rubbed my thigh like it belonged to him. He hadn't twisted his arm around mine and let all his fear shine through while the doctor reduced his shoulder. He hadn't insisted I join him in bed and he absolutely, positively had not flattened me underneath him and slept like he wanted nothing but me for the rest of his days. I would've been content with that burst of amnesia. I would've appreciated it too, as I couldn't make sense of the alarming rightness of being possessed by him, caged in his arms and kissed on the head while his mother and sister reminded him I wasn't Millie.

And the trouble with all this, the thing I really should've known from the start, was I wasn't meant to like him or his ooey gooey. I was supposed to encounter this man, this beautiful, flawed, tender man…and walk the other direction because he wasn't for me. Not me, not now. Probably not ever. It didn't matter whether his glares gave me the best belly flips or his growls actually raised my body temperature. That fitting in wasn't something I'd experienced once, not in any of my thirty-one years on this planet, and even though we fought and it wasn't always fair, this fit better than anything else, ever.

But this wasn't how I was supposed to start over. I wasn't supposed to argue with a man on my getaway flight and fall into bed with him and then make friends with his mother and sister. No, no, no. I was supposed to leave, figure myself out, make a plan and stick to it, find a place to live for more than a weekend, buy some houseplants and Fiestaware, get militant about organizing my closets. Maybe then, after sustaining both the plants and the crockery, I could allow men into my life again. They'd be astounded by my aggressively structured spice cabinet and find my spider plants sexy as fuck. They'd respect my self-sufficiency and never, *ever* presume to trample it. I'd know how to be myself then, with my grass-green plates and my windowsill garden and my hard-won independence. I wouldn't be the grown woman who ran away anymore. I'd be the woman with the life she'd built for herself, one precisely labeled cupboard at a time.

There was something critical about starting all the way over and allowing myself to feel everything I did while arguing—and cuddling—with Ash didn't fit in that process. He couldn't and he wouldn't, if this morning's tantrum was to be trusted. He wanted me as his assistant and, as it turned out, we'd also share his apartment until I found alternative arrangements.

I'd start over with my plants and crockery and closets then.

Mrs. Santillian ("call me Diana") shifted on the tufted leather sofa to face me. "So," she started, a whole load of meaning in that tiny word, "Zelda. Tell me everything."

From the tailor's pedestal, Ash glared. "Leave her alone, Mom."

"You have the very important task of standing still, Ash," she replied, wagging a maternal finger in his direction. "Please don't stop to interfere with our girl talk."

"This is pointless," he continued. "I have plenty of suits. Why do I need a new one?"

"Because I only get married once," Magnolia answered.

He glanced down at the dark blue fabric. "I have navy suits."

"I'm sure you do," she replied. "But you won't match the other guys and I don't want my photos to be odd because you can't deal for half an hour."

"This is ridiculous," he muttered.

"So is your attitude," she sang.

"Zelda," Mrs. Santillian drawled, tucking my hair over my ear, "tell me all about you, sweetheart. Your hair is lovely. So thick!" She studied the stripe of blue and I shrank, both emotionally and physically as I anticipated her disapproval. I'd learned to shrug off judgment ages ago but it was more difficult when it came from people who mattered and I knew this woman mattered. "Who is doing your color? There's a gal at my stylist's shop who is a whiz with all the funky colors you kids are doing these days. I'm sure you'd love her, if you're ever looking for someone new."

"Oh, thank you," I said. "I had this done in Denver so—"

"Denver? Ash, didn't you just return from Denver?" Mrs. Santillian asked, whipping her head toward him.

He met my gaze in the mirror, a muscle jumping in his jaw. "Last night."

Mrs. Santillian stared at me while I continued watching that muscle. "Is that where you met? In Denver?" she asked.

To the tailor's frustration, Ash jerked his shoulder up. "Essentially, yes."

"Then," Mrs. Santillian continued, "this is new? Recent, I mean."

"Amusing is what it is," Magnolia murmured, tapping her fingertips against her lips.

The corner of Ash's mouth tugged up into a hint of a smile. My belly flopped and my toes tingled and I wanted to step onto the pedestal and claim my space under his chin and in his arms because I fit there. The only appropriate way to respond was, "I'm going to be helping Ash in the office. That's all."

"Oh, sure," Magnolia replied, bobbing her head and rolling her eyes. "'In the office.' That's an experiment with an obvious outcome but good luck anyway. I'm rooting for you both."

Mrs. Santillian patted my hand. "No explanations required, Zelda. I'm just thrilled to meet you."

"I'm just thrilled she's not Millie. I didn't want that wedge of iceberg lettuce at my wedding," Magnolia added.

"Magnolia, I swear to god, if you start with that again," Ash warned.

"Oh, stop it, Ash," Mrs. Santillian chided. "We're not bickering this morning. Your sister's new eyelashes are too fragile for dramatic squabbling."

"Don't explain that to me," Ash said. "Whatever it is, don't tell me."

Ignoring him, Mrs. Santillian turned back toward me. "You're coming to our family dinner tomorrow," she announced.

Ash gasped. *"Mom."*

"Oh yes, you're definitely coming to dinner," Magnolia said, gesturing toward me with her phone. "I'm calling Linden right now. I'll bet you my life savings he's forgotten he's supposed to be there."

Again, I met Ash's gaze in the mirror. His brows pitched up as if he was asking whether I wanted him to jump in front of this speeding train for me.

I stared at him for a moment but then I glanced away because—because I didn't know what I wanted anymore.

———

I GAZED DOWN THE STREET, WATCHING THE CAR CARRYING ASH'S mother and sister inching through the jammed intersection. It was a hot summer day and everyone in their right mind should've been out of the city. This was a beach day, a lake day. An anywhere but here day.

But Ash and I, we were here. We were here *and* alone on the sidewalk. Again.

He was right behind me. I could feel it just as much as I

could feel the plump water molecules in the air and the sweat gathering at the back of my neck.

"I, uh, I—or, we," he stammered, his words coming from over my shoulder, a distance too close to be considered polite. He wasn't polite. No, that wasn't how I'd characterize my boss. He was direct and assertive, and at times, abrasive. "I need to get some work done. I completely lost yesterday and the coming week is packed, so I can't let that slide. I should go home and—and catch up. You don't have to come with me. You can do whatever you want. I'm sure you know that," he added, mostly to himself. "You've probably had enough of me."

Direct, assertive, abrasive. Also ooey gooey like a perfectly underbaked brownie.

"Not sure what you're planning on doing but I need to remind you about the one-hand situation." I shifted to face him. A thick layer of scruff covered his jaw and even though it was the worst idea in the world, worse than packing my life in the middle of the night and hopping on the first flight to the East Coast with nothing more than a Post-it note of explanation in my wake, I reached up and cupped that scruffy jaw. Just for a moment. Just to feel him against my skin. "I do believe it is I who hasn't been willing to be shaken loose."

He laughed at that and I realized I enjoyed the feel of him laughing as much as the sound. I pulled my hand away, shoved it in the pocket of my jeans. At that, Ash's smile fell. His brows pinched and the warmth in his eyes—all that soft brownie goodness—chilled. I glanced at the street again. It was one thing to be on the receiving end of that chill when it was his prerogative but another when it was self-inflicted.

"Do you want me to get a cab for you?" I asked, stepping closer to the curb. "I'm not sure but I don't think it's that far back to your apartment. We could walk but maybe you should prob-ably take it easy, considering"—I tipped my head toward his shoulder—"all of that."

"It is too fucking hot to walk around the block, Zelda," he replied with that well-worn exasperation he favored so much. "Sorry but I'm in no mood to hike through the Common, down Charles Street, under an overpass, up Cambridge Street, and across Haymarket Square to my building."

I stared at him, blinking, my hand in the air as I hailed a cab. "Are you ever in the mood?"

His lips parted and his eyebrow bent up. I didn't expect him to reply and he didn't, not when he held the car door open for me, not while I scooted across the seat, not when he dropped down beside me, not when I rattled off his address, and not when the driver lurched us forward despite the crush of traffic.

He didn't say a word to me in the cab and I didn't expect any. When Ash didn't want to share his thoughts, he locked them down. I imagined there was a large strongbox in his head and it was overflowing with thoughts and feelings he didn't want to examine. And I was certain he believed that was a smart, effi-cient way to operate.

Not that I was much different. I didn't bury the things I didn't want to confront. I ran away from them. I found a brand-new disaster, another world to tape back together and resent for being broken in the first place, and then I'd run away from that one too.

Wasn't that it? Wasn't that the highly defensible thesis of Zelda? And wasn't I bound to do it again? Every single time I thought I was finding the gig, the place, the people, the guy, the state of comfort with myself that would finally translate into being a grown-ass woman whose life was greater than the contents of a backpack and more stable than a Jenga game, I slipped right into those old patterns. I bailed on grad school, took the go-nowhere gigs, settled in the wrong places, fell in with shallow friends who wouldn't notice I'd gone, hooked up with a guy who was no prize, and kept on wrestling with which part of this misshapen construct of myself I should smooth down next.

Some would say it was easy. I was taking the *easy* way out. There was nothing easy about this. It wasn't easy to meander from place to place, the totality of myself contained within a hard pass of a résumé and a storybook of tattoos and a bit of blue hair because I'd tried everything else.

This wasn't easy and it wasn't going to be easy when my current disaster ended. I'd have a pocketful of moody glares and gooey moments and my complete inability to know better.

"Wait," Ash called from behind me as I climbed out of the cab and marched toward his high-rise building, walking as fast as I could without running. "Zelda, *wait*."

I stopped at the doors but didn't turn toward him. "What are you working on today? How can I help? Better yet, let me page through your email and your calendar. I'll figure it out from there."

His hand met the small of my back and I startled, skittering forward a step. "Sorry," he murmured, his hand still pressed to my sweat-dampened t-shirt. "I didn't mean to—"

"Let's just go upstairs and get things sorted out." The words tumbled out in a breathless heap, each one more panicked than the one before. Though it wasn't panic, not really. It was the moment when the rush of jumping without a fully sewn parachute transitioned from exhilaration to desperation and I started working double time to piece it all together before it was too late. "You'll feel better when you have everything sorted. I always do."

Or, I imagined I'd feel better if anything was sorted, ever.

Glancing to the side, I saw him nod. His hand stayed fixed on my lower back as we walked through the upscale, modern lobby with its wall of succulents and slate, waited for the elevator, rode to the ninth floor.

I couldn't decide who this touch served, me or Ash. Hunger came in many forms and yesterday Ash was starved for comfort. I'd known that as soon as he'd fallen asleep on my shoulder. Today was different. The excitement was wearing off and I wasn't immune to my own needs anymore.

When we stepped inside the apartment and surveyed the wreckage of luggage we'd left not long ago, Ash barked out a laugh. "It looks like there was a struggle."

"The only thing missing is a few bloody handprints," I said, collecting Ash's laptop bag and setting it on the countertop.

He hung his keys on the tidy set of hooks near the door. "Some broken glass."

I righted the suitcases abandoned near the entryway bench. "Or a ransom note."

"Or?" he repeated. "Come on. It's *and*. And a ransom note, Zelda."

"Okay, sure," I murmured, pulling the handle on my luggage. "*And* a ransom note." I swept a gaze over the apartment. "I should put this away. Somewhere that isn't the middle of your entryway. If you still want me to stay—"

"I need a shower," he announced, cutting me off before I could open the escape hatch all the way. He shifted toward me, running his good hand over the straps keeping his shoulder in place. "Will you help me?"

I swallowed. I bit my lip. I stared at his hand for a moment. Remembered his hand on my back, keeping me still and—and safe. This new disaster, the one I'd barreled into with both hands, had the power to crush me. This was the one I wouldn't be able to save before splatter.

"With…?"

I glanced up at him. This was my chance. My fingers were curled around the handle of my luggage and my purse was over my shoulder and I could walk away now. I could leave. I could go somewhere—anywhere—and not risk another moment with a man who didn't know how to fight fair or feel his feelings or live outside his self-imposed idiosyncrasies for one second. I could stop this and find a new disaster, a better, simpler disaster. A disaster where I didn't fit and I didn't want to stay. A disaster that didn't ground me with his touch because he knew—though he'd deny it—I needed it.

"With—what, exactly?"

TEN
ASH

I knew what I was doing. I couldn't pretend otherwise.

I knew exactly what I was doing and I did it anyway. I shot a helpless glance at my sling. "Can't do much, can I?" Not waiting for Zelda's response, I continued, "Help me take this off and wash up."

Her lips parted as if she intended to reply but she stopped herself to stare at my busted shoulder. Maybe if she stared hard enough, she'd solve that problem the way she solved everything else.

"And—and by that," she stammered, "you mean *what*, Ashville?"

I shot an eyebrow up, silently challenging her to read between the lines. Which was all kinds of deranged since I'd drawn a line in the fucking sand and then spent the morning being a dickface jerk to her. That, and freaking the fuck out because she was *still* making noise about leaving to crash on some random couch.

Leaving. *Fucking leaving.* I could manage many things but the idea of her slipping out of my grasp wasn't one of them. Not without knowing exactly where she was going and seeing to the comfort and security of that couch myself.

But I couldn't do it and I'd tried. For thirteen and a half seconds this morning, I'd lied to myself about that being the best choice. When that was over, she'd taken it upon herself to chastise me so hard, I was already plotting ways to earn my next punishment. Already asking for it.

What the hell was it about this woman? She had some blue hair and a lot of earrings. Her work history was insane. She was going somewhere but she was also stopped, suddenly rooted in my world. None of it made sense. She didn't make sense and when I was close to her, neither did I.

I wanted an assistant. I wanted distance and proper boundaries. I wanted to scream at her about her ambling, directionless professional life.

And I wanted to feel her skin against mine so badly, it seemed like I was suffocating without it.

It didn't matter how many times I gathered these line items and attempted to make assets and liabilities of them, they wouldn't balance. I'd stood on the pedestal, glaring at her reflection in the mirror while the tailor stuck me with a thousand pins and mentally clicked through the if-then tree from hell.

If she left, then I'd lose my fucking mind because—because I would and there didn't need to be a reason.

If she left, then she might never come back and I'd never know why this woman mattered and that was un*fucking*acceptable.

If she left, then I'd find her. Then I'd bring her back, which made fine sense to me even if it did sound like an abduction plan.

If I brought her back, then I'd never let her out of my sight again and that also made fine sense while sounding rather criminal.

If she stayed at my apartment, then I'd want to touch her because she was a living, breathing magnet.

If I wanted to touch her, then she'd let me because she needed it as much as I did.

If she let me touch her, then I couldn't have her work for me because there was a limit to the number of complications I could supervise at any time.

If she couldn't work for me, then I'd lose my fucking mind. And I still didn't need a damn reason.

That'd pissed me off to no end, right up to the point when she'd stood in my entryway, looking like she didn't know where she belonged.

Right here, I wanted to say. You belong right here.

Instead of saying that or anything close to it, I made a half-assed suggestion about taking a shower. Deranged. I was absolutely deranged. And the worst part? I'd dedicated ten solid minutes to this sideshow. I still didn't have a functional watch to confirm that but I knew. I knew what seventeen percent of a billable hour felt like.

"I can help you out of your sling." She reached for me with both hands but stopped herself before making contact. Stepped back. Folded her arms. "I can do that, if you want. If that's what you're asking."

"Come here." I beckoned her closer. She didn't move. "Zelda, please. I can't do it by myself."

A shaky breath burst from her lips. Then, "I bet you can. You're very capable, after all. You don't need anyone and you're the first to remind everyone of that fact."

"You should know by now I need you more than I care to admit." I scratched my jaw with the one useful hand I had left. "It's rather convenient for you. Is it possible you're the reason I was knocked on my ass in the terminal? Now, tell me the probability of you setting off the chain of events that sent me cartwheeling over a kid."

She untangled her arms as a laugh shook through her body. God, she was pretty when she laughed. "I'm not calculating those odds."

I took a step closer. She did the same. "I thought you liked a challenge," I said. "I thought you liked to invent statistical proof for your mental math games."

She pursed her lips and bent an eyebrow as she started loosening the sling. "And I thought you were busy performing a one-man show. Go on. Show me how you do it all yourself."

I couldn't stop myself from asking, "You're staying, right?"

She glimpsed up at me while disengaging the cinches and straps, her lips still pursed. "I don't have to. I don't want to invade your space and—"

"You're staying," I interrupted.

"That seems like a not-great idea," she replied. "It isn't a problem for me to call some friends. It might be better that way."

"It might be better if you stay," I argued.

She slipped the sling from my arm and flattened her hands on my chest. Aside from the fact everything hurt like hell, it was exactly what I needed. A million more doses of this and I'd be right as rain.

"Tell the truth," she said. "You're after one of my breakfast sandwiches."

I pressed my hand on top of hers. "Let me introduce you to the café on the ground floor of my office building. You'll never eat another serving of pocket eggs again when this place is through with you."

She grinned at me but then her gaze shifted, sliding down to the spot where my hand covered hers. "You couldn't wait to get rid of me yesterday."

"That was yesterday," I replied.

"You were extremely clear about my *role*"—the word sounded like a slap in the face, one I'd definitely earned—"this morning."

"That was this morning," I replied.

"And tomorrow? What will that bring?"

"I don't know," I admitted.

A brittle laugh filled the space between us as she shook her head. "Perhaps you can see my dilemma, Ash."

This was why I needed two functional arms. One to hold her hand to my chest, another to hold her close to me. To keep her. And fuck me if that made any sense. "As you've mentioned, I'm moody."

"I'm not going to be a casualty of your moods," she replied. "You can't try to get rid of me one minute and then—"

"Listen to me, Zelda." I shifted my hand to tip her face up, meeting her gaze. "I'm temperamental as fuck and you're more than comfortable calling me on that shit. None of that is changing any time soon. But here's what I know for sure. I need you to put my office in order because it's a hot mess right now. I need you to do your bizarre little Mary Poppins thing where you smile, blink, and fix my whole life. But I'm not having you shuffling from one futon to another in Allston or Brighton or some other collegiate crime den when there's a perfectly good bedroom for you right here."

Without missing a beat, she said, "And you'd like me to help you into the shower as well."

Yes. Yes was the answer, the only answer. I wanted her in my bed, my head on her shoulder, and yes, the shower. All those places where I could simply *be.*

But— "I needed you to get me out of that sling. I would've dislocated the other shoulder trying to do it by myself. I'm sure I can manage the rest on my own."

She closed her eyes as a knowing smile pulled at her lips. It looked like she was holding back a laugh. "Collegiate crime den," she muttered. "What…what does that even mean?"

"You know damn well what it means," I replied. I had no idea what I'd intended with that.

She took a step back, turned in a circle like she didn't know where she was, and power walked into the kitchen. I tipped my head to the side, watching her hips sway in those vintage jeans. I realized then I'd missed a critical amount of Zelda's assets in yesterday's audit. I'd spent the flight focused on that streak of blue hair, the ink on her skin, her mismatched eyes. At no point had this perky backside figured into my assessment.

Another reason I needed two functional arms: grabbing this woman's ass hard enough to leave marks. Now, that was a new urge.

"Just log me into your email and I'll figure the rest out myself. Unless, of course, you don't want me in your email. Which is also fine. I can start with your calendar. Are you a Google Calendar kind of kid or are you all iCal? While many things about you do scream 'Outlook!' I doubt that's your prefer-ence. Right? Where are you at with this, Ashville?" When she turned, my laptop bag in hand, she tracked my gaze to her back-side. "Yes?" she asked, laughing.

"Do you have, you know"—still staring, I scratched the back of my neck—"office clothes?"

"Sure do," she replied. "Should I change now? Is that the ludicrous thing you need at this moment?"

Goddamn, I wanted to rub my face against that ass and I knew I'd never in my life thought that before. Not a single time ever had I wanted anything like that.

"Nope," I answered, moving toward her. I grabbed my laptop from the bag, opened it, and banged out my password. "All yours. Email is open." I backed away, moving toward my bedroom. "Go ahead and remove those job postings, if you don't mind."

She glanced up from the screen, her lips parted. "You don't want to leave them open? In case—"

"The position is filled," I said, closing the bedroom door behind me.

I marched into the adjoining bathroom and flipped on the shower. Stripping while the room filled with steam, I realized another reason I required the use of both hands: one to flatten against the shower wall while I jerked off.

———

BEFORE STEPPING INTO THE SHOWER, I HADN'T GIVEN MUCH thought to erections. I mean, I'd thought about them in the sense I noticed when my dick was hard and when it wasn't. But I'd never contemplated the erections I'd racked up in my life. Certainly never compared them.

There was no need to compare them, not when my dick was as predictable as the rest of my life. Most of the time, I was good for a respectable length and girth that jutted straight out. If you didn't have a protractor, you could use my shaft to find a right angle.

But this—the monster throbbing against my belly button—more closely resembled a flexing forearm than any erection I'd ever experienced. It was a personal best. I was going to remember this one.

Another thing I was going to remember? The amount of rueful regret I felt over using my hand on an erection of this quality. It deserved better than a shower jerk-off. If I could've swapped out this one the way I swapped good ties with better ties when I had important meetings, that would've been amazing. Put this one in the back of the closet on a special hanger and save it for a long night, a soft bed, a warm, wet woman who felt like joy and looked like a miscalculation, one with a half dozen earrings and stripes of blue hair and—

"Oh my fucking god," I choked.

Heat blasted through me like an electrocution. Honestly, this fucking hurt. My spine arched, my abs trembled, my arm burned as if I'd done more than take my cock in hand. I couldn't see anything, couldn't hear anything. The only sense at my disposal was feel and the only thing I could feel was my blood hammering in my veins. The water pounded my skin and my breath rasped out of me and my entire body shuddered as my orgasm painted the tiles.

Since I was now in the business of comparison, I couldn't help but note I hadn't come like a cannon blast...ever. I stared at the streaks on the shower wall as I panted, my chest still heaving. I'd never done this before. I was always so careful about coming in my hand or angling toward the drain.

I'd never done any of this before.

"Ash? Ash! What happened? Are you all right?"

The door flew open and bounced off the wall and the force sent it slamming back in Zelda's face. It would've been funny if it hadn't made my balls hum and my cock spurt once more. She pushed it open again, this time keeping a hand locked on the handle.

"I heard a crash," she said, her eyes wide and alarmed. "Are you okay? What happened?"

I glanced down at the bottles of shampoo and conditioner gathered around my feet. Soap and body wash too. I didn't know when I'd knocked them over. It didn't matter.

"I'm fine," I croaked.

Her hand twisted on the knob and I saw the exact moment she realized this shower was a crystal clear glass box and I was stark naked. "Oh, shit," she murmured, angling her body away from me. That would've been helpful if she hadn't turned toward the mirror and found another eyeful of my bare ass and the hand still curled around my dick. "Oh my god. Okay. You're fine. I'll leave. Sorry about"—she clapped a hand over her eyes—"oh my god, everything."

"Don't," I barked, suddenly bothered. Why did she keep running? Where did she think she was going when she clearly belonged here?

Her hand still pressed to her eyes, she said, "I am sorry about barging in here. I heard noises and I thought you might've slipped and I—I'm sorry."

"Don't be," I replied.

"Well, I am," she said, laughing. Her cheeks were red. She looked adorable. "You're not going to change that."

I bent, grabbing the soap. "What can I change?"

Her gaze still averted, she said, "I don't need you to change anything, Ash. I'm good." After a pause, she added, "I need to stop barreling into disaster. That's what I need and it's not something you can do for me."

I watched her as I ran the bar over my body. "What kind of disaster?"

"It's nothing. I shouldn't have mentioned it," she said.

"But you did," I said, leaning into the shower spray. "And you're here, making sure I don't fall on my ass, so you should tell me. Maybe I can help you."

"Yeah, that's the thing," she said, laughing. "I'm good at fixing. I don't like to be fixed."

"Is that what you're doing to me?" I asked. "Fixing me?"

She shot a glance at me, careful to stay well above the waist. "And if I am?"

"Then it's only fair I do the same for you," I replied.

"I can't see how that's accurate."

"You can't—what?" I snatched the shampoo off the floor. "Of course it's accurate."

She shook her head in the same, tight way I did when people couldn't understand simple math. "It's not symmetrical," she said. "You're you, I'm me, we're different people and the things we have in need of fixing are different too. Based on this alone, it's obviously not symmetrical and therefore this idea of fairness —that you do something for me because I'm doing something for you—will always be misaligned."

"I mean, well, no, no, that's not right," I stammered.

"It's absolutely right." She shifted, facing me. "You need me to run your office because there is—shockingly—a limit to the number of jobs you can do at once. I need"—she ran a hand through her hair as she shook her head and glanced away—"I need a job. And a place to stay. And some time to figure out all the important things I should've figured out years ago, while you find someone who gives a shit about accounting."

She dragged her gaze back to me, still avoiding the fact my cock was behaving like a puppy who'd heard the word "walk."

"Sounds proportional to me." I ducked my head under the water to rinse away the shampoo and skip out on her protests. When I emerged, I said, "And listen, if you need help, you should tell me that."

"It's not proportional." She turned in a circle before opening the narrow closet beside the shower and plucking a towel from the shelf. "It stopped being proportional a long time ago."

I wasn't convinced I agreed with that. Not the way she told it.

"Why does it need to be?" I asked, turning off the water.

Zelda held the towel open for me and I stepped into her waiting arms. "This is such a bizarre conversation," she said, forcing a laugh.

"All of our conversations are bizarre, Zelda." I closed my good arm around her shoulder and pressed my lips to the crown of her head. There was no way she couldn't feel the ridge of my shaft between us, just as there was no way I mistook her wiggling against—and not away from—it. "I see no reason to change that mandate now but I would like to know why you're hell-bent on—what is it?—symmetry."

She dropped her head to my chest. "Because I don't like getting caught in situations where everything is asymmetrical and I'm the one bending and scrunching and giving away everything to fit into my tiny slice."

Steam and heat filled the room but cold snaked over my shoulders. "Who put you in that tiny slice?" She started to shake her head but I tilted her chin up to meet my gaze. "Zelda, love, you will tell me right now who did that to you."

Casting her eyes down, she sawed her teeth over her bottom lip and said, "I did."

ELEVEN
ZELDA

It was true.

What they said.

About shoes. And feet.

And penises.

It was all true.

For the hundredth time in ten minutes, I stole a glimpse at Ash over the laptop's screen, my cheeks flaming hot enough to sear a scallop. Seated at the other end of the dining table, he was studying something on his tablet while simultaneously keying numbers into the battered old calculator at his side and then frowning at the readout. Always frowning. That little TI-whatever from eleventh grade trigonometry was pissing him off.

It was so freaking true.

I hadn't intended to get a faceful of naked. I had *not*. But I'd heard noises—things falling—and my first instinct was to verify Ash was unharmed. While I knew he was showering when I'd heard those noises, my run-and-check-on-Ash thought process hadn't accounted for him also being naked and wet.

The wet part really pushed matters over the edge. Not the

muscular grooves cut into his torso. Not the Coppertone-baby-inspired tan line. Not even the shaft that proved the best of the urban legends.

Not that I'd gotten a good look at it. The tan line. Of course, the tan line. What else would I not look at?

"Hey. Zelda. What's up?"

"What?" I leaned back in my chair and blinked up at him. "Nothing." Grabbed for the pen at my side, pressed it between my palms. "I didn't say anything."

Getting caught noodling over memories of my boss in the shower while extremely wet and naked was much like burning yourself with a curling iron. You knew the blazing hot fire wand was *thiiiiiis* close to your face but you were too busy shaping your tousled waves to realize and now you had your very own Harry Potter scar. Ten points to Gryffindor.

"I didn't…" He tipped his head as if seeing me from a different angle would help. He could stop right there because I knew it wouldn't. Then, he chuckled. "How's my calendar looking?"

I glanced down at the screen. It was a rainbow of overcommitment. "If you were hoping this week would be the one you make time for a new hobby, I have bad news for you."

He shook his head, allowing himself another low laugh. "I haven't had time for hobbies since I was fourteen."

I set the pen down, folded my arms on the table. "What happened when you were fourteen?"

"Nothing *happened*," he drawled. "I just—I don't know, it was high school. I was taking a full course load and I had a job and—"

"And the first thing to go was fun," I said. "Yeah, Ashville. I can see that being one of your moves."

"It wasn't a move," he argued. "It's growing up. People do that all the time, Zelda."

"Sure, they do," I replied. "You're not one of them."

He glared at the ceiling, sighed, and asked, "What the hell are you trying to say?"

"That you were an adult the minute you were born," I replied. "Call it being an old soul or whatever you want but you grew up at birth. I'm sure of it." I gestured toward him. "What was the hobby you gave up at fourteen?"

His brows shot up and any semblance of a smile he might've had fell. He studied his tablet for a moment before asking, "How's the inbox?"

Finding Ash's sore spots was almost as fascinating as finding the sweet spots. He was sensitive in the most delightful and unexpected—and *telling*—ways. He didn't like being wrong and he hated losing control but more than that, he didn't want to be found lacking. Somewhere along the way, someone told Ash he wasn't good enough and he'd never been able to shake that.

Probably because nosy people like me kept poking that sore spot and driving it deeper into his soft tissue. I hadn't meant to nudge him where it hurt. If anything, I wanted to find another one of those sweet spots. Just as I was certain he was an old soul in a pleasantly young and virile body, I was also certain he'd rest his head in my lap and fall asleep while I ran my fingers through his hair.

He was starved for affection. I was starved to give it. And I liked him. Oh, hell, did I like him. He was fucked-up in the best ways. He was an egomaniac and couldn't imagine a world where anyone was smarter or better or more competent than him. He didn't know how to ask for help and he was liable to burst into flames if he tried. He was demanding and impatient and occasionally rude, and I liked it because he never hid from me. Not really, not in any duplicitous way. He was grouchy in a fashion that made me want to smother him in joy and silliness and snuggles. I wanted to sneak cookies into his briefcase and argue with him about things that didn't matter and force him to play drunk Jenga because it would be profoundly amusing. He was salty as fuck and secretly adorable and he didn't look at me like I was a shopping cart with a wonky wheel. He looked at me like I was magic.

All the pieces fit, save for him being my boss and me being in the most discombobulated stage of my life imaginable. Just those teeny, tiny, wee issues.

"Hmmmm. About your inbox." I dragged my lower lip between my teeth. Ash's email was a never-ending avalanche. Each time I removed a chunk of pointless "thank you" and "got it!" messages, another horde appeared to take their place. "I've weeded out the nonsense and prioritized the ones that looked important but there's more to work through."

"It will never be done," he said, punching a string of numbers into his calculator. "Inbox zero isn't something I'll live to see."

He glanced at his wrist, scowled, and tapped the tablet twice. Since today was the day when I noticed every last thing about this man, I knew this wasn't the first time he'd eyeballed that bare wrist. "Why are you doing that?"

"Doing what?" he asked, not meeting my gaze.

"You've looked at your hand every few minutes since you sat down," I replied. "Considering we've been sitting here for about three hours, you've done it at least fifteen times."

With a sigh, he dragged his hand down his face, saying, "*Fuck*, Zelda. Just...fuck." He laughed in a way that made me want to join in. "How do you do that?"

"Did I stumble upon a vast conspiracy?" I asked. "I've always wanted to uncover a conspiracy, so I hope it's that. Or is it the pain meds giving you some weird creepy-crawly feelings? When I had my wisdom teeth out, they loaded me up on the good stuff but it felt like there were bugs all over me."

"No conspiracy, no hallucinations," he said. "Billable hours are divided into six-minute segments. I mark the file I'm working on to keep track."

"Okay, part of that makes sense." I gestured to the tan line at the base of his forearm. "I'm still wondering why you look at your wrist."

"Because it's where my watch used to be," he replied. "Before you knocked me on my ass in the terminal and it broke. Back in Denver."

"I was not responsible for that," I said. "You tripped over your own feet, sir. It's not my fault they're enormous."

"For your information, I tripped over a child," he argued, a laugh ringing in his voice. "One I didn't even notice before catapulting over. I don't know how I blew out my shoulder and busted my watch while that kid walked away unscathed."

"Right. Resent the child for being uninjured. That's great. You know, it's a good thing I found you, Ashville." I closed the laptop, leaned forward. "You need full-time supervision."

He tipped his chin at the computer. "Finished?" When I nodded, he continued, "I'm hungry. Let's go out. There's a place I like. I want to bring you there."

My life was an aerial shot of a town destroyed by a tornado right now. Nothing left standing, just shards of existence strewn over miles of flat, unforgiving land. Rebuilding was the only course of action for me. I couldn't spend time lingering on the belly butterflies that took flight each time he demanded my attention. I couldn't bask in the warmth of his embraces. I couldn't devote sun and water to growing this thing between us when the rest of me was an uprooted, wilting mess.

I couldn't—but I did.

"If you like it, I'll like it," I replied. "We both know you're the hardest to please."

"That is a gross misrepresentation of the facts," he said, pushing to his feet. "I'm highly adaptable."

"I'm sure you are, sweetie," I cooed. I slung my bag across my chest. "If you're not going to die of the hungry horrors, let's get you a new watch first. You're highly adaptable but you're going to keep on looking at your wrist and it's still half past the freckle until we put a timepiece there."

Ash swung his arm around my shoulder and steered me toward the door. "I have no doubt in my mind you'll uncover a conspiracy one of these days."

ONCE AGAIN, I FOUND MYSELF TUCKED BESIDE ASH IN THE BACK seat of a car.

Once again, I didn't hate it.

There was something special about sitting beside him, close enough to observe his mannerisms without getting caught staring. The way he manspread like a champ. The way he drummed his fingers on his knee when stopped in traffic. The way he glanced at his wrist every few minutes, only to shake his head or arch an eyebrow as he looked away. The way he leaned into me, his shoulder nudging mine.

The last thing I should've done was respond by brushing my elbow against his forearm. I was in no place for shoulder nudging and elbow brushing. No place for back seat moments of any sort.

"Where are we going?" I asked, our bodies still pressed together in strange, bony ways. It was a noncommittal form of hand-holding. We weren't prepared for the implications of such a gesture and weren't sure we wanted *that* much of each other but needed a little something.

"Back Bay," he replied, shooting me a quick glance. "I figure we can eat and then walk over to the Apple store. It will be cooler by then. Won't be so horrible walking around."

I stared out the window at the blaze of sunset over the city. Boston sunsets were nothing like Denver sunsets. No mountains changing color along with the sky, no peaks for the sun to dip beneath. None of it was the same. I wasn't the same.

I barely recognized the person I'd left behind in Denver. I wasn't her, not anymore. That knowledge hit me like the morning after my first set of push-ups in ten years—I was sore in unexpected spots but I also felt good and strong and right. I was aware of myself in ways I hadn't been recently, each step away from Denver aching and burning a bit as if my body was telling me *this hurts but it will be worth it.*

When we pulled up at the restaurant, Ash stepped out of the car and held the door open while I scooched across the bench seat and thanked the driver. I joined him on the sidewalk, waiting for him to lead the way. The finger drumming continued on his thigh while he stared down the street, frowning.

"Do you like cheese?" he asked. Again, all the awkwardness in the world blossomed between us, a reminder we barely knew each other. Even though we very much did. "As in…different kinds of cheese?"

"Different kinds of cheese?" I repeated. "Yeah, of course. What's not to like?"

"I've learned to stop being surprised. You have blue hair and the phases of the moon on your arm, and you're an archaeologist from Denver. Not eating cheese would fit in with all that just fine." He rubbed his palm over his brow. "I want to make sure you can order something you'll enjoy. It'll piss me off if you sit there, picking at a tiny bowl of olives." He pointed toward a restaurant called The Salty Pig and then brought his palm to the small of my back, urging me forward. "Come on, Zelda."

"Thanks for asking," I mumbled, letting him lead me inside.

I needed to say those words out loud but I wasn't certain I wanted him to hear them. This wasn't about him being decent enough to inquire as to my preferences. It was about me recognizing I deserved to engage with people who paid attention to me and my preferences. It wasn't expecting too much. It was barely expecting anything at all.

"I didn't catch that," Ash said, ducking his head to speak directly into my ear. The hand on my back pulled me closer to him. "What did you say?"

"I just said I always knew you were a cheesy guy. You're going to have great dad jokes someday."

He laughed, his forehead at my temple and his nose on my cheek. "Your faith in me is admirable."

We sat at the bar, still side by side, still connected in small, unlikely ways. His knee on my thigh, my shoulder on his bicep, our forearms brushing each other as we inspected at the menu.

"What's good here?" I asked.

"Everything," he replied, overflowing with enthusiasm. That was a new look on him.

Laughing, I asked, "What do you usually order?"

"Everything," he repeated, pressing his arm against mine. "Last time I was here, it was with my sister and her fiancé. We shared two pizzas, a charcuterie board, an order of meatballs, and some fried brussels sprouts."

"So…yeah, that's everything," I said, glancing back at the menu. "It all sounds great."

"Do you trust me?" he asked.

"With what, Ashville? Cheese? Sure. No problem." I jerked my shoulders up as I flipped the menu over to inspect the cocktail choices. Terrible idea. They all sounded amazing and the last thing I needed to be around this man was tipsy. "Do I trust you to pick out an eye shadow palette or use a blowtorch? Not on your life."

"All right. I'll order for us," he said, a wide grin on his face. "You should know I'm plenty capable with blowtorches."

"Agree to disagree," I said, waving him off. "I don't want you wielding fire, thank you very much."

"And why not?" he asked, ballsy enough to be insulted.

I skimmed the wine list. Not that I knew anything about wine but it was fun to read the names and origins. "Why would you even need a blowtorch?"

"I don't," he replied. "You brought it up."

The bartender stopped in front of us, folding his beefy forearms on the bar as he smiled. "What can I get you folks tonight?"

Ash tapped his finger against the menu, pointing to his selections as he spoke. I didn't know what the Vermont verano or the Blue Ledge camembrie were, but they sounded good. He ordered a beer and requested an extra dish of Marcona almonds.

"And for the lady?" the bartender asked. "What can I pour for you?"

Ash looped his arm over the back of my chair as I asked him, "What kind of beer did you order?"

"The Allagash is a sour ale," the bartender offered. He gestured toward my hair as Ash cleared his throat. "It's brewed with real blueberries."

Ash shifted his arm from the chair to my shoulders, tugging me closer. "Would you like that?"

It was unfair. Completely and truly unfair. Why did I have to wait until now, when my life was spinning like a blender without its lid, to realize how desperately I needed someone to ask me that question? It didn't matter whether he was asking me about beer or blowtorches or anything else in the world. And I wanted to answer him—answer myself. I wanted to know what I wanted and where I belonged and who the fuck I was after all these years of searching and shrinking down to fit the tiny crevices available to me.

I wanted to answer but all I could say was, "Maybe."

Maybe. Maybe I liked sour blueberry beer. Maybe I liked it when my boss glared at a bartender and pawed me like I was marked territory. Maybe I liked leaving the lid off the blender because now—finally now—I didn't have to pretend I cared about the mess I'd made. The mess that was made of me. I didn't have to keep it anymore. It was out, sprayed all over the ceiling and walls and everywhere, and it wasn't inside me.

"I'll put your order in and bring you a sample of the Allagash," the bartender said, pushing away from the bar with a wink in my direction.

Ash's lips were on my temple before the bartender made it two steps.

The twinges that felt good and right? I felt them in all the places Ash touched me.

TWELVE
ASH

Well, I'd lost my fucking mind.

That was the singular explanation for my manic reaction to the bartender who'd given Zelda an altogether too thorough once-over. He'd eye-fucked her cleavage while she studied the menu and, for the first time in my life, I wanted to grab another man by the collar and slam him up against a wall. And that asshole thought her blue hair somehow translated to a preference for blueberry beer. Of all the ridiculous, reductionist things.

Then, I'd tugged her closer, whispered into her ear, kissed her forehead. Watched as she sampled several different beers, scrunching up her face and shaking her head at the taste of each one. Wanted to find the one that would make her smile more than I wanted anything else.

Yeah. I'd lost my fucking mind.

That was why the hand not enclosed in the sling was shoved deep in my pocket as we walked up Dartmouth Street toward the Apple store on Boylston. This was a rare moment where having one useful hand helped rather than hindered matters. It was hard enough minding that hand when I wanted to run my fingers through her hair or brush my palm over the small of her back or squeeze the rounded backside she kept wrapped like a birthday present in vintage jeans.

I wasn't this guy. I didn't fight off the urge to grab anyone's ass. I didn't notice physical attractiveness unless I stopped and made myself focus on seeing it. I didn't think I'd ever touched a woman's hair because I'd wanted to feel it on my fingers and I didn't understand that reaction now. I wasn't this guy.

Now that I was thinking about how much I wasn't that guy, it was worth noting I didn't spend much time thinking about sex. The world wanted me to believe that was uncommon. Some kind of anomaly. I didn't care. I'd had sex. I'd enjoyed sex. I'd never found a reason to let it dominate my life and I appreciated the hell out of that because I had too much on my mind as it was.

And then Zelda Besh came along and quite literally fucked me up. Oh yeah, she made me this guy. I must've hit my head when I fell in the airport. Knocked something loose. Traumatic brain injury was the only explanation for my newfound desire to —to fucking consume this woman.

That traumatic brain injury must've also accounted for my manic lapses in judgment because there was no way in hell's sandcastle I'd interact with an employee like this otherwise. She wasn't technically employed as she hadn't signed an offer letter or standard confidentiality agreement, and hadn't completed an I-9 or W-4. In that sense, I was only flouting ethical business practices in theory. Like that made it any better.

When I stepped back and looked at the way this week came to a close, I wasn't positive I knew how it all added up. Millie had broken up with me; I'd broken up with the normal functioning of my shoulder. Then Zelda swept into my life and now I had a new assistant, a new roommate, a new case of grabby hands, and a fuckton of new problems I didn't care to solve.

And I wasn't that guy.

Leaving issues to linger on the fringe of my consciousness made me restless and irritable. More irritable than usual. I didn't like leaving work for another day.

"This is a perfect night," she remarked, her face tipped up toward the sky. "I like nights like this, when it's never fully dark until midnight and there's no reason to be inside."

I didn't do this. I didn't want this. And yet—

Rising up on her toes, she turned in a circle like a punk rock ballerina. The tall, gleaming windows of the Boston Public Library reflected her movements, forcing me to choose between the glowing silhouette of her and the real thing. Both were enchanting but it was the silhouette that never made me wonder why she was running away from home. What she was running from. How I could help her.

"These are the nights you remember," she said. "They're the ones that go down in your memories as emblematic of summer, and when it's dark and cold in January, this gets you through the worst of it. You never remember the days of disgustingly oppressive heat or the bug bites. The sunburns are forgotten and only the gorgeous morsels of perfection remain. Memories are good to us that way. They help us forget the rough spots and crave the bright ones."

She twirled again, her arms held over her head in a proper pirouette. I stopped to watch. People swerved around us on the sidewalk but I barely noticed. Zelda was right, it was the perfect night. But I wasn't sure about my brain forgetting the rough spots. I wasn't sure I worked that way.

I held out my hand to her when she stopped spinning.

"Come on," I said, nodding toward the Apple store ahead. Her lips quirking in an odd grin, she placed her hand in mine. "Let's get this done. Then we can walk some more."

When we reached the store, it was blessedly empty and the staff sprang into action to replace my device. I had to drop her hand to retrieve the dead watch from my pocket and I couldn't decipher Zelda's sigh when I did it. I wanted to ask her whether it was relief or disappointment, or something else altogether, but I couldn't seem to start that sentence. Instead, we circled the display tables while we waited.

She stopped in front of the watches, examining the samples closely. "You really dig this thing, huh?"

I turned away from the iPads on the adjacent table and stepped up to her from behind, my chest brushing her back. "It works for me, yeah. It also tells me when to calm the fuck down so I don't stroke out over inappropriate expense reporting."

"Always helpful," she murmured, still fingering the watch.

"Do you want one? Here, I'll grab one for you and you can give it a shot," I said, glancing around to find the genius assigned to me.

"No, no, no. Slow down, Ashville."

Her hair brushed my chin as laughter moved through her. I leaned in, pressed my lips to the crown of her head. This—my body against hers, her scent all around me, my arm itching to band across her belly and hold her the way I wanted—was a bright spot I'd never struggle to recall.

"Slow it way down," she continued. "I neither need nor want one of these Jetsons watches. I don't like having that much personal information mined. They know where I am and where I've been, who I'm with, when I'm sleeping, when I'm not sleeping. They've run an MBTI and my credit score. They've determined exactly which ads to feed me and clocked the number of times I've watched the dinner party episode of *The Office*. They're planning my future by placing all these digital flags in my path and telling the government all about it. They know about my under-the-table babysitting money too. They're listening to everything and the real truth is, I don't need anyone hearing my rendition of 'Born to Run.' I don't want to give anyone all that information."

Of course she liked Springsteen. And of course it was "Born to Run." God damn, this woman. I could forget every rough spot in the world when I held her close and shut my eyes.

"Ah, so you want to uncover a conspiracy theory and you also want to live in one," I said into her hair. "Good to know."

"Oh my god, Ashville," she muttered, tilting her head to the side. She wanted me to pay attention to her neck. She wanted my mouth there and I was not going to deny her because who the hell could say no to a request like that? "It's not a conspiracy theory. They're listening. You know that. And you know they're selling all your data. That's not even tinfoil-hat shit anymore, that's front-page news."

"All right. Let me get you a phone. For work," I added, brushing my lips over the sweet column of her neck.

"I don't need a phone," she replied, her words soft. "But thank you."

I wanted to slip my hand under her shirt and explore the tender skin below her navel the same way I was exploring her neck. Light, delicate passes of my lips over her skin, just enough for her to know I'd forgotten everything I'd said before, erased all the lines I'd drawn. "I'm not taking no for an answer."

"That's not something you can say in this day and age," she quipped.

"I'm not taking no for an answer," I repeated, a growl ringing through my words. "There's a phone in your back pocket. It's been there all day. You haven't taken it out once. You used my phone to find the urgent care and order the car service last night. I'm betting yours hasn't been switched on since leaving Mountain Time. Let me get you a new one so you can avoid yours a little longer."

"You noticed all that?"

"I notice everything." I flattened my free hand on the table, caging her in as much as any guy with a bum arm could. "You can tell me anything...but you don't have to. You don't owe me any explanations. Just let me do this, love."

She stared down at the display watch in her hands. I expected a refusal. I expected an argument. I expected another conversation where we talked in circles around the fact we were tangled up in each other in nine different ways.

Instead, Zelda melted against me, nodding. "Okay, Ash. You get your way this time but don't say I didn't warn you about the constant surveillance thing. The machines are learning about human behavior from us."

"That seems unwise," I murmured. "The part about learning from us. The machines should listen to other people. You and me, we're way off the tail ends of the bell curve."

A laugh rippled through her body, the vibrations coursing into me as the sound passed her lips. She tucked her hair back over her ear, saying, "You get me, Ashville. You really get me."

WE WALKED HOME FROM THE APPLE STORE. IT WAS A BIT OF A distance but it seemed we both had energy to burn.

We didn't talk, didn't touch, but we walked close enough for anyone to know we were together. The precise type of together was still unclear to me.

I kept remembering the way she'd tilted her head for me in the store, granting access to her neck and quietly ordering me to that beautiful spot. There were at least ten occasions on the walk where I seriously contemplated grabbing her around the waist or shoving my hands into her hair or twisting her shirt in my fist and yanking her against me. I wanted to take the energy crackling between us and make it explode, and I couldn't say I cared if I burned in the process.

I didn't care though I stopped myself every time.

Maybe it was the lingering sting of Millie dropping me like I was the human equivalent of junk mail—what'd I been thinking with her?—or the whirlwind of my time with Zelda. Whatever the origin, I didn't trust myself to read the situation accurately. And I wanted to get this right. If I hauled her into my lap and kissed her the way I wanted to—and the way I wanted to involved no clothes and a bed—it was possible I'd lose a friend, a roommate, and assistant in one swoop.

More than all that, I could lose Zelda.

Desire could boil me through and through and I'd endure it. I'd wait as long as I had to, even if I waited forever. I knew that as well as I knew the tax code.

Once inside my apartment, Zelda leaned back against the door and twisted her fingers around the strap of her purse. She kept her gaze away from me. I watched her as I hung up my keys and toed off my shoes. Eventually, I asked, "What's up with you?"

She shook her head and flung open her arms as if she intended to say something enormous but then she looked up at me and whatever she'd meant to say evaporated as she studied me. "Do you need anything? How are you feeling?" she asked.

I need to kneel at your feet and beg for the honor of touching you.

A soundless laugh shook my chest. I'd do it. I'd kneel for her. I'd earn it, I'd kiss my way from her belly button down, and I'd kneel.

"I'm fine, Zelda." I stepped closer, tucked her hair over her ear. "What about you?"

"Oh? Me?" She ran a hand down the center of my shirt, over the line of buttons. "I'm fantastic. Like, completely fantastic."

I flattened my hand on the door at her back. "Are you sure? It's been a day."

"It's been *a day*," she repeated, lifting her gaze to mine.

We stared at each other for a full minute. Sixty whole seconds passed, I was certain of it.

At the exact moment I asked, "Do you want to hang out?" Zelda pointed down the hall, the one leading to the guest room, saying, "I'm kind of tired. I should get some sleep."

"Oh, yeah. Of course," I replied.

"But I could stay," she said.

"No, no," I argued, stepping back. "You're right. It's late and—"

"And we're visiting your family tomorrow," she added.

I dragged my hand down my face, groaning. "Oh my god, you're right. I can't believe I agreed to drive out there on a summer weekend."

"In that case," she said, moving toward the guest room hallway, "we should both get some rest. It sounds like tomorrow will be a busy one."

"It will be something," I muttered, staring after her as she walked away from me. "Good night."

She raised her hand in a wave and called, "Good night" as she stepped into the bedroom.

I stood there, barefoot and lost, longer than I should've. But as the minutes passed and her absence shifted from a cold snap to a dull ache, I forced myself into my bedroom. I did my best to get out of my clothes without fouling up the shoulder brace contraption too much, and once again I marched into the bathroom with the singular objective of jerking my want for Zelda right out.

I required that quick release to satisfy some of the hunger inside me. I needed it to make a dent in the overwhelming desire to consume Zelda, body and spirit. And I needed it to provide me enough momentary relaxation to get some sleep without resting my head on that gorgeous woman's body.

It didn't.

All I got was another streak on the shower wall and a buzz in my body that seemed to say, "Great warm-up. When's the real game starting?"

I tossed and turned in bed as much as I could, considering the busted shoulder situation. I slept for minutes here and there. My dick was hard the entire time.

After three hours of nocturnal torture, I heaved myself out of bed and went in search of some pain medication. Instead of the pills, I found Zelda curled up on the sofa wearing what I could only describe as nothing.

"Oh," she yelped, scrambling to the corner and tucking her legs under her. "I didn't mean to wake you up."

"You didn't," I said, my voice only slightly gentler than a bark. "I've been up."

Her gaze dropped to my boxers. "I can see that."

THIRTEEN
ZELDA

There were two things you should know about me. Probably twenty things, but for the present situation two were most important.

One, I didn't sleep well. I'd never been able to rest my head on a pillow, shut my eyes, and drift off to dreamland. I had to wiggle around in bed and make unrealistic plans for the next day and reevaluate every time I'd ever said supremely cringey things in otherwise ordinary moments. I couldn't wind down until my head completed its Rockette-style high kicks for the night. Most of the time, I avoided the mental spinout with reruns of *The Golden Girls* or *The Office*, melting into the comfortable predictability like chocolate bars in the microwave. Even then, I drifted for hours in a groggy state that was neither asleep nor awake.

And two, I didn't own any pajamas. No one believed this but it was the damn truth. I slept in underwear and t-shirts, and not baggy sleep shirt-ish ones from Homecoming 2008 but actual t-shirts. The same ones I wore most days with jeans. They weren't big or holey, or otherwise pajama-y. Sometimes, I opted for a tank top. When it suited me, I skipped the shirt altogether and stuck with undies—or nothing at all. I couldn't justify buying clothes to sleep in when I was perfectly cozy without. The only exception was a pair of boxer shorts I'd owned since high school, back when it was "fashionable" for girls to wear boxers as clothing. Now, nearly twelve years later, those boxers were faded beyond recognition and washed so soft, they were threadbare. Any sudden movements and those things were bound to fall apart.

Like I said, you should know this. It made the whole *lounging on Ash's sofa in the middle of the night wearing men's underwear and a tank top* thing a lot less unusual.

There was no explanation for my inability to stop staring at the erection trapped behind his boxer briefs. I mean, nothing beyond the knowledge of what that thing looked like when wet and what it felt like pressed against my thigh.

Ash glanced to the television—*Parks and Rec*, tonight's elixir—and then back at me. Brows furrowed, he asked, "Why are you awake?"

Blinking at him, I jerked my shoulders up. "Why are you?"

"Because..." He tapped his fingers against his hip, forcing my gaze back to his boxers. Either he liked the attention or he had no idea what was happening down there. "Because I couldn't sleep. My shoulder hurts and—and I don't know. Maybe I'm still on Mountain Time."

"You don't seem like the kind of person who lets pesky things such as time zones interfere with your life," I replied.

Annoyance splashed over him like a spilled bowl of soup. "What kind of person is that?"

"There's no reason to take offense, Ashville." I stood, straightening my tank top straps in the process, and headed into the kitchen. I returned with his prescription painkiller and a glass of water. "We both know you like things a certain way. Nothing wrong with that or the fact your body does recognize when it's in a different environment, even if you wished it didn't. The fact is, you need what you need."

He tapped his fingers on that hip like he was sending a very important telegraph. Tapped for the length of a dog food commercial. Then he accepted the pill and water, gulped them down, and said, "Right now, I need you to clarify what you're saying to me."

I ran my tongue over my top lip and glanced at the television before settling back into my corner of the sofa. Most of the time, there wasn't a reason for my sleeplessness. I never called it insomnia because I did sleep for a couple of hours each night, once I'd chilled out enough to get there. But I couldn't sleep tonight because I was overwhelmed the way a fountain gushed and billowed when a bottle of bubble bath found its way into the water. Everything was so much.

But somehow, Ash—the human spreadsheet who couldn't stop bringing my attention to his standard deviation—wasn't part of that overwhelm. Not really. The push and pull between us didn't send my mind whirling in an up-all-night way but I couldn't ignore the feelings he stirred in me. They were danger-ously close to becoming the kind of feelings that grew roots and sprouted limbs. And they demanded I acknowledge them.

"Zelda. Explain it to me," he said, dropping a knee onto the sofa. "Please. I don't want to misunderstand. Explain it, love."

When I'd decided to leave Colorado, I knew the summer would involve soul-searching. Some effort devoted to finding myself and deciding how that person wanted to live her life. Men and sex weren't part of the plan.

If someone had asked me that morning, before boarding the flight to Boston, whether I'd beckon a man toward me so we could watch sitcoms at three in the morning while dressed in nothing more than our underwear, I would've laughed.

I would've argued it was time for me to prioritize my needs —hell, recognize the existence of those needs!—and inviting a man to nestle between my legs and rest his head on my belly wasn't on the path to self-actualization. It wasn't the way to figuring out this new chapter of my life and putting the past behind me.

I would've insisted I was finished being a vessel for others, a stepping-stone to help them achieve their dreams while mine went unfulfilled.

I would've said I needed to do this outrageously selfish thing and I had to do it *alone*.

But here I was, a handful of days and thousands of miles removed from Colorado, with Ash's body pressed against mine as another episode of *Parks and Rec* started. It was the one where a guy handcuffed himself to Leslie's office radiator over the *Twilight* books. A solid episode.

"Is this all right?" he asked, his cheek flat on my torso and his arm around my waist. "Are you comfortable?"

I'd expected the summer to be difficult. Listening to and validating one's needs wasn't like getting bangs. It took months, maybe even years, of unlearning destructive, harmful habits. You didn't wake up in the morning, decide to give a shit about yourself, and then live that way by lunchtime.

But then Ash Santillian snuggled me on a sofa in the middle of the night, his cock harder than ever on my leg, and I discovered it could be that simple. At least when my needs sat on the same level as his, it could plant those seeds.

"This is good," I replied, sweeping my hand down his back. "I'm good."

I was asleep before the end of the episode.

————

W‍HEN SUNLIGHT SWALLOWED UP A‍SH'S LIVING ROOM, I WOKE AND found us wrapped together, legs twined, our arms locked around each other. None of this should've been comfortable enough to allow for sleep. His hand was under my shirt, steady between my shoulder blades as his breath came in even puffs against my neck. Mine sat at the small of his back, my fingertips edged beneath the band of his boxers. I didn't remember consciously choosing to take my touch into that territory but then again, I didn't remember how *any* of this happened.

I knew the facts of the matter and I knew the logistics that brought me and Ash here, stripped down to nearly nothing and snuggled like lovers while his hips lazily bucked against mine in sleep but I didn't know how this had become my new world. I didn't know how I'd abandoned all the weight of the past months and years seemingly overnight and I didn't know how the atoms inside me combined to shed the skin of lifetimes past and replace it with fresh newness and a keening desire to be held by *this man alone*. I didn't know the sequence of words and moments and touches that brought us to this. For as much as I wanted to excavate and study each of those incidents, that required stepping away and examining this from a distance. I didn't want to do that. I didn't want this to end.

If I could stay right here, just like this, I could avoid all the reality bound to catch up with me. I could pretend Ash was clinging and rutting because he wanted me in all of my randomness, my me-ishness, rather than desperately needing his affection tank refilled. I could allow myself to believe I hadn't blown up my life and I wasn't trying to outrun the blast.

Ash shifted, stretched. His body was so—*oof*—taut against mine. "You hum when you think." His words rumbled against my neck, rough and sleepy. "It's really cute."

I glanced down at him but his eyes were still shut. I snatched my hand back from the band of his boxers. "I didn't mean to wake you up."

"I'm not complaining." He fumbled for my hand and when he found it, returned it to his lower back. "Since we're talking, would it be all right if I asked you a personal question?"

I studied the thick stubble on his jaw and above his upper lip as I considered this. "I hate to break it to you, Ash, but we're past the point of requiring permission to ask personal questions. This is all one big personal question."

"Is that a yes or a no, Zelda?"

"Yes, go ahead," I replied.

He dragged his hand from between my shoulders to my waist, *slow slow slow* like he wanted me to record the feel of his fingertips all over my skin. "What the hell are you wearing?"

"It's a shirt."

He fisted his hand around the fabric. If he gave the tiniest of tugs, it was bound to rip. "Is it really?"

"Yes," I snapped, failing to keep a laugh out of my voice. "And shorts."

He released the shirt, then traced his knuckles along my vintage waistband. "I'd really like to know whose boxers you're wearing."

"Who? What? Oh, they're mine," I sputtered. "Yeah. These are mine."

He stared down at the boxers, frowning. "I can't decide if I'm surprised or relieved."

"No?"

"No," Ash replied. "And that's not the greatest complication in this matter."

"What would that be?"

His frown morphed into a grimace, his brows gathering. "There's the issue of me being irrationally troubled at the prospect of you sleeping in some other guy's underwear."

Stifling a laugh, I said, "I like that this is when you decide to recognize the irrationality in your thoughts."

"If you liked that, you're going to love my next irrational thought." He dragged his knuckles from my hip to my belly button, making my heart pound in hard, dizzying whomps as he picked up the pace of his sleepy thrusts. "You should wear this *every* night."

Then, because when the universe blessed me with the treasured gift of making everything uncomfortable all the time, it blessed with many hands, I said, "Maybe this works for you but I don't usually wear much of anything to bed. I'm only dressed now because I'm not in bed."

Ash blinked at me, blew out a breath as ragged as hurricane gusts, and rocked his body against mine like he couldn't help but get the last word. He was thick and hard, and if he hadn't frowned at me after holding himself against my body for a heavy-lidded beat, I would've locked my legs around his waist and begged him to finish what he started.

But I'd made it uncomfortable and now Ash was busy overthinking.

"Why did you tell me that?" he asked.

There were no words. Truly, no words. I didn't have an

answer for him and even if I did, the erection throbbing against me was the only thing on my mind. The words available to me now included *yes, condom,* and *please.*

Fortunately for me and rhetorical questions everywhere, Ash continued. "Why do you want me to know that, Zelda? Do you want me knowing there's nothing between you and the sheets? Do you want me thinking about you that way?"

Since I didn't know how to help myself, I said, "I think you'll do it anyway."

There was a moment when he was completely still and silent, and I was even more aware of the places where our bodies touched and formed a new topography. Ash dropped his head to my chest, asking, "And if you're right about that?"

His words reverberated against my breast and I stayed quiet a few extra moments in case this was another question not meant for an answer. Also, I really loved the sensation of him speaking directly to my breast. Eventually, I said, "You tell me, Ash. What does it mean to you if you're thinking about me naked?"

With that, he climbed off the sofa. He gave me his back, not allowing me the pleasure of seeing his war of arousal and agony. I believed I would've enjoyed that. Would've enjoyed it very much. Watching him struggle against the things he believed he wanted and the things he actually wanted was becoming one of my favorite pastimes.

"Fuck, I need to take another shower." As he stalked toward his bedroom, he called, "Do me a favor. Don't come in here, love. Even if it sounds like the ceiling has collapsed and I'm pinned under a ton of rubble, don't come in."

"Got it, boss," I replied, though I was certain he didn't hear me over the slam of his door.

———

FOR SOMEONE WITH AN EXTENSIVE TRACK RECORD OF SHATTERING ordinary moments with extraordinary feats of strange and unusual, I was rather skilled at smoothing over even the stickiest of situations. My method was ridiculously simple: pretend the stickiness didn't exist. Deny, deny, deny. It hadn't happened and you were nuts if you thought it did.

Nothing was easier than that.

Case in point: a handful of years ago, I was walking down the center staircase in the Clark building at Colorado State. That place had more wings than a 1970s-era maxi pad and at least a million stairs, give or take a couple thousand. There I was, descending the stairs like everyone else until I snagged the heel of my shoe on my too-long pants and went for a tumble while everyone watched. I was bruised to shit and broke several fingers in the process but I wasn't about to acknowledge that stickiness in any fashion. No, I stood up and walked away as if my ass and legs weren't already black and blue from thumping down the stairs, as if my pinky finger wasn't bent at an unnatural angle, as if I hadn't felt a damn thing.

And I did the same this morning.

While Ash showered, I rifled through his kitchen cupboards and refrigerator. For someone who'd spent the last week away from home, there was no shortage of fresh ingredients. That was curious yet not unexpected. He struck me like a man who always had everything in order.

I made him a breakfast sandwich because I was required to return the ribbing he'd given me. But I did him one better than the hastily slapped together sammy I'd packed for myself before hitting the road; I whipped up some silver-dollar pancakes in place of toast. The pancake sandwich was the top dog in my breakfast repertoire.

I didn't wait around to inform Ash of this or watch while he picked at the syrupy tower of pancake, egg, bacon, and cheese. As much as I liked watching him experience all manner of things he'd convinced himself he neither wanted nor needed, this wasn't the time for that. It was the time for pretending away the moment we shared this morning and the one from last night too, and all the other moments when we'd wandered too close to the borderlands between emotionally needy cuddling and emotionally needy fucking. Though I wasn't the one with the erection or the rhythmic thrusting, I'd dragged us straight into that land long enough for Ash to regret it.

And I couldn't leave it to him to know better. For once in my life, I had to know better. I had to avoid hurtling toward the edge with my parachute in shreds. In this reincarnation of me, I didn't rely on men to know better, to do better. I relied on me and that meant teaching myself to trust me too.

Leaving the pancake sandwich for Ash, I retreated to the guest room I had yet to use for its intended purpose. I showered and did my best to assemble a *summer weekend dinner party with friends and family* outfit though I'd never experienced such a thing. Then I spent five pointless minutes fussing with my hair. I knew it wasn't going to do what I wanted, not without backup from a curling wand or round brush, and neither of those had earned a spot in my luggage.

But the fussing gave me something to do. The alternative—being still and quiet and settled enough to hear my thoughts—was too daunting for a pancake sandwich Sunday kind of day.

In truth, I needed several more pancake sandwich Sundays before I could contend with my thoughts. The murky ones I only acknowledged in the worst of times, the dangerous ones that made me examine my choices and motivations in a way that invited gasping, overwhelming shame.

Yes, those thoughts could wait. They always did. And until I was ready to plunk myself down in the thistle and rip out the roots, I'd fuss with my hair and smooth my suitcase-wrinkled skirt. After all, I'd run away from my life with nothing more than a vague note in my wake because *I had to*. I was allowed to fixate on my hair and skirt.

After an appropriate amount of obsessing over insignificant things, I emerged to find Ash in the kitchen, his hand on his hip while he glared at his phone in the other. He wasn't wearing his sling but that was the last thing I noticed because he was wearing a polo shirt that must've been tailored to fit every inch of his torso to perfection. His hair, still wet from the shower, was boyishly floppy. The most bizarre urge to slide my hands into the pockets of his navy shorts and feel the body beneath the fabric consumed me.

Without glancing in my direction, he grumbled, "You didn't have to cook for me."

"I know. I did it anyway." I spotted his plate beside the sink, a streak of maple syrup the only remnant. "Hated it, didn't you?"

This earned me his full attention and he'd barely blinked before saying, "Goddamn. What are you wearing?"

Frowning at my plum paisley skirt and its topography of wrinkles, I held my hands out. "Calm down, Ashville. Long, summery skirts aren't meant to be perfect. I'm currently operating as if this is a crinkle fabric. I'm not changing. You need to deal with—"

"I'm not sure what you just said," he growled as he approached me. He lashed his arm around my waist, closing the remainder of the distance between us. "I didn't catch any of it but I don't want you to change a single thing."

Something happened to me then, something like altitude sickness mixed with a tequila buzz, all divided by hunger pangs as if I hadn't eaten in days. It was a strange dizziness that made my eyelids heavy and my lips part and my body *want*. And it wouldn't let me dismiss Ash's words. I couldn't form a response. It wouldn't take shape. The only thing I could manage was "Where's your sling?"

"Don't need it," he said, still holding me tight.

I watched as his gaze traveled from those heavy lids to my parted lips and then down, down to my sleeveless top in the palest of pinks. It wasn't the top that interested him. It was the space between my breasts, the valley only visible from his vantage point.

I didn't have a lot going on there, nothing more than the average, but the way he sucked in a breath and growled at that valley like it belonged to him only made me dizzier, hungrier.

With his gaze locked on my cleavage, he said, "I need you to know something, Zelda. If we do this, if we go to my parents' place—"

"Well, of course we're going," I interrupted.

In that measured, managerial voice he favored so much, he repeated, "If we go, you won't be able to undo it. I need you to know that."

"Why does that sound like an ominous warning from a practiced skeptic? Like, one doesn't simply sneak into Mordor."

"Because it is, love. You can back out of this. Stay here. I'll handle the explanations."

"Why don't you want me to meet your family? That is, the

portion that didn't invite themselves into your bedroom the other day."

He tapped a finger against my belly. "For one, they'd want to keep you."

"What's so bad about that? Your mother and sister are amusing as hell, especially when they literally stared at us in bed and carried on a conversation where they took turns insisting I'm Not Millie. Given this, I'm sure everyone else is equally amusing. And I'm not against being kept. As you might've noticed, I'm not that difficult to collect."

He waited as if he was indulgently allowing me to thatch together my childlike argument. Then, his brows low, he said, "Shall I remind you how *you* informed me that my mother was about to break out the knitting needles because all the grandchildren we're going to give her will need blankets and hats? I'll wager she'll have one finished by morning if I bring you home with me today."

My eyes widened at the thought of his mother's lingering gazes on our visit to the tailor. Yeah, Mrs. Santillian struck me as the type who asked forgiveness rather than permission. "Oh, right, right, right."

"And for two, I don't share." He dipped down, brushing my hair from my shoulder and replacing it with his lips. "I don't share, Zelda."

He kissed my neck the way he knew I liked and I slipped my hand under his shirt the way I knew he liked, and for that beat and breath, the only thing that mattered was the way we fit.

"What you're saying is," I started, "you won't have as much time to be obsessive and tyrannical when your family decides I'm their new favorite thing? Because I'm good at being the flavor of the week, even if there is some wishful knitting involved."

I'd always had a knack for being the friend everyone's parents loved, the one invited to stay for dinner, spend the night, join their summer camping trip. I'd learned early how to make myself invisible yet also indispensable.

"You're not hearing me, love," Ash whispered. "I know you and I know—"

"Hold up, Ashville. You don't *know* me."

He hummed against the juncture between my neck and shoulder but he didn't pull back to look me in the eye for this conversation. He went on kissing me as if he required it. I did. "Maybe I don't know your favorite of the Indiana Jones films—"

"Those movies are such terrible representations of archaeology, they should come with a warning."

Smiling against my neck, he continued, "Like I said, I know you. I know my family too. They'd keep you and toss me."

"I wouldn't let that happen, boss."

And that does it.

Ash's body tightened against mine, a rope stretched to the point of fraying, and a husky breath rattled out of him. Then, "You're sure about this, Zelda? You're allowed to say no."

I was allowed to say no.

While I knew that in an abstract sense, I wasn't sure I knew it in the practical, make my own limits sense. Not until Ash granted me the right.

I scraped both hands up his back, holding him as I had all night. "I want to go," I said. It was good to touch someone this way. Good to gather him in my arms and hold him together while he nibbled my neck. It fed a need in me that'd gone untended too long. "Do you?"

"No," he replied, laughing. "I have to talk to my dad about business matters and I know it won't go smoothly."

If we kept this up, we'd while the day away with circular conversation and unending embraces. The trouble was, I was certain neither of us saw an issue with that. "Why?"

"Because—" He stopped himself, shook his head, and stared down at my breasts again. "We don't see eye to eye on the running of the firm."

This was one of those instances where there was nothing appropriate for me to say and thus silence was the only solution. I'd only learned to spot these situations in the last year or two. Before, my cringeworthy motormouth would've said something snarky about Ash's micromanaging or his leadership by doing everyone else's jobs for them. It'd taken too long to realize it but those comments weren't edgy, they weren't funny, and they weren't helpful.

Silence lingered between us though Ash seemed to find enough entertainment from frowning at my breasts to keep him busy. Eventually, he loosened his hold around my waist and dragged his gaze up to my eyes, saying, "We should head out. Summer traffic is ridiculous."

I followed him out of the apartment, down the hall, into the elevator. We didn't speak but somewhere between locking the door and pressing the button for the basement garage, we agreed to the terms of a new game where every touch had to be reciprocated. It was a twisted, grown-up iteration of the game we all used to play where the only objective was to keep the ball from dropping. And I was absolutely positive Ash didn't know how to lose a game.

Elbows grazed forearms, shoulders slid across chests, hands glanced down backs and over hips. Our hands lingered over each other as we walked toward Ash's car, a surprisingly cool vintage Porsche. I almost lost the game for us when I skittered to a stop several paces ahead of the hunter green roadster but he hooked his arm around my waist and urged me onward.

"I would not have expected—" I pointed at the car as Ash shot me a sidelong glance. "I didn't expect this from you, Ashville. Very nice."

"You might know me," he replied. He opened the door for me, his fingers grazing my backside as he helped me settle into the passenger seat. He crouched down, tucked my hair over my ear. "That doesn't mean you know everything."

I smiled to myself as he rounded the vehicle. I hadn't intended to like this guy. Not this much. I'd wanted a job and I'd wanted to be better than a hard pass. There were obvious reasons for these intentions too. I was in no condition to grow feelings for anything more sentient than a spice rack. Plus, it was clear he'd recently stepped out of some sort of fucked-up situation. I didn't need the whole story to understand everyone's shock at me being someone other than the notorious Millie.

However, the deep, dark, true reason I didn't plan on liking him—or anyone—this much was I didn't know how. I knew how to handle my boss, whomever that was at the moment, but that was more a matter of topping from the bottom than anything else. I could do that now. I could muddle along, anticipating his moods and managing his office and melting into his arms, but I didn't trust myself for anything else.

Inside the small cabin of the Porsche, our game continued in earnest. I rested my hand on his knee as I bent to retrieve my purse. He ran his hand down my arm as he glanced out the rear window. I passed my hand over his when he reached for the gearshift, a thick groan tumbling out of him in the process.

"Are you gonna survive?" I asked, my hand returning to his as he scrunched his eyes closed. "I'm not sure driving a stick shift is on your list of approved activities for a few more days."

He flexed his hand on the knob and choked down another groan. "All good."

Though I didn't entirely believe him, I kept that to myself. We'd know within a couple of minutes of city driving whether he could manage and that gave me the opportunity to ask him the question I'd stored away since commandeering his kitchen. "Do you have a grocery service?"

Ash barked out a laugh as we emerged from the underground garage and into blinding summer sunlight. "Yeah. It's called Diana Santillian Is A Busybody. Great service but the fees will kill you."

Because I truly did not understand, I asked, "What does that mean?"

"It means my mother takes it upon herself to leave her home on the southeast coast of Massachusetts, drive to Boston, and stock my kitchen with whichever items she believes I need."

Again, I truly did not understand. "Why?"

"You're asking for some long-form history if you want the answer to that, Zelda," he said with a chuckle.

I gestured to the highway entrance on the other side of the intersection. "We have time."

At first, he didn't respond. He squinted at the traffic, took a sip from his stainless-steel water bottle, plucked his wallet from a back pocket and dropped it in the center console. Then, "The food is the byproduct, it's not the primary driver here. We grew up as free-range kids, probably more than others from our generation. We were allowed to wander and roam and make our own kinds of trouble. Encouraged, even. My parents were all about us exploring without them hovering while we did it. And it wasn't just traipsing through forests. It was everything. We were responsible for our schoolwork, for dressing ourselves to get out the door on time, all that stuff. And that autonomy took different forms in each of us. It still does. But the problem with growing free-range kids is—as far as my mother is concerned—they turn into independent adults."

It was amusing to me, in a gravely bitter kind of way, how Ash and I both knew independence at early ages but his was the result of intentional parenting and mine was the result of, well, neglect. I'd been clothed and fed and sheltered but neglect had dimensions. It had shades.

"It's fascinating, if not a bit cloying, how my mother is so much more concerned with looking after us now," Ash continued. "She'll plan her entire week around preparing meals for me, Magnolia, and Linden and delivering them to us while also bringing paper towels and dish soap and whatever else crosses her mind. She'll figure out what we're eating—and not eating—as a method of checking in on us. And maybe it's my adult view on the matter. Maybe my mother did hover when we were kids and we just didn't notice it. Maybe that's the gift we didn't know we were given."

He was right about that. It *was* a gift and Ash was perceptive enough to recognize it as such. He wasn't a complete tyrant. He wasn't a tyrant at all, not in any true sense of the word. He just preferred things a certain way and hoarded responsibility because he didn't know how to live without simultaneously proving himself to someone or something that surely wouldn't notice his efforts.

"But like I said, it can be cloying," he continued.

"She cares about you, Ashville. Plenty of people would kill

for a parent who cares. Take it from me. It's not the worst thing in the world."

The second he swung that pinched-brow, sharp-eyed gaze in my direction, I knew I'd said too much. Way too much. Even as he returned his attention to the road, he watched me with thoughtful frowns and inquisitive furrows. Too much, too much.

Of course, I overcorrected for that slip by cramming every breath with mindless chatter. *What was that rainbow-painted tank on the left? What's the story with that billboard? How did you pronounce the name of that street on the off-ramp sign?*

Ash answered all those questions in a clipped, distracted way as he continued with his frowns and furrows. Then, "Who knows where you are right now?"

"I'm thirty-one years old, single, and owe money to no one. The only person who needs to know where I am is me."

"My siblings and I share our locations with each other. Either of them can open up the app and find me at any time," he replied. "It just…I don't know, it helps. It's smart."

I feigned a ton of interest in a large pond beside the highway. "Is it smart because it was your idea or is it smart because it's served a meaningful purpose on occasions unrelated to your micromanagement compulsion?"

"Meaningful purposes, for sure," he replied. "Whenever we're supposed to meet up and Linden says he'll be there in five minutes, I can track his location and know he's still on the coast and at least ninety minutes away." He tapped my outer thigh. "You can't trust that guy to show up on time because his only concept of time is the sun. I mean it. He doesn't wear a watch, leaves his phone in the truck. He looks at the sky to tell time. If Magnolia and I didn't track him, we would've missed the first half of every game we've planned to watch together because we were waiting outside the stadium."

"I'll grant you that one," I conceded.

"What about you? Any siblings?"

I ran my fingertips over the back of his hand. "Sort of."

A quick breath of laughter shook his torso. "I don't know what that means."

I shrugged. "You don't have to know."

He shot me a sidelong glance. "Let me ask you again. Who knows where you are?"

Since the lady protesting too much never improved her situation, I said, "There's you and me, which makes two whole people. And the artificial intelligence unit assigned to tracking everything I do."

He groaned but this time it wasn't the strain of downshifting with an injured shoulder. "Zelda," he said, in one breath my name twisting into a sigh, an admonishment, a sympathetic embrace. "What the hell is that all about?"

"I'm not sure what you're asking." *When in doubt, pretend it didn't happen.*

"We have a solid hour ahead of us. Use some of that time to tell me more about your relocation plans."

"No," I replied simply.

The stunned laugh of a man unacquainted with roadblocks and refusals echoed inside the car. "No?"

"I understand it's difficult to hear something exists outside your reach, Ashville, but you being unhappy doesn't mean I should roll over on my limits."

Even his sharp exhale was wrapped in exasperation. I imagined this was a strange experience for Ash, what with not getting his way and all. But this piece of me wasn't on the table for consumption. I shouldn't have allowed the story of his doting mother to trigger a reaction from me. I was better than that. I was *beyond* that. And I just didn't discuss my family life with anyone. All anyone ever knew was we weren't close, and when spoken with enough finality it paved over the possibility of follow-up questions.

Except for Ash.

He ran his knuckles over the outside of my thigh. I grazed his bicep with my elbow. "I'm sure someone is wondering where you are, love. If you were gone from me, I'd, well," he paused, reaching for my hand, "I'd want to know you were safe."

Yeah, except for Ash.

The truth of the matter was, Ash was a yard sale of exceptions. He was every mismatched emotion, every incomplete set of desires, every vintage experience I'd missed out on along the way. And I could have all of it, all of him, for the low, low price of my dusty, old secrets.

"There you go again with the sweet words," I said, affecting a breezy tone I didn't feel. "Much more of this and you won't be able to maintain your reputation as a tyrant."

He kept his focus on the road though returned his hand to my thigh, offering a quick squeeze. "I'd want to know, Zelda, and I'm sure I'm not alone in that."

And because I didn't run away—as much as any thirty-one-year-old single woman with no debts to pay could run away—to cut and shape myself into bite-sized pieces for anyone ever again, I said, "That's nice of you to suggest but I've never had a mother concerned with stocking my pantry."

He shifted his hand to tangle his fingers with mine. "Now you have my mother. Let's give it a few months and then you can tell me how wonderful it is for her to call in the middle of the day, ranting and raving about how much cinnamon we're going through."

"Why *are* we going through so much cinnamon?"

"Probably all the French toast we eat." He ran his thumb over my palm as he said this, as he allowed us to stop talking about the reasons no one cared to know where I'd gone or why I'd left home. "Seems like the next logical step, no? After the pancakes?"

He continued exploring my palm while I watched the passing scenery. It was different here—*I* was different here—and it was never as obvious as when I glanced upward only to find a wide blanket of sky. Nothing interrupting the serene blue, not a single mountaintop to be found.

"Here's a story I don't share every day," Ash said after the subject of cinnamon was miles behind us. "My parents are hippies. Flower children in the first degree. Peace, love, and the rest of that bullshit."

"Wait, what?" I peered at him. "I've met your mother. She was wearing Tory Burch sandals. I'm sorry to be the bearer of bad news but Tory didn't follow the Dead, and any true hippie would've gone barefoot before walking around in a luxury brand."

"I don't know anything about sandals but that sounds like my sister's handiwork," he replied.

I thought about Ash's very posh, very beautiful sister. "I can see that."

"From what I've gathered, the free-range parenting approach was out there at the time," he continued. "That's the general thesis of growing up in my family. It was all a bit out there. We had the most random toys and were the only kids at school with home-made almond butter and cherry preserve sandwiches and—"

"Those sound amazing," I interrupted. "Who do I need to beg for some cherry preserves?"

"Offhandedly mention to my mother you like that sort of thing and we'll have a case of jam in the fridge when that season rolls around," he said. "You'll have more than you'll know what to do with."

"If that's my biggest problem, I don't have any problems," I said. "Back to you telling me how extremely difficult it was to have a mother who canned her own preserves for your school lunches. Because I sympathize with that, Ashville. I really do. My heart goes out to you. Thoughts and prayers for your difficult time. I can only imagine the hardships of eating real, unprocessed foods and playing with an abacus or some other wooden instrument because everything at Toys'R'Us was too commercial and consumerist. And clearly, it's had a terrible impact on you. You only have one graduate degree, the refrigerator in your apartment has just a few of the features I'd believed to be exclusive to the space program, and you're driving a car that's older than I am yet fully tricked out with sat-nav and cupholders. I get it. You're struggling big time."

He was gracious enough to look affronted. Good man. "All I'm saying is growing up with recovering hippies for parents is not nearly as amusing as it sounds."

"Yeah, I get it. You have nice shiny things now because you were only allowed to play with sticks and rocks," I replied. "I'm not sure I can allow you to caucus with the Society of Banana Babies unless you want to share a juicy story about the first girl to break your heart or the time you were passed over for something really important and that's why you work your tail off to avoid the tiniest suggestion of failure now."

Ash was silent a minute or two before saying, "I don't think anyone's ever broken my heart."

Without thinking *at all*, I replied, "That's funny because everyone breaks my heart."

Why was I doing this? Why now, why here? I'd always managed to keep a lid on it all. No one ever knew my true stories because I never gave them reason to look for one. No one looked at me and saw loss or fear or abandonment. I'd always been cautious about letting loose the frayed, knotty bits because I couldn't take them back once they were out. Yet here I was, unraveling those knots with Ash as my witness, nearly begging him to pull the threads and tear it all apart for me.

"Zelda." He plucked my hand from my lap and slipped his fingers between mine. "What's the Society of Banana Babies?"

"People who grew up in completely, unbelievably, indisputably bananas situations."

"Give it to me. Let me take it off your hands."

My defenses gathered around me, rising and closing until I could only speak in fast, snappish words designed to fill the gaps in my armor. "It's weird. The weirdest thing ever."

"Weren't you the one who said something about being outside the mainstream wasn't grounds for disparagement?"

I knew what he was doing and I fell into the trap regardless. "All right, Ash. You want to know, I'll tell you. My mother and father aren't my mother and father. They're my grandparents. My sister is my mother. Since my life is an actual mistake deep fried in shame and regret, I have interacted with them no more than a handful of times in the last ten years." I yanked my hand back because I needed everything inside the crispy shell of my defense mechanisms. "So, no, Ash, my family hasn't noticed I'm gone. The truth is, they're much happier when my sister-mother's teenage lapse in judgment doesn't trouble them."

"I heard you when you told me to fight fair. Now I want you to listen to me about sharing fair." Ash reached for me again, his touch gentle yet steady. "Take yourself away from me if you need space. Don't do it because you're bracing yourself against my saying something terrible. I told you I could take this. I meant it."

I nodded. "Okay."

"Can I ask how—how that all happens?"

I stifled a bitter laugh. The leather-wrapped steering wheel protested, an impolite squeak of skin I wouldn't have noticed if not for the sudden silence between us. I followed his white-knuckled grip to the bulge and twitch of his forearm muscles up to the stiff set of his jaw. "Which part?"

Ash cut a hooded glance in my direction, his eyes burning dark and serious like a storm. "The part where anyone could ever look at you and see a mistake."

FOURTEEN
ASH

I DIDN'T UNDERSTAND.

Not the part about the sister-mother. I had a decent idea how that one shook out. It was the piece where Zelda dipped out of her own family and they didn't care whether the door hit her in the ass.

The Zelda I knew gathered up asshole men and carted them off to urgent care clinics, she stayed with those assholes when they were drugged and punchy, and she accompanied them to Sunday dinner after fair warning about those gatherings.

The Zelda I knew was loyal to a fault. She was smart and caring and perfect.

"I mean it," I added. "I don't know how anyone could see a mistake in you, love. They must be deeply confused."

I lifted our joined hands to kiss her knuckles because, yeah, we did that now. Whatever that was, whatever the fuck was happening with us, I was here for it. Even when a sizable portion of my brain drew up lists and decision trees and indexed arguments as to why this was not a good idea, not at all, I was here for it.

"Actually, yes. They were confused," she replied. "They didn't know what to do when Deanna got pregnant. She was fifteen. I'm told she was an otherwise exemplary child without so much as a lunch detention to her name. But it all happened around the time Roseanne—that's my mother, or Deanna's mother—accepted a new job in Utah. She's a college administrator, and Kevin, the father figure in all this, is a research librarian. Apparently, it was a time of big change for everyone and they figured with the move it would be best for Deanna to have a fresh start at a new school. And that's how it went. They just raised me as little as possible. I spent a lot of time with babysitters." She shrugged in a stiff, defiant way that yelled *I don't have to care about any of this, you can't make me.* "They should've given me away. I don't think that dawned on them until it was too late and people knew about their later-in-life oops baby. I know it sounds harsh but I truly believe they would've offered me for adoption later on if it wouldn't have been socially complicated for them."

I wanted to pull over, stop right here on the shoulder of the highway and drag her into my arms. Zelda was all *try* and *care* and *give* and, according to this disclosure, no one tried or cared or gave for her. I wanted to drag her into my arms and I also wanted to hop on the next flight to Utah or wherever the hell her family lived now and tear into them for a solid hour.

More than any of that, I wanted to keep her. Carve out a space beside me and keep her right here, a world away from anything that could cause her pain.

Oblivious to my warring urges, Zelda continued, "I started working at summer camps when I was seventeen. I'd gone away to camp every year since, I don't know, forever, and I always loved my camp families. I always looked forward to going back.

One year, after the end of the season, I didn't return to Roseanne and Kevin's house. I was in my last year of college—U of U, because it didn't cost them anything to send me there—and I decided to stay with friends instead." She tucked her hair over her ear as she sucked in a rough breath. "They didn't call to ask where I was for six weeks." She shifted, staring directly at me. "I can assure you, Ash, they're not concerned with my whereabouts."

I pressed our joined hands to my chest because—because I had to. "I know you don't want me to say I'm sorry you went through this because you don't want anyone feeling sorry for you but I *am* sorry. So fucking sorry."

"It's okay."

"It really isn't, Zel. Not at all," I replied. "Do you see them around the holidays or—wait, I don't know if that's appropriate for me to ask."

"You sleep with your head between my boobs, you can ask me whatever you want. Doesn't mean I'll answer."

Her bright laughter filled the car and she rubbed her fingertips over my knuckles. Life was all right.

"As you know from your extensive review of my CV, I went to grad school in Colorado," she continued. "I didn't make it home for most holidays but there were a few years when they asked me to visit. Mostly for show. The year Deanna brought her boyfriend home and he proposed. The year they were first married. Times like that. I went. I played along."

"Have you always known? Or was it a secret? About your sister-mother, I mean."

"It was supposed to be a secret but Roseanne's a heavy drinker in the way many people are heavy drinkers but since they have good jobs and nice families and don't look like your stereotypical alcoholic, everyone lets it slide. Right on cue, you can count on her to bring it up between her third and fourth bottles of wine for the night. I didn't understand what she was talking about until I was at least eleven, maybe twelve. I'd known I was a mistake but that was when I realized I wasn't *her* mistake. It made a difference, somehow."

This time, I did pull over. I shot off the highway, down the ramp, and into a Dunkin' Donuts parking lot, stopping only long enough to engage the brake before flinging the door open and climbing out of the car. When I reached the passenger door, Zelda asked, "Do you need coffee? Iced tea? A strawberry glazed donut? What is it, boy?"

"Could you just come here? I'm gonna dislocate the other shoulder if I try to snatch you out of there."

"You're a lot of things, Ashville," she said as she disengaged the seat belt, "but I never took you for a guy who required an escort into a donut shop."

The moment she stepped out of my car, I scooped her into my arms as best I could. I didn't have any of the right words, any of the words she deserved, but I had this.

"Okay, so, you have really big feelings about coffee and donuts. I get it. I sympathize. Maybe not to the level of burning rubber off the highway but—"

"Would you just shut up and let me have you?"

She held herself still for a moment before softening and sliding her hands up and down my back. "You're too sweet, Ash. Sweeter than you let on. But you don't have to worry about me or my WOAT childhood. I'm okay. Really."

"What does that mean?"

"Weirdest of all time," she replied.

"Oh, well, that's handy. And I'm not worrying. I'm—" What

the hell was I supposed to tell her? That I'd be her family and my siblings and parents could be hers too, and I'd keep her safe and loved? No. No way in hell. Those weren't words I could speak, not today. Not in a parking lot. Not yet. "Thirsty. And undercaffeinated. I really do need an iced coffee."

"Oh, honey. You are so special." She patted my back as she said this and I pressed my lips to her neck, just the way she liked. "Don't stress over it, okay? How someone grows up is only one piece in their puzzle. There are so many other pieces that make them into a whole person. Mine was super weird and yours was free-range, and now you're dangerously close to giving me a hickey in an off-ramp shopping plaza parking lot which is one way of saying we came from different worlds and landed in the same place."

"Yeah," I said to her neck. "What are the odds?"

"Are you asking me to run the probability? Because you know I can."

"I am not challenging your competence, love."

I stared at her lips because it was the closest thing to kissing her without actually doing it. *Not here, not yet.*

"Then let's get you caffeinated." She took my hand and led me into the shop. "That's one thing I can do without fail."

One thing we weren't was simple. No, Zelda and I were as complex as any two people with a shot glass full of history could be. Maybe we were past complex and there was no sense trying to force us into a simpler state of being. But I knew I couldn't kiss her right now. It was the one line I'd drawn, the one intended to keep complex from slipping into chaos. Because if I kissed her, I'd want to kiss her back at my place too—also known as the land of beds. And if we fell into bed together, I didn't trust us to ever leave.

That wasn't something I could afford. It was no exaggeration. My ass needed to be in my desk chair, turning out audit reports and churning through financial documents. I didn't have anyone to delegate any of it to—not that I'd ever met anyone I trusted with much of anything. The sad, boring truth was I didn't have time to keep a woman in bed with me for days on end.

What if the bed doesn't matter? What if keeping her is all that really matters?

My car was small but I'd never fully comprehended that fact until I had Zelda *right there* beside me. And that skirt, my god. Who knew an ankle-length skirt had the power to ruin me? I wanted to reach over and drag it up. Better yet, I wanted to watch *her* drag it up. Tease me while I couldn't look away from the road.

And that was the thing about being around Zelda—she made me irresponsible. She made me forget every obligation I'd ever accepted. She helped me ignore the lines between airplane seatmates, between boss and employee, between roommates, between temporary saviors. She pushed me to chase the things I wanted rather than the things expected of me. She granted me permission to touch her and be close to her and be vulnerable with her, and I—I didn't know the right way to handle that. I didn't want to do it wrong. I *couldn't*.

But goddamn I wanted to kiss her. To shove my fingers through her hair and take her lips the way she deserved. To twist those fingers into a fist, pin her down, claim my place between her legs.

Holy fuck. What the hell was that and where did it come from? Fuck. *Fuuuuuuck.*

I was certain of little but it wasn't about the shitshow family.

That just pushed it over the edge. It also confirmed a few things for me.

First, Zelda was not leaving my apartment. She wasn't going anywhere. Whichever random friend was willing to put her up could forget the offer. Zelda's days of couch surfing were over.

Second—and most importantly—we'd make this ill-fitting job work. I was keeping her and I didn't care if that meant I still needed to find a competent auditing assistant. We'd make it work. I was unwilling to accept any other option.

———

MY MOTHER COMPLETELY IGNORED ME WHEN ZELDA AND I ARRIVED at my childhood home in New Bedford. She swatted my hand away from Zelda's lower back and scooped my girl into a tight mama squeeze. I had to work overtime to prevent myself from cutting in and snatching her back.

I'd meant what I'd said earlier: I didn't share—and I didn't care if I sounded like a pouty child because my mother was busy hugging the life out of Zelda.

As if my mother could hear my thoughts, she clucked at me over Zelda's shoulder. "Stop it, Ash. You can spare Miss Zelda for a minute. I promise I'll give her back." She lifted her palms to Zelda's cheeks, framing her face and grinning at her. "Look at those beautiful eyes. I don't believe I've ever seen anything like it."

"Thank you," Zelda replied.

"Blue and green," my mother continued. "How very special and lovely, just like the rest of you." She patted Zelda's cheeks with the kind of fondness that killed most of my possessive scowl because yes, Zelda was special and lovely and it was about time everyone noticed. "I'm so happy you didn't allow my son to talk you out of joining us today."

"Thank you for having me." She aimed a conspiratorial smile in my direction. "And for what it's worth, I didn't let him try very hard."

If my mother hadn't already fallen for Zelda in the tailor's shop, she fell here and now. She slapped her hand on her thigh, muttered, "Hot damn, honey, I like you," and linked arms with Zelda, steering her deeper into the house.

They went back and forth at my expense before my mother transitioned to explaining how she'd recovered the dining room chair cushions by herself, crediting the wonders of YouTube and staple guns for her success.

Once we reached the kitchen, my mother waved me away, saying, "You don't have to supervise, Ash. I won't take a bite out of her."

Zelda caught my eye and offered a smiling shrug that seemed to say, *I wouldn't mind if you took a bite out of me.*

Aaaaaand now I was thinking about scraping my teeth over her neck, her shoulders, her—oh, fuck me, I couldn't think about this in the middle of my mother's kitchen. Hell, I couldn't think about this while wearing thin shorts or with several hours of family time ahead of me. Or, hell, anywhere outside the blessed privacy of my apartment.

I returned that suggestive shrug with a *what are you doing to me?* glare. She stifled a laugh and leaned in as my mother insisted on showing her something related to the wedding. While my mother unfolded a long sheet of butcher paper dotted with tiny stickers, Zelda tucked her hair over her ear and—oh my god, she'd bent her head and brushed back her hair and all I could see was the long expanse of skin extending from her neck to the thin strap of her top. Maybe I wasn't too disciplined, too private to gather up the woman who'd consumed my existence and nip at her neck while my mother complained about the science of seating charts. Maybe I could—

"Your father is in the den," my mother announced, punching a hole through a solid plan to maul Zelda here in the kitchen. "Spend some time with him. He's been interested to hear more about your travels this week. And let me be clear, there will be no business talk at the supper table."

"Only wedding talk," I said.

My mother shooed me away. "That's enough from you. Get all the work out of your system and leave us ladies be."

I ran my hand down Zelda's back. "Be careful with this one. She'll try to sell you raffle tickets for a church feast or convince you to join her the next time she hits up the flea markets."

"That doesn't sound problematic at all," Zelda replied. "I could get down with a good flea market."

"Would you get out of here?" my mother yelled in the same exasperated, put-upon voice she used when we would dump our backpacks, shoes, coats, and sports gear in a heap in front of the door. "Now, Zelda, I have to tell you about the specialty cocktails we have planned for next week. They're just adorable. Do you like Moscow mules? Because I've convinced my future son-in-law he does and that's why we're putting one on the menu."

Zelda gave me a quick wave and I forced myself to head in the direction of my father's den. The conversation we needed to have today was long overdue, and after the new business I'd secured last week, it couldn't be put off any longer.

The glass-paneled doors to the den were open as always and he was seated behind a heavy banker's desk, his silvery white head bent over a page of old-fashioned ledger paper, mint green with slightly darker green column lines. His left hand rested on his ten-key adding machine, the tape curling as it calculated sums.

This was one of the most familiar sights of my childhood, one I associated with home more than my mother's cooking or piling into bed with my siblings because we hadn't learned how to sleep apart until we were seven. It was the rhythmic clack of keys and the grunt of adding machine tape, the scent of dusty paper that lived only in this room, the wide ridge of my father's shoulders against his desk chair.

This was home to me.

And I had to go to war with my home.

That made it sound dramatic in gross, silly ways but my father and I couldn't agree on anything and we couldn't muddle along in that way any longer. It was the three-legged race from hell because I had none of the leverage but all the responsibility to get us across the finish line.

I rapped my knuckles on the door and waited for his acknowledgment. Interrupting someone engrossed in numbers by speaking words was rude. Almost as rude as speaking numbers.

He beckoned me inside with one hand, his other still consumed with keying in figures. It wasn't a power move. My father didn't do anything like that. He wasn't a shark and he wasn't out for blood. The truth was he lived with a singular vision for his accounting practice and when he'd invited me to leave my work at one of the world's leading firms to join him, he'd hoped I'd come around to share his vision. I should've known his willingness to move in new directions and accept change and do the things I proposed wasn't rooted in reality but deal-sweetening concessions he'd never intended to actualize.

I dropped into the chair positioned in front of his desk, a mauve-and-burgundy situation my mother gleefully collected from the side of the road one day. It was better now that she'd gotten rid of the fleas.

A ring of laughter floated in from the kitchen as I folded my hands in my lap. I wanted to sprint in there, tuck myself next to Zelda, and witness every laugh, every meaningful shrug, every glance. There wasn't a moment we hadn't shared since Denver and now…now I didn't know how to exist without her *right there.*

My father tore a strip of tape from the machine and stapled it to the ledger. He preferred paper to any accounting platform in existence. It was one of his most old-school quirks, one I accepted with gritted teeth and waning patience. There were tons of reasons it was better, safer, and smarter to store this work digitally but his ways were forged in fire. And it wasn't a matter of him coming up in an era when computers and accounting software packages didn't exist. They'd existed. They hadn't been the first line of defense back then but he'd learned his way around an Excel spreadsheet to be sure.

Regardless, he kept his work in handwritten ledgers which he handed off to his secretary to key into a software program so antiquated it was operated on a computer with a floppy disk drive. Since those files were technical dinosaurs, I couldn't translate or reformat them unless I wanted to do it all manually. And the process of hand tabulating followed by ancient computer processing was time intensive. This was a problem because my father also accepted every client who walked through the door, without concern for scheduling or capacity. He often didn't have the time which left me to make sense of the files I could only access from his secretary's computer in his New Bedford office.

Yeah, commuting between Boston and the southeast coast of Massachusetts whenever my father overbooked himself was fantastic. A really good time, ten out of ten, would recommend.

He loved to help out local businesses and I admired that, I really did, but the scope of work was limited to managing their books and filing tax returns. As far as my father was concerned, there was no reason to extend his scope beyond that narrow slice—and I wanted to do everything *outside* that slice. I wasn't looking to take over the world but I needed a job more challenging than repeatedly running the financial equivalent of an oil change to keep me going.

"You were in Colorado this week, right? Your mother mentioned something of that," he said after tucking away the folder in front of him. "What's doing there?"

"Fieldwork for the Thanapoulis LLC audit. Then, meeting with the CFO of Orculus Solutions about their upcoming audit which will require a good deal of time considering they've acquired nineteen entities in the past year. Last, I sat down with Shadyside Brewing about getting their expansion business. They're opening six beer gardens across the country."

His brows pinched together in his usual brand of confused contempt for my initiatives, he asked, "Why the devil would you want to do any of that?"

"Which part? I've been contracted for the Thanapoulis audits for three years. Orculus is an emerging biotech and conducting their audits will pay for my office space for the *year*. And Shadyside is interesting and fun for me, not to mention setting them up to do business in four new states over the next three years and training their teams how to run those systems and manage local requirements will be hugely profitable for us. It's the kind of work that will grow us from tax returns and P-and-Ls to an organization with multiple deep revenue streams which is the reason we're having this conversation. That's why we formed this partnership, Dad."

"You're getting carried away again," he argued, waving me off as if I pulled this stunt all the time. I did, if you considered a once-monthly revisit to this stalemate *all the time*. "We don't have the setup for that. We don't have the staff and it's not the kind of work we do."

"It can be," I boomed, too frustrated to temper myself. "And I *am* set up for it. I've been scaling up for this since the beginning. Remote staff, info tech resources, connections. Like I told you then, it's what we need to build the next generation of this business."

He stared at me for a long minute but I knew from the brackets around his mouth he was using this time to curse the day he sat me down to say he was making plans to step back, to transition into semi-retirement. He was cursing the assurances he'd made that I'd be able to bring his work up to the present century and court the kind of clients that interested me. He was cursing his promise to allow me to work as I saw fit and not exactly as he did because he respected my training and experience, and he didn't expect me to abandon that when I teamed up with him. He was cursing the whole damn relationship we'd brokered to bridge our worlds.

"We're not about to agree on this matter," he replied. "My priority is meeting the needs of my clients. I'd like it to be yours too though it's clear you find that boring."

This was how he played it *every time*. It was never about smart decisions but me rejecting his world, his clients. More to the point, it was about me rejecting his approach. In the beginning, I'd humored him on this. I'd allowed him to feel his feelings. But instead of him seeing my side of the argument, he leaned deeper into his. Another one of my madly successful strategies working out for the worst.

"It doesn't *bore* me." I glimpsed at my watch. This conversation was a terrible use of a billable hour. "It isn't what I signed on for. It's not the reason I opened an office in Boston and went after new business opportunities rather than spending time on your client roster."

"I don't know why you can't service my existing clients using the systems that haven't failed me once in thirty years and leave these projects of yours on the side."

If it were that simple, I would've already taken that route. But the audits and consulting contracts I was going after wouldn't leave time for wading through handwritten notes and dot-matrix printouts. I couldn't spend three hours on round trips from my office to Dad's because he accepted more work but didn't have the capacity for it given his mule-and-cart process.

"I can't do that, Dad. I hate to say this but I'm *not* going to do it. I thought you were going to start declining new clients since you've pulled back. I figured you'd offload some existing clients onto another firm or—"

"There has never been talk of sending clients elsewhere," he snapped. "If that was what you expected, you didn't get that idea from me."

"Fine. Great. Hearing you loud and clear now." I ran my fingertip over my eyebrow in a feeble attempt to ease the tension headache coiling there. "Then I'll hire and supervise a junior accountant to manage those clients. Is that acceptable to you?"

"When did you become so dismissive of these family operations? These people who are our neighbors and friends, they're our community. And you want to cast them aside to consult for big corporations."

"Not that it matters here but Shadyside and many others on my roster *are* family businesses," I said, mostly to myself.

Too engrossed in his own argument to my counterpoints, he continued, "Why would you think I'd want these clients, the ones I consider family, handled by some no-name twenty-four-year-old in your Boston office? They come to us because they trust us and that's a fact you refuse to accept. You just don't understand this business and I don't think I can try to teach you anymore."

The thing about wars was they weren't fought over one thing. It was never the pinpoint reason found in history books. Wars exploded out of a sequence of events that built over time, a series of pressure points twisting and closing in, a process of buckling down and hardening up. Then a line was crossed and there was no going back.

It seemed, in my throbbing-head view, we'd crossed several lines in the span of this hour.

"I don't want to say this," I started, "I haven't wanted to say it for months. A year, even. But I don't have any other choice. If you are determined to be the only person who makes decisions, if you want to continue focusing on your client roster while working fewer hours, and if you're going to block my way at every turn, I can't grow a future for this practice. It's time to stop forcing this arrangement and let me walk away. I'll call my attorney in the next few days and get her started on revising the LLC."

Without pausing to breathe, he replied, "That's not an option.

You have to get these ideas out of your head and do the real work of—"

I didn't hear the rest because I made good on my promise and walked the fuck out. Storming down the hall, through the kitchen, out to the backyard. My feet carried me forward without conscious thought, skirting around my mother's raised vegetable beds, past the old cherry tree, down the mossed-over brick path to the brambly section of the yard my siblings and I long ago claimed as our hideout. It was the space at the far end of the lot, where the property line was cornered with two granite markers and the land gave way to the woods, where bushes and vines and trees gathered together to form a quiet, protected understory.

I walked out because I couldn't take it anymore. Because I'd heard it all before. Because the path forward was clear to me but not my father. No, the path was an offense to him. At once a dismissal and an indictment of his practice. But that wasn't it. I wanted to build something for myself—and by myself—just as he'd done. I didn't know why I had to do the same thing he did and I didn't know how he'd convinced himself I'd want that.

I didn't startle when I felt an arm slide around my waist or a head nod against my bicep. Part of me knew Zelda would follow. The other part wished for it.

"How much of that did you hear?" I asked. "The walls in that house are tissue paper."

"Enough," she replied, her knuckles gliding over my flank. "How are you doin', Ashville?"

There was a split second where I considered lying to her. Blowing it all off and insisting I was fine, this was fine, every-thing was *fine*. But I'd never succeeded in telling Zelda anything but the absolute truth. Every single one of my lies and omissions came back to kick me in the ass. "It's frustrating, you know?"

"Yeah. I know." She paused, probably waiting for me to disembowel myself further but when I didn't say anything, she continued, "I think the hardest part is the doubt. You let yourself believe that people understand you, they get you. You let yourself believe they trust you to do the right thing too. But then someone says they don't get it and they don't trust you, and maybe you're wrong for thinking you could be trusted or understood. And you just doubt that anyone will ever be able to do those things for you."

She ran her hand along my spine in elegant, artful passes like she was drawing a map to my salvation there and all I had to do was open my eyes and see it. I felt a tremendous surge of emotion, as if pins and needles and goose bumps had colonized my skin and now I was a man-sized nerve ending hiding in an overgrown canopy of summer green with a woman I fully and irrevocably required in my life.

"Yeah, Zelda," I said, turning my gaze away from the woods for the first time since I'd marched out here. "The doubt."

I hooked my arm around her shoulders, yanked her tight to my body, and kissed her. I wasn't especially kind in the manner I took her. There was no gentle brushing of lips, no respectful hand placement. It was rather unhinged—*I* was unhinged—and my body seemed to interpret this as the proper moment to calm down and tighten up all at once. I could breathe again, I could think beyond the headache behind my eyes, and I also wanted to burn down anything that dared to separate me from this woman. I already knew her subtle scent and the way she felt against me, and now I knew I should've done this a long time ago.

She flattened her hands on my chest and bunched my shirt in her fists, forcing me closer, pressing me harder to her torso.

"Yeah?" I murmured against her mouth. I needed her to want this the way I did. Unhinged and fiery and all this overwhelming relief.

She reached up, cupping her hand around the back of my neck. *"Yes."*

"Thank god."

Everything fell away as I melted into Zelda. My hands roamed over her body, cataloging her with more than a little entitlement while her tongue wiped out everything I'd ever known of kisses and affection and desire, replacing it with a screeching kettle of instructive lust. She was delicious comfort, one that lulled me into a sense of buoyant peace—before biting my lip and laughing as I blinked down at her in delirious awe.

"Again," I managed, and she complied, taking my jaw in her hands and raking my bottom lip between her teeth.

She smiled up at me with those strange eyes and the smile that understood unspoken things. "Like that?"

"Again. More."

There was a second where Zelda paused, her eyes glittering as she no doubt held in a quip about my domineering ways. If she only knew the half of it.

She pushed up on her toes to meet me as I locked my arm around her lower back, my hand coming to rest on the tender round of her ass. When we crashed together this time, in this backyard jungle with a mountain of disapproval and meddling waiting for us on the other side, I knew there was nowhere else I wanted to be. There was nothing else I needed.

A twig snapped behind us and I groaned into Zelda's mouth

because only one person arrived at my parents' house by way of nature walk. "My brother has terrible timing," I whispered.

"Just passing through," Linden said. "Don't mind me."

I kept my lips fused to Zelda's as I cut a glance in his direction. He raised a hand in greeting as he passed, the other wrapped around the neck of a growler of beer. Since Linden minded his own business like a champ, he kept his gaze fixed on the path toward the house.

"On your way, then," I called.

He waved once more and made an effort at eliminating himself from our hideaway but the moment was gone. When he disappeared past the branches and vines, I said to Zelda, "There are fifteen different things we should talk about right now but I'd very much prefer to kiss you again. Would you allow that?"

Zelda locked her arms around my neck. "That depends. Will those fifteen things drive you crazy and distract you while you're kissing me?"

I dropped my hands to her thighs, gripping the thin fabric of her skirt. I had to grit my teeth to keep from ripping it, instead really edging it up as I spoke. "There's nothing in the world that could distract me from you. Not a single thing has distracted me from you since you sat down and started hollering at me, and that's the rock-solid truth. My mother could come out here and whack me with a rolled-up gossip magazine. My father could launch into another lecture about my priorities. Hell, currency as we know it could end and I'd just want you to bite my lip one more time."

"Why now?"

"Because I've figured out you're something I need," I replied helplessly. "And I think I might be something you need too."

She sucked in a breath and I didn't miss the watery shine in her eyes before she buried her face in my shoulder.

"Are those good tears? Like, *He finally did something right and didn't fuck it all up* tears? Or hurt tears?" I asked.

She shook her head and I assumed—risky as that was—she was saying no to the latter.

"If they aren't hurt tears, tell me I can kiss you again. If that's what you want."

Zelda kept her head in the crook of my shoulder long enough to start me wondering whether I'd gotten it wrong, whether I'd miscalculated everything. She lifted her head and looked up at me with unshed tears pooled in her eyes and it seemed certain I'd fucked it all up.

"Are you going to change your mind later?" she asked.

I dropped her skirt because the only clear, direct instinct I could find among the clutter of lust and stress and hunger was to wrap my arms around her and hold her tight enough to feel her heart pounding against me. And, yes, perhaps rocking my shaft into her belly would relieve the throbbing ache there. "What are you asking, love?"

"I want to know if you're going to want me when it's convenient and push me away when you remember you're the boss and I'm—"

"No, I'm not doing that again. I hate that I've done it more than once, hate that I've done it at all. I've tried pushing you away and in case it wasn't clear, I missed you too much every time I did it. It was a shoddy attempt at trying to keep all the out-of-control pieces of my life in order."

"If you shared some of those pieces maybe they wouldn't feel out of control anymore," she said.

"As you've noticed, I'm not great at that," I admitted. Zelda laughed, sudden and bright, and I walked her backward until she was wedged between me and the first available tree. "And maybe you've also noticed I'm obsessed with you, you adorable evil genius."

"You don't have to say that because we kissed. What I do need is for you to stop throwing me away when your thoughts get the better of you."

"I said it because I meant it," I replied. "And just so you know, you're never inconvenient. The rest of the damn world is inconvenient and you…you are not that."

She tipped her chin up as her lips curled into a playful grin. "That's a funny way of saying you don't know what to think of me."

I think I could fall in love with you.

I didn't say it out loud but as I studied her mismatched eyes and the strands of blue woven through her dark hair, I wondered where those words came from. I'd never spoken them to a romantic partner before, never came close to it. Yet every time Zelda asked me for some confirmation of my intentions, a promise to be less of a jackass where she was concerned, I responded with more certainty and affection than I believed I possessed. I leaned into it. I took another step on shaky ground because I'd already blown up my relationship with my father and my world was a fresh mess and *I wanted her*. That was it—I wanted Zelda in every possible way, for as long as possible. And here, with her back against the tree and my palm sliding down her thigh and her hands clawing at me, I dipped my head to taste the sweet spot on her neck and said, "I think everything of you."

"You think I'm an evil genius," she whispered as she drove

her fingers through my hair. God, I loved that. "Somehow I've never heard that one before."

"*Adorable* evil genius," I said, punctuating each word with a kiss to her neck. "What if you've never heard it because not everyone can see it?"

I leaned back, watching as Zelda considered this. I couldn't explain the reasoning but I needed her to agree with me on this. I needed to be the one who saw her because she saw me too and it was both distressing and incredible.

She raked her fingernails over the nape of my neck and scalp as she stared at me, a glint in her eyes that appeared cautious. A moment loaded with all the things we didn't say passed before she ran her tongue over her top lip. Then, "I'm happy that family wasn't seated together. I'm happy I yelled at you too. And I wish you hadn't been injured but I liked being the person who took care of you. I'd do it all again."

I did the only reasonable thing and sealed my lips to Zelda's as I thrust my aching shaft against the heart of her. I hitched her knee to my waist and there was no confusion about my intentions. I wanted her—and I wanted that thought building between her legs until I got her behind closed doors again. It was the most brazen, shameless thing I'd done in this hideout— or anywhere—in at least twenty years.

"Promise me you won't freak out later," she whispered. She said this as she hitched her other knee on my waist and fought her way into my mouth with her tongue.

I heard one of her sandals hit the ground, then the other. With her ankles locked at the base of my spine, she urged me closer, squeezing out every bit of air and light until we were as connected as any two fully clothed people could be. This wasn't the first time we'd stolen all of each other's space and blanketed ourselves in vulnerability but this was the first time we did it while accompanied by an abundance of deep-dug truths. "I have no intention of freaking out later. Later involves taking you to bed and hoping to hell you make good on that threat to sleep naked. With me. While I kiss every inch of your adorable evil genius body, if you're amenable to that. Just promise me you won't make any more noise about leaving to stay with strangers on the other side of the city."

Zelda dropped her head back against the tree trunk and a downpour of winged maple seeds fell around us. "Be honest. It was the pancake sandwich that sold you."

I shook my head. It wasn't the pancake sandwich. Just as wars weren't launched in response to a single incident but a progressive mounting of tension and shows of aggression, neither was love. "Quiet now, love. Let me have you. Let me keep you."

FIFTEEN
ZELDA

Following Ash out the back door and into the yard after overhearing that argument wasn't an option. I had to go and I didn't question whether he'd want my presence. Ducking out in the middle of a conversation with Diana and Magnolia about the ice cream sandwich bar planned for the wedding's after-party wasn't the best show of manners but I hoped they'd understand.

He'd been a walking pile of rubble, a man demolished, and for the first time since he'd curled up on my shoulder and slept, I believed he needed *me* rather than any warm body offering comfort.

I'd heard almost everything Ash and his father Carlo said and it nearly killed me to stay put in the kitchen. There was no way I could've allowed him to escape into the yard alone after that. I couldn't do that to him, not when I knew the dirty secrets he didn't want to share.

All along, I'd suspected he was proving himself to someone who'd convinced him he wasn't enough of something. Now I'd identified the who and the what.

Knowing Ash—because yeah, we did know each other in a

thorough, inexplicable way—I didn't expect he'd take to kicking rocks or bloodying his knuckles on tree trunks or even screaming profanity into the woods. But I hadn't anticipated finding him so thoroughly lost, as if there was nowhere for him to go. And I hadn't anticipated the blistering firebolt of need lancing through me when we'd kissed.

In this thicket of unexpected, the biggest one I hadn't seen coming was my insistence he play fair if he was certain he wanted to *play* with me. I'd never set boundaries like that before or held firm to them when going with the flow was always the most serviceable, obvious solution.

Perhaps growing and healing was nothing more than making one right choice after another, even when those choices felt like the opposite of everything I'd always done.

Also, allowing my casually controlling boss-roommate-snuggle-buddy to pin me to a tree and kiss me like our lives depended on it was a completely right choice.

"Your mother is going to be wondering where we are," I managed between kisses.

"We could leave now. Just sneak out the side and go. They won't even notice. Magnolia is the main attraction this month."

"Mmm-mmm," I murmured, the only disagreement I could manage with his tongue in my mouth. "I think they'd notice."

"If anyone's waiting for us, my mother would ring the—" Right on cue, the clang of a bell broke the woodsy silence. *"Fuck."*

I wrapped my arms around Ash's shoulders when he dropped his head to my chest. "That sounds like a chuck wagon bell."

"It is," he said to my breast. "When we were kids, my mother never wanted to holler out the door for us to come in. Then she found the bell."

When Ash kept his head down and my legs locked around his waist, making no movement whatsoever, I asked, "How about it? Ready to go back in there?"

After an exaggerated sigh, he eased me down to my feet, wincing as he shook out his injured arm. "It's nothing," he said before I could ask. "It's fine."

While I smoothed my skirt and tucked my shirt back in, I glanced around the sheltered space. Gesturing toward the far end of this alcove, I asked, "Is that what I think it is?"

Ash turned, looking in the direction I pointed. Then he belted out a deep laugh. "If you're thinking it's my mother's secret herb garden, it is."

That nice lady with the reupholstered dining room chair cushions was growing a field of marijuana. Who would've guessed? "Are you serious?"

"I told you, my parents are hippies at heart."

"And that's why your mother has a bumper crop of weed hiding behind her blackberry bushes?" I asked.

He shook his head like dealing with his mother's antics was a real hardship. I knew it wasn't and I enjoyed his impatience for that reason. "It's on the edge of the property and insulated from view well enough to prevent notice. If anyone asks, she pretends she has no idea what it is. She told one of her neighbors it's an invasive but *protected* species so they shouldn't treat it with any chemicals."

"This isn't the last thing I would've guessed about your mother but it's not in the top quartile," I said.

"She used to tell us she used the leaves for brewing salves and tinctures." He dragged a finger down my arm, raising goose bumps as he went. "It made sense since she was always drying her own herbs and canning vegetables and god knows what else."

"Salves and tinctures," I repeated to myself. "And to think, you gave me shit about working at a spirituality shop."

"What can I say? You're rather overwhelming. I handled that by being a dick." He shoved his hands in his pockets. "I feel like you know this about me."

I wasn't certain when I'd become overwhelming or what it was about me that overwhelmed but I'd heard this enough along the way to know it was a core piece of my me-ishness. *You're a lot.* It was the kind of comment that slapped on both sides while leaving the crumbs of a compliment in my lap.

Perhaps those words wouldn't have landed with such force if I hadn't spent so much time crimping myself into a shape that others could accept and embrace. But that was the gravity of it all and it hurt now because I'd realized it should've hurt before.

"You know this, right?" Ash prodded. "You know I have occasion to be a dick and you know how to put me back in my place for it." He waited a beat. "Right?"

I touched my fingertips to my lips, tracing the freshly swollen lines as I replayed his words in my mind. "I'm not overwhelming. You were overwhelmed. That's about you, not me."

"Okay." Ash watched me as he rubbed a hand over his shoulder. It seemed to be bothering him. He probably shouldn't have held me against that tree. Even if it was the single most spectacular event of my life as I knew it. "Okay, yeah. I was overwhelmed. I was fucking leveled by you—and I still am." He reached out his hand to me and I took it. "What does that face mean? What did I do wrong just now?"

I let him lead us along the path toward the house. "Nothing." I shook my head but he probably didn't see. "I'm just thinking."

"No, your thinking face looks like gears turning behind your eyes and you chew on your bottom lip." When the path narrowed between the raised beds, Ash stepped behind me, settled his hands on my waist, and steered me through the garden. "It isn't your worried face because that one involves defined frowns. I wouldn't wager money on it but it isn't your irritated face either since that one is all about slicing me in half with your killer eye beams."

"When did you have time to catalog my faces?" I asked, all while knowing I'd unconsciously done the same to him.

"I'm a man of many talents. One of those talents is being able to think about multiple things at once." We stopped at the base of the back steps and I turned to face Ash. "One more thing before we go in there."

He slipped his hand along my cheek and into my hair as he leaned down to kiss me. I sighed and softened when he gathered my hair in his fist, holding me steady as he banished all consideration of my overwhelming effect on people.

Nearby, someone cleared their throat while Ash's tongue flicked over mine. He rumbled a grumpy *mmm-mmm* in response and banded his arm around my lower back.

"I wouldn't mind but the food is getting cold," his mother called. "And I'm not about to allow Zelda to sit down to a cold supper."

"But it's acceptable for me?" he asked, his lips hovering over mine.

"You're not a guest. I'm stuck with you, young man, and nothing I put on the table is about to change that," she replied.

"But I'd like Zelda to come back again. That's not likely to happen if her rice is cold and dry."

"I see how it is," he replied with a chuckle. "We'll be there in a minute."

"I'll be watching the clock." The screen door banged shut behind Diana as she returned inside.

He delivered a quick kiss to the corner of my mouth. "What did I tell you about my family wanting to keep you?"

I busied myself with straightening his collar and brushing away nonexistent dust. "Will you make it through this? Will it be all right for you?"

He glanced at the house, giving it a scowly study. "Yes, for two reasons. First, my mother doesn't allow any work conversation at the table. And second, despite the disagreement you overheard, my dad is a laid-back guy and won't continue being upset once a conversation has ended. He isn't resentful. He doesn't hold on to anger or grudges. We don't agree on matters of business but it doesn't overflow into other areas, thank fuck for that. All things considered, he's remarkably easygoing."

"Must be all the weed."

Ash replied with a deep nod. "You're right on that front."

"It must be frustrating though," I added. "Having a heated disagreement one minute and then sitting down at the table as if nothing happened the next. Maybe not frustrating but—I don't know—disequilibrating."

He stared at me for a moment, his jaw stiff and his head cocked like I'd said something terribly incorrect or maybe invasive. No, his cool study told me it was *very* invasive and he wasn't accustomed to anyone invading him.

Then, "How did you know that?"

I flicked a bit of pollen from his shirt. "Because it's how I'd feel. Like I never knew where I stood with someone. But maybe that's just me."

"No, it's not you. That's exactly it. One minute we're tearing everything apart, the next we're bullshitting about the Bruins. It wasn't always like this but now—" He blew out a breath as he blinked up at the roof and chimney. "It's a mess right now and I don't know how to fix it. I don't think I can."

"We'll figure it out," I said, meaning every word of it. I'd solve this problem. I could solve nearly any problem so long as it wasn't mine. "But not right now. We should get in there before we get another warning."

He led the way inside the house and toward the dining room —the one with the newly upholstered seat cushions courtesy of the bolt of fabric bartered for two old crockpots, which was all highly important for me to know and admire, I'd learned. Diana was always on the hunt. She intercepted us in the hallway, her hands loaded down with a large dish of rice topped with meat and shellfish.

"I was about to send out the search party," she said. "And Zelda, sweetheart, you have some maple seeds in your hair. Those little wingy thingies. They're everywhere. Such a mess. Ash, help her, would you?"

She shot a meaningful wink in my direction that said she was aware we'd been fooling around in the woods like oversexed teenagers just now and her only concern in the whole affair was for my bird's nest hair.

"My pleasure," Ash said as he plucked out the seeds.

"Come along, then," Diana said, hoisting her platter in the direction of the dining room. "You'll sit between me and Ash, sweetheart. I'd keep you all to myself but I imagine my son would pitch a fit."

"You imagine right," he said to her. To me, he murmured, "Told you so."

Another thing you should know about me was other people's parents always loved me. I'd meant it when I told Ash I was accustomed to being the flavor of the week. The part I'd omitted was becoming that flavor required real strategy and I'd honed that game hard. I knew how to be the fun friend kids sought out and the respectful, courteous, *tidy* friend the parents wanted in their house. By the time I was eight years old, I knew how to coax my friends into following their parents' directions and doing their chores, sometimes doing them myself if that meant keeping the peace well enough to stay for dinner or spend the night. Twentysomething years had passed but I still remembered folding a load of the family's laundry because my friend Aimee was in a mood and refused to do it. I couldn't look at her father the same way after handling his briefs.

I cleaned up after myself—and everyone else—because leaving a room better than I found it guaranteed an invite back. I took up the parents' and siblings' interests to keep the conversation flowing. I knew how to make myself invisible when the parents argued or my friend got in trouble and I knew how to smile and play nice even when a member of the family hadn't earned that from me.

Carlo grinned at me from his seat at the head of the table but I offered that make-believe smile because I'd heard the whole damn conversation he'd had with Ash and he was nowhere near earning a real smile from me. I wasn't letting him off the hook for a word of it but I knew better than to tear a stripe off my host at the start of dinner. Not that I had a clue what to say about their business issues—not yet—but I hated the way Carlo had questioned Ash's intentions. The man could be a whole bunch of bossy but he wasn't underhanded. Ash wasn't out to screw anyone over. He was a good guy wrapped in an assertive shell and doused with an overbearing sauce.

"I don't believe we've met," boomed a deep voice from across the table. The resemblance between Ash and his brother was striking because it was something of a mirage—they looked exactly alike but only when in an unfocused glance. I could see how they would've been nearly identical children though as adults, he was thicker and darker than Ash, and the beard was a definite difference. "Not properly, at least. I'm Linden. The third one."

"Third?" I repeated.

"Second," Magnolia said, holding up two fingers. She pointed at Ash. "First."

"What are we talking about?" I asked Ash.

"Birth order. We always get that question," he said, holding up a bottle of wine. "Would you like some?"

I held my thumb and forefinger apart. "Just a bit, please." Then, realizing I'd ignored my half of the introductions, I said to Linden, "Sorry, I got caught up in the triplet speak. I'm Zelda. I'm Ash's"—I stopped myself because I had no idea which word came next. The man in question dropped his palm onto my leg, his fingertips pressed deep into the private skin of my inner thigh, and he gave me a greedy squeeze. An invisible cord cinched around my chest, forcing out a quavering gasp in response. "I'm Ash's."

"Pardon this old man's memory and give me a second to catch up here, would you?" Carlo peered down the table at us. "What happened to Millie?"

"I can*not* believe this," Magnolia muttered. "Do you not recall the conversation we had ten minutes ago, Dad? When I explained to you and Lin that everyone—but especially you two —was to be on their best behavior tonight because we don't want to traumatize Ash's new person the very first time she meets all of us? And how that would be an issue because I don't want her feeling uncomfortable at my wedding which is in"—she angled her wrist for the group to see her smartwatch—"six days?"

Carlo offered a sheepish head shake. "We had this conversation *tonight*?"

Rob, the fiancé I'd met before chasing Ash through the backyard, took hold of Magnolia's wrist and lowered it to her lap. "Take the loss. You can't win all of them."

Ash handed the bottle to Rob. "Have some wine," Ash said to his sister. "Have the whole bottle."

"That's funny," she quipped. "As if I'm not well into hip flask territory these days."

"Yes, Ash arrived first," Diana said, lacing her fingers together in front of her plate as if still caught up in the birth order discussion and oblivious to everything after. "He was in a big hurry to meet us and Magnolia was quick to follow but Linden would've been content to have the place to himself for a time."

"In my defense," Linden started, "it was very crowded in there. Anyone in my position would've enjoyed the solitude."

"Unless you were in *my* position," Diana said with a wistful laugh. "There's no modesty when you're birthing three babies over twenty-eight hours. No shortage of hands inside you either."

"I warned you about the childbirth stories, Mom," Magnolia said. "I told you to get into the habit of not talking about your uterus so it won't be so difficult next weekend. Remember that?

Remember my wedding and the three hundred guests we have attending?"

Rob emptied the remaining contents of the bottle into her wineglass, holding it vertically while the final drops dripped out. "You gotta let some of these go or you're going to run out of steam before the evening's over."

Linden glanced up at me and gestured around the table. "You can see why I still prefer my solitude."

"At least half of them have already heard some version of that story," Ash said. "She'll only overshare to the other half."

"Yeah, that's the problem," Magnolia replied. "I'd like the other half to live in blissful ignorance."

"You need to stop hoping for impossible things," Linden added.

"Truth," Ash said. "When you look at it that way, this is entirely your fault."

"Zelda, did you know Ash built a library in his bedroom when he was a kid?" Magnolia asked, pointing a cheeky grin at her brother when she pushed away her empty plate. "He made little pockets and cards to go inside each book and hounded me and Linden for money when we didn't return them on time. He fined Lin nine *hundred* dollars for misplacing an R. L. Stine book."

"I don't believe I've paid that." Linden gave his beer a thoughtful frown. "Then again, Ash manages my money so what do I know?"

"That is delightful," I said, meeting Ash's gaze with the biggest heart eyes I could manage. "Do you still do that?"

He shook his head, saying, "No, I—"

"He has a stamp now," Magnolia interrupted. "Look inside

any of the books on those shelves in the living room. All stamped. Most dated with when he read them too."

I pressed a hand to my chest. "That's even more exquisite than the library fines. I'm totally checking when we get home."

He shrugged this off with an eye roll but he didn't mean it. He was an adorable little nerd and I loved that shit.

Now that everyone else was finished eating, their plates and utensils tucked together and pushed aside, Linden pulled the serving dish of spicy shrimp toward him and dug into it, asking, "When did you move in—wait, never mind. I didn't say anything. It wasn't me. Blame someone else."

Diana folded her arms on the table as she leaned toward me with a conspiratorial glint in her eyes. "Is it official, then? You're living together?"

"Um, it's mostly, well," I stammered.

"Baby blankets," Ash murmured to me.

"We'll just see where the summer takes us," I said.

"I hope it takes you into autumn because the church puts on a darling fall festival and I just know you'd love it, Zelda," Diana said.

Ash squeezed my thigh again, his thumb stroking high enough to glance over my panties like a proper perv. "I'm sure Zelda enjoys a good fall festival as much as the rest of us," he said. "But we have an early morning at the office so we should—"

"At the office?" Rob echoed, glancing between us. "I didn't realize you're in financial services too."

I shook my head. "Oh, no, I'm—"

"Zelda has an extensive background in customer-facing operational systems and employer-side federal and state compliance as well as quantitative analysis. I'm fortunate she accepted my offer to get my house in order as I'm now in a position of needing to rapidly scale up," Ash said.

This was met with a moment of collective eyebrow lifting though it took me the duration of a full minute to realize the response wasn't because these people doubted a word he'd said about *me*. Everyone at this table knew Ash rarely invited anyone inside the house, never mind letting them put it in order. Those eyebrows were all for Ash.

Life was a real trip. One day you were busy hearing you didn't have what it took to make it in academia while simultaneously writing—ahem, make that *proofreading*—someone else's graduate thesis for them, and the next you were the brains of the operation and no one doubted it for a second. Life was a real fucking trip.

"We should grab lunch sometime this week," Rob suggested. "My office building is a few blocks away from where you guys are on State Street and your schedule"—he paused to smile at Magnolia—"is pretty flexible up until Thursday, right?"

"Depends how my final fitting goes," she said ominously. "I might not be allowed to eat the rest of the week."

"Stop it. You're eating. Yes, you are," he replied.

"Maybe not after Tuesday," she argued with a hearty laugh. "The seamstress will break my ribs if that's what it takes to get the corset laced up. Honestly, though, I will turn into a ball of fire if it's too small again. Actual burning fire."

"I told you to try the green juice cleanse Heather from the yarn store recommended," Diana said. "She looks fantastic."

Magnolia leveled a glare at her mother. "Not another peep about that, you hear me? I'd rather wear three layers of Spanx than get married smelling like cabbage and garlic."

Rob set his elbows on the table and rubbed his forehead. "I

still don't understand why you bought a dress two sizes too small."

"It was a designer trunk sale," Magnolia replied. "It's a limited edition dress and I was able to get it for one-tenth of the price. There was no other option."

"I still don't get it," Rob grumbled. "I would've paid the other ninety percent and saved us the misery."

Diana shifted her attention back to me. "You should come with us to the fitting, Zelda."

"Did you ignore the part where I mentioned Zelda is essential to the continued functioning of my business?" Ash asked.

"Yeah, drag the nice girl along because it sounds like such a good time," Linden muttered. "Hangry Maggie, broken ribs, great balls of fire. You're really trying to put Zelda through the paces, aren't you?"

Diana patted my hand. "I didn't raise them to be such rude boys. Ignore them. I do."

"It's okay," I said, laughing. "They don't scare me."

"I like you," she said with a wink.

"You should totally come with us," Magnolia said. "You'd be doing me a huge favor by subjecting yourself to my mother's ceaseless meddling while I'm brutalized by a very small but very strong seamstress."

"Meddling? I don't meddle at all," Diana said. She spoke in a tone that suggested she truly believed it too.

Carlo pushed away from the table and collected two empty serving dishes from the center of the table. With a glance to Rob, he said, "Best of luck."

"We're not about to debate whether you meddle," Linden said. "It's accepted as fact. Let's move on."

After muttering something about her children needing her

meddling in their lives, Diana returned her attention to me. "The shop we're visiting has lots of lovely pieces. I'm sure they'd have something perfect for you to wear next weekend if you'd like to browse for yourself. I'd be happy to help you look."

"Oh, that's not necessary," I said, suddenly flustered. I didn't know why I reacted this way but I could feel heat crawling up my chest and neck like an allergic reaction. "I'm all set."

"Mom," Ash warned.

"What did I say?" Diana held up both hands. "What did I do now? I'm being *helpful*."

"More than enough," Ash replied.

"There aren't many people in the world today who have a range of options for a formal seaside summer wedding with only a few days' notice," she said. "And since I want my oldest son's companion to feel as radiant as ever, I'm going to keep doing more than enough." She gripped my hand. "All right, dear? Very good. I'll drop by the office on Tuesday afternoon around four and we'll walk to the shop together."

When Diana and Magnolia fell into a discussion of the wedding reception's seating chart, Ash leaned in, brushing his lips over my exposed shoulder. "I'll handle the dress shop issue and the nineteen baby blankets she's going to knit in the next two days," he whispered. "And I won't drag you onto my lap or pull your hair and kiss you while my entire family watches which is why I need you to get your sweet ass up and assist me in making a swift exit. Can we do that?"

I blinked at him for a sweltering second before reaching for Diana's hand, saying, "Thank you so much for welcoming me into your home. The meal was exquisite and you've done a spectacular job on these cushions. I'm so sorry we have to step out before the evening is over but I know we'll have plenty of time to catch up on Tuesday afternoon."

"No apologies allowed," Diana said. "Have a safe drive back to the city."

Beside me, Ash stood and held out his hand for me. When I joined him, Diana tackled me in a fierce hug. I gave her a polite pat on the back but she didn't let go and soon I realized this wasn't an ordinary hug. It was the kind that transfused affection from every point of contact and the longer it lasted, the more I felt my parched and fractured places filling with kindness and love. My own stores of affection seemed fuller now, as if I could now give more because I'd received this.

"Please give her back," Ash said. "She's mine."

"I know, honey, I know," Diana said, bussing her palm up and down my back. I blinked hard because I could've cried if I hadn't fought it off. I was plump and overflowing with emotions that seemed too large for me to bear, too permanent for me to accept outright. "I'm just so happy, I can't help it."

"Probably because she's not Millie," Linden muttered from the table.

"None of you can be trusted," Magnolia said with a groan. "None of you."

Once Diana released me, we made a quick exit. Ash held the car door open with a glance at his watch, saying, "Four minutes. You're amazing."

Since I was still the girl who ran straight to the edge with her parachute in shreds, even after a million right choices and all the deepest hugs, I dropped into the seat and said, "I thought I was overwhelming."

He crouched down to meet my eyes. "And I've found I love being overwhelmed."

WE PLAYED ANOTHER ROUND OF THE TOUCHING GAME AS WE returned to the city but there was nothing mild or innocent about this iteration. It was all deep, lingering thigh squeezes, rough fingertip scrapes, clasped-hand knuckle kisses with a side of teeth. Everything about it was aggressive—and intentional.

The elevator ride from the basement garage to Ash's apartment was quiet and close, our arms tangled around each other as if we would drown otherwise. It seemed absurd to think that but when I caught sight of us in a mirrored panel, I knew it was true.

Instead of climbing inside my mind to examine why we always resorted to lifeboat-style embraces or analyze any of the other emotional stones I'd overturned today, I rested my head on his chest and granted myself permission to experience this. This man wanted me and cared for me and drove me a bit crazy, and none of that was impacted by my past decisions. I didn't have to live inside those decisions anymore. I wasn't required to be that person anymore. I could make one right decision after another and build a brand-new me.

We were completely civilized when we exited the elevator, strolled down the hall, stepped inside the apartment. I slipped out of my shoes and set down my purse. Ash hung up his keys and secured his phone in its charging station. Completely civilized.

Then his hand was on the back of my neck and my body was flat against his and I could taste the way he wanted me. It was a smoky heat, almost bitter, like he'd burned for me all this time and could only now show me the charred truth.

I liked that. Probably too much. And I liked the way he'd

reached for me like I was his to take as aggressively, as imperiously, as unapologetically as he wanted. There was a violence to it, one I felt in a desperate, sacrificial sense. I wanted to be *taken*. Stolen away from the polite domesticity of phone charging and shoe removal, and stripped down to our most basic, elemental pieces—the ones that seemed to fit together without us knowing how or why.

"We can't do this tomorrow," I whispered to his lips.

"What's tomorrow and why the hell not?" he asked, gathering my shirt in his fist as he took my mouth again.

He was going to rip it if he wasn't careful.

I hoped to hell he wasn't careful.

"Tomorrow," I managed between kisses. "Monday. We can't do this at work. Not at your office."

He pulled back from my mouth, his eyes pleated at the corners. "Not at the office."

"It's just—we can't."

That neck grab cemented a few things for me and now I knew there was no way I could do this *and* work even a tiny bit because I'd want it all day. The almost-torn shirt and the arrogant hand on my neck. No work would be completed in that office, not a minute of it. "We shouldn't. There have to be limits. Ground rules. I won't get rug burns from kneeling under your desk and—"

His lips slammed into mine, biting the words off my tongue. These weren't the kisses we shared in the backyard. These were a narrow belt of electric heaven which offered the merciless savagery necessary to shutting down the loud and anxious parts of my brain. They were the deliverance I'd come in search of.

After he dragged my bottom lip between his teeth, he gripped my shirt tighter, saying, "Show me what that looks like."

"Sh-show you?" I stuttered.

A muscle in his jaw twitched. He blinked at the hardwood floor. "Kneel."

The options weren't *kneel* or *don't kneel*. They were *give him what he wants* or *get the hell out*—which sounded atrocious when taken outside the context of me very much relishing this. I didn't have a curated set of sexual requirements or conditions to orgasm though I knew without hesitation I wanted Ash precisely as authoritative as he was about everything else.

And maybe I wanted the power that came with relinquishing control to someone who'd earned it from me.

Since I had no intention of running for the hills, I dropped to my knees. Instead of releasing my shirt as I went, Ash yanked it over my head, pitched it to the side. "Much better." He motioned toward his belt and zipper. "Go ahead."

That tone undid me.

The executive too busy to be bothered with unfastening his clothes, freeing his erection, even participating in this—this *servicing* of his body. No, he had no intention of participating at all. That was the dirty work carried out by dirty mouths and he cared nothing for the heartbeat between my legs.

He threaded his fingers into my hair as I peeled down his shorts and boxers. His shaft bobbed up near his navel, full and ruddy like it couldn't believe it hadn't been put to good use yet. I couldn't stop myself from trailing my nails down his thighs and up again, and watching with delight as he dropped his head back with a groan.

"Enough, enough." Ash curled his fist around his base and swept the head of his cock over my lips. I already knew the scent of him but it was different like this, different in a way that stirred low in my belly. "Get to it. Show me what you'd do under my desk, love."

There was a solid minute of tentative licking as if I hadn't had a popsicle in years but then I curled my tongue around his head as I stroked him. A jagged, rusty *Fuuuuuuck* gusted out of him. I peered up, grinning as wide as I could manage.

"Just like that," he panted, weaving his fingers through my hair again. "Fuck, Zelda, yes, *just* like that."

I was out of practice but Ash didn't seem to care. He growled and groaned when I got it right, twisted my hair around his fist and told me what to do when I didn't. It wasn't long before I was torn between the satisfaction of pleasing him and the need to hear more of his sternly spoken commands.

My eyes watered every time he snapped his hips forward and his shaft bumped the back of my throat. "*Keep going,*" he ordered. "I'll tell you when you're allowed to stop."

We both know that wasn't accurate and he'd stop if I gave him any sign of needing to do so but the *suggestion* I didn't have a choice in the matter gouged out my belly and arrowed heat between my legs. It wasn't about being taken against my will or being used but rather handing over the decision-making to someone I could trust with that responsibility.

And if there was anyone to be trusted with a responsibility, it was Ash.

He released my hair to cup my chin, tipping my face up a bit as he did it. "No kneeling at the office, you say." His brows arched as he covered the fingers I'd wrapped around his length with his own and eased out of my mouth. He hadn't finished but that wasn't the point. This was only the start. "That's your request?"

I didn't know it was possible for every inch of skin to throb and burn until right now, when I insisted upon a conversation about our working relationship while also wanting to be violated in very twisted, beautiful ways. "Yes."

"And what of bending over desks? Is that forbidden as well?"

My core gave a painful clench around nothing. I nodded. "Yes."

"And if I want to spread you out on a conference room table? Or pin you to a door? Are those options available to me?"

I was dying here. All I needed was one flick to my clit and the ache inside me would subside. "No. Not at the office."

"Perhaps I ask you to inch your skirt up and pet yourself while I watch," he continued. "Will I be allowed that?"

I pressed my thighs together, shook my head. "No."

"That's right." Running his thumb over my lips, he said, "I already knew this but that demonstration was worth revisiting the topic."

"You—you already knew that?" I sputtered.

Ash reached for my elbow, whacking me in the face with his hard cock in the process, and helped me to my feet. "I did. I'm aware you'd rather watch technically inaccurate archaeology movies than play secretary games and if I can be quite honest with you, I'd be out of business before the end of the week if I was allowed to have your mouth on me from nine to five. However, watching you squirming and squeezing your legs together is a divine thing and I intend to see it again soon as it in no way controverts the agreed-upon limits."

"Oh my god, no, please don't," I sobbed. "Please don't make me wait."

A cool, almost bored chuckle sounded. "I didn't mean right now, love, though it's pleasant to know I have you on the edge."

He spun me around as he searched for my skirt's zipper and

did it again when he didn't find one. I hooked my fingers under the waist, saying, "It's more obvious than you think."

With that riddle resolved, my skirt hit the floor and he lashed an arm around my waist, jerking my back to his chest. "What do you want?" he asked. "No, don't tell me. I already know."

"That ego of yours." I wiggled against him, against the insistent thickness of him.

"Just you wait." A laugh rumbled in his chest but it might as well have been a lion's roar for the way it called up all the anticipation inside me. "Tell me what you don't want, love."

I knew he was asking this in a logistical, boundary setting sort of way but I couldn't stop myself from saying, "I don't want you to regret me."

He released another rumble. "Only a fool could regret you, Zelda. I promise you that won't happen." I shuddered then but ducked my head to play it off as a reaction to his scruffy chin tickling my neck. "I'd like to be finished with this discussion and well on my way to learning what you look like when you come so tell me, Zelda, is there anything else you don't want?"

"No. Nothing at all."

I wouldn't generally share this but given the situation, it was something you should know. I've had some good sex in my day. Summer camp was a hot bed—literally—of dirty, instructive sex for teenagers. Camp counselors knew how to get down after hours. Some of us were real filth monsters with serious freaky streaks. In a good way.

And Ash was a serious filth monster in the best, most surprising ways. The second he'd kissed me in the woods, it was like a switch had flipped in him and the rigid, moody accountant disappeared and a coarse, demanding man took his place.

I loved everything about Sex Monster Ash.

SIXTEEN
ASH

THERE WAS A QUICK CONVERSATION OF PROTECTION—CONDOMS would do just fine—and the matter of separating Zelda from her remaining clothes while I marched her down the hallway to my bedroom.

"On the bed," I ordered, giving her a slight shove between her shoulder blades. "Get comfortable."

Behaving this way was new for me. It was like walking into a lake and immediately finding myself at the deepest point where I couldn't touch the bottom unless I allowed myself to stop kicking and just sink down. It gathered around me that way, at once mightier and stronger than me, but also rendering me fully weightless. I could do anything and be anything here but only if I was terribly careful.

I tossed my shirt aside as Zelda climbed onto the bed, giving me my first good look at the tattoo on her lower back. The one I'd worked hard at not referring to as a tramp stamp. Indeed, there was nothing seedy about the black and white dragonfly inked in ultra-thin lines. It more closely resembled a scientific diagram than the whimsical clip art that often found its way to tattoos in that location.

The rest of her body was fascinating in a manner that demanded exploration. Dark olive skin giving way to much lighter olive skin where a bathing suit would keep her covered. Small, teardrop-shaped breasts with nipples the color of sunset. A gently curved belly and full hips bracketing a patch of midnight curls. Just fucking fascinating.

I wanted to stroke and suck and bite every inch of her.

Blinking away from that fantasy, I found Zelda nestled up against the pillows. It was almost the exact position I'd found her in on the sofa late last night—legs folded, ankles crossed, head pillowed on the arms layered over her knees.

I crossed the room, jerked open the top drawer of my bedside table and tore off several condom packets. Dropped them on the bed coverings. "That's not how I'm going to fuck you."

"You told me to get comfortable." I could hear the pout in her voice. "So, I did."

I took my cock in a loose fist, stroking it just enough to catch my breath. "Show me the pretty pussy I'm making mine."

Zelda complied because of course she did. Because she was right here, seated at the bottom of the lake alongside me. Because the weightlessness allowed her to transform into someone wilder, someone even more unfettered by convention than she already was—and maybe it didn't matter whether her natural state was one of unconventionality and pocket eggs. Maybe that meant she required weightlessness even more.

I dropped a knee to the mattress and prowled toward her, stopping only to wrench her legs apart with more force than required. I didn't hurt her, not in any real sense. "That's better. Don't even think about moving." Kneeling between those glorious thighs, I shoved my hands under her, kneading and squeezing and separating her ass cheeks while her eyes flared big and dreamy. No, I hadn't hurt her *at all*. "What will happen if I fuck you with my fingers?"

Her hips rolled in an erratic rhythm as they searched out friction. "I'll come in a hot second."

I ghosted a finger over her clit, her seam, her ass—and watched her body flutter and pulse in response. "We can't have that." Notching a finger against her back channel, I asked, "And if I tease you here?"

She pressed her hands to the sides of her face like she couldn't stand this—the questions, the foreplay, all of it. "Same. Oh my god, *same*."

I reached for a condom, rolled it into place. Tugged her ass up the slope of my thighs and hooked her ankles over my neck, settling her into the most gratuitous position my mind could conceive. My injured shoulder hated that but it couldn't be helped. This was how I had to have her and I didn't care whether I ached from it in the morning. I'd ache regardless, but this way, it wouldn't be from giving her only half the things she deserved.

"Zelda," I said, tapping my cock against her clit. "You'll come when I'm good and ready to let you."

"Oh my god," she breathed, her hands still on her face and her body tightening like a bow stretched back before shooting.

I filled her with one merciless thrust and that was enough to make me dizzy, make me delirious. By the time I banded my arm over her legs and slammed into that honeyed heat again, I was already thinking about the next time and the time after that and all the other times I'd push inside this cunt and know it was under my care.

"You're gorgeous when you're wet and desperate." I traced her swollen petals where they clung to my shaft, where she stretched around me. I couldn't look away. I'd never seen anything as perfect, as *right*. "Fucking gorgeous. You make me want to tear this condom off and spill all over you."

Zelda hummed in agreement as she met my thrusts as best she could in this position, asking, "Is that all you want?"

I didn't even have to think about it. "Not hardly," I said, speeding up because I couldn't slow down. Couldn't draw this out, couldn't wait to feel her coming on me. "I want to tear it off and spill *inside* you. Want you bare, want nothing between us." My skin was too tight and my bones were hollow, and I was breaking, just fucking shattering under the strain of holding out. "It's not like I can protect myself from you, Zelda. I haven't for a single minute so why shouldn't I fuck you raw? Why shouldn't I give you everything I have and then take everything you give me in return?"

There was the deep part of the lake and then there was the dark part. It was just as vast and powerful as the deep but it lacked all the clarity. It wasn't enough to be careful here because the darkness made it impossible to know when I was upside down, right side up, or drifting off into the abyss. I had to know what I was doing if I wanted to dive in these waters—and I wasn't sure I knew anything. Not when my words were dangerously close to crossing the line from dirty talk into real, guttural urges.

"Wh-what do you want me to give you?" she asked.

Because all this honesty left me feeling a little ragged, a little mean, I pushed a finger into her ass. She clamped down around me and I was *done*. This was over.

Despite my request to wait for permission—who the literal fuck did I think I was with that?—her body quaked and shook, a million tiny flutters moving through her muscles as goose bumps swept over her skin. If I wasn't wrong, her eyes rolled back in her head as I blasted into the condom. "Which part of *everything* was unclear to you?"

Zelda's only response was a long, moaning, "*Ash.*"

WHEN MY ALARM SOUNDED AT SIX THIRTY, AN HOUR AND A HALF later than usual because my shoulder hurt too much to even think about hitting the gym, Zelda slapped my ass and said, "The first shower's yours."

"It could be ours." I buried my face in the crook of her shoulder and ran a palm over her bare belly and yes, *yes*, she was right about sleeping naked. This was so much better like this. "Consider the facts. We'd conserve time and water."

She scraped her nails up my spine and I accepted that invitation to grind my erection against her thigh. At that, she laughed, her fingers moving into my hair and closing around the strands. "Are you really telling me you're up for some communal showering? After you groaned into every downshift last night?"

"That happened two times," I argued. "Three, at the most."

She made an indelicate noise, something between a laugh and groan that seemed to say, *Okay, whatever.* I burrowed deeper into her shoulder as she added, "Not to mention we don't know each other well enough for that."

I pointed to the bed. "Were you here last night? The first

time? Or the second? Perhaps the third then? You took me three times, love, I think we know each other fine."

Another one of Zelda's bright laughs sounded in the morning stillness, cracking open the day and promising everything would be as wonderful as waking up with her naked skin and the burn of muscles overworked beneath the sheets.

"There's a difference between knowing someone for sex and knowing someone for a Monday morning shower."

Already prepared to shoot down this notion, I shook my head, asking, "And what is that difference?"

"It's a whole bunch of things. Everyone looks like a fool during sex—"

I shook my head again. "I don't agree with that."

"Go ahead and shock me some more," she murmured.

"I have it on good authority you don't look like a fool during sex. I was here. I watched. You look like spring in full bloom."

"That's kind of you but I promise it's something else when I'm hunched over shaving my legs. Before you tell me how you're sure that's as charming as baby chickens, please remember you're still healing. You can't argue your way out of that and the only reason I'd join you in the shower is to supervise."

"I would've appreciated that supervision the other day," I mused. "I would've jerked off on your skin instead of the wall."

"I'm sure you'll get a chance to do that eventually," Zelda promised. "We don't have to cram everything into one day."

We stayed there for several minutes, my hips rocking as she scratched my neck, my back, while I dragged my lips over her neck and shoulder. "I saw you checking out my shower the other day."

"I was checking it out because you were standing in it while extremely nude." She slipped her fingers over my scalp. "I was attempting to be polite."

"That's good of you. One of us should be."

"Trust me, I knew it wasn't going to be you since you practically begged me to ogle your body." She tipped her head back to shoot me a knowing grin. "You couldn't have grabbed a washcloth or something? A loofah? Anything to at least pretend you didn't want me staring?"

"No, I couldn't pretend that because I did want you staring," I replied. "If you'd walked in a minute or two earlier, I'm sure the whole experience would've been less unsatisfying."

"Mmm, yes. Your struggles are significant." She slapped my ass again. "Hurry up now. I'll bet you're a stickler for being in the office by a certain time and I won't be much use to you without the proper combination of toast, eggs, and cheese so you need to get a move on."

"Did you think I'd forgotten about that? How could I, after you whipped out pocket eggs at thirty thousand feet. Fuck, no. Your breakfast needs are my top pre-eight-a.m. priority. You're going to love the café on the ground floor of my office building. Excellent coffee too."

When I didn't move because why the hell would I move when I had a soft, naked woman beneath me, Zelda said, "If you're expecting me to kick you out of bed, you've underestimated yourself, as you are a large slab of man."

I traced the jut of her collarbone with my lips. "I don't know if that's a compliment."

"Think it over while you're in the shower."

With great reluctance, I shifted away from the cocoon we'd constructed from blankets and bodies. Standing beside the bed, I held out my hand to Zelda. "Come on. I swear I'll be good. I'll even look the other way when you're hunched over to shave your legs."

She accepted my hand but replied, "A lady needs her secrets. Some other time."

I wrapped my arms around her and pressed a kiss to her hair. "Promise?"

Bobbing her head against my chest, she said, "Promise."

———

HALF AN HOUR LATER, I EMERGED FROM MY ROOM TO FIND ZELDA staring at her phone and—"What the hell are you wearing? Take that off."

Her head snapped up. "Pardon?"

Helpless grumbles rose in my throat as I waved at her navy blue skirt and ivory blouse with a dreadful bow-sash-tie situation at the throat. "Don't you have anything more…Zelda?"

She crossed her arms over her chest. "I vividly recall you asking if I had office attire."

I recalled it too but now I couldn't cope with so much standard issue corporate wear on a woman who was neither standard nor corporate. "Yeah but…that doesn't look like you."

"Are you sure that's the direction you want to go?"

That was a warning shot and I knew it but I pressed on regardless. "I liked what you wore yesterday."

She tapped a finger against her lips. I envied that finger. "Unfortunately for you, this is one area you cannot micromanage." She laughed, saying, "Don't give me that face. It's too early for glowering."

I wasn't glowering but I turned away from her all-seeing eyes anyway. "Fine. All right. Whatever. Let's go."

Zelda followed me into the hall, asking, "Can I get more information about this café? I need my breakfast brain ready to make these critical decisions."

I caught another glance at that horrible blouse, the one that'd certainly come from a bland women's store where everything was neutral toned and ruffled in superfluous ways. Okay, maybe this blouse wasn't *that* bad but it was a disservice to Zelda. It smothered all her wonky weirdness. It even appeared to fade that stripe of blue hair behind her ear.

"Don't tell me the sandwiches are canceled because my office attire is too office-y for you."

I huffed out a laugh. As if I'd deprive her of anything she wanted. "Not canceled," I replied. "But I fully intend to say perverted things to you while we wait in line."

Zelda tapped the elevator button for the ground floor. "Pssh. Like I'd mind that."

———

AFTER PROCURING BREAKFAST AND ASCENDING TO THE NINETEENTH floor of my office building, I held the suite's door open for Zelda and followed her inside. "This is us."

I studied her as she swept a gaze over the small waiting room and receptionist's desk but her expression remained cool and curious. She knotted her fingers around the strap of her purse and tucked her hair over her ear three times.

"We have a conference room right here." I pushed that door open to illustrate though it was pointless given the walls were floor-to-ceiling glass and she could see this for herself. "Offices on either side. Supplies, storage, and restroom down the hall.

My office is over there," I said, pointing to another glass-walled enclosure.

When Zelda didn't move or react in any obvious way, I brought my hand to the small of her back and led her into my office. We'd sit, we'd eat, we'd figure this thing out.

I set my coffee on the small meeting table near the door and deposited my laptop bag on my desk chair. Shrugging out of my suit coat hurt like a motherfucker but it had to be done. I couldn't work in that thing, not all day.

With the coat cloaked over my chair, I started rolling up my shirtsleeves. It wasn't until I flipped open the second cuff that I realized Zelda hadn't said a word since stepping off the elevator. Peering up at her, I found she was still glancing around the space, her lips pursed and her fingers tangled on that strap.

I beckoned her toward the table. "Why do I get the sense I'm going to need all of this coffee in my system before you start asking questions?"

"No, no, it's fine," she replied as she craned her neck around to squint at the receptionist's desk. "No fortification required."

I sat down, rested my hands on my thighs. "Then what's wrong?"

"I wouldn't say anything is wrong."

I stared at her because it was too soon to drag her into my lap. Not that I was allowed that pleasure here. "What would you say?"

She shook her head, busied herself with unpacking the bag. "I'm just wondering, Ash, where is everyone *else*?"

"Everyone else," I echoed.

"Mmhmm." She popped the lid off her iced coffee and wrapped both hands around the cup. "You have all these offices and desks. Even though it's ludicrous to think you're all by yourself here, it doesn't look like they belong to anyone." Her eyes locked on me, she lifted the cup and took a long sip. "So, where is everyone else?"

I started to speak but stopped myself to fuss with my coffee. Not that there was much to do to it but I made meaningful work of swirling the cup until the lingering wisps of milk assimilated into the blackness. Eventually, I said, "It's complicated."

"Oh, Ashville." Zelda gave me a great, overlarge frown, her plush lips popping into a moue that demanded my urgent attention. Leaning over the table, I took her chin in my hand and sealed my lips to hers. It was quick and a bit brutal, and my ass was back in the seat in time to catch her swiping a finger over her top lip and whispering, "Whoa."

"You knew I had a job opening. Or two," I added.

She blinked at me as if she was struggling to process my words. Then, "Tell the truth, Ash. Did you drive off a perfectly competent staff?"

I unfolded my breakfast sandwich from its wax paper wrapping. "Competence is a matter of opinion."

Zelda and the rest of the world might argue that point with me but the fact remained, if I had to spend more time explaining to someone how I wanted a job done than it would've taken me to do the job myself, there was no benefit to keeping them on the payroll. Did it leave me looking like an impossible manager with even more impossible expectations? Yes. Did it mean everything got done right the first time? Yes. Mostly.

And that was how I found myself with a skeleton crew for an office staff.

"The phones are forwarded to a remote call center. I get an update from them every morning at six. IT is also outsourced. I have someone who handles payables and receivables. Offsite though Hazel does stop into the office about twice a month," I offered. "And there's an intern from one of the local colleges."

She flung her arms out wide. "Where?"

"He's only around during the school year." I ignored her aggravated murmur as I unwrapped her sandwich. "Eat. Please. We can index my issues once your stomach's growling has quieted to a low roar."

"Growling," Zelda muttered while she rearranged her food. "As if I'm the one growling here." She spared me a glance. "Since I'm going to need to do more than organize your calendar, this would be a fantastic time for you to explain to me what it is you do. You know, beyond Grumpy Businessman."

"Grumpy Businessman is not my job," I replied.

"Funny, I was convinced otherwise."

She jerked a shoulder up as she bit into her sandwich and I didn't know how the hell I was expected to survive a full day of her *right there* without making things exactly as indecent as they were in my head.

"I'm an accountant. I specialize in financial auditing. I've told you this before."

She patted a paper napkin to her lips, saying, "You have, yes, and you'll need to hold your grumpy grumblings about that for a later date. So, what do you account for? Paint me the picture, Ash. Walk me through it and pretend I don't know where you're taking me."

"Can we bring a blanket and a picnic basket? Because that sounds like something I'd enjoy."

"Unfortunately for your blanket, I'm only interested in talking about accounting and auditing." She snatched a pad of sticky notes and a ballpoint pen from my desk. "I want to hear about the work you do. Help me understand so I can help you."

I reached for my coffee while I gathered my thoughts. I knew how to answer her question but there was something nuanced about answering it for the woman who'd stepped into my world and created a new place for herself beside me. "I started off focused exclusively on financial audits where I'd spend a week or so in fieldwork. I'd go through an organization's books, come back here to churn through it, and write up a report. That was the deal I made with my dad, actually. He'd hang on to his existing tax and small business bookkeeping clients, I'd develop a new base of auditing clients."

"Except it hasn't gone that way," she said.

I shook my head. "Not at all. He picks up new clients every time he leaves the house which would be fine except for the issue of him scaling back his time in the office and having hardly any support staff—"

"So it's a genetic condition," Zelda said. "That makes more sense."

I pitched a brow up as I sipped my coffee. "At first, I didn't mind running a few individual tax returns. In most cases, it's quick work. But then it wasn't just tax returns. It was bookkeeping for a meat market in New Bedford, it was an annual report for a church, it was payroll for a dance studio."

"All while you're trying to pick up audit clients," she said.

"Yeah and it wasn't difficult to delegate that work to an accounting assistant."

"Back when you had one, that is."

I rapped my knuckles against the table. "It's almost like you pleasure in reminding me that I can't keep anyone on staff."

Sidestepping that comment completely, Zelda asked, "What are your big projects right now? Is it still auditing with a side of your dad's strays?"

For a minute, I debated keeping this part of the story to myself. I didn't have a good reason for it aside from not wanting to hear another person tell me it didn't make sense. But this was Zelda and fuck me if I could keep anything from her. "For the past year, I've been taking on clients with different needs. Consulting with organizations about tax strategy. Setting up payroll systems for new or expanding companies. Or whatever they need."

"And you're enjoying that," she said.

"Yeah, it's a nice addition to the audit work," I agreed. "It's interesting. I get to tackle new problems every day while still allowing enough time for fieldwork."

She hooked a thumb over her shoulder. "Don't forget the part where you're signing for deliveries at the door and managing the accounts of a meat market. Are you also washing the floors and emptying the wastebaskets in the evening? Do you perform maintenance on the copier? I'm torn between wanting to see that more than I can explain and fearing the blunt-object damage you'd do."

I finished off my sandwich and balled the paper in my hand. "I pay for those services."

"Thank god," she murmured.

"Does that answer your questions?" I asked.

Her bottom lip snared in her teeth, Zelda bobbed her head as she scribbled on the sticky note. "Mmm. Yeah. We need to find a way for you to do the things that fill your bucket, delegate the things that don't, and keep the wheels turning without you having to change any tires."

"I imagine you already have a plan on how you'll accomplish these goals. Perhaps one with fewer mixed metaphors."

She continued bobbing her head as she wrote. "Oh yeah. Give me a few days, Ashville. I'll get you under control."

I pushed to my feet and gestured toward the receptionist's desk outside my office, saying, "I'll leave you to it."

Zelda stared at me as my quietly spoken challenge hung in the air between us. When she stood, she said, "You're not the first man to doubt me and you're not likely to be the last."

"I don't doubt you at all, Miss Besh," I replied. "But I do need you to stay out of arm's reach or I fear I'll break our agreement before lunch."

"Mr. Santillian, please," she said with a huff. "That agreement was broken before I finished my sandwich. Speaking of which, I need another."

———

I MADE IT FORTY-FIVE MINUTES BEFORE CALLING ZELDA BACK INTO MY office. That was forty-five minutes of watching her through the damned glass walls and listening to her hum and talk to herself. Forty-five minutes of forcing myself to stare at my computer screen and ignore the heaviness growing between my legs. Forty-five minutes of huffing and scowling every time she dragged the toe of her shoe up the back of her leg or squatted down to collect a file from the bottom drawers. Forty-five minutes of debating whether I could close up shop for the day, the week, the rest of the fucking year if it meant sitting with her, listening to her, keeping her.

"What do I have going on today?" I asked, mostly to myself as I rustled through the papers on my desk. "There's the audit work to wrap up from last week and—"

"You have calls at one, two thirty, and four, an amended

proposal to send back to the Shadyside team before close of business, and a dinner meeting at seven thirty at Abe & Louie's with the leadership from Ferryman Brothers."

Fuck, I'd forgotten about that dinner. It was too late to cancel. Considering those guys holed up in Nantucket most of the summer, I'd have to wait until September to get on their calendar again and that was too long.

Zelda noticed me thinking this over. "Don't worry about me. I can entertain myself for a few hours."

"You could come with me," I said but I knew it wasn't a solid idea. The Ferryman guys liked to talk a big game while having their hands held through their annual audits. And they spooked easily too. I couldn't bring my new associate along without plenty of advance assurances I wasn't about to dump their account onto someone else.

"Instead of doing that, let's see what's behind door number two," she replied. "Ah, yes. It's me being fine on my own."

"But, Zelda—"

She held up a hand. "Listen, Ash. There is plenty for me to do here"—she gestured to the mess of folders, mail, and stray paperwork she'd gathered—"and your meeting doesn't require me or my presence. It wouldn't make sense for me to sit through that so let's wrap up that argument. I can't say the subway system makes any sense to me yet but—"

"You'll use my car service account," I interrupted, not that she noticed.

"— I'm a big girl and I'll find my way. I'll feed myself too so don't you worry about anything."

"Give me your phone." I held out my hand. When she responded with nothing more than a tolerant smile, I added, "Please."

"I don't need your car service."

"You might not," I said, my hand still outstretched. "But I'll need to know you made it home without accidentally taking the Red Line to all the way down to Braintree instead of hopping on the Orange and riding it to Haymarket."

"That seems like a worst-case scenario."

"I'll spend the whole evening worrying, you know. I'll ignore my clients because I'm busy checking my phone. They'll drop me as their auditor and I won't even notice because I'm texting you for the four hundredth time. If anything, you'll be doing me a favor."

Taking care to reply with both an eye roll and an impatient sigh, Zelda snatched the phone off her desk and slapped it into my hand. "You have some peculiar theories, Ashville. More peculiar than some of my conspiracy theories."

"As you didn't argue with me on the odds of winding up in Braintree versus Revere Beach, I'll count this peculiarity as a win." I downloaded my preferred car service app and several food delivery apps too. My neighborhood wasn't nearly as lively as the North End or Back Bay come evening and she'd need to order out if she didn't find anything she liked in the fridge.

"Only because I don't know where either of those places are or the relative ease of traveling in the wrong direction on public transportation."

"It's all about knowing inbound and outbound," I said, my focus on the device as I logged into my accounts and switched the system preferences to save my passwords. To the contacts, I added my number, Magnolia's, and—against an entire canyon of better judgment—my mother's. "It doesn't always get you where you think it should." I handed the phone back. "Tell me you'll call a car instead of giving the T a shot."

She took the phone from me, slipped it into a hidden pocket in her skirt. "You're taking this a bit too seriously. We're talking about one evening where I, a capable adult woman, will return myself to your apartment before the late summer sun sets and the cast of *Cats* takes back the streets."

She was right about that. I was taking this far too seriously and I was worrying in unnecessary, unproductive ways. Yet I didn't care and I wasn't certain I could help it. I didn't know how I'd leave her for a meal bound to last three hours. I didn't know how I'd sit through the first round of drinks without an update on Zelda's journey back to my place not because I sincerely doubted her ability to navigate the city but because I didn't want to be separated from her for that long. And yes, there was a part of me that wanted to look after her and protect her, even if that made me an infantilizing dick.

Then again, I could always take her home and then leave for my meeting—

"Whatever you're thinking, don't," Zelda said.

I pushed out of my chair because I had too much energy coursing through me to sit much longer. "Tell me you'll take the car service."

"I am under no obligation to make such promises." She tipped her chin up and shifted to inspect the pile of junk collecting dust on the corner of my desk. "You're making it far too simple to push your buttons."

I snatched the papers she'd gathered from her hands and stepped into her space. "Is that what you're doing? You're toying with me?"

She shook her head, keeping an indifferent gaze on the junk pile. "No, I'm reminding you I'm able to get myself from point A to point B without incident, without the aid of anyone's car service, and without any male prerogative to guide my way."

I dropped my hands to her waist, tucked a finger under her skirt. "Tell me you'll do it, love."

"You want me to agree because it will make you feel better about something that isn't a real concern because this city is generally safe, and even if I did get lost on the subway, I'd find my way back eventually. However, you've invented this concern because it gives you a handy place to store the emotions you don't know how to name," she said.

"Zelda," I protested because it was the only thing I could say.

"Is it possible that making you feel better will also succeed in making me feel small and powerless? Because I have to tell you, I just climbed out of that box and the process was *grueling*. You're not going to put me back in there only to unbox me when you want a bad bitch in bed."

"For fuck's sake, Zelda, no. That's not what I meant."

She flattened her hands on my chest, pushed up on her toes, and delivered a quick kiss to my lips. "What did I tell you about your buttons?"

Turning to collect the papers from wherever I'd thrown them, Zelda shot me an obscene wink. I had to press my fist to my mouth to keep from growling when she bent over to retrieve a file from the floor because that skirt was awful but it was also torture. The fabric hugged her backside, outlining the twin globes and enough of her panty line to make me dizzy with want. Actually fucking dizzy before ten in the morning.

The fist was of no use because I growled anyway. My hands were itching to touch her, to ruck up that skirt and palm her where she was warm and wet, to press my shaft inside her while her knuckles went white clutching my desk. I balled my hands as she reordered the papers and straightened, smoothed her skirt. I shook them out as she tucked her hair over her ears. Balled them all over again because she was here in my office—and my bed—and something had changed. Something significant, something big enough to alter everything because it'd never before crossed my mind to have sex in my office. Now I wasn't positive I'd survive the day if I didn't.

And goddamn, the swell of…I didn't know what it was but my chest was tight and full and I was about to burst.

"If you're going to hover until I capitulate to your improbably patriarchal request, you should know that's a terrible use of a billable hour." She gathered an armload of my junk collection and headed toward the door. "Why don't you just shoot irritated glares in my direction every few minutes while you make headway on wrapping up that audit?" When I didn't reply because I was fantasizing about tasting her through her panties, she stopped, glanced over her shoulder at me. "Do you need some cookies? Would that help?"

I needed tits flat on my desk and her cunt clenching around my cock while I teased her ass and I also needed to know she'd make it home without incident but yeah, cookies would do. As good a substitute as any. That was why I beckoned her toward me. "Bring me your phone again."

She shifted the files to her other arm. "Dare I ask what now, boss?"

"I want to enable contactless payment under my corporate card. If you're fetching cookies for me, I want to expense them."

Instead of arguing, Zelda drew the phone from her pocket and held it up. "Will this make you happy?"

Leaning across the desk, I plucked the device from her fingers and set to keying in the information. "I don't know about happy but since I know you're not going to come over and get that skirt out of my way—"

"You know you're a sex monster, right?"

I glanced up from the phone. "Meaning…what, exactly?"

"Meaning you're a dirty, filthy sex monster," she replied. "And you secretly eat cookies in the morning."

"Can you clarify for me whether this is an issue for you or a glowing review following a night you'll never forget?"

"I like how your ego has no limits," Zelda mused. "It's really endearing."

Since I was a dirty, filthy sex monster, I dropped down into my desk chair and made an unmistakable gesture toward my fly. "Come over here and say that to me."

We stared at each other longer than any two people should stare at each other. It was heated and intense, and a million things passed in the moments between blinks. And then—finally—she set down the papers, the phone, and she rounded my desk, straddled my lap, laced her arms around my neck. It seemed she had no issue with me being a sex monster despite the pejorative nature of that label. And, fuck, I'd be the best sex monster she'd ever had. The best, the only one she ever wanted.

"You are full of feelings today, aren't you, Ashville?"

I touched my lips to the smooth line of her jaw. "Yeah."

"Don't know what to do with any of them, do you?"

I kissed my way down her neck as far as her filmy blouse's collar would allow. "Not really, no."

She took my face in her hands and she drew half-moons from my cheekbones to my lips. And then she gifted me a slow, sweet kiss that turned everything else off. It didn't alleviate my desire to rip that skirt up the back or bite her clit through her panties but it picked up the pieces of my frantic need and put them away in a manageable order.

When she broke the kiss, she leaned back, her fingers pressed to my lips. "I'm going to get you some cookies now. When I come back, you're going to work on that audit and I'm going to make sense of all the little fires around here. Then you're going to Abe & Louie's and I'm going back to the apartment on my own, and I won't be informing you about my mode of transportation because I'll tolerate only this much"—she held her hand up beside her shoulder—"insanity from you. Not an inch more. When you return from your meeting, you're welcome to be a filthy, filthy sex monster all you want. I'll look forward to it." She granted me a brief kiss before sliding off my lap. "Now tell me. What kind of cookies do you want, boss?"

THIS DINNER MEETING WAS RUNNING THREE BOTTLES OF MALBEC too long.

Not that I'd enjoyed much of the heady red. Why would I when I could nod and laugh along with my clients while waiting for an opening to step away and check my phone for an update from Zelda confirming she'd arrived home without incident? Or better yet, why imbibe when I could replay the strangled sob I'd forced from her lips when I'd pushed inside her last night? Why, indeed.

Her message landed shortly after the appetizer plates were cleared, a one-word note of "home" accompanied by a photo of her outside my building. I'd thought about telling her she wasn't home until she was behind the closed doors of the apartment, that god-awful shirt in the trash and her feet bare while she lounged on the sofa in *my* boxer shorts, but I had to get through this evening without my dick throbbing. I replied with a stiff "thank you" and made a note to scrub my calendar of dinner meetings wherever possible.

While I wasn't one to cram my weeknights with these gatherings, I'd never understood why some of my clients were in such a rush to get home. I could give a pass to the ones with small kids but when it came to the dual income, no kids crowd, I didn't get it. Didn't those people have enough time with their partners? Couldn't they manage an evening apart without sighing into their gin and tonics? Why did anyone need to sprint home for a couple of minutes with their partner when there were deals to be made and hours to bill? I'd never been able to make sense of it.

Until tonight.

I understood it all and that understanding came with a dose of resentment for know-nothing fools such as myself who insisted on finalizing agreements after hours.

I didn't want to be here, didn't want to do this. Nothing mattered besides getting back home where I could set down my troubles and simply be with her. And inside her.

Though it wasn't all about the sex. The sex was a fine bonus but it was everything else, all the pieces of her I'd discovered and claimed as my own. Plus all the pieces I'd yet to collect, the ones I didn't know but required nonetheless.

As soon as the business conversation gave way to the well-traveled paths of golf handicaps and vacation destinations, I excused myself to settle the bill—another bottle of Malbec tossed on for good measure—and made my exit. I didn't need to be here for the rest of this. Not when it was the same pointless chatter that always populated the tail end of these gatherings.

Sports, industry gossip, political grousing. I hadn't noticed the rigid three-point waltz of it before but now that I saw, there was no missing it.

While waiting on the curb for the car service to arrive, I snapped a photo of the receipt and uploaded it to the Ferryman Brothers' expense file. I could've walked back to my place and on any other night, I would have. Get in some steps, burn off the wine, think through tomorrow's work. It was time well spent. Yet I didn't give a single fuck about tomorrow because I had a strange, beautiful woman at home and tomorrow would arrive whether I worried over it or not.

The ride to my building was quick and silent but once I stepped into the lobby, everything slowed down to heavy, aching seconds. It was like a roller coaster climbing to its first peak, every grind forward loaded with anticipation and the knowledge these were the last moments of relative calm before the splashdown, the next upswing, the spin and whirl. It was anticipation and it was also relief—*I'm getting what I came for*—and the end of all my staid predictability before Zelda upended that too.

Low light and the rhythmic hum of the washing machine greeted me when I stepped inside and locked the apartment door behind me with a gentle twist of the deadbolt. I leaned back against the door, the key ring still hooked around my fingers as I listened for Zelda.

The cobalt blue flats abandoned near the bench informed me she was here and that only heightened my awareness of the roller coaster plunge to come. She was here and I had to find her if I wanted my world turned upside down.

Once free from my suit coat and shoes and my pockets emptied, I surveyed the living room. The television was off, the throw blankets artfully arranged over the back of the sofa. I moved toward the bedroom but she wasn't in there either. The bed was in the same crisply made condition we'd left it, the adjoining bath dark and empty. Save for those cute shoes near the door, it seemed like she'd existed only in my imagination.

I retraced my steps, casting gazes all over for signs of Zelda. She could've stepped out. That was reasonable. She could've gone to the local market or the drugstore. Maybe the pizza place around the corner. It was late but not outrageously so, not too late to run out for a few things.

I turned in a circle when I reached the kitchen and trailed my palm over the stone countertops. Why wasn't she right here, exactly where I wanted her, when I wanted her?

Then I caught sight of the hall leading to the guest room. More often than not I overlooked that section of my apartment. It served only as a crash pad for Linden or my parents when they had occasion to come into the city and wanted to avoid a long ride home at night. Magnolia too, before she and Rob found a place in the South End. And now it was Zelda's— though she never did sleep in there.

Restlessness fractured the quiet still as I marched in that direction, my socked feet rasping against the rug, my fingertips pressed to the wall as if I was searching for a pulse. The door was ajar, a soft slice of light melting into the hall. I flattened my palm on the panel, eased it open. There I found Zelda face down on the foot of the bed, still dressed in that aggravating skirt and blouse. Her head was pillowed on her arms while one foot dangled off the side. My discombobulated beauty.

I lost track of how long I stood there, watching while she slept. It was more than a minute and less than an hour, and I regretted none of it as there weren't many moments where I'd been able to catch Zelda at rest. She was always the first one awake and more than that, she was always in motion. Always occupied with something. Rare were the instances when she was stationary long enough for me to get a good look.

She must've been exhausted to fall asleep like this. Not the discombobulated part—she was an eternal state of glorious disarray—but in here, dressed for work as if she'd intended to sit down though found herself bowled over by sleep instead.

As I scanned the small room, the evidence seemed to mount in support of that theory. Her luggage was open on the floor with tidy piles of clothing stacked on one side, books on the other. I counted three pairs of jeans, five t-shirts, a plum cardigan, two dresses, and a few more of those crepey blouses —and at least eight academic journals and four beat-up textbooks.

A dark gray skirt and short-sleeved pink sweater were laid outside beside the books, her choices for tomorrow. Both of her phones—the beat-up one she hadn't turned on and the one I'd insisted she have—sat on the floor beside her hot pink sneakers. All of it combined into a statement that screamed *temporary*.

Tomorrow we'd handle the matter of her living out of a suitcase while there was a serviceable closet calling her name, plus all the space for her on the other side of the apartment, in my room. One of these days we'd deal with her phone and whomever it was she intended to avoid. And someday soon, we'd make this far less temporary.

Tonight, however, we'd sleep.

I stripped down to my boxer briefs and deposited my clothes on a chair in the corner before starting in on the blankets and sheets. The tricky part was peeling off Zelda's clothes without waking her. A girl who preferred sleeping in the buff would never survive a night confined to a slim-fitting skirt and a noose-neck shirt.

Against all odds, I removed her skirt without incident. It was the least Zelda article of clothing in the world and I hated it with a fiery passion though I hung it in the closet with care. The top proved more difficult. As I inched it up her torso, she came around with several bleary-eyed blinks.

"Help me get this off you, Zelda," I whispered.

"Oh shit," she rasped, her eyes drooping shut. "I didn't mean to fall asleep." I lifted her arms and drew the shirt over her head. Once it was free, I pitched it toward the closet. I'd send it out with my dry cleaning in the morning. "I just wanted to put my head down for a minute. I had things to do."

I ran my thumb over her cheek. It was flushed from where it had laid against her arm. There was more of her to take in—the way those black cotton panties stretched over the curve of her ass, the thin tank top rucked up past her belly button, the purple bra straps sliding down her shoulders—but this, her cheek, her lips, this was enough to send me on another dip and rise of the roller coaster. "I know, love. I know."

As much as I wanted to scoop her up and settle her under the blankets, I couldn't do that. I might've ditched the sling but my shoulder still hurt like hell and the last thing I wanted was to fuck that situation up any further.

"Come on now," I crooned, sliding my good arm under her arms. "Rest your head on the pillows for me. There you go, there we are. Good girl."

Zelda murmured and nodded like a sleepwalker as she flopped down. I circled the bed, climbing in on the opposite side and drawing the blankets up around us. Everything about this was foreign—the mattress, the pillows, the light cutting in from the window—yet all the restlessness inside me fizzled when Zelda nestled her back against my chest and tucked herself into my notches and grooves.

I was almost asleep when she bolted up, murmured "Fuck this" and whipped her bra off through her tank top's arm.

When she reclaimed her spot beside me, I smoothed her hair from her face. "Better?"

"Much," she replied.

As usual, she was right.

SEVENTEEN
ZELDA

ONE MORE THING TO WARN YOU ABOUT WAS MY STUPIDLY TOLERANT nature. It coordinated nicely with my occasional obliviousness, like a dress that always looked *just right* with an old jean jacket.

I had a storied history of accepting the worst behaviors from others and keeping myself in harmful situations past the point of reason. Part of the trouble was I couldn't help but accept everyone as they came. I believed everyone was doing their best with their circumstances. Believed it past the point of knowing better. Believed it past the point of self-injury. That was stupidly tolerant for you. It wasn't until someone else showed me the toxic sludge I was choking down that I was able to see the poison I'd chosen for myself this time around.

No, I couldn't have helped the circumstances I was born into but I did the best anyone could've expected from a child and I made it through. Though it hadn't been until trading small teenage tragedies with my camp counselor confidant Gunnar DeWitt when I was nineteen that I'd opened my eyes to the reality that my family life was marked by abuse and neglect.

I could remember her reaction as clear as if it'd happened

yesterday. I remembered every minute of it. There was no mistaking the face people made when introduced to homemade horrors. It was one of shock and distress but it was also pity. Always pity. The worst part of pity wasn't feeling powerless or small. It was the shame that stole the oxygen from my chest and blocked out the sun.

In keeping with our usual late night gatherings, Gunnar and I surrounded ourselves with chips, cheap wine, and gossip. But that night, I'd tripped into a well of honesty when I told her about the worst sunburn of my life. I was fourteen and I'd tried to develop a base tan on my torso before debuting a new summer bikini. But I'd missed the mark and scorched my skin far past the point of an average sunburn. There were blisters and cracks and an alarming amount of peeling skin—it was gross. It hurt like nothing I'd experienced before and my body treated the entire incident as if it was suffering from the flu. But the real victory, the success of this experience was my ability to conceal it from my parents. I'd slathered myself in creams, kept a cool, damp cloth layered under my clothes, and popped painkillers around the clock until I could exist in my skin without crying. And they never suspected a thing.

I hadn't expected the words to flow as freely as they had and I knew I'd said too much when Gunnar blinked at me, the wine bottle frozen on its way to her lips and pity scrawled over her face. She'd wanted to know why I hid the burn, why I hadn't asked my parents to bring me to a doctor, why hadn't they *helped*. Parents were supposed to care for their children, even when those children did boneheaded things like frying their skin off in the name of beachwear. Then she'd wanted to know everything else about my home life.

She'd informed me it was curious that I'd spent most of my

high school years staying with an assortment of friends and only visiting my home once every few weeks. It wasn't okay for my mom to drink to excess every day and say cruel things to me. And leaving me to figure out how I'd get to and from school as a kid wasn't a practical experience in self-reliance or independence. It was abuse—all of it was abuse—even if it didn't leave cuts or bruises.

I hadn't mentioned the sister-mother piece. I didn't tell anyone about that.

Gunnar was the first person who told me it shouldn't have been that way and it didn't have to continue being that way, and I could change it. I hadn't realized how detrimental it was until she'd shown me, just as I hadn't known my life in Denver had simmered down to the same type of scorched terrible until Leesa Bruno, the owner of the spirituality shop, started pulling tarot cards one uneventful afternoon. She asked about grad school and I was forced to tell her I'd put a hold on my studies. Like any good witch, she wanted to know why.

Explaining a flawed, fractured relationship to someone unaware and uninvolved had a way of pulling apart the scar tissue of shame until the whole thing broke in my hands. Shame was the root of it all, of course. It wasn't the shame that followed an awkward moment or saying the wrong thing at the wrong time. This was the shame that accompanied me everywhere, a parasitic passenger determined to weigh me down until I stopped moving altogether.

Leesa had listened, just as Gunnar had. She'd pointed out the problems, the fallacies, the unacceptable behaviors too. She'd tapped her finger on the cards and told me it was time for me to go into the world and find my way again.

Then she'd fired me.

———

ASH PROPPED HIMSELF AGAINST HIS DOORWAY TO HIS OFFICE, HIS back pressed to the jamb while he crossed his arms over his chest. He did this exact thing several times each day. He'd leave his desk, walk to the door, and say nothing while he settled into the Hot Boss pose.

I couldn't determine whether this was a performance for me or an innate mannerism not unlike a jaguar perching in a tree to study its prey in the most comfortable pose possible. Either way, I'd learned to pay this behavior little attention. I didn't spin my chair around to watch anymore. I didn't prompt him to speak. I stayed focused on my work until the last moment because the Hot Boss pose was the best and worst type of power play.

It was both best and worst because Ash was already in control here. There was no dispute in that matter and he didn't have to roll up his shirtsleeves or pace his office while on conference calls or station himself in the doorway to communicate his authority. It seeped out of him and scented the air. I could no sooner avoid it than hold my breath all day.

There was an extra layer of goodness because he didn't do any of these things with the intention of being arrogant or outwardly dominant. It came as naturally to him as his mercurial moods. He had no idea how much raw, assertive confidence shone like a halo around him.

I had to admit there was another reason I didn't give him my full attention during these moments. If I devoted any time at all to watching him lean against the door or stand behind his desk with a hand on his waist while he frowned into a phone conversation, I'd probably rip his pants off. No exaggeration.

"My mother texted just now," he announced. "She'll be here in fifteen."

I shot a glance at the wall clock. "Wow. Where did the afternoon go?"

"You can skip this dress fitting thing for my sister. I'll take care of it."

Still seated at my desk, I asked, "Are you offering because you think I can't handle your mother and sister or because you don't want to go to the doctor alone?"

"I know you can. I'm saying you don't have to," he replied, dodging all talk of his visit to the specialist. All day, he'd insisted his shoulder was nearly back to normal and when he didn't think I'd notice, he hit up the tiny bottle of over-the-counter pain reliever in his desk drawer.

"And you don't want to visit the doctor all by yourself," I added, busy organizing documents for tomorrow. I needed everything in place now because I didn't want to be running around crazy while the first part of my plan to get Ash's office functioning at top speed launched.

He made a noise, something that suggested he wouldn't admit anything of that sort, then said, "If you're sure about doing this dress thing, I'll meet you there when I'm finished."

"You don't have to make it sound like we're parting for sixteen years." Finally, I swiveled my chair around to face him. "It's only a few hours, Ashville. You will survive, I promise."

"I know that," he grumbled.

"You're in a mood." I eyed him, the haughty fold of his arms, the scowl dug into his face, even the broody way he cocked his hip. "What's that all about?"

He lifted his brows by way of explanation, his eyes widening as if that were adequate in defining the afternoon's issues.

"Mmhmm." I shifted back toward my documents and files. I couldn't say I understood everything about accounting but I'd figured out how to tee it up for the people who did. I'd also figured out a few things about Ash's moods. He was obsessively efficient but if he didn't feel like tackling a task, it didn't matter what his schedule required of him, he wasn't doing it. He brought his A game to meetings and calls but he fell quiet once they ended, as if he was running low on words after spending so many. Cookies helped with that.

It shouldn't have surprised me after he'd released his inner filth monster but Ash devoted full minutes to growling as he watched me move around the office. Perhaps that wasn't indicative of his moody tendencies so much as the zealousness of his libido. I should've known from the moment I sat down beside him on the plane that anyone as tightly wound as him would be an almighty beast in bed.

"I'll meet you at the dress place," he said. "We'll get dinner somewhere. I owe it to you after last night."

He meant the part about leaving me to brave the big bad city on my own while he was out for a posh business dinner, not the part where he snuggled me up like a baby doll when he arrived home to find me passed out between loads of laundry.

I bit my lip to keep my sloppy grin in check. Even with Ash at my back, I was certain he'd see it otherwise. I wanted to give him my sloppiness, I wanted it very much, but I knew he'd dip his chin and frown in that way of his and say something about there being nothing heroic in putting someone to bed.

For all I knew, it was as everyday as holding the door open for the person coming in behind you yet that didn't make it any less foreign to me. I couldn't remember anyone gathering me up and tucking me into bed before. No one had ever held me through a night not punctuated by sex of some sort. No one had ever held me like I was important enough for them to hold on.

The daffy part of this was I'd slept through most of it. I was a light, fitful, somewhat insomniac sleeper though I barely remembered him stripping me down or settling me beneath the blankets. It was as though my mind and body knew to trust Ash, knew we were safe here with him, and we didn't need to be on guard all the time.

"You must stop agonizing over last night," I said.

"I'm not agonizing. I'm stating I want an evening with you without the interruption of clients or sisters." He grabbed the back of my chair, spun it toward him. He flicked a hand toward the documents. "Put that down. Come here."

"You can wait a second." I swiveled back to the desk, taking care to set the papers I'd sorted on one side and those still in a garbled mess on the other. I did not want to start this process all over. That, and waiting was good for Ash. It gave him something new to growl about and took his mind off everything else.

When I was ready, I pushed out of the chair and into his waiting arms. He kissed my hair like always and held me tight, exhaling softly as if this contact came as a relief. It was a relief to me too. His touch had put me at ease since he fell asleep on my shoulder and all the fear and anxiety I'd accumulated in my break from Denver and its associated parts hushed.

I chose to accept this about us rather than analyze it. Nothing good could come of me annotating the reasons I'd thoroughly melted into this man's life nor him into the new construct I called my life.

"I already know you can hold your own with my mother and Mag but don't let either of them pump you for information." He skimmed his hand down my spine and under the thin cotton of my sweater to rest on the small of my back. "They'll ask lots of nice, innocent questions and then they'll be back at my apartment, taking measurements of the guest room to turn it into a nursery."

"Don't be obtuse. They'd require us to move out of the city first. Somewhere with room to *grow*."

He made a deep, raspy sound in agreement that I felt as much as I heard. "At least two bedrooms for the babies. Maybe three."

"Why stop at three when you could have four?" I joked.

Another rasp, another growl, and then a hand clamped on my hip. "Why ask that question when I'm not inside you?"

There wasn't a single earthly reason to find that comment arousing. I was starting my life over, inventing a new way for myself and putting my pieces back together all at once, and the last thing in the world I needed was an eager pair of ovaries egging me on. And yet— "Because it'll give you something to ponder between now and when you come find me."

And to be sure, none of this was real. There were no babies, no nurseries, nothing more than a truly unsafe-for-work conversation between people who felt better when they touched.

"Oh my god." Ash ducked his head to my neck, his lips and teeth connecting with my skin as if he intended to mark it. "It's like you're asking me to fuck you in a dressing room."

Since I really enjoyed some virile male swagger and was guaranteed a special kind of sex monster in bed with me tonight, I said, "Identify the problem in that for me."

"*God*, Zelda." He shifted his hand to my ass, jerked me up against his body hard enough to acquaint me with his erection. "I don't know what you think you're doing right now."

"Nothing you don't want."

"Fuck me if that isn't the truth," he murmured to my cheek.

"Your mother will be here any minute."

He rolled his hips, groaning as he palmed my jaw to kiss me. "Don't you dare let them put you in anything that isn't, you know, *Zelda*."

Since this wasn't the moment for button pushing, I kissed the corner of his mouth and said, "I won't."

"And don't accept any candy from my mother," he added. "She never remembers to mention her candy is the recreational variety."

I rested my head on his chest. "Your mother is a national treasure."

He gave a snort that shouldn't have been adorable on a man who traded in being the smartest guy in the room. "She's extremely—" Before he could finish that thought, the main door swung open and Diana stepped in, phone pressed to her ear and a binder wedged under her arm.

"I specifically requested wisteria and stated repeatedly that wisteria was non-negotiable. If I'd known you wouldn't be able to deliver, I would've selected a different florist," she said in the tone of voice reserved for women who knew how to speak to a manager. Holding up a finger, she mouthed *one minute*. "I am not interested in a substitution."

"She's extremely," Ash murmured.

I kept my head on his chest and let him hold me a bit longer. "I can see that."

"If you're unable to source the agreed-upon materials, I will expect a revised contract with a steep discount for the trouble I've incurred. I will also be forced to climb a ladder and cut down the wisteria growing in my backyard because I am unwilling to consider any alternative," Diana said.

"That's a terrible idea," Ash said to her. "Don't climb anything. Please."

"I'll anticipate a follow-up call within the hour," Diana continued, ignoring Ash. "That's much better. Thank you." She dropped the phone into her shoulder bag, set the binder on my desk, and approached us with outstretched hands. "How do you get more gorgeous and glowing every day? Oh, I cannot wait to dress you up in pretty gowns."

"Thank you but gowns aren't my style," Ash said.

"Would you stop it, son." Diana hit him with a pursed-lip frown. "You know I was talking to Zelda."

"And here I was, thinking you'd noticed me at all," he said. "Apparently not."

Stifling a laugh, I asked, "Is everything all right with the flowers?"

She gave an epic eye roll. "It will be, even if I have to get in there and arrange them myself." Deciding she was done with that topic, she patted the binder twice. "We should make our way over to the shop. It's a quick walk. You don't mind, do you? I hate to give up a good parking space once I've found one."

"Sounds great." I tipped my head back to meet Ash's steady gaze. "You'll have to let me go, you know."

"I know nothing of the sort," he replied.

Diana headed back toward the door, calling, "Ash, we don't have time for this territorial nonsense. Save it for another day when I don't have a schedule to keep."

"I'll text you the address of the shop and I won't accept candy from anyone," I said to him, low enough for it to stay between us. "Go get that shoulder checked out. I want you in full working order, boss."

He kissed my forehead. "Pick a dress I can fuck you in, okay? Nothing too complicated."

From the door, there was a slight gasp and "Jesus, Mary, and Joseph."

I nodded. "I'll see what I can do."

———

"I don't have to breathe. Breathing is highly overrated," Magnolia said from the pedestal in the center of the shop. "I will be fine without breathing for, like, eight hours."

"If you continue stressing like this, you're going to give yourself hives," Diana called from somewhere in the racks of white silk and tulle. "Or worse, a pimple. We don't have time for an emergency dermatologist visit this week."

Magnolia caught my eye in the mirror while two seamstresses pinned the bustle into place. "I love this dress," she said. It sounded like an apology. "I do. It's totally perfect for me and the venue and all, but I'm halfway terrified I'm going to look like an overstuffed sausage in my photos."

I tipped my head to the side as I studied the stunningly simple ball gown. The skirt was full and sumptuous, and the sweetheart neckline was precious on her. She was right about it being totally perfect. "You don't look like a sausage at all. You look incredible."

"Thank you." She lifted her arms, glanced down at the dress. "Seriously, thank you for coming along for this. I know it's a lot to ask."

I waved away her words as I collected the flute of champagne I'd abandoned following our arrival. I'd been too busy trying on the dozen or so dresses Diana plied me with to consider champagne. Now, with a divine backless floral print floor-length dress bagged and hanging near the door, I could derive joy from my beverage and all the associated frills of visiting a bridal boutique. The velvet sofa, the billowing satin draped behind the mirrors, the plush ivory carpets. This was new to me, the whole bridal thing.

No, that wasn't true. I hadn't forfeited my share of save-the-dates or bachelorette weekends. I'd attended plenty of weddings for camp and college friends. YouTube once taught me how to sew a strapless bra into a bridesmaid dress because alterations weren't in my budget. I'd consumed an ample quantity of *Say Yes to the Dress*.

However, I'd never witnessed a mother-of-the-bride dressing down a florist or acting as the bride's shoulder of support during her final fitting. I'd never really been *in* it.

"Don't mention it," I said. "This is fun."

Magnolia stared at her reflection in the trio of mirrors surrounding the pedestal. "It is fun." She said that as if she'd only now realized it. "I have to remind myself it's really just a big party with a random assortment of sacred choreographies to make it difficult but also awesome."

"Don't forget about the embedded patriarchal structures and unattainable social standards," I added with a laugh because we weren't dismantling the marital-industrial complex today. Just kicking a few rocks at it while drinking champagne.

"Right? God save me if I accidentally use my third cousin's colors from her wedding nine years ago or the same first dance song Rob's sister's maid of honor played when she got married. Don't get me started on some of the traditions. I know they have significance to some people but, dude, I arrived at this point through some majorly non-traditional paths and a lot of that stuff feels uncomfortable to me. I'm too old for someone to give me away, you know? And it's not about my dad because he's awesome and he'll do anything I ask." She met my eyes in the mirror. "My father is walking me down the aisle but I couldn't hang with any of the 'who gives this woman' language in the ceremony. I give myself. No one else has that right."

I felt that in my bones. So much that I couldn't respond for a moment for fear of a blubbering flood of words falling from my mouth. Instead, I took a sip of the now-flat champagne and nodded. "That's fair. I get it."

"Thank you for not telling me I'm a selfish wench for not wanting my father to essentially hand off ownership of me to my future husband in front of three hundred people," she replied.

Though there was a part of me that didn't get it, not because I wanted to be given away but because it hadn't crossed my mind anyone would wrestle with the degree to which their father would be involved in their wedding ceremony. I couldn't sympathize with Magnolia too much as I still didn't know what an ordinary father-daughter relationship looked like. To my mind, it was much like wondering how I'd handle an extra toe. You'd paint the nail of course but did you play it up with a ring or anklet or live life like it didn't exist?

I didn't know the answer to that one but I nodded along with Magnolia just the same.

"These are good problems to have. I'm aware of that," she continued. "I'm fortunate to have all this and I shouldn't whine about being given away or abandoning all my anti-diet mindsets to squeeze into this dress. I'm surrounded by blessings and I get to marry my favorite guy in a few days and my life is good."

"But a cheeseburger would be real nice right about now."

Magnolia pointed at my reflection. "Bingo."

From the other side of the shop, Diana called, "Zelda? Zelda, where did you go, dear?"

"We're right here, Mom," Magnolia replied. "Just turn around, take a few steps away from all the white and fluffy stuff, and—there you go. See? We didn't go anywhere."

Diana shot her daughter a huffy glare. "Zelda, I found the most unbelievable dress for you."

"I already found one," I said. "With the spaghetti straps and the full skirt? Floral print, no back?"

"That's for *Magnolia's* wedding," she replied, clearly amused at my confusion. "This is for *your* wedding."

I wasn't even drinking the champagne and I choked. "What?" I asked between coughs.

A sales assistant appeared beside Diana, a pool of silvery fabric spilling over her arms.

"You have to try it on," Diana insisted.

My stomach was both in my throat and on the floor. "Oh, I can't—"

"Mom, you're being pushy."

"It's not pushy when it's helpful," Diana replied. "What would it hurt to try it on? We're here and we have time, and who knows? It might look like a secondhand beet sack."

The sales assistant's eyes popped at that comment. "I'd be happy to help you if you'd like to step into a fitting room," she offered in a tone that said *ma'am, this is no beet sack.*

"What would it hurt, Zelda?" Diana asked again as she crossed the room toward me and tucked my hair over my ear in a move that was so purely maternal it cracked something inside me. "You're not required to like it. If you hate it, you hate it. You can't hurt my feelings."

"That's false," Magnolia said as the pair of seamstresses guided her off the pedestal. "Don't believe her."

Ignoring her daughter, she set her hands on my shoulders and smiled like this moment, us here in the dress shop, was the highlight of her day. Like *I* was the highlight. "If you love it then that means you know what you like when the time is right."

When I hesitated—because there was no obvious right choice ahead of me—the sales assistant grasped the hanger and held up the diaphanous gown for me to see. "It is lovely," she said.

Diana was right about it being unbelievable. The skirt was full but delicate, lacking the volume of Magnolia's. Embroidered petals and leaves blanketed the top layer of the moonlight fabric. Wispy, raw-cut tulle elbow-length sleeves and a deep v-neck made it sexy and bohemian all at once, like it was meant to be worn without shoes or undies.

"Okay," I heard myself say.

I followed the assistant—her name was Stacy, she reminded me—back to the fitting room where I'd tried on everything else Diana had selected for me.

There was something sacramental about stepping into a dress designed for one specific moment in a woman's life. It was a threshold, one I hadn't expected to cross any time soon.

This is just part of the fun. This is what mother-daughter shopping excursions are all about. It's just a dress. It doesn't mean anything.

I continued telling myself this as Stacy zipped and buttoned and laced me into the dress. She made noises about the color being a good complement to my skin and the style flattering my shape. I didn't dispute those points but that had more to do with me tracing the narrow raw silk sash at my waist and trying to reconcile the quiet in my head where there should've been noise. So much noise.

I'd never thought much about my father giving me away because I'd never thought much about getting married. My life was a landscape dappled with exits rather than commitments. I abandoned things like it was my purpose for existing. I packed up. I walked away. I didn't look back. At least not when anyone was watching.

Choosing a person, a place, a future—that wasn't something I knew. The champagne and the wisteria and the nearly sheer layers of star-glow fabric were for someone else, someone who'd earned herself a wedding gown.

And that wasn't me being tough on myself. No, my future was a giant question mark, an ongoing diet of figuring it all out and fixing myself up. I was in no condition to slip on a dress and wonder who'd walk me down the aisle.

When I stepped onto the pedestal and Diana launched into a string of squeals and coos high enough to summon forest animals, I had to force the words "it's just a dress" into my mind. Had to tell myself this was a game of make-believe, not the first spike of wedding fever.

It's nothing. It means nothing.

"Okay, Mom," Magnolia said from beside her on the sofa, out of her gown and back in her sundress and sandals. "You were right about this."

I shifted to get a look at the translucent back and Diana seized that opportunity to say, "You love it. I can tell."

Because deflecting was my best friend, I replied, "Oh, well, I don't know. It's very pretty but it doesn't...and I can't...and—"

Putting an end to my word salad, Diana cut in, "Yes, you can." She pushed off the sofa and moved closer to the pedestal, gathering the short train and letting it flutter behind me like a shimmering fog. "You can, my dear, and you *know*. Your face says it all."

Yet I couldn't say it all, not until I understood what I was saying. I pressed my fingers to my lips.

"I wish I could pull off boho," Magnolia said. "It just looks so effortless and cool on you."

I forced a laugh because it was the only thing I could do to stifle the keening pressure to know what was happening to me, to understand everything about this immediately. "You looked effortless too, I promise. And classic, which is just as good as cool. That dress was meant for you."

She locked her fingers together around her phone. "By that logic, this dress was meant for you."

That wasn't the direction I'd expected this to take. I wasn't prepared to slip on *the one* this evening and I didn't know how to put my feelings about this in the proper order.

I turned back to the mirror, again surprised to find myself in the reflection. Stacy tucked a headband behind my ears and put a bouquet of silk flowers in my hand while she explained something about the fabric or the designer. I didn't hear much of it.

The boutique's door chimed as it had several times since we'd arrived. I noticed a spot of shine on the gown's bodice and realized several of the embroidered petals were studded with seed pearls and gems. I liked the subtle sparkle of it as much as I liked the open back, the drapey sleeves, the airy fabric that seemed to weigh nothing. It was all of my things, all at once.

Who knew there was a dress for me and all my me-ishness? One unique and funky and also achingly romantic? It shouldn't have made sense, shouldn't have looked like a dream come to life. And it shouldn't have found me now when it was the last thing I needed.

"Yes. Hello. I'm just here for my—"

My attention snapped to the deep, demanding voice on the other side of the shop and found Ash staring at me, his lips parted and a slight twist of confusion on his brow.

"Zelda." He sounded breathless.

"You can't be here," Diana cried, advancing toward him with her arms raised like she was trying to chase a raccoon away from her kitchen garden. "You can't see the dress—"

"Not now, Mom."

Ash crossed the shop, Magnolia and Diana watching him as he rounded the pedestal to stand between me and the mirror. I sensed a hot flush climbing up my chest and neck, settling at my cheeks.

He didn't say anything as he took in the dress, the headband, the bouquet. Then, he cupped my flaming cheek and leaned in for a kiss almost as airy as this gown. "Now this is what I mean when I say I want you in a Zelda dress."

Behind us, Diana let out a cheer and Magnolia said something about not letting it go to her head but neither of us paid them any attention.

Ash leaned in, dragged his lips up my neck, and asked, "How quickly can you get out of this? I need to know for right now and the next time you wear it for me."

EIGHTEEN
ASH

"Don't you think we should say goodbye?" Zelda asked as I led her out of the dress shop, my hand fisted on the waist of her skirt like a true savage while she waved to my mother and sister.

It wasn't as though I was truly dragging Zelda away or I doubted her willingness to leave the shop under her own free will. It was that I rather enjoyed the visceral satisfaction of claiming her, possessing her. It was that *she* rather enjoyed it too, and there was no material difference between fisting her skirt on a sidewalk and cinching my belt around her wrists in the bedroom.

God, the things this woman made me feel and think. The things she made me *want*.

"I think finding you in a wedding dress calls for the suspension of all polite conduct," I replied, scanning the street for the arrival of our car service.

"And why is that, boss?"

I couldn't wait any longer. I just couldn't. "They've had you all afternoon. It's my turn now." With my hand still gripping her skirt, I brought my lips down to hers.

"I didn't plan that," she whispered between kisses. "I mean, I didn't expect to try it on."

"Doesn't matter," I murmured to her cheek. "Damage is done, love."

She leaned away, scowled up at me. "What do you mean by that? By 'damage?'"

"It means I won't be able to scrub the memory of you standing there like a glowing moonbeam bride and I don't believe I care to scrub it anyway. Not when I know I want to see you just like that again."

The car pulled up and I handed Zelda into the back seat. Rush hour—or *hours*, as it was in Boston—meant we inched through traffic one jerk and stop after another though we were too busy touching, kissing, leaning into each other to care.

"What did the doctor say?" she asked, her lips on my jaw. "Let's talk about that. Tell me about your shoulder."

I kissed a line up her neck. "It's fine. No surgery."

"More," she demanded. "There has to be more."

I shook my head. I wasn't getting into the doctor's recommendation of light activity and physical therapy if I didn't regain full range of motion in a few weeks. Unimportant to my present needs. "Nothing else to report."

She laughed, saying, "I doubt that. Details, please."

I flipped open the top buttons of her little sweater, only enough to reach inside, and ran my knuckles over the gentle rise of her breast. "Fuck the details."

Zelda covered my hand with hers as she glanced at the driver. "Ash, I don't want—"

"No one gets to see you but me," I whispered into her dark

hair. I scraped a finger over her nipple before buttoning her back up.

Eventually, we made it to my building though we were forced to ride the elevator alongside a pair of men who felt that was the appropriate venue for their disagreement on grocery spending. Zelda gazed up at me with her chin on my chest as we listened, not bothering to pretend otherwise. It was a good diversion from all the emotions I'd experienced since finding Zelda on that pedestal and the way they swirled together, melting and melding into a fervent, boundless desire to keep her—and not simply in my bed, in my presence but in my future. I couldn't imagine the next week, the next month, the next year without her right here beside me, and that was a vast new ocean of emotions I was helpless to handle on my own.

Fortunately, I had Zelda to put me in order.

She led me down the hall, inside the apartment, into her arms, though I required much more than that this evening. With both hands on her waist, I walked her backward toward the dining table. She edged up onto the surface and brought her palms to my chest.

I wedged her legs apart, stepped between them. Unbuckled my belt and drew it through the loops with a swish that vibrated like a warning. "Answer me this, my moonbeam bride." I leaned in, my hands flat on the table and my mouth a breath from hers. "Will I fuck you before the vows or after?"

She closed the distance between us, nipping at my bottom lip. "Does it matter?"

"It does." I slanted my lips over hers, sighing into her mouth as I tasted her tongue. "It matters if you're walking down the aisle full and wet from me or waiting until after you're mine."

Zelda hummed for a moment, her eyes shut. "I know which way you want it."

I unbuttoned my shirt, unzipped my trousers as I watched her considering it—and what a strange, strange thing it was to speak this way about a marriage we'd never discussed yet accepted without hesitation. "Is that right? And how do I want it, love?"

"You want it before." A feline smile curled her lips and sparkled in her eyes. "You'd want to keep a secret like that while everyone watched us say very polite and chaste things to each other."

I could see it as if it'd already happened. Zelda alone in some quiet, cloistered room as she waited for the ceremony to begin. Me sneaking inside without a word. I'd skim her panties down and her dress up, and I'd fuck her from behind while she clutched her bouquet. I'd use those panties to mop up the mess I'd made between her legs, then I'd tuck them in my breast pocket.

Certainly, grooms were entitled to keep up the tradition of something borrowed.

Zelda shifted her hand to my gaping trousers, stroking me over the fabric. "That's it, isn't it? I can see you thinking about it."

I tore her sweater over her head, tossed it behind me. The bra followed. Rucked her skirt up to her waist because I intended to use it for leverage. "The bite mark I'll leave on your thigh will be my something blue."

"That's not the kind of wedding gift most brides receive," she said, lifting up her bottom to help me free her of those panties.

"It's a fine thing you're not most brides, love." I bucked into her hand, my entire body tensing, tightening as I dropped my head back and let loose a snarling sound. "There's a condom in my back pocket. See to that for me."

I thrummed my knuckles down her breasts, snaring her dusky nipples while she opened the packet. She sawed her teeth over her bottom lip as she sheathed me, her mermaid eyes clear and focused on each deep, twisting stroke.

"Zelda," I rasped, the table biting into my legs as I edged closer.

"Yes, Ash?"

I smoothed my hands up her thighs. "Open for me. Show me what's mine."

With a starved gasp, she settled back on her elbows, her legs parted wide. She was luscious and ripe, her folds blooming like a summer rose. "All yours."

These words, they were dangerous. They made promises—promises I intended to keep. "Good girl," I said, taking hold of her ankle. I set her foot on my uninjured shoulder and raked my teeth up her shin, and my chest was tight like I'd forgotten how to exhale. "Keep your eyes open, Zelda. Pay attention. I'm going to fuck you just like this after I marry you."

The first thrust was like my first ever, new and raw and over-poweringly *right*. As it was, that rightness threatened my ability to stand unaided, inhale properly, and last through the next thirty seconds.

"Oh my god," she whispered, her hands stretched flat on the table. "*God*. You feel like you're in my throat."

It was her lips I focused on as I fucked her, plump and barely pink. Lips I loved seeing wrapped around my shaft, pressed to my skin, parted on the most beautiful cries of pleasure I'd ever seen. I focused on those lips because if I glanced down to watch my cock moving inside her, I was certain to come on the spot and say something irrevocable while I did it.

Something like *I'm falling for you. Falling so damn hard.*

To stave that off, I pressed two fingers to her ass and grinned while her entire body shuddered.

"I'm right there," she panted. "*Right there.*"

Honestly, this came as a massive relief. There was no way in hell I'd leave my girl wanting but my body wasn't interested in long, thorough loving right now. This moment existed for the purpose of possession. Loving would come later. We had all night for that.

"Right there, right there, *riiiiiiight* there," Zelda continued.

I lashed an arm around her waist, yanked her up. "You're not there yet," I snapped.

Defiance shined in Zelda's eyes but then her lips found my neck and that seemed to keep her close enough to the edge without sliding over as I hammered into her.

"There you are," I crooned as her cunt gave a vicious clench. "There you go. Take it, love, take it all."

Everything hurt. Everything, every last stitch of me, and I was burning up. We'd only been at this a few minutes but my muscles were wound tight and my heart was slamming into my ribs and every one of her deep, rolling spasms clamped down on my cock like she meant to keep me inside her always.

The idea of that, as impractical as it was, shot fire down my spine. I came in a panting, roaring burst and the only logical response was touching Zelda everywhere, kissing her everywhere. I needed her to know everything.

"Zelda, I—" I stopped myself because what the hell did I intend to say? What was the *everything* I needed to share? What did any of it even mean? I knew I wanted to snatch all the joy and permanence I felt with her and shove it into a jar so I'd never be without it again.

She ran her fingers through my hair, nodded. "Yeah."

"Yeah? You…?" I asked.

What was I asking? We could've been agreeing on the merits of wedding day fantasy sex or determining we needed to eat soon. And we could've been saying the most important things we'd ever said.

Another nod, a small kiss on the corner of my lips. "*Yes*."

NINETEEN
ZELDA

BY MIDWEEK, WE'D LOCKED INTO A SOLID MORNING ROUTINE WHICH started with lazy cuddles and heavy petting. More often than not, this turned into the kind of rumpled, squishy, slightly rude sex that asked little of technique and everything of intimacy.

Kicking off the day like that, with Ash's arms lashed around my body and obscene words delivered straight to my skin, was better than any breakfast sandwich I could cook up. Not that I'd tell him that. He was already rather impressed with himself as a matter of fact and if he knew, he'd make sure to whisper something filthy in my ear while we waited for our orders at the café in his office building—the café that served breakfast sandwiches so scrumptious I'd taken to ordering two and saving one for my midday snack.

Ash was helpful as ever in this matter, terming it desk eggs. He couldn't understand why I didn't return to the café at ten or eleven, when my snack needs activated, and get a fresh sandwich. This, from the man who scheduled his work down to six-minute increments.

Besides the morning sex and needlessly controversial sandwiches, there was a mountain of work to move at Ash's office. In a surprising show of restraint, he actually handed over several mid-level tasks to me *and* did it without an hours-long explainer or buzzing around my desk to "supervise" and "help."

Even better for my mountain-moving purposes, I was alone in the office today since Ash was scheduled to participate in a daylong strategic planning meeting with a corporate board of directors. I didn't know the specifics aside from him billing them for five full days on account of all the preparation this event required.

This was the perfect timing for getting him out of the office since I couldn't put my plan into action with him looking over my shoulder.

That sounded terribly sinister. It wasn't. Hell, I didn't even know how to be sinister. Regardless, Ash's staffing situation needed a quick solution and I was prepared to deliver—assuming his meeting didn't end early.

———

THE MEETING ENDED EARLY.

Of course it did.

Ash froze at the conference room door, his eyes flashing confusion as he took in the candidates gathered there. He shook his head. "Zelda…what is this?"

I skirted the table and met him at the threshold, my hands shooing him back. He was supposed to be at that meeting another hour or two. He was supposed to be there because I needed that time to wrap up these interviews. "Let's chat in your office."

"Or right here."

I kept shooing. "Nope. Office."

He glared at me for a moment and then strode to the next room. Instead of waiting for me to close the door, he immediately started in with, "What the hell are you doing?"

"Deep breath. Calm. Listen, first, don't freak out—"

"Save the new age shit for another day," he snapped. "Explain to me why you have ten people—"

"Actually, it's only eight."

"—in my conference room and handling confidential documents," he said. "Do you have any idea of the ramifications of sharing NDA-secured information?"

I held up my hands and lowered my voice as he paced the wall of windows overlooking the city. It was a remarkable view when not bisected by a furious man. "First off, they aren't handling any confidential—"

"I know what I saw," he yelled.

Oh, wonderful. Let's introduce everyone to Ash's tyranny right off the bat.

I cleared my throat. "The identifying information is blacked out. I redacted everything before preparing those performance tasks."

This did nothing to assuage his anger. "Why are they doing performance tasks with redacted client files, may I ask? And who are they and where did they come from? Or are these questions I'm not allowed to ask now that you've decided you run the joint?"

"Don't be belligerent." I crossed my arms, watching while he continued pacing. "You told me to close your job postings. I did—and I selected a handful of applicants for on-site interviews and brief work samples to get a true sense of their skill level."

He stopped pacing, peered at me, then rubbed his temples. "Since when are you qualified to evaluate that?"

An acidic laugh sounded in my throat.

It was funny how those words would've leveled me before leaving Denver. Funny in the way I'd allowed others to distill the value of my contributions down to tiny nuggets of nothing. Funny that I'd believed it, I'd bought into it, I'd sold my hopes of geeking out over pre-Columbia North American burial traditions down the river over it. Funny in the way it wasn't funny at all but if I didn't yank a bitter, burning laugh up from my depths, I'd cry.

And there was no way in hell I was going to cry. Not over this.

"You're right, boss," I said. "I can't evaluate the nuances of accounting work well enough to spot the tiny errors that make all the difference. But you know what I can do? I can cull through the applications and line the bench with viable candidates. Then I can call them in and verify their résumés aren't loaded with marshmallows and gum drops. I can check their references and confirm they didn't embezzle from their last employer. And the other thing I can do is whittle down the vetted prospects to a small, manageable number and let you use all your qualifications to evaluate them. That way, you can confidently delegate and buy yourself the time necessary to meet the needs of your clients and your dad's too. Did I mention I have candidates who can work remotely or out of the New Bedford office? Yes, I do, because that would help alleviate the backlog of work from there and also minimize your dad's concerns about shipping the work off, away from the home base of those clients."

Ash stared at me while he gripped the back of his desk chair as if he meant to dismantle it with one quick snap. Then, "You should've told me before you did all this." He waved at the wall shared with the conference room. Thank god it wasn't like most of the glass walls in this office but a solid slate of whiteboard on both sides. "You can't go and—and do whatever the hell you want. We aren't doing tarot card readings here."

"What did I tell you about fighting fair?"

"Then don't keep secrets from me," he roared.

"That's not how it works. You fight fair all the time, even when it's inconvenient." I folded my arms over my chest and leaned back against the door. "What are you actually upset about right now? Because I've already explained that the docs are redacted and your NDAs are safe. There's nothing outrageous about calling people in for an interview. Worst-case scenario, I reach out to them tomorrow and tell them we've decided to go in a different direction. Nothing tragic there. So, what's your real problem?"

His whole body got in on the action of being affronted— rolling the eyes, shaking the head, cocking the hip, fisting the hands on the waist. If I wasn't mistaken, there was also a snicker or two.

"I expect you to keep me updated. For reasons I cannot comprehend, you let this initiative fly undetected all week. You didn't mention it to me once, Zelda, and you sprang this maneuver the minute I was out of the office for more than a few hours."

"Can't comprehend?" I echoed. "How about the micro-managing tyrant who likes to come out and play whenever things don't meet with his fanatical expectations?"

"Have you considered the possibility it's important for this work to meet my expectations? Or, I don't know, those of the

Internal Revenue Service, the Securities and Exchange Commission, any of the states in which my clients operate? That this matters beyond *me*? That this might not be about me at all?" He reached for the laptop bag and suit coat he'd abandoned on his desk. "I have a meeting on the other side of town," he murmured. "I'll be out of the office the rest of the day."

"A meeting? Where? With who? There's no meeting on your calendar."

He shrugged his bag over his shoulder, avoiding my eyes, and said, "Guess I'm not the only one who can keep a secret."

I watched him leave, all bluster and bullshit. I banged out a quick email before returning to my interviews. This man didn't make it uncomplicated for anyone, least of all himself.

———

Mr. Santillian,

Despite the fact I'm currently living out of your guest room and sleeping with you most nights, I am writing to announce my resignation effective two weeks from today.

In other words, I'll locate someone who is both obscenely overqualified and willing to devote their days to the handful of tasks you are able to wrench from your perfectionist, micromanaging grip. It may be difficult to find a Nobel laureate genius looking for basic filing work on such short notice, but I'll do my best.

Don't worry about your sister's wedding this weekend. I still plan to attend as your date, assuming you've finished hating me by then.

Thank you in advance for your understanding.

Zelda

TWENTY
ASH

Ms. Besh,
Resignation not accepted.
I'll see you at home.
Ash

———

I SCOWLED INTO MY TUMBLER OF WHISKEY WHILE MY FUTURE brother-in-law roared with laughter.

"This isn't funny," I muttered.

Rob slapped my back as he went on laughing from his barstool beside me at Ginger Man. It was mostly empty, not yet packed with happy hour crowds.

"Shit, man," he said, grabbing the napkin trapped under his pilsner glass and mopping the tears from his eyes. "I needed that today."

"It's not funny."

"You can't see it the way I do," he said. "If someone came into my office and basically did everything I needed without asking me a single question or even involving me, I'd give them a spot bonus." He barked out another laugh. "You, my friend, yelled at the genius running your shit, called that genius an idiot, and compelled her to quit all in one afternoon."

"I did not call her an idiot." I frowned at my untouched whiskey. "I mentioned she doesn't have the knowledge or experience to make hiring decisions."

Rob held up his hand for the barkeep's attention. "I need sustenance if I'm gonna help you unpack your problems." He chucked the menu toward me. "What do you want? I'm getting the Reuben because we're only eating iceberg lettuce at my house right now and I'm feeling a little anemic these days."

"That's awful."

Rob snorted out a laugh. "I'm counting down the minutes, man."

Once we'd ordered, he shifted in his seat and set his hands on the bar top like he meant to diagram his analysis of my problems. "First things first, you have to get comfortable with other people having a hand in your work. Yeah, there are times when it might be quicker and less stressful to do it yourself but that's not a long-term strategy and it will choke out your growth. Teach people what to do and then get the hell out of their way."

"Did you spend two years getting an MBA to learn that pearl of managerial wisdom?"

"Fuck you. I have an MFin and you know it." He lifted his beer, saying, "And I learned that pearl from my last boss who refused to pay people if I wasn't going to let them do their jobs."

"When you put it that way," I grumbled.

"And it's not my place to say this but if Zelda can work out a way to get Carlo off your back, let her run with it. You can't have your father's business strategy holding you down."

"He'll never go for it," I argued.

"Take a page from the Book of Diana and act first, ask forgiveness later."

"I have a feeling I'm going to be apologizing later regardless," I said.

"Oh, hell yes," Rob replied. "Based on your synopsis, I'd bet you'll be apologizing and groveling and buying a field of flowers tonight. And you'll need to explain you're the only idiot in the situation."

A server set our plates down, plunked a bottle of ketchup between us, and promised to return with another round. I didn't need any more whiskey as I'd only gazed at this one but I knew Rob would put the surplus to good use. Better still, he was buying. That was what he'd vowed when I flung myself into one of his office chairs and told him we were having an off-book meeting today.

"You had to know something like this would happen when you hooked up with her," he said between bites. "I wouldn't be able to pull it off, man. Being the boss and the boyfriend? I'd rather originate GSE debenture debt all day."

"Let's not talk derivatives, okay? Especially not the government-sponsored variety. My day has been rough enough."

"Happily." He balled a paper napkin in his hand. "But the fact remains, you work with Zelda, you sleep with Zelda, *and* you live with Zelda. That takes a whole new kind of managerial finesse unless you want to fuck up your entire life."

I stared down at my plate while Rob plowed his sandwich. I didn't have that finesse, not a single drop. And I'd effectively fucked up my life today, I knew that much. This was why I'd wanted to isolate Zelda in one discrete corner and prevent the lines from blurring but I couldn't enforce that any more than I could keep my mouth shut in bed.

What a fucking mess I'd made. And instead of finally getting one evening without clients or bridal gowns getting in the way, I was here with Rob, dousing my problems in whiskey and french fries.

I'd known I was fucking it all up before I grabbed my things and stormed out like the tyrant Zelda accused me of being. But I'd still felt an overwhelming urge to keep anyone from destroying the carefully constructed system I had in place. I needed things to work a certain way and I didn't know what I'd do if it collapsed on me.

Zelda probably knew what to do. She probably had plans and structures to handle that very event in the time it took me to pick out a tie. I couldn't figure out how she did it, how she saw solutions where I'd knocked my head against a wall for a year.

She was right about me not fighting fair too. I'd really fucked up there. I didn't have a good excuse—not that I deserved to be excused—for my reaction. It violated everything we'd agreed upon and I had to fix that. I had to make it better.

Zelda didn't show it when she was hurt. She didn't lash out or melt down. She just took it and I didn't know anything for sure but I had the sense she'd taken more than her share. I hated that, but more so, I hated being another person who did that to her.

"When you say 'field of flowers,'" I started, "what do you mean by that?"

Rob swapped his plate for mine and swiftly yanked the tomato off the burger. "With Magnolia, it's at least ten new houseplants. But that's Magnolia. Houseplants might not work on Zelda. What does she love?"

I was prepared to confess that I didn't know but I realized that wasn't accurate. I pulled my phone out of my pocket and fired off a response to Zelda's newest message.

Ash,
This isn't how resignations work. When someone says "I'm out," you aren't allowed to debate that choice with them.
Please make an attempt at understanding.
Zelda

Zelda,
I understand completely but that doesn't mean I have to accept it. I'll be home soon.
Ash

Hopping off the stool, I clapped Rob on the back, saying, "Good meeting. Thanks for the drink. I gotta go."

———

Ash,
If you won't permit me to do the work necessary to keep your office moving along, there's no reason for me to work there. I would expect you to know this, given your ongoing concerns for efficiency.
Zelda

Zelda,

Traffic is the fucking worst today and everything is taking twice as long but we need to pause this conversation until I get home. I don't like talking to you when I can't enjoy the faces you're making.
Ash

WHEN I ARRIVED, I SEARCHED THE APARTMENT UNTIL I FOUND Zelda in the most unlikely of places: the dryer.

Rather, only part of her was in the dryer, her legs hanging out the open door.

For the second time in a matter of hours, I asked, "Zelda, what the hell are you doing?"

"Of fucking course," sounded from inside the appliance. "Why can't I *ever* do these things without an audience?"

I decided I didn't need the details this time. "All right, love," I said, straddling her legs. "Let's get you out of there."

I hooked my only useful arm under her hips and hauled her out, setting her on her feet. She waved a hot pink bra by way of explanation. Then, "Got stuck. Couldn't get it un-stuck. Resorted to desperate measures."

I ran a glance over her body, intending to check for injuries but lingering over jeans and a pale, pale yellow t-shirt she'd changed into since leaving the office. Her hair was tied back in a low ponytail that showed off her blue streak. "Evidently."

She wagged a finger—and the bra—at me. "Don't do that. No up-and-down eyes. I'm not having that with you right now."

After banging the dryer door shut, she marched down the hall to the guest bedroom with me following close behind.

Zelda busied herself with a basket of fresh laundry on the bed, angling her back toward me when she noticed me in the doorway. "I need you to stop what you're doing and come with me."

"Ashville." She sounded tired—or tired of me. "I'm busy here."

I clutched the doorframe to hold myself steady. This would've been so much easier if I'd pulled her out of the dryer and then immediately put her in a car with me. "*Please* come with me. It's important."

"You traffic in importance," she replied. "Forgive me if I'm suffering a touch of importance fatigue."

"You need to let me apologize," I said, knowing precisely how much it would tickle her into responding. Sometimes, I was an asshole and sometimes, she liked that.

"As a matter of fact, I do not." She shook out a towel with a vigorous snap. "And I believe I'm entitled to set the terms and conditions when I'm the one owed the apology."

"I can accept that," I hedged. "But only if you'll let me buy you some pancakes first."

She snapped out another towel. "I know you're all creative with the dirty talk but you've lost me on that one. Not to mention, I'm not having sex with you right now."

Right now was a world apart from *not ever*.

"I'll admit that makes me sad because I'm sure I could apologize *thoroughly* if you were interested," I said.

She laughed, a real, true, gorgeous Zelda laugh. "I'm not."

"Right, well." I shoved my hands in my pockets. "We have to leave now. For pancakes."

I left Zelda there with her whip-cracked laundry to change out of my suit and tie. By the time I stepped out of my closet in jeans and a polo, she was stationed in the middle of my bedroom with her hands fixed on her hips.

"I don't get it," she said. "Where are we going?"

I slipped my wallet into my back pocket. "You'll find out when we get there." I grabbed her hand, grinning when she didn't swat me away. "Let's go, love."

Zelda allowed me to hold her hand as we rode the elevator to the street level and settled into the car I'd ordered. She positioned herself in the middle of the bench seat knowing she'd be pressed up against me which was the equivalent of her lowering the drawbridge and allowing me back into her good graces. Neither of us spoke as the car inched through traffic in the Theater District and Chinatown.

I didn't know whether we both tended toward this independently or it was a product of our relationship but there were often times when we didn't need to speak. Sometimes it was pensive, like tonight, and the silence settled around us like heavy woolen cloaks while we worked out our problems within ourselves and the worlds we knew. Other times it was a quiet that required no words because we'd replaced them with touch and the cellular connection we'd formed. Then there were the golden moments, the ones we often shared at work when we understood and anticipated each other without any form of language. It was like synchronized swimming or a perfectly executed pass run.

This silence tested my limits. More than once, I nearly blurted out, "Promise me you're not actually quitting."

By force of will alone, I survived the ride without doing that but only because her coming along and all but snuggling up beside me seemed like positive signs.

When we climbed out of the car, Zelda said, "This is a diner." She stared up at the authentically retro South Street Diner. "You actually meant…pancakes?"

"Yes." I reached for her hand again. "You said you love blueberry pancakes and cheesy omelets and crispy bacon but you never have time to make that and—and I've fucked up everything so you have to let me give you the things you love."

She shot a longing look at the diner's shiny aluminum trim and the giant coffee cup perched on the roof. "What I have to do is require you to fight fair," she said. "Pancakes can't change that limit."

"They can't," I agreed. "Let's get a table. I want to talk through this and I want to hear your plan to staff up Dad's office."

After a pause that lived in my chest for an eternity, she asked, "These are good pancakes?"

"Excellent," I replied.

She folded her arms over her chest and scowled like she was posing for a reality cooking competition. "I'll be the judge of that."

And now my heart was able to beat semi-normally again.

We stepped into the diner and I steered Zelda toward a booth in the corner. If nothing else, this location offered a great vantage point for prime people watching. If I fucked this up any further, we had a city full of people to stare at instead of each other.

Zelda plucked a menu from the metal holder near the window. She read each item listed as if she was studying up for an exam and ignoring my entire existence in the process.

I probably deserved that.

No, I definitely deserved it.

I didn't know why I had to be an asshole all the time.

Once again, no. That wasn't true. I was an asshole because I couldn't cope with anyone taking control away from me. But I wasn't on a maniacal power trip. That wasn't it at all.

I didn't like offloading responsibilities on anyone and more often than not, I was the one collecting responsibilities from them. It used to be sheepdogging my siblings, now it was sheepdogging Dad and his clients. And I didn't trust anyone else with these tasks because I was the only one who'd care about my family the way I did. Even when I was at war with my father, even when Lin and Magnolia didn't need me herding them anymore.

I was an asshole because no one could care about these people the way I did.

Except for Zelda.

Maybe. Possibly.

Probably.

I'd meant to open with this admission but she beat me to it, saying, "There are zero circumstances in which you are allowed to use the things you deem weaknesses as leverage against me in a disagreement. You've done it twice and I'm telling you there won't be a third time."

"I know. I should've—"

She held up a hand, tipped her head to the side, closed her eyes. "I'm not finished."

I slumped back against the booth. "I'm sorry."

She laced her fingers together on the table. "If you actually think I am incapable of doing this work—and not because you've permanently flipped your Control Freak Boss switch to *yes*—then we need to end things."

According to the pressure in my chest, I was now running wind sprints. "No, Zelda. That's not—"

"I'm. Not. Finished. Yet." She leveled me with a glare I'd swear was cold enough to freeze vodka. "I can help you, Ash, and I *want* to help you. But I'm not going to continue playing this game where you allow me to make some progress only to shut it all down when you see your autonomy slipping and you choke."

I'd never had my ass handed to me with quite so much specificity before.

The waitress appeared while I was busy recovering from that blow. We rattled off our orders—an omelet for me, a little of everything for Zelda. Then we were alone again.

"You're thinking a lot of thoughts right now." She gathered the menus, tapped them on the table. "It's okay if you don't know which order to put them in or how to use them. You don't have to do any of that tonight. You have two weeks until anything really changes and by then, I'll have a worthy replacement on hand to smooth the transition." She returned the menus to their holder. "Now I'm finished."

I had to work at keeping myself seated in the booth and not snatching those words from the air and shoving them away. All I could do was rub a hand over my forehead. "I'm not accepting your resignation."

It was the wrong tack to take first but I did anyway. Why start helping myself now?

"I'll find you someone who knows a bit more about your line of work," she offered.

"I don't want someone else," I replied with all the asshole arrogance I had in me. Which was a lot. "I want to hear about this plan of yours. The great caper you tried to pull off while I was out of the office today."

That brought an inkling of a smile to her beautiful face. "You can't handle my plan."

"*I* can't handle the plan?" I shot back in my best Jack Nicholson voice. "*You* can't handle the plan. This whole plan is out of order."

Laughter shook through Zelda as she buried her face in her hands. "I'm trying very hard to set limits with you but then you decide to be cute and funny and adorable, and now my very serious conversation is shot to hell."

I pried her hands away and held them in mine. "I fucked up today, Zelda. Fucked it all up."

She shrugged. "Pretty much."

"Whether right or wrong, it was like the rug was pulled out from under me when I walked in this afternoon. I was flat on my ass." I squeezed her hands. "I'm not good at handing over the reins. I want to trust you. I want to let you work your magic. Give me another chance to get it right, Zelda. Let me do better."

"All you need to do is less," she said with a laugh. "You're doing too much. That's why I'm trying to get some extra hands to pick up the excess from your dad's office."

"Walk me through the proposal," I said, still holding her hands like they were my only lifeline. "While I was having my tantrum, you mentioned something about a few candidates who could be based in New Bedford, right? Or did I fuck up my recollection of the conversation too?"

"No, you heard that through your asshole earmuffs just fine," Zelda replied. "The way I see it, you and your father are looking at this from an either-or perspective when it should be both-and. Not Boston or New Bedford but Boston and New Bedford, remote and New Bedford, and any other combination. People are open to these flexible arrangements, more than you might assume. That's the part I want to capitalize on because it eliminates your father's issue of his clients seeing their accounts shipped out of town. I have to imagine there's some big city resentment, even if it's misplaced. Right?" I nodded while I pressed my lips to her palm. "Right, okay. So, instead of leaning into the *big city accountant who doesn't care about your smaller city meat market* drama, we embed staff in New Bedford and train them to use your systems."

"I've attempted that move," I said gently. "It was interpreted as a criticism of his methods and management."

"Then adapt the move, don't abandon it."

I kissed her palm again as I considered this. All I knew was my father and I couldn't get on the same page. I didn't see how I'd be able to change that with the same dance set to a different song.

"I hear you though I've tried all the adaptations I can think up. I have actually tried to solve this on my own, Zelda. I haven't been ramming it through."

"That's right because you reserve ramming for the evenings I visit bridal boutiques."

I groaned into her hand. "Don't bring that up. Not unless you're asking for a repeat."

Pleasure danced in her eyes as she asked, "Would you like that, Ashville?"

More than anything in the world.

The waitress returned at that moment with our plates, forcing me to release Zelda's hands and withhold the response burning on my tongue. But I didn't take my eyes off her.

When we were left with pancakes, eggs, bacon, and everything else she'd ordered, I said, "I am not accepting your resignation."

She lifted both hands as if weighing my words. "Is it up to you?"

I inclined my head. "I'd like to think so."

"What about me? Don't I get a say?"

I snagged a piece of bacon from her plate, chewed it thoughtfully. "Of course you do. I'd send you on your way with a glowing recommendation if you actually wanted to go but you don't. You want me to be better. You want me to get my shit together and you want to stay."

She doused her pancakes in syrup and licked a drop off her finger, effectively converting my blood to lava. "There you go, Ash. That's how you fight fair."

TWENTY-ONE
ZELDA

I was halfway through folding the load of laundry I'd abandoned earlier when I felt Ash watching me from the guest room doorway. He'd changed into a t-shirt and gym shorts when we'd arrived home from the diner though in the past hour—or his way down the hall—he'd lost the shirt. Not that I was complaining.

His stare was constant and thorough, as if he could see through my clothes, through my skin, all the way down to the aggregate pieces of me. He saw it all and if he'd noticed I was in disarray, he didn't care.

Part of the fun came from ignoring him. Shaking out shirts and snapping towels, pressing them into precisely folded piles, pretending a bossy, growly man wasn't watching the whole thing.

The other part of the fun was waiting for the moment he'd push away from the threshold, saunter across the room, and tell me what he wanted. It didn't matter whether I'd laid into him this afternoon or issued a very real threat about leaving his employ. He was still going to fuck me like he owned me tonight and I was still going to ask for more because being owned *just like this* was the best, most liberating experience of my life.

I was preoccupied with a fraying t-shirt hem when Ash brought his hands to my hips, an undercurrent of urgent insistence in his touch.

"You're so hot when you're mad. So fucking hot," he said, flipping open my jeans. "Stay right here and let me watch you work it out of your system."

In direct defiance of his request, I swished my backside over his cock and dropped my head back against his chest as he dipped his fingers inside my panties.

"Just for that," he rumbled, "it's going to be so much worse."

I didn't respond because in the calculus of this, worse didn't mean worse and begging wasn't going to make it better—or lessen the degree of worse.

"Ignoring me, are you?" he asked.

"Just letting you slip into sex monster mode uninterrupted."

"Fair enough, Miss Besh." He nudged my feet apart and slicked up two fingers in my arousal, then pressed them to either side of my clit. "Though don't say I didn't offer adequate warning."

At first, he offered the type of light, inadequate strokes that barely registered as petting—and it pissed me off. This had been *a day* and I didn't have the patience to play around after all the drama I'd put up with even if it was part of his *much worse* plan. Yet those strokes seemed to build on each other, climbing and mounting one after the other even though the pace and intensity hadn't changed.

He gave me nothing more than those two fingers *near* my clit —not even direct contact—and I was hot and gasping as pressure gathered behind my clit, filling and expanding like a balloon. I was so close, so—

He stopped. *He stopped.* No more than one stroke from triggering my release, he retreated, pulling his hand from my jeans and popping those fingers in his mouth. He met me with a smug grin when I rounded on him, flushed and hollowed out and desperate for—for *anything* but most of all, him.

"Was that disappointing for you?" he asked as he kicked back on the bed, his ankles crossed and the tips of those fingers lingering on his lips. He was being a complete bastard but he was wise enough to do it without disturbing my laundry. "Unsatisfying, perhaps?"

I shoved my hands through my hair. "What the hell was that?"

He crooked a finger in my direction. "Take your clothes off and get over here."

"And then what?" I cried, dying a little from every clench of my core. This emptiness *hurt*.

He pointed at my jeans. "Off. Now."

My default reaction was to comply but his highhanded tone —after all the highhanded words I'd heard from him today— had me glaring, my arms crossed over my chest. "Would it kill you to ask nicely?"

He shook his head. "No, it wouldn't. But it would kill *you* to spend another minute inside your head, figuring things out and making decisions. So, as I said, take off your fucking clothes and get over here."

There was a minute where I didn't say anything. Didn't speak, didn't move, didn't look away. I replayed his words in my head on a slow loop because I still didn't understand how he knew what I needed, even when I didn't.

For his part, Ash plucked a condom from his pocket and kicked off his shorts and boxers. He parted his legs in a fundamentally uninhibited manner and fisted his cock, stroking while I stood there with my hipshot stance and sulky glare.

"Come, now," he said, patting the bed. "Before I make you put this condom on me with your mouth. And enough with the pouting, love. You're making me think this cock has better places to be than buried in your cunt."

I peeled my t-shirt off, flung it at the mouthy bastard's head. Gave my bra the same treatment.

"If you think I won't jerk off on this shirt or use your bra to bind your hands behind your back and make you watch while I do it," Ash mused, "you're incorrect."

He pressed the shirt to his face, sucking in any lingering scent of me. I had to look away as I stepped out of my jeans because there was something primitive about him breathing me in like that, something I wanted to categorize but couldn't find the words to begin that process. And it still hurt like hell. This kind of twisted-up need had to be unraveled, unwound. It couldn't be overlooked. I threw my panties at him too.

"These," he said, holding up the black cotton bikinis, "are a gift and I'm keeping them. I might not be allowed to fuck you in my office but last I checked, there's no restriction on coming in your panties while you sit six feet away from me in another one of your very prim secretary skirts."

"If you can find time in your schedule tomorrow—" I snatched up the condom and ripped open the package. With my hand curled around the root of his shaft, I kissed the rubber down his length. "—you're welcome to play with my panties all you want."

Ash reached for my hip, urging me closer. "Get up here. Sit on my cock."

Since I didn't want to argue anymore, not even to play-fight, I dropped a knee onto the mattress and levered myself into his lap. I let him tease his shaft between my folds, let him position me as he wanted, let him dig his fingers into the soft of my hips, my ass and let him slam me down until I was certain I felt him pulsing somewhere in the middle of my chest.

"Ride me," he ordered, moving my hips to match his thrusts. "I want to watch those tits bounce."

My tits were not the variety to bounce but I couldn't tell Ash this because his cock was splitting me in half and my clit was rasping against the base of him and his fingers were digging cruel divots into my skin. Every snap and jerk of his hips sent electricity spiraling through me, each jolt stronger and sharper than the one before.

"Ash," I gasped, my hands flat on his chest for balance though I knew he wasn't about to let me fall. "*Ash*."

"Do you think you're ready to come for me, love?"

Some wailing, hysterical sob burst up from my chest as I nodded, saying, "Yes, please."

"Then I'll get you there." The muscles in his jaw and neck coiled and jumped as he deepened his thrusts and he moved me faster, his thumbs drilling into my bones as he made me work for it. I closed my eyes because I couldn't keep them open, couldn't experience these sensations and watch the bunch and stretch of his abs, the hard line of his shoulders, the greedy, molten way he gazed at the place we were joined.

The orgasm took me by surprise, one brutal clench of my core followed by a rolling wave of sensation that started small and didn't stop until I was sprawled out on Ash's chest, gasping and shuddering and shivering from the force of it.

Though I hadn't caught the particulars, I remembered Ash squeezing my ass and chanting my name as he came. He hadn't said anything since, only folding me into his arms, smoothing back my hair, kissing my forehead. He held me tight for a long time and that was when I heard the words gathering in my mind.

I could love him.

I might already *love him.*

I wanted to press my face to his neck and deliver him these confessions and then I wanted him to return those confessions to me. I wanted him to know he was wrecking and ruining me because he knew down to the decimal what I needed and now I was a wrecked, ruined mess of woman who only wanted more, all of it, everything.

"I don't believe you're disappointed now," he said, his voice hoarse.

"How did you know I needed it just like that?" I asked.

He ran his fingertips between my shoulder blades as he said, "Because I know you. I don't have to think. I touch you and I know."

I blinked up at him, wondering if he also knew he'd ruined me.

TWENTY-TWO
ZELDA

One thing you probably didn't want to know about me was the hellacious nature of my premenstrual syndrome. You could set a watch by that bitch. Without fail, ten days before my cycle was due to restart, an eighteen-wheeler of symptoms backed right over me.

There was the infamous duo of cramps and moods, and I always had a day or two of exhaustion before it was on to headaches and hunger, chills and digestive wonkiness, and loose clothes on account of the bloated belly and milkmaid boobs.

Oh, and the horny thing. That part was *extreme*.

At this point in my reproductive life, I was well acquainted with the way my body worked and I knew how to manage through. It was an inconvenience, for sure, but I knew enough tricks to keep going.

Except when everything hit at once. It was only on special months when those symptoms converged on the same day rather than ambling out over several.

That was why Ash found me draped over the printer on

Thursday afternoon like I was washing ashore after a shipwreck. In truth, he first passed without looking up from his phone but then jogged backward, asking, "What's happening here?"

Still flopped over the machine, I said, "It's warm. Like a heating pad."

He reached out to settle his hand on my back but changed his mind at the last minute, shoving it in his pocket instead. "Are…are you all right?"

"Yep." The machine's heat offered such glorious relief. "Just taking a minute."

"With the printer?"

"Yep."

Finally, he brought that hand to the small of my back and I almost cried with joy because the light pressure he offered was perfect. "Why don't you tell me what's wrong?"

"Because I'm all good. Promise." I pushed off the machine and forced my shoulders back. What I wouldn't do for a big, slouchy sweater right now. Something fuzzy and gray and shapeless. The best slouchy sweaters were always gray. "Did you need me to get something from the records room? You were headed that way."

He tucked my hair over my ear, frowning. "Stop lying to me. You look pale and you're hugging the hardware. No part of that qualifies as 'all good.'"

As I didn't have the energy to shelter Ash from the reality of women's bodies and their assorted functions, even if I didn't know how to forge this territory with him. I made a vague gesture toward my abdomen, saying, "It's just some cramps. They'll pass."

There were seven seconds of total, blank confusion in Ash's eyes before he understood my meaning. Seven. Then he nodded to himself and consulted his watch. "Let's head out for the day. We'll get something delivered. What would you like?"

I pointed toward his office. "You need to finish the—"

"I did," he interrupted. "I printed the last draft to give it a final read tonight." He reached into the output tray and held up the papers as proof. "What do you want, love? Please tell me."

I stared at my shoes because I didn't know how to do this. How to share this part of myself with someone else though it wasn't a matter of shame. Rather, I'd always handled it on my own. I'd managed through my first period by myself and all the ones that followed. I'd escorted myself to the gynecologist when I was seventeen and managed my birth control choices without the guidance or support of anyone but my doctor.

"I don't want to make you uncomfortable," I said.

When it came to divulging these things with my boss-room-mate-sex-monster, I didn't know what was normal. I was aware the polite obliviousness thing was a sketchy way for men to pretend vaginas were only intended as their playgrounds but I hadn't realized some men didn't plug their ears and la-la-la it away until this conversation. I didn't know there were real men who cared.

"Not being able to make it better is uncomfortable for me," he replied.

I wrapped my arms around my torso and offered him a quick shoulder lift. "Maybe we could order pizza."

Ash winced, shoved his hands in his pockets. I didn't know if that was a reaction to pizza or something else.

"What kind of pizza?" he asked. "Thin crust, deep dish, brick oven?"

"Thin crust," I said. "If that works for you."

He made a sound of approval. "What are we putting on this thin crust pizza, love?"

The air-conditioning vent above us roared to life and I was presently dying of hypothermia on a summer day. Good *god*. Whenever a chill struck me, there was nothing I could do to get warm. I just had to wait it out. "Peppers, mushrooms, and pepperoni," I managed.

He offered another rumble, another nod. "And what are we drinking?"

I rubbed my palms up my arms. "What about beer? Something like Blue Moon."

"That's going to be a Trillium wheat in this neck of the woods but sure," he replied, swiping his phone to life. "Anything for dessert?"

I shook my head as goose bumps climbed over my chest, down my legs. "No, I won't need chocolate for a few more days."

"For fuck's sake, come *here*," he said, thumbing away at his phone. "You're shivering." I went into his open arm and slumped against him. "Do you need…anything? We have over-the-counter pain relievers at home but I don't have anything else you might require."

I flattened my palms on his torso because he was so damn warm, like a human hot water bottle. "Not until later next week. This is just—it's just the prelude," I replied. "If it helps, please know the opening act is worse than the main event."

Ash finished with his phone, returned it to his pocket, and kissed my temple. "I've tossed this over in my head a few times and I don't think there's a way for me to tell you to stop apologizing without sounding like a tyrant but I'm saying it. I don't care if the entire show is difficult. In case you haven't noticed, I can't get enough of you and your body. And I'm sure you haven't forgotten how you looked after me when I needed it. I plan on returning the favor and you need to accept that. No apologies allowed. No pretending you're fine. No protecting my fragile male consciousness because you're worried I'm squeamish."

If the emotion filling my chest at this moment wasn't love, I didn't know what was. In fact, I didn't want to know. I didn't want to live out my days waiting for something better than the vast, glowy feeling cracking my chest open.

"Thank you," I said.

"Don't mention it." He ushered me into his office, pointing at the pair of seats in front of his desk. "Sit down."

After snatching his suit coat from its hanger on the backside of the door, he cloaked it over my shoulders. "Give me a minute to pack up."

I nodded, my hand clutched around the lapels to keep the coat from sliding off. I watched while Ash filed away his laptop and the report he'd fetched from the printer. He cast a hesitant glance at his desk, as if he couldn't decide whether to straighten the stray documents or take another project home with him. Eventually, he turned his wrist and blinked down at his watch, saying, "Our car will be here in five."

"We don't have to take a car," I replied. "I can walk. Or take the subway. Really."

Ignoring this protest, Ash tipped his chin toward my desk. "I'm going to grab your purse and log you out of your computer. Is there anything else you'd like me to do?"

I pushed to my feet, saying, "I have systems. Don't foul any of that up for me."

I swatted him away from my things and made quick work of closing out. Once I was finished, I followed him out of the suite and into the elevator. When he held his arms open to me, I paused, first shrugging out of his suit coat before nestling up against him.

"Did you warm up?"

I shook my head. "I don't want to walk through the lobby looking like tonight's A-block on the evening news. You know what I mean. There's always some tragedy porn in that segment. A dead-eyed woman swallowed whole by an over-sized coat or blanket. People on their front lawn in pajamas. Someone who lost their shoes in an accident of some type. That sort of thing."

"You don't have dead eyes," he said.

"You're kind." I leaned my head against his bicep. "And tolerant."

His scruffy chin scraped over my cheek. "No. Neither."

"Then your mother and sister taught you—"

"No. Not that either." He held his arm over one side of the elevator door when it opened, gesturing for me to exit first. "The car should be here now."

He led the way, his hand steady on my back as we crossed the lobby and stepped outside into the wall of summer humidity. That left me cold yet sweating, an ever-pleasant combination. A spasm curled down my abdomen as he swung the SUV's door open and boosted me onto the bench seat. I went with a grunt that was graceless even for me.

Ash hopped in behind me, asking, "Could you dial down the air conditioning? Thanks, man. Appreciate it." He smoothed a hand over my hair and folded me in his arms. "What else can I do for you?" As if he knew I was about to shut down his offer, he added, "By that, I mean do me a favor and let me feel useful right now. Give me something to do for you, some way to help.

If you don't, I'll invent my own solutions and god knows those will be some hot fucking messes."

A laugh worked its way up my chest. "There's one thing you can do."

———

ASH TIPPED HIS BEER BOTTLE BACK, DRINKING DEEPLY. HE RELEASED a satisfied groan when he set it down empty on the floor. "Fuck, this is nice. Is it inappropriate for me to request we do this every month?"

I flicked some water in his direction and reached over the side of the deep soaking tub in his bathroom for another slice of pizza. "Not inappropriate. Just…unusual. I'm not accustomed to being open about certain things."

Ash studied me for a moment, his brows lifted as if he was waiting for me to elaborate. When I didn't, he said, "There's nothing you can't share with me. Nothing that would change anything for us."

This wasn't about the ups and downs of my hormones anymore. It was about all the things left unsaid, unexplained. The story of where I'd been, why I left, why I had to stay gone— and all the reasons I couldn't get my hands around what it meant for a man to care about me the way Ash did.

I devoured my slice while he watched me, his golden hair dark from running a wet hand through it, water glistening on his broad chest, his legs layered between mine.

On the surface, this seemed like the perfect time to unload it all. Just unpack every volume of the history I'd planned to ignore in this new rendition of my life and show him the half-sewn parachute too.

But this wasn't the night. It wasn't. The water was already cooling and the pizza was almost gone. It didn't make sense to start a story I'd have to pause for the *dry off and dress* process, not to mention the *clean up the pizza and beer consumed in the bathroom* process, and restarting a story after those breaks was like eating rice with a steak knife. Plus, we had to leave for his sister's wedding tomorrow. There was too much going on right now. Better times would come and when they did, I'd be able to explain everything.

"I know," I replied.

Ash stared at me for another minute and though it seemed like he wanted to push the issue, he eventually cut his gaze to the six-pack on the floor. "Do you want another?"

I nibbled my last bit of crust. "No, thanks, but I'm wondering if you'd conduct an experiment with me."

He settled his arms on the rim of the tub. "What's the experiment?"

I glanced at our legs under the water, his shaft full and thick against his belly. This was not an experiment in the sense I was curious about the outcome. I was well versed in reaching this outcome—alone. I'd never enlisted anyone else to help with this particular matter. Not at this point in the month. "The one where you relieve cramps with orgasms."

After a pause, he asked, "You're up for that?"

I nudged his knee with mine. "This is weird for me, remember? I wouldn't ask if I wasn't."

Ash pushed to his feet, sending a wave of water rushing to my end of the tub and a small downpour off his body. "Stay there," he ordered as he stepped out and secured a towel around his waist.

With one quick scoop, he gathered the pizza box and beer

bottles and left the room. He returned a moment later, shaking out some fresh towels. "I'm ready to start this experiment whenever you are."

When I climbed out of the tub, he swaddled me in several towels which created more of a straitjacket-meets-burrito effect than he'd intended but it succeeded in drying me in record time.

There were no artfully choreographed moves when it came to us falling into bed and that was the best part. We simply crawled between the sheets, our skin still fresh from the bath water and our blood humming from the beer—and a bit of anticipation too. We settled back on the pillows, kissing and touching like we had all the time in the world with each other.

His hands coasted over my breasts, always glancing up at me for approval before rubbing, pinching, biting. My belly followed and he skimmed his palm over my skin in gentle, reverent strokes as he moved down and dipped between my legs. His shaft was heavy on my thigh and I knew it would feel incredible inside me, kind of like a premenstrual vagina massage. That needed to be a thing.

"You're too tender for me to put my weight on you," Ash said against my lips. "Could we try something different?"

In my head, that translated to *I changed my mind and I don't want to fuck you tonight so we're going to watch reruns of* The Office *now.*

"Oh. Okay," I said. "If that's what you want."

"Good girl," he murmured, shifting himself—and the cock I'd enlisted for that vagina massage—off me. "Now roll toward the window for me."

This was awesome. Just…awesome. I needed to remind myself to never suggest sex studies ever again because I'd end up staring at a wall and have zero orgasms for my trouble.

I went but said, "It probably makes more sense for me to hang out in the guest room."

"What? Why? No. You're staying right here." Ash slipped his hand under my knee. He stroked his fingers over my mound, giving me only the barest of touches with each pass. He was devastatingly good at the light, teasey thing. I hated it. I arched into him because I also adored it. "I can't see you so you'll have to speak up if you're uncomfortable. Okay?"

Ohhhhhhh. He wanted me to roll over to fuck me from behind. Okay then.

"Zelda. You have to speak to me, love."

"Yeah," I managed. "Yeah, this is good."

"We're going for better than good. What are the secondary objectives of this experiment? Are we talking one exceptional orgasm, the kind where you look at me all dazed and speechless after? Or as many as I can get out of you *and* looking all dazed and speechless?"

"Yes," I answered, arching into his touch.

He laughed and the crinkle of a condom wrapper sounded behind me. Once that matter was handled, Ash banded his arm around my waist while his other hand secured my bent leg over his which was exactly as Twister-inspired as it sounded.

If I thought about this position for more than a second, I'd realized I looked like a tin of sardines with the lid peeled half open. This wasn't the kind of sex I'd wanted photographed for the memories. I didn't really want *any* sex photographed but especially this, where my leg was up and my sardines were out and my body was as plump as Thanksgiving dinner.

But goddamn it felt good.

"Are you ready?" he asked.

"Yes though please don't reinjure that shoulder. We don't need both of us wrecked."

He kissed the space where my neck met my shoulder. "Won't allow that."

Then he pushed inside me, his shaft heavy and demanding. I cried out, something between a sob and a plea for more, and I surrendered to the fullness of this position. I was pinned down and stretched wide and there was nothing else I could do but take it.

When he stilled, I reached back, squeezed his granite-carved ass cheek. "Don't stop."

Ash settled his hand low on my belly, his fingers spanning the distance between my navel and my clit though he didn't tease. He held me steady as he moved in me, his gaze fixed on the place where we were joined. Mumbled curses and broken growls fell from his lips as he pulled out. I felt his thick crown hot and pulsing on my folds and I ached at the absence.

"Don't stop," I repeated. I dug my nails into his backside, his thighs. Tiny bites of pain as my core clamped painfully around nothing. "I need you."

"For experimental purposes? That's why you need me?"

"For all the purposes," I sobbed.

Ash lifted two fingers to my lips, saying, "Be a good girl and suck."

His fingers tasted like my arousal—and also pizza. If it was possible, he swelled and lengthened as I sucked him, every hard inch of him filling me in a way that was incredible now and would twinge tomorrow.

"That's right," he drawled, shifting those fingers between my legs. "Let's get you what you need."

I was certain about it now. This was love. It wasn't bouquets of roses or cute social media posts or sparkly things. No, love didn't sparkle at all. It didn't shine and it didn't traffic in flowers or candlelight. Love was beers in the bathtub. It was helping to fold laundry and insisting it go into the closet, not back in the suitcase. It was prying your person out of a dryer and requiring her to scope out a menu to make sure there was something she liked before going into the restaurant.

Love wasn't any of the glossy, glorious things I'd imagined it to be. It wasn't even sex—not really, not when it came down to it. Love was a sturdy old workhorse that showed up every day and did whatever was necessary to keep the wheels turning.

As tears filled my eyes—hormonal tears because they couldn't be falling in love tears, dammit—I said, "Talk to me. Tell me what you're thinking. Don't go quiet on me now."

He kissed along my shoulder as he found a sedate yet intense rhythm. I was going to feel this *all day* tomorrow. Every time I sat down.

"What am I thinking?" he rumbled. "I'm thinking about pinching your clit right now but I'm not sure you want—"

"*Ohmygodplease*," I panted.

A laugh shook his chest as he said, "Remember you begged for it, love. Remember that."

As promised, he pinched my clit between the pads of his fingers like he was searching for the root of all orgasms. I screamed, not for the pleasure but the pressure. It was a sudden, brilliant burst of pressure from somewhere behind my belly button and I would've hated it if he hadn't been lighting me up with deep, potent strokes at the same time.

"I'm thinking I'm going to work your pussy until you can't take it anymore and then I'm going to camp out between your legs and devour you until you fall asleep." He released my clit to draw lazy circles around it which was both better and worse in that I loved clit-adjacent contact but also wanted that crazy, blinding pressure back. "I'm thinking about turning you over and sliding into you from behind," he continued. "I'd shove a pillow under your hips and two fingers in your ass and I'd last three minutes at the most. You make such a mess of me, Zelda. Such a fucking mess."

He pressed on my belly though only enough to magnify the force of him moving in me. It nearly did me in, nearly broke the dam holding back the orgasm, the tears, the emotions throbbing behind my breastbone.

I could withhold the words but I couldn't stop a tear from spilling over my cheek which was more alarming than anything else because I didn't cry real, actual, sobby tears out of my eyes. What was the point? It never solved anything and no one who cared ever noticed.

"What's this?" Ash stroked a finger down my cheek. "I need to know if I'm hurting you *before* you cry, love."

"You're not hurting me." I tried to shake off his attention but our limbs were knotted together and he was deep enough inside me to steal my breath.

"Then what is it?"

"I'm a mess too. Okay?"

Our eyes met as he thrust into me again and my orgasm unfurled like he'd snapped his fingers and made it so. It was as though he'd taken control of my body, everything from my belly button down now operating under his command. I wasn't mad about it.

"Maybe you're not a mess at all," he whispered. "Maybe you're exactly as you're supposed to be."

I felt the unmistakable pulse of him filling the condom and

the reflexive kick of his hips as the spasms twisted his spine, and I couldn't reach enough of him to give me what I wanted right now. I wanted to map every inch of his skin with my hands and taste all his favorite places and keep these pieces in a place that would last forever as mine and mine alone.

TWENTY-THREE
ZELDA

ASH STIFLED A YAWN AS HE ASKED, "WHAT DO I HAVE THIS morning?"

We shuffled forward in the queue to order. I peered at the chalkboard menu while Ash checked his watch for the third time since wedging our way into this café and claiming a spot in line with the rest of the caffeine-starved commuters. "First up, a quick call with the people from Shadyside because they have questions about one piece of your proposal. My sense is they really just need some hand-holding, maybe a pep talk."

"I'm not the person anyone comes to for a pep talk," he said as he scrolled through emails on his phone. "They can't possibly want that from me."

"Then consider it a pep talk for you," I said. "I think they want you to confirm you've got this one tied up, nailed down, and all the other brutal metaphors involved with telling someone you've got them covered."

Ash dropped his hand to my lower back and pressed a kiss to my hair. "That, I can manage."

"Great because you're on with them at ten. After that, the

CEO of Furylight has an hour scheduled with you though I don't know the details on that one."

"It's a standing meeting. He enjoys picking up the phone for an info-dump of his plans once a quarter and I enjoy billing him for a full hour."

I blinked at the menu again. Too many good choices. What did I want, *what did I want*? "Then you have a call with the team from Pantheon Partners. They're growing and will be hiring hourly and salaried staff—"

"Right, the payroll tax conversation," he said, mostly to himself. "That will be quick and entertaining. It's always fun to explain taxation to finance guys. It's like they blew off the entirety of their accounting coursework when they went to B-school to go golfing."

We stepped up to the counter and ordered the same breakfast sandwiches and coffees we'd ordered every morning. Since food didn't always imitate life, I was the sausage, egg, and cheese traditionalist where Ash was the wild child with spinach, mush-rooms, peppers, and feta accompanying his eggs.

"If all goes according to plan, we'll be closed up by lunchtime," I said as we waited near the pickup counter. It was a good spot to ogle sweet rolls and some voluptuous muffins, neither of which I'd sampled yet but I had big plans for next week. "Let the wedding weekend begin."

"Closed, yes," he replied. "I have an hour or two beyond that before I can sign off for the weekend."

"That's reasonable. I can work with an hour or two."

When our order was called, Ash gathered our coffees and took hold of the paper bag. "Regardless of anything my mother has told you, we don't need to be there until seven tonight."

We crossed the lobby, our elbows bumping together in

another silent game of Touch Each Other Always. "If you're proposing we simply work all afternoon, I'll remind you I moved all of hell to protect that time from all the people who want a piece of you."

He jabbed at the elevator call button. "We could find something else to do this afternoon."

We shared a meaningful glance as we stepped onto the elevator. "What comes to mind?"

"There are several ways to consider this concern," he started.

"Says the accountant."

"We could find somewhere interesting for lunch. I could introduce you to roadside clam shacks. You know you're in New England when you're eating freshly fried littlenecks on the side of the road, especially if that shack backs up to a coastal marsh. If not bivalves, maybe hit up an arcade near the shore. Those are always a good time. There's also wandering around Bristol, the little town where the wedding is taking place. The downtown area has to have something exciting for us."

I sipped my coffee as Ash unlocked the office door. "I can't tell if you're intentionally skipping over the part about us having a hotel room all to ourselves or if that part hasn't occurred to you yet."

"It's occurred to me," he said as he marched into his office. "It's also occurred to me we have that room for the entire weekend. Pace yourself, love. I can't have you walking down the aisle on wobbly legs."

"Fair point." I started unpacking the food while Ash woke up his computers. "So we have clam shacks, arcades, and small town wanderings for our non-bed options."

"You know I don't require a bed," he quipped as he joined me at the round table.

That was true. He didn't. And neither did I.

———

"Hey, Zelda," Ash called from his office. "If you have a second, could you grab the Castavechia Family Trust file from the records room? My digital file has to be missing a few things and these people won't get off my back."

I poked my head through his doorway. "Anything else?"

He glanced up at me from where he stood behind his desk, shirtsleeves rolled to his elbows, one hand perched on the notch of his waist while the other held a sheaf of papers. He looked like a slice of bossy deliciousness as he dragged a deliberate gaze up and down my body.

"I can't answer that," he said, his attention stuck somewhere between my hips and breasts. "Not until after I dispose of this issue and lock the doors."

"Then finish it," I said, walking backward from the threshold. "Remember, we have an entire weekend and you promised me cornhole at this shindig."

"I can promise you we won't be spending much time on cornhole," he called after me.

A smile plastered on my face, I ducked into the records room, a space more akin to a large closet than the type of room deserving of a name. I set to locating the Castavechia file but discovered it wasn't where it should've been, and as I hunted for it I found several others in the wrong location and tucked them under my arm. Humming to myself as the files in need of rehoming grew, I almost missed the voices floating down the hall. That was unexpected. It didn't sound as though Ash was on a call and he'd concluded all his meetings for the day. We didn't get walk-in visitors. All the delivery services had already passed through.

The files still in hand, I stepped out of the records room, moving toward the front of the office when I heard Ash ask, "Is there something *specific* I can help you with?"

I knew that tone. It was his *why the fuck are you bothering me?* tone.

Before I reached the end of the hallway, a response lanced through me. "I'm meeting my girlfriend here."

Oh my god, no. Please no.

"Your…girlfriend," Ash repeated. "Are you sure you have the right suite?"

"Quite certain, yes."

How the hell did he find me?

"Who might that be?"

He cleared his throat in that condescending manner of his. "Her name's Rose. Rose Besh."

"*Rose*?" Ash asked with as much hostility as he could pack into four letters.

"Yes," he replied. "I believe she's here. Is that correct?"

Since my brain was busy commanding my legs to carry me forward, it missed the panic switch cue from my gut to run, hide, fight, claw, kick. Whatever it took to hold on to the world where I didn't have to be small and invisible, that was what I had to do. As I rounded the corner and came face-to-face with the reason I'd pined for an organized spice rack and a life belonging to me. The reason I hadn't been asked if I liked cheese in years.

I stopped in the reception area, a shoulder's width of distance between me and Ash and an entire ocean between me and Denis. I folded my arms over my chest, clutching the files with both hands until the edges bit into my skin. Then I held them tighter, welcoming the grooves and cuts as frustration—no, anger, this was *anger*—drenched me like a summer storm.

"What are you doing here?" I asked Denis.

"There you are. I knew I was in the right place." Denis put on a show of clutching his chest before motioning to Ash. "Thanks for your help. If you don't mind, I could use a minute alone for a private discussion with my girlfriend."

"You're in my office. I'll stay, thanks," Ash replied.

"We have nothing to talk about," I gritted out. Ash was staring at me and hoping for some kind of explanation, I knew this, but I couldn't offer him that yet. That would come later, when I'd fixed this.

"We have everything to talk about, Rose," Denis replied. "What were you thinking, going off on your own? This isn't good for you. It's not *smart*." He blinked at the modern office space like it was a cold, empty shell not unlike his impression of my brain. "Did you really think you'd be able to do this? By yourself?" Not waiting for a response, he continued, "Come along. We'll go home where you belong. Where you're needed. We'll forget about all this nonsense and get back to our routine."

"I am not going anywhere with you. Not now," I said. "Not ever again."

Denis pressed his teeth into his top lip as he chose his response. "This isn't the time to let your emotions get the best of you, Rose. Call up some maturity, would you? You know I don't appreciate when my girlfriend acts like a child in front of others."

"I am *not* your girlfriend," I replied. "I have nothing to say to you. We're finished."

"Now that's not true and you're well aware of it," Denis said in that lofty, professorial voice he'd cultivated while I'd juggled jobs to cover our rent. "Please, Rose. Stop making a fool of yourself. I haven't the time for your juvenile games."

"Watch yourself," Ash growled.

"I know you think that's going to shut me up because it's worked all the other times you've thrown those words in my direction," I replied. "But it's not working anymore. I've given you enough of my time. You should leave."

"Yes, you should," Ash said.

Denis ran a hand over his thin, straw-colored hair as he stared at me, his lips parted and his jaw working as he searched for a sharp response. Those didn't come quickly to him. Eventually, he said, "I'm unimpressed with your behavior today but I do require a minute, Rose, as you have something of mine." He glanced at Ash. "In private. At the minimum, you owe me that much for everything I've done for you."

I didn't understand how I'd wasted years of my life on this man. How I'd ever looked at him and thought, *this guy is going places and I want to go there with him*. More than that, I didn't understand how I'd accepted the ever-shrinking box he'd fashioned for me without complaint.

"I owe you nothing," I said. "You shouldn't have come here. I don't even understand how you found me."

Denis held out his hands, offered a stiff shrug. "You really must learn how the world works, Rose. Airline tickets, credit cards, cell phone tower pings, email logins. Very simple to track."

I stomped my foot on the floor. "How did you find me *here*?"

"You really don't understand anything, do you?" he mused.

"What did you say?" Ash boomed. "No, don't repeat it. Just get the hell out of my office."

Denis eyed Ash again, this time with unshuttered suspicion. If I had to bet on it, I'd say he was trying to figure out what Ash was getting from me. There was no other purpose to keeping me around.

Denis replied, "All I had to do was ask my brother to run some checks down at the station. Your new boss doesn't waste any time getting you paid, does he?"

That damn cop brother of his. There wasn't an ethical bridge he wouldn't burn. The arson extended to legal bridges as well.

"Since you weren't returning my texts or calls," Denis continued, "I had to come here for myself. Considering you left town in such a rush and with some critical documents in hand, you left me no choice."

"That's not true," I argued. "I have no reason to keep a single thing of yours."

Denis brought his fingertips to his forehead and muttered a string of ripe profanity, banishing the refined professor act as he curled his hands into fists. It was then I realized this man *scared* me. Perhaps it hadn't always been that way and perhaps I'd felt this cold tingle before but I'd scribbled over that reaction and renamed it something more innocuous, something less dangerous. He'd been passionate and zealous, short-fused and sensitive. He was a whirlwind, a great, dusty mess of a man. And I'd believed him every time he insisted I didn't comprehend, I wasn't intellectual, I didn't have the acuity for academic work. Oh, and by the way, did I mind gathering all his research, revising all his work, and ultimately drafting his papers for him? Because those little things would really help and what good was I if I couldn't at least *help* him with the enormous undertaking of it all?

Denis was all of these grand and overpowering things, and I

couldn't bear the sight of him anymore because he'd used it against me and then he'd used *me*. I didn't know much for sure but standing in front of a person who borrowed the most advantageous bits of you for his personal benefit while you both knew the truth was almost as awful as letting yourself be used in the first place.

"She asked you to leave," Ash said. "She was more courteous than required." He reached for the telephone on my desk, tapping out an extension before leveling Denis with a glare. "I'm not asking and the security officers won't be courteous."

Ash kept that glare on Denis while he spoke in hushed tones to the security office. I could feel Denis's temper sparking and everything inside me screamed to move, to go, to get the hell out of the way before he blew up. I knew what that was like and while he had never put a hand on me, words had the power to be just as violent as fists.

But I couldn't move. I wasn't convinced I could breathe.

Ash dropped the headset into the cradle. "You have about ninety seconds to leave before you're forcibly removed. I'd recommend you take this time to exit my office and this building, and never contact Miss Besh again unless you'd like to find yourself the recipient of a restraining order."

I knew the minute the tide turned in Denis. I'd seen it a hundred times if I'd seen it once. The professorial demeanor vanished and in its place was an irritable man who felt the world owed him everything. "This doesn't involve you," he snapped at Ash. "I didn't invite you into this conversation but since you're here, you should know she lied to you. She doesn't know shit about accounting."

"You're vitally incorrect on each of those four points," Ash replied. "Not that I could take you seriously when you've spent the past five minutes on blatant intimidation moves."

Denis shifted and took a step toward me, his hands outstretched and those old familiar eyes of his, the ones that asked for everything and promised the moon in return, flashed hot and desperate. "I know you have it. I'm not leaving until you give it to me."

Ash gave a beastly growl as he blocked Denis from advancing on me. "You must not want this to end peacefully, do you?"

"I don't have it, Denis." A shiver moved through me. "I left everything for you, all of it, even my notes and annotations. The entire outline is there. I put it all on your desk. There's nothing else for you to take from me."

"But it's not finished," he roared. "What the fuck am I supposed to do with half a dissertation?"

I hugged the files to my chest as if they could block his words from permanently lodging in my soft tissue. "You're going to have to write the rest by yourself. It's about time you earned something without me."

Propelled only by the power of speaking these words to Denis, I turned and marched back to the records room. With my back against the closed door, I dropped the stray files to the floor and welcomed the velvet rush and sting of blood flow back into my arms. Raised voices filtered through the door though I resisted the urge to listen. I couldn't do that, couldn't go there. Not when the shock of Denis's appearance still flickered in my chest. Tears warmed my eyes but I wasn't crying now because I had more important things to do. There was a cabinet in need of order and then a wedding to get to and muffins to sample next week and perhaps a new, larger pot for Kirby the cactus after that.

Fifteen minutes later, the drawers of the disemboweled cabinet hung open and knee-high stacks of files sat around me like beige toadstools. It was a haphazard mess and I'd invented new work but it was better than beating myself up one more time over past decisions. Not that it would help anyway. I already knew all the missteps I'd made with Denis. It took me far too long—*years* too long—to see those missteps but I saw them now. There was no reason to relive any of it.

By the time Ash edged the door open, I was plopped down on the ground and busy alphabetizing the tallest of the toadstools. He started to speak but stopped himself as he surveyed the damage. "What the hell is this?"

"I don't know who you had keeping your records in order, Ashville, but they weren't in any generally agreed-upon type of system and now I'm correcting that."

He sawed his teeth over his bottom lip. "Right," he murmured, shifting the piles with the side of his shoe and stepping toward me.

"I have this under control," I said.

"Of that I have no doubt." He held his hands out to me. "Come here. Please."

"I need to finish this. You asked for the Castavechia file and I found it but I don't know where it is anymore."

"Zelda. Love. There isn't enough space in here for us both to sit down so I need you to take my hands and come with me."

Reluctantly, I set the stack aside and allowed him to help me up from the floor. He led me into his office, his arm swung around my shoulder. His posture was concrete stiff though he held me as if he was truly concerned I'd shatter under anything more than the lightest touch.

That wouldn't happen. Even if Denis's appearance had acquainted me with the very real and very shitty emotions he generated in me, I could survive this. After all the cliffs and unpacked parachutes of the past thirty-one years, I could survive anything.

Ash sat me in one of his guest chairs and dragged its mate closer for himself. When he lowered himself into the seat, our knees wove themselves together.

"Are you all right?" he asked.

There was no mistaking the weight of those words. He wasn't only asking about this present moment but all the ones before too. "Yeah." I nodded quickly. "Yes. I'm all right."

"You're sure? You're not hurt? You're—you're okay?"

Another quick nod. "Yes."

Ash stared at me a second before shooting out of the chair. "Then please explain to me what the fuck I just witnessed because I can't make sense of it."

"I'm not still with him."

"Obviously."

"Obviously?" I echoed.

"You wouldn't be in my bed if you were still with him." He lifted his shoulders, inviting me to disagree. When I didn't, he continued. "Why did he call you Rose?"

"It's my middle name."

"My brother's middle name is Wolf and even though he could carry it off, no one calls him Wolf."

"Maybe we should give it a shot," I said. "See if it sticks."

"Zelda, for the love of god, save it for later. You know, when I'm not in a blind, murderous rage. Okay?"

"I mean, if that's going to make you happy, sure," I replied.

Ash blinked at me, his brows gathered in tight slashes and his hands on his hips. "But why did he call you Rose?"

I ran my palms up my forearms. "He said I couldn't be taken seriously in higher ed with a name like Zelda. Rose was better."

"I paused on the summer camp line of your résumé for a second and you threatened to castrate me."

"I did nothing of the sort," I replied.

"Close enough." He paced between his desk and the door. "You've never once backed down from a fight with me, but that guy"—he waved toward the reception area—"that guy, he—"

"What are you looking to hear from me?" I cried. "Tell me what would make you leave this alone and I'll say it."

"I want—" He shoved his fingers through his hair as he stared at me. "—I don't know what I want. Just tell me how it happened because you should know I have the worst explanations going through my head right now. I need to know if I should've decked him when I had the chance."

"It happened the way everything happens. It's a series of tiny steps and little things that aren't okay but there's no sense making big issues out of them. It's expecting things to get better once you reach a certain point or when difficult times have passed. It's inches and inches and inches that add up to miles in the wrong direction but once you realize it you're so far down that path you're not sure how to reverse course." I crossed my legs and glanced out the window. "It's complicated. Maybe it's not actually complicated at all but it feels that way to me and I don't want to explain the rest of it right now. I just can't, Ash."

Ash returned to the seat and took my hands in his. "That's your call, love. I won't demand anything from you unless you give me that permission first."

I hadn't known the importance of respect until upending my world and claiming Ash's as my starting-over site. I'd only known respect in name—real respect, the kind rooted in wanting another person's joys and successes and journeys as much as your own—but never in practice. Respect didn't leave space to owe each other anything, it didn't tally the gives and takes, it didn't allow for unequal footing. No one held all the cards in a relationship founded on respect.

"One of my sister's best friends is an attorney. Mostly real estate but she's very knowledgeable in other areas. She'll be at the wedding but if you want to talk to someone about a restraining order, we can call her now."

I shook my head. "He won't come back."

Ash slid off the chair to kneel in front of me, dropping his head onto my lap as he went. "You are far too important to take that risk and I'm not sure I'll ever be able to let you out of my sight again without some assurance you're safe."

"It's not like that," I argued. "He's just a spectacularly lazy person whose only accomplishments in life are getting other people to pay his way and do his work because he fundamentally believes he's deserving of such things and others owe it to him."

"And he stalked you across the country," Ash said to my skirt. "Where he openly and repeatedly attempted to intimidate you. I was damn close to dropping his ass to the floor."

I ran my fingers over the nape of his neck. "Why didn't you?"

"You had it under control," he said as if it was the most obvious fact known to humanity.

I'd wanted my new life—the one with a windowsill herb garden and a place that felt like home—to be free of the histories I'd left behind. Denis, my family, my failed attempt at grad school. I wanted to sever it all like diseased limbs and then continue onward as if I didn't have a collection of wounds in varied states of healing.

Even with all the best decisions, I was beginning to see that wasn't how it worked. "I haven't always had it under control."

"Neither have I," he admitted.

Sanding my fingers through his hair as I searched for the next right choice, I said, "Look at us. A pair of cool cats who can't keep it all together."

Ash lifted his head to meet my gaze. "Can I keep *you*? That's all I need to know."

Yes. Yes, of course. I wanted to give him that but I needed a minute. I just needed a minute to glue the pieces of my life back together one more time before I could do anything else. "I don't know," I admitted.

Ash leaned back, nodding. "Then tell me when you do."

————

I could feel Ash's gaze on my skin, his watchful if not wary stare following me as we closed up the office, returned to the apartment, and then piled into that spiffy little Porsche of his. I was aware of the glances he tossed in my direction every few minutes and the pinched lines bracketing his mouth.

He was searching for answers I couldn't give him, assurances I didn't have. He wanted me to convince him I was okay, the connection we'd forged out of thin air was okay, everything was okay. I didn't have those words for him yet because I wasn't okay, not all the way.

We had so much to discuss but also nothing at all. I had a history behind me and the worst of my recent years showed up in our office this morning to demand more unpaid and uncredited work from me. What else was there to say?

So, I said nothing.

As we crawled through heavy summer traffic with Ash's glances pinging off the side of my face as I stared ahead, I wondered how I became *that woman*. The one who didn't notice she was being manipulated until she'd written several peer-reviewed journal articles and a graduate thesis without being able to claim credit for any of it. The one who agreed it was a good idea to abandon her academic plans because some guy told her she wasn't up to the challenge. The one who accepted a loveless, emotionless relationship because that guy promised her everything would be better after finals, after the internship, after field work, after defending the dissertation she wrote for him. The one who let him call her by her middle name and wouldn't let her attend university events with him because she was just *too much*. Too, too much. The one who ran away only to have her beautiful, safe new life interrupted because that guy wanted her to finish the paper that would give him the highest degree in the field and her absolutely nothing.

I was *that woman*. I couldn't even bury that truth under all the other sticky, thorny truths I possessed because Ash saw the whole thing play out in the middle of his office. He knew all my truths and now he couldn't stop himself from dousing me in pity and cautious concern, the kind that stared and frowned in a way that seemed to suggest I'd fall apart under those truths like a spent daisy.

He didn't even want to play the touching game.

It was late in the afternoon, nearly evening when we finally arrived at the hotel in the seaside town of Bristol, Rhode Island. Late enough to keep Ash's phone buzzing with near-constant calls and texts. He ignored them all, not that it reduced their frequency. We had a bit of time before we were due at the rehearsal but knowing Magnolia and Diana, they weren't taking any chances with Ash.

He killed the engine yet made no move to climb out of the car. Instead, Ash trailed his fingers down my arm and gathered my hand in his. "You don't have to do this," he said with a nod toward the stately colonial.

The rehearsal was being held at the historic Blithewold mansion, not this hotel, but I understood his meaning. I could play the Toxic Ex card and lick the wounds of my severed limbs in private if I wanted.

"If you're not up for it," he continued, "there's no reason you have to spend the evening around a bunch of loud people who will want to know everything about you."

"I'm all right, Ash."

I wasn't lying, not really. Part of me was quite well—and newly angry. Not only angry at myself but also at Denis for being such a major weasel. Another part of me was assessing the bumps and bruises incurred in the whole affair of leaving Denis behind and finally, finally standing up for myself. Some of those bruises were big and nasty. They were sure to turn putrid shades of green and yellow as they healed but the greatest myth about healing was that it didn't hurt. That was bullshit. Healing hurt like a motherfucker and nothing you could do would save you from that pain because it was inescapably essential to being whole again.

"Besides," I added, "if I'm not there, you know your mother will go berserk. She'll drive you up the wall with questions and she'll probably hold up the entire rehearsal because of it."

"I have several decades of practice with her driving me up a wall. I'd take that over putting you through an event you can't handle—"

"Don't do that," I interrupted. "I'd prefer if you didn't tell me what I can't handle. Your intentions are good but please don't do that."

I couldn't have that from him. I couldn't let him look at me with sad, searching eyes. I couldn't be his damaged little woman in need of rescue because that wasn't the way it worked around here.

He paused, exhaled, and said, "Okay. I won't. What else?" His phone buzzed—then it buzzed again, and again. He yanked the phone from his pocket and tapped the settings to silent without consulting the messages. "Sorry about that. Please tell me."

"It can wait," I said with a tight laugh. "The bride, however, cannot."

"We don't have to stay long," he said, giving my hand a final squeeze before opening the door. "Actually, I tried to get out of this thing. My mother offered to disown me."

"We'll stay as long as we should." I reached into the back for my weekend bag. "I'm sure it will be a really nice time and I'm not surprised in the least you wanted to avoid such a thing. You have a troubling aversion to enjoying yourself."

"False," he barked, plucking the bag from my hand and swinging it over his good shoulder. "Factually incorrect. Just because my idea of entertainment is reading the newest edition of Publication Sixteen from the Internal Revenue Service doesn't mean I am any less fun than you, love."

And there it was, our quippy little equilibrium. More than any serious conversation, any painful realizations, any storm of emotions, this was what I needed tonight. The way we always were together—banter and bullshitting and picking at each other as we had from the start, when we knew nothing of sore spots and over-the-line exes. I needed a hug from Diana too and some Santillian family noise to drown out all the breathtakingly overwhelming moments I'd lived through today.

And the tender way Ash called me *love*. I needed that the most.

———

ONCE WE CHECKED INTO THE HOTEL, DROPPED OUR BELONGINGS, and changed into attire befitting a rehearsal dinner, we were out the door again. I was thankful for the snug schedule and the hectic evening of meeting Magnolia and Rob's friends and family, rehearsing the ceremony, and then retiring to a local restaurant for dinner with the wedding party and guests traveling to the wedding from out-of-town. It saved me from accepting any of the concern Ash desperately wanted to dole out.

Another thing saving me was the train wreck of a rehearsal. This beast went off the rails within the first five minutes.

Magnolia's heel snapped off when she stepped out of the mansion and onto the garden path leading toward her aisle, resulting in a twisted ankle and several scraped toes. Her pedicure was trashed.

The officiant referred to Rob as Raymond multiple times, once insisting to Magnolia it was, in fact, Raymond when she attempted to correct him.

Linden wandered away in the middle of the rehearsal to inspect a tree.

The redheaded bridesmaid stepped away to vomit in the

bushes. The rumor mill was betting on morning sickness with that one.

And then a crack of lightning lit the skies and an almighty downpour soaked us all before we could take cover. Not that the mansion's staff allowed us inside dripping wet and muddied but they did open up a covered porch area for us to congregate while the storm blew through.

We were still soggy when we arrived at the restaurant but that only amped up this group's excitement. I was thankful for that as much as I was thankful for the hellish rehearsal. It felt good to laugh, to get back to myself.

There were toasts upon toasts, bottomless bottles of wine, and servings of tiramisu larger than my head. Diana fussed over the funky way my hair dried from the rain and the mud splatters on the hem of my sundress after wrapping me up in the best hug of my life. I got everything I needed plus several more hugs from Ash's aunts, each of whom chastised him for not calling or visiting enough. They left the party with promises he'd do better—and a promise from me to hold him to it.

I hadn't known it but I needed that too. I wanted to be more than the friend parents loved to have around, the tag-along kid they didn't mind setting an extra place for at the table. I wanted to belong somewhere and to someone, and it had to be more than temporary.

After the final toasts were made and most of the guests were on their way back to the hotel, Ash looped his arm over the back of my chair and leaned in close, his lips almost on my ear. "We stayed for the entire event and now I'd really like to get you alone."

The words were no sooner spoken than Ash's father Carlo

cleared his throat behind us. "Your sister is looking for you out front."

"This ought to be good," he grumbled, his arm shifting to my waist as we stood.

We followed Carlo outside and found Magnolia barefoot on the sidewalk, Rob and Diana flanking her. The street was still wet from the storm and now a warm mist moved in lazy swirls through the quaint downtown. It walked the line between spooky and dreamy which made it my favorite thing ever.

"My presence was requested," Ash said by way of greeting as he checked his watch.

"We need to have a sleepover," Magnolia cried, shooting her arms in the air and wiggling her fingers at the stars. "Just like we did when we were little. Oh my god, do you remember when we were small? Like, tiny humans." She cupped her hands in front of her. "Our feet were this big."

"What is happening to you right now?" he asked.

"We'll go back to the house we rented for the weekend," she continued at a volume that far outstripped the needs of this conversation. "The one Rob wanted so no one would hear me being slutty on my wedding night."

Rob ran a hand up the back of his head. "That…is not what I said."

"Just think, we can hang out together, just the three of us, the way it used to be," Magnolia said. "We can watch a movie and eat the kind of candy Mom never lets us have. Come on, please? Please, please, please."

Ash shifted to face Diana. "On a scale of one to Woodstock, how high is she right now?"

Diana offered a non-committal shrug. "She needed to calm down so I gave her a gummy."

"Two," Rob added. "This is what you get from two gummies."

"And how many have you had?" Ash asked Diana.

She smiled. "No more than usual."

Magnolia shrieked when Linden joined the group, throwing her arms around his neck. "Lin, we're having a sleepover. Isn't that great?"

"Oh my god." Ash rocked back on his heels. "Rob, you need to get this under control."

He shook his head. "I've been banished for the night. It's the one tradition she's holding on to and she's doing it with fists of fury."

Ash turned to his mother while Magnolia rambled off popular teen movies from twenty years ago. "Mom. Deal with this."

Diana held up her hands, saying, "She wants some time with her brothers. What would you like me to do about that?"

I patted Ash's chest. "You should do this. I'll find my way back."

"Zelda," he started, a warning in his tone, but Carlo was quick to jump in.

"I'll walk you there myself," Carlo said, offering his arm. "I'll look like a real cock of the walk with a fine pair of ladies with me."

"Oh my god," Ash muttered again.

"Did my father just say cock?" Magnolia yelped. She clung to Linden's arm as a fit of giggles vibrated through her. "*Cock*. He said cock."

Linden nudged Ash's elbow, saying, "She's gonna crash in an hour or two. We'll watch something from Sarah Michelle Gellar's catalog while Maggie laughs herself to sleep." He tipped his head toward me. "We'll be back where we belong soon enough.

Then you can have all the soulful eye-gazing missionary sex you want."

Ash stared at his brother. "How many gummies did you have?"

"What?" Linden asked. "Why?"

Ash shook his head. "Never mind. Isn't this what bridesmaids are for? Like, by definition?"

"My maid of honor is ovulating tonight so she's in pound town," Magnolia announced. "But that isn't the point. We were born together, you guys. I'm not going to be a Santillian triplet after tomorrow." She hooked a grumpy thumb at Rob as tears shone in her eyes. "I'm going to be Mrs. Russo tomorrow and it's not going to be the same anymore so we have to do this tonight. Together." She stepped away from Linden, turned in a circle, and pursed her lips. "Does anyone else smell pizza?"

Swearing under his breath, Ash guided me away from the group. "I don't want to leave you alone," he said when we'd gained some privacy. "I need some Zelda time."

"Well, your sister needs some triplet time," I replied. "You know what? This is good. I need a moment to decompress and maybe write an anonymous letter to Colorado State University on the topic of academic integrity." I nodded as if confirming this decision with myself. Yeah, that would do it. "I want you to spend some time with your sister but please keep her away from the pizza. She'll regret it tomorrow when she can't breathe in her dress."

He stared at me a moment, those concern brackets taking up residence on either side of his mouth and those same old crinkles cutting into his forehead again. Then, he took my face in his hands and kissed me. It was a sweet kiss, nothing rough or demanding as he usually preferred, and I didn't resent that change as much as I thought I would. It felt like it always did with Ash—like I belonged right here.

"My dad's going to dine out on this two ladies story for months," Ash murmured against my lips. "Do you see what I mean about them wanting to keep you?"

"Maybe I like being kept by them."

He made a grumbly, growly noise of dissent I knew he didn't mean and asked, "You're sure about this?"

I replied with a quick kiss and a pat on his rock-solid chest. "I am. You know where to find me later."

When we rejoined Ash's family, we found Magnolia asking, "What is the actual difference between rocky road and Mississippi mud? Does anyone know? Because I'd like to explore that now. Where can we conduct this important research?"

"Baby, we're not going out for ice cream tonight," Rob said, slicing a hand through the air like that was his final word on the matter. "Go back to the Airbnb with your brothers. Get some rest. Call me when you wake up—or whenever you want."

"That will be on our wedding day," she shouted. "I'm getting married tomorrow."

"Okay, that's it," Rob muttered as he stepped forward and swung her up into his arms. "I'm putting you to bed."

"No," she cried. "We have to be separated tonight. It's the *law*."

"It'll never hold up in court," Ash said.

I elbowed him in the ribs for that.

"I'm just taking you home, baby. You're going to get yourself arrested for disturbing the peace if this goes on much longer and I'm not interested in bailing out my bride."

He marched away from the restaurant, Magnolia babbling on

the topics of ice cream and movies and something about land-scape renovation budgets.

"That's our cue," Linden said, gesturing for Ash to join him.

"Mine too," Carlo said, presenting his arm to Diana. "I'm going to get a reputation for myself if I'm out with two beautiful women at this hour."

"Keep that up," Ash said to his father. "It's hilarious." He gathered me in a tight embrace and pressed a kiss to my hair. "Text me when you get in. Okay?"

"I will," I promised.

He walked backward in the direction Rob and Linden had traveled, making little effort to catch up to them while I hooked my arm in Carlo's elbow.

"Are we ready, ladies?" Carlo asked.

I held up my hand, waving to Ash as we turned in the opposite direction. He did the same.

When I knew Ash was out of earshot, I patted Carlo's arm and said, "Since I have you here, may I bend your ear on the topic of business for a minute?"

"I can't think of a better topic for a moonlight stroll," he replied while Diana snorted. "What's on your mind, my dear?"

"I think I might be able to give you more time away from the office," I said. "But only if you're up for some creative solutions."

"I can't wait to hear this," he replied. "I'll do anything to cut my hours."

I almost laughed at that as I knew he'd stonewalled all of Ash's proposals. Almost. "Then you're going to love the plans I've developed."

TWENTY-FOUR
ASH

IT WAS A LITTLE AFTER THREE IN THE MORNING WHEN I MADE IT back to our hotel room. It would've been sooner but I'd nodded off somewhere in the middle of *10 Things I Hate About You*.

The lights were off and the curtains drawn but the television was on, a hazy old episode of *Cheers* playing, the sound barely audible. I found Zelda on top of the blankets, curled up in the mass of pillows. She was awake in a cloudy sort of way, her blinks slow and her gaze distant. A mountain of balled up tissues sat beside her and her eyes were red.

"Waiting up?" I asked as I stripped out of my suit.

She gave me a drowsy headshake-shrug response and lifted her legs when I tugged down the quilt and sheets. I climbed onto the bed and held my arms out to her. "Come here, love. It's no good sleeping without you."

I'd also suffered no fewer than five heart attacks in the past twenty-four hours, not that I was sharing that issue with Zelda. She didn't need to absorb the weight of my worries on top of dealing with the wholly unwelcome appearance of her fleabag ex.

My office building's security firm was already on alert about him, as was my apartment's management company. He wasn't to be allowed inside under any circumstances though that didn't seem adequate. I didn't believe anything could ever be adequate so long as he was capable of tracking Zelda down.

All I could do was trust Zelda's belief he'd go and stay gone. I couldn't hide her away or hire a private investigator to keep tabs on him in perpetuity. Couldn't hire a hit man either, as much as that appealed.

The list of things I couldn't do in this situation was extensive but so was the one with everything I could. There was no restriction on loving her the way she deserved or honoring her boundaries when she asserted them. I was free to give her the affection —and sparring—we both required on a fundamental level.

Right now, I intended to do just that.

Zelda tucked herself up against me, her knees folded to my torso and her toes pressed to my bare thigh. "How's Magnolia?"

A soundless laugh rattled in my chest. "She should know better than to take anything from my mother's stash but otherwise fine. She reminisced for a few hours before passing out."

"I tried to do that," she said. "The passing out, not the reminiscing. I've relived enough today." She peeked up at me from her spot on my chest. "But you probably have questions you want to ask."

I shook my head even though I had no fewer than a million. Plain and simple, this wasn't about me or my questions. "You said you didn't want to talk about it. You said you're all right. That's all I need to know."

"You want to know how I let it happen," she continued, as if I hadn't offered an end to this conversation. "How I didn't notice that he was bad news or how I didn't know better but—"

"No, love. No. I'm not thinking that at all," I interrupted.

"—but the thing you have to understand is nothing ever happens all at once. It isn't terrible from the start. It isn't until you've made tons of tiny sacrifices that you see the giant hole where you used to be and the person who consumed it without regret." She pressed her hand to her sternum. "Now, I get to start over without Denis's shadow leering over me and that means windowsill gardens and green plates and—and *you*, Ashville. I get to start myself over with you."

Though it was exactly what I wanted to hear, I had to ask, "That's what you want?"

"If you're worried about being my rebound, you should worry about something else. My relationship with Denis was closer to roommates, I guess. If one roommate used shreds of validation and praise to coerce the other into writing academic papers and paying his rent."

I was working my ass off at staying quiet because I wanted to let Zelda say everything she needed but I must've reacted in some way.

She paused, peered up at me. "We're not going to be upset about it, Ash. That's a waste of energy. I made these mistakes, I've learned from these mistakes, and I sat down beside you on that plane because I was ready to leave those mistakes behind. All right? That's where it stays, behind us, never to be relived again."

I wanted to believe her. I wanted to accept all of her words and use them to pave the path forward but something tickled the back of my brain in a way I couldn't shake.

Since I couldn't explain this tickle in a meaningful manner and it was the middle of the damn night, I ran my finger down

Zelda's nose and over her lips. "You're tired, love. Let yourself rest now."

———

It was late when I woke up, the morning's sunlight poking in through gaps in the curtains and the sounds of life from the downtown below fracturing the tender quiet we'd found. Zelda, for her part, was undisturbed by the bright and the noise, still fast asleep in her threadbare boxers and a tank top that seemed more like a suggestion of a shirt than anything else.

According to my watch, it was nearly noon. A little more than three hours separated me from my groomsman duties. From there, I'd surrender the day to a carefully calibrated procession of photos, the ceremony, more photos, drinking-eating-drinking, toasting, dancing, and a bit with a flying bouquet.

I planned on positioning a very specific woman in the path of that bouquet.

I climbed out of bed, hit up the bathroom, and then shuffled through the papers and brochures we'd received last night. I'd abandoned it all on one of the side tables because we'd been pressed for time and had to make our way to Blithewold mansion for the rehearsal before my mother gave herself an eye twitch.

But now I couldn't find—

"What are you looking for?" asked a sleep-roughened voice behind me.

"Don't move," I ordered, still paging through the documents. "I can't feed you breakfast in bed if you're not in bed."

Zelda linked her arms around my waist, rested her head

between my shoulder blades. "I don't need room service. Forget about that."

I turned, taking her in my arms and dropping a kiss on her forehead. "Then what do you need, my love?"

She blinked up at me, her eyes still swollen and bloodshot. I didn't like seeing that, didn't like knowing she returned to this room alone last night and cried. It left me ragged on the edges, empty and aching in the middle.

Zelda ran a hand through her hair. "Let's start with a shower."

"Sure. I'll get the water warmed up for you."

"After you do that," Zelda started, "will you join me? In the shower?"

"Yeah," I said, nodding. I bit back the tease waiting on the tip of my tongue because I didn't need to remind her of the times she'd declined my offers. She knew all about that and she knew today was different. "Of course."

That was how we ended up in the shower together, Zelda's head tucked under my chin and her arms linked around my waist while the water washed over us. We didn't care about the time we stood there, doing nothing but holding each other and ignoring my dick's desire to be the center of attention.

Until Zelda swayed against me, her hips pressing into mine in a fatally soft move that eliminated all questions of *if* she wanted me this morning and replaced them with *how*.

Her lips found my chest, my neck, my jaw, my arms—every bit of skin I had to give her—and she covered it all in kisses, licks, timid bites. She was like a baby vampire, unsure of precisely how she planned to kill me, but the truth was she'd already done it. I'd been hers from the start.

When the kisses and little bites no longer fed her desires and her body seemed to tremble with need, I brought my hand to the back of her neck. "I'd love nothing more than to pick you up and fuck you until there are grout lines on your back but—"

"Don't you dare," she cut in. "Not until you stop groaning in agony every time you put on a suit coat."

"That's why I need you to turn around and put your hands on the wall, love." I held her tight, my fingertips pressing into the corded muscle of her neck. Her breath caught and her lips parted on a sobbed sigh but she didn't move. "If I have to stare at those lips a minute longer, I'll come on your tits and leave you squirming the rest of the day. Do as you're told and put your hands on the wall. Understand?"

There was a yawning second where Zelda's eyes flashed with defiance, resentment, exasperation, and interest—in that order. It was then that I knew why I'd played that card, why I hadn't opted for some gentle petting or a sweet, safe fuck void of these rough-scraped commands. It was because she pushed her wet hair from her face and planted her hands on the wall, steadying herself in place while shimmying her ass at me. She didn't need anything sweet or safe today. Her ex was an abusive prick and I had to get over that fast because he didn't get to rob her of the intimacy she deserved—even if it was rather rude and depraved.

I ran my fingers down her spine, over the dragonfly tattoo at her waist, between her cheeks. "I'd prefer it if you responded to me with words, Zelda."

Arching her back, she tossed a glance over her shoulder. "Yes, Ash. I understand."

Despite the teasing in her tone, her message to me was clear.

You can tell me what to do but I'm always in charge.

You have my body and more importantly, you have my trust.

You get to have me because I chose you.

It was exactly what I needed to hear.

"Good girl." I dragged my fingers down the line of her ass again, massaging her there because it turned her on like nothing else. Truly, her body could singe sheets when I played with her back channel the right way. If we played like this for a couple of minutes, she'd boil the bathwater too. "I didn't come prepared, my love." She rocked her hips against my hand, silently ordering a finger inside her. I complied. "If I leave you here a moment, can you promise you won't move?"

We'd had a brief conversation the other day on the matters of protection when Zelda mentioned needing to find a pharmacy to transfer her birth control prescription. We discussed an appropriate amount of health history to decide we could *go forward* without condoms when the time was right.

"I will not give you a second. Not even one," she replied as she worked herself over my finger. With this view, I wasn't certain I'd last more than two, three thrusts once I got inside her. As if that was anything new. "I want you right now and I don't want to wait."

My cock had a pulse and I could hear it pounding in my ears. I closed the last breath of distance between us as a growl climbed up from the bottom of my chest, low and primal like it was meant to warn my prey to take cover. However, my prey knew exactly what I was capable of and she loved it.

"You want me to fuck you without anything between," I said, tipping my head to the side to get a better view of the swollen lushness of her cunt. "That's how you want it?"

Instead of answering me, Zelda reached between her legs

and took my shaft in hand, notching my crown inside her. Taking what I'd planned to give and turning up the pulse in my head until I could hear nothing, nothing but white noise fractured by throbbing bass and the echo of *mine, mine, mine*. Yet it had nothing to do with the absence of the condom. That was merely a fringe benefit.

"What did I say about putting your hands on the wall?" I asked, coiling her hair around my hand.

"You told me to put them there *once*," she replied, a moan peppered into her bratty words. "You said nothing about keeping them there."

The way I thrust into her was no less loving for its brutality but this kind of love—the strange, stitched-together one we'd found together—*was* brutal. Though there was no excuse for the way I teased her ass while my cock fucked the oxygen out of her lungs. That was plainly impolite and how she liked it best.

"I'll be more precise in my requests next time, Miss Besh."

I pulled out with the intention of making her gasp and beg but made the fatal error of glancing down at my shaft and staring as the bare skin glistened with her arousal and it stretched her open. As her body worked to take me inside, keep me inside.

Fuuuuuuck.

If this was nothing more than a quick romp in the shower, I would've come right then. Blow it all and promise to make it good for her the next time. But this was Zelda and Zelda was everything.

"If you had any idea how you looked to me right now, you'd thank me for lasting this long," I said, my words twisting out in a snarl. "If you don't get there soon, you're going to miss out. You're going to wiggle this precious ass all through the ceremony. You'll be begging me to yank up your skirt and rub your clit before they cut the cake."

"So arrogant," she whispered.

"What was that?" I added another finger to her ass while the smooth suck of her flesh around my cock made my vision hazy. "You want me to make you wait for it?"

Zelda clenched her inner muscles around me and I was lost to every sight, sound, and thought beyond this woman.

"Don't you dare," she said.

I released her hair and closed my fingers around her wrist, bringing it between her legs. "Let's get you there." Our joined fingers parted her, settling on that sweet, swollen button. "This is what you'd want me to do, isn't it? After I've left you empty and wanting all day, you'd want my fingers right here."

A frantic noise burst from Zelda, one that vibrated through my fingers, up my arms, into my chest. I wanted to pin her to the wall and I didn't care if I dislocated my shoulder again in the process. I wanted to hold her down, mark her and claim her in every way I could. I wanted to be a little mean and I wanted it to hurt in the good ways, and I wanted her to know she was safe with me. I'd deny her and I'd tease her and I'd invent new ways to defile her—and I'd protect her from everything.

I pumped into her in a fanatical, frenzied rhythm and dropped my head between her shoulder blades because I was dizzy and senseless, saying, "Come for me right now or I'm putting this cock in your ass."

That was all it took.

"Oh my—*Ash*," she cried, her hands slapping at the shower wall.

She came the way a tangled knot unfurled from the inside out—one small, nearly imperceptible loosening somewhere near the center, then another and another, and then she was fully undone.

As if my shaft knew its place in the pecking order, I exploded inside her the second those spasms slowed. It was a devastating sort of orgasm, the kind that made me wonder whether it was actually possible to fuck my brains out. Heat and prickles filled my limbs, white noise was still playing in my head, and words failed to form on my lips despite my best efforts.

Then my watch buzzed to notify me I'd closed a few activity rings. Well done.

We didn't move for several minutes, save for straightening into a position that didn't require Zelda to take the brunt of my weight, and that seemed right. I hadn't known until now that love was a full-bodied action, a response requiring everything inside me like a sacrifice. I hadn't known I'd want to sacrifice everything.

She reached back, patted my thigh. "I needed that."

I kissed her neck. "I know."

"You always do," she whispered. "Thank you."

I gave her backside a thorough squeeze. "You're welcome."

"I know you said we don't have to talk about, you know, everything," she said. "But maybe we could grab some lunch and—"

"And you can tell me as much or as little as you want," I added, meaning every word of it. Part of me wanted to live in a universe where I knew nothing of that bastard because the mere thought of him gave me ideas about digging a shallow grave. The other part of me needed to hear this so I could help her recover from everything he put her through—and that side won out. "We'll eat. You'll get this off your chest. Then we'll enjoy the hell out of this insanely expensive party my sister and Rob are throwing."

The soap and shampoo and leg shaving came along eventually, the awkward choreography of it all too, and then we found ourselves locked together under the spray once more.

And that was how we operated best—snuggly then rough then awkward then love.

TWENTY-FIVE
ZELDA

There was something inherently naked involved in explaining an unhealthy relationship to a person who knew very little about it. In sitting down at a perfectly ordinary table in a perfectly ordinary café and conducting a postmortem. But it was the worst kind because you had to live through the process of laying out all the ugly, misshapen bits of yourself while praying that person never determined those bits were too dreadful and misshapen—*you* were too dreadful and misshapen—for their affection.

The trouble was, you couldn't hide behind justification or rationalization or any of the other lies you'd told yourself when starting with "Everything was fine in the beginning."

And, "It started with us studying together. We were in a statistical methods lab class and he said my eyes were a chromosomal anomaly that would've led to my expulsion from ancient societies. He struggled with that class. He relied on me to get him through it and he appreciated it so much when I did."

However, "We weren't exclusive. We only moved in together

after a year to save money and—and labels and restrictions were nothing more than social constructs."

Then, "It just didn't make sense for me to continue on with grad school. He was working on his dissertation and we needed to put all our attention on that. It was more important for him to focus on his research while I took care of everything else. I could always go back later. It was better that way."

Although, "Once he started his doctoral work, he nearly drowned in it. Between all the research and the annotation and the outlining for a dissertation, he needed me to pitch in more. Sometimes, I helped with his teaching assistant responsibilities too but only because he would've been kicked out of the program otherwise. I didn't mind the grading."

And, "It wasn't awful. Really, it wasn't. He studied. I worked. We were making it through. To my mind, that was how real couples did it. They sacrificed for each other. I sacrificed for him and after graduating, he'd find a corporate archaeology job and my turn would come."

But, "He stopped talking about life after graduating. He laughed when I mentioned my turn coming. He said I wouldn't make it in academia and it wasn't worth my time to go back to school."

And, "I didn't know how I ended up there or why I gave up everything to gain nothing, and I didn't know how to leave without making it worse. All I could think was I had to go. Go now and don't look back."

These were naked words and there was nothing I could do to cover up, to protect myself. There was no graceful exit to be had and no good place to put my hands. It was a matter of standing still and enduring the truth of it, blanking your eyes and mind enough to keep the overwhelming discomfort of it from spilling over.

It should've been easier considering this was the second time I'd taken myself apart and explained it all but explaining it to Leesa at the shop in Denver was like nothing compared to Ash.

He reached for his coffee but set it down without drinking. "I have five different things to say about this but I need you to know none of it matters. Obviously, it does matter but not to me. You are the same little Mary Poppins moonbeam you've always been and nothing can change that for me."

I picked at the remains of my sandwich, pressing my lips together. I couldn't decide whether I was holding in a smile or tears or a delirious laugh because a minute ago, I was dreadful and misshapen and *bare* and now I was a moonbeam.

"Next," he started, tapping a finger on the table, "that guy is a dirt bag. An actual bag of dirt."

"I know. I see that now." My shoulders slumped. "I should've seen it a long time ago."

He tapped the table again. "Don't do that. I won't allow it."

"You won't allow it," I said, fully amused.

"Not for a fucking minute, Zelda. I'd like it very much if you pursued a restraining order against him but that's not my decision. It's yours."

I bobbed my head. "I'll think it over."

"Another thing—no. No." He shook his head like he was carrying on a debate with himself. Lifted his mug. Set it down. Consulted his watch. "It can wait. The bottom line, for the purposes of this conversation, is you're here now and you're staying here—assuming that's what you want."

I had to laugh. "Ash. Sweetie. I'm attending your sister's wedding in a few hours. Your aunts pinched my cheeks last night. I'm getting a pedicure with some of the bridesmaids next week because that's apparently a thing they all do. I wouldn't be in Rhode Island with you and doing all these things if it wasn't what I wanted. Trust me when I say I'm better at boundaries and limits now."

"That's a relief." He reached for the mug, this time drinking before returning it to the table. "And speaking of the wedding, we have to get a move on. I have to be at the Blithewold mansion in an hour for photos."

I watched him glance at the check and count out a few bills. "I know. I've been tasked with getting you there on time."

Ash pushed to his feet and held out his hand for mine. "By all means, Miss Besh. Keep me in line. I'll be returning the favor to you tonight."

THE WEDDING, OF COURSE, WAS AMAZING AND BEAUTIFUL AND ALL the precious things weddings should be, and I watched it from the front row, beside Ash's parents. Before Magnolia's procession, Diana whispered to me that they weren't going to seat Millie with them but I was family and they were just so thrilled I wasn't Millie.

One of these days, I had to meet this Millie for myself.

The Blithewold grounds were gorgeous, the bride was radiant, and the groom cried at the right moments. And I was overcome with a hot, buzzy sensation that felt a lot like comfort. Maybe even belonging. I didn't have a parachute to pack or a collision to avoid anymore but a life to simply…live.

As this settled over me, I glanced up at Ash where he stood with the other groomsmen in their crisp navy suits. He met my gaze and pressed his hand to his heart but something went terribly wrong and he muttered, "Fuck" loud enough to catch the minister's attention. Snagging the handkerchief from his breast pocket, he said, "Please continue."

One last thing you should know about me was I loved this guy to pieces.

TWENTY-SIX
ASH

Today was perfect.

It was also imperfect in a thousand paper-cut ways but it was mostly perfect and I knew that when Zelda caught my eye and I attempted to cover the heart hammering in my chest for her with my hand but succeeded only in stabbing my finger all the way through on the corsage pin. There was blood, too much to address while my sister said her vows, so I sacrificed the silk hankie artfully arranged in my breast pocket and shoved the whole mess into my trouser pocket.

When I glanced back at Zelda, I found her eyes twinkling as she pressed her fingers to her lips to hold back the laughter I'd earned with my brief interruption of the ceremony. I still didn't believe in signs, not the ones outside of mathematics, but I believed in Zelda. More than that, I believed in me *and* Zelda. Us, together. Always.

And that was why I had to ruin it all.

———

I held out my hand to Zelda when the dessert plates had been cleared and the crowd on the dance floor had thinned. "Will you walk with me?"

She laced her fingers with mine. "Where would you like to go?"

I tipped my chin toward the far side of the grand reception tent, toward the waters of the Narragansett Bay. "This way? Or back toward the mansion? Your choice."

"Let's wander. We'll find out where we want to go when we get there."

We strolled for several minutes, wending our way through the grounds as bursts of music and exuberant shouts echoed from the tent.

"I'm happy you're here with me," I said.

"Not Millie?"

I barked out a laugh and tugged Zelda close, holding her tight to my chest. "Not Millie. Not for a minute."

"I'm happy I'm here too. I don't know if you've noticed but I like hanging out with you."

That was my opening, plain as day and waiting for me to seize it. "Have I mentioned you look incredible tonight?"

She raised our joined hands over her head and twirled, sending her floral skirt billowing between us. "An average of once an hour for the past seven hours. So, yes, you have."

"Once an hour? Couldn't be. I was with the bridal party for an hour before the ceremony, the only thing I said during the ceremony was a 'fuck' heard around the world, and I didn't see you for the first half of the cocktail hour. Not until my mother decided she needed you in the family photos since she's knitting baby blankets and keeping you forever. That's at least two and a half hours where I didn't get to tell you how much I want to crawl under this skirt or that I need all of your dresses to be backless from this point forward."

The number of times tonight I'd contemplated licking my way up from the dragonfly at her waist to the graceful juts of her shoulder blades was in the triple digits.

"Ah but I didn't say *every* hour. I said an *average* of once an hour. Back those two and a half hours out of the overall seven and distribute your generous if not fully obscene words over the remaining time. That averages out to one compliment every thirty eight-ish minutes."

"I love you."

She took that overripened truth from me and turned another pirouette, a laugh rippling out as the air caught her skirt. I wished the wedding photographer was lurking nearby because I wanted to remember this up close and also far away. I wanted to see the moonlight glowing on her skin and the flutter of her skirt and the unbound joy on her face. I wanted every side of this memory.

"There you two are! Di, they're over here."

We turned to find my father bounding toward us, half jogging, half strolling as if he couldn't pin down his level of urgency. His tie was loose, his suit coat was gone, and he clutched two flutes of champagne in his hands. And he looked happier than I could ever remember.

"We've been looking for you all night," he said.

I caught Zelda's eye and stifled a laugh. "We sat across the table from you through dinner and dessert. Did you not notice?"

My father dismissed these points with a wave of his hands which sent champagne sloshing over the sides. This didn't seem to bother him.

"I hope you know you have a hot one on your hands," he said with a nod toward Zelda.

Knowing my father meant recognizing this as a comment on Zelda's skill rather than her appearance. He also referred to kids and young people as *chicks* because—in his mind—they were new and youthful like spring chickens. He held tight to the expression *bitchin'* and generally struggled to understand how any of these words made for questionable choices.

My father was as complex and imperfect as the rest of us and it only took me thirty-five years to figure it out.

I rested my hand low on Zelda's bare back. "I noticed."

My mother bustled over, her high heels now swapped out for flip-flops with watermelon slices printed on the straps and the skirt of her long dress bunched up and knotted at her knees. "We've been looking for you all night," she cried. "Why did you leave the reception? The after-party is starting soon. You have to stay for that!"

Before I could dispute any of these claims, Zelda jumped in with, "I wanted to see more of the grounds. We won't miss the after-party."

I groaned at that but only Zelda noticed, responding with a light pat to my chest intended to shut me up.

"I've been thinking about our discussion last night," my father said to Zelda.

"Which discussion was that?" I asked.

Zelda's lips pulled up into a smile. "We had a chat on the walk back from the restaurant."

"You have some smart ideas." My father gave her a wink before running an appraising glance over at me. "Zelda thinks I can spend two full days each week out of the office. Maybe three come the new year."

I bobbed my head in the best show of blindsided agreement I could manage. "That's right."

"And without fielding frantic calls from my clients or finding them on the doorstep, wondering why some suit in the city"—that was me, I was the suit in the city, the villain in this story, apparently—"will only communicate with them through email and internet portals, like some corporation."

"Of course," Zelda replied, appropriately aghast at the idea of anyone putting up with a *corporation.*

My father considered this, taking a sip from each flute of champagne. Then he lifted his shoulders, saying, "Let's do it."

"About time," my mother muttered.

He held out his hand, first to Zelda, then me. "I trust you kids to get it right."

Before I could ruin this unprecedented moment of peaceful professional coexistence with some kind of asshole comment about always getting it right, Zelda replied, "We will. This means as much to us as it does to you."

Tears gathered in my mother's eyes. She hooked her arm in my father's, saying, "Two of my babies are happy tonight, Carlo."

"What happened to Linden?" he asked, frowning down at her.

"Nothing *happened* to him," my mother replied. "That's the problem."

"I don't understand anything you're saying." He drained one flute, then the other. "What's the issue with nothing happening to him?"

"It's not one we can solve tonight." My mother cast a feral gaze back at the tent. "Although—"

Zelda hid a laugh behind her hand.

"What were you saying about the after-party?" I asked because the last thing my brother needed was a Diana-sanctioned night with a bridesmaid. It wasn't like he didn't see plenty of action from his lumberjack beard alone but a fix-up would ruin any and all of his plans to get wet in Bristol's waters. "Where is that? What's the plan? Magnolia mentioned something about chocolate chip cookie ice cream sandwiches and I hope to hell she wasn't lying."

I held Zelda close to my chest as my mother lapsed into a thorough explanation of the next leg of this event. There was to be food and drink, music and games. My sister had a special dress for this, something called a romper. And yes, chocolate chip cookie ice cream sandwiches.

Then, my mother stepped toward us and brushed Zelda's hair back over her ear. "I love your stripe of indigo," she said. "It suits you."

"You're sweet. Thank you for saying that," Zelda replied. "We'll be along to the party soon."

Since they adored her and hung on every word she said, my parents accepted this and turned back toward the tent. If I'd said it, they would've dragged me along by the collar.

Once we were alone again, I asked, "Is there anything you can't do?"

"Many, many things," she said, laughing. "Can't walk in heels at all. Can't pick out a ripe melon. Can't mix a cocktail. Shall I continue?"

"You can but I still won't believe it."

She squeezed my arm. "You're adorable. Even when you work real hard at making people think you're not."

Instead of responding, I pointed at a bench nestled between two massive rhododendrons and guided Zelda there. Once we were seated, I lifted her legs onto my lap and watched her gaze out at the slow-lapping water.

I knew three absolute, incontrovertible truths as we sat there, my hands traveling over her legs and her smile outshining the stars.

One—I loved Zelda in a gasping, defenseless, bottomless way and I'd wait an entire lifetime for her to love me back.

Two—she saved me in every way one person could save another and it was possible I saved her too.

Three—I had to fire her right now.

TWENTY-SEVEN
ZELDA

For the first time in as long as I could remember, I didn't need my parachute. The one I'd never finished mending, the one meant to rescue me from all my choices, situations. From myself.

I didn't need it tonight. I wanted to believe I didn't need it anymore but I knew better than that. Eggs in one basket, crops before the harvest, chickens before they hatched. All those farming metaphors applied here.

Though today felt like a turned corner. I knew I wasn't lost in my own life anymore. I wasn't dogged by fear and dread and *waiting waiting waiting* for something right to happen.

Weddings had that effect. They made life feel like it was overflowing with possibilities and there was hope for me and you.

Maybe that was why Ash blurted out that *I love you*. Maybe he was as caught up in the rush of all this as I was.

I hadn't replied because I was preoccupied with the amazed way those words slipped over his lips. Like he couldn't believe it —he couldn't believe me.

That was all right. I couldn't quite believe this either.

He circled his fingers around my ankle, tickling just a bit, and drew me out of my thoughts.

"You have fixed...everything," he said.

"I just pushed a few things around and found the right order for them."

"You fixed everything," he repeated. "Remember when I freaked out because I thought you didn't know what you were doing and I didn't want to let anyone else call the shots?"

"This sounds familiar," I joked. "Give me a minute. The memories are coming back."

"I was wrong about it but I still reacted." I nodded, not sure where Ash was taking this. "Keep that in mind, okay?"

A shiver crossed my shoulders. "What do you mean?"

He pulled in a breath, blew it out. "I accept your resignation."

I blinked. "What?"

"You fixed everything for me and now I have to fix something for you. I can't let you work for me. I can't—I *won't* be another guy who expects you to give up everything you want only to make his life better. I won't let you spend your days riding herd on me and running my office when you belong elsewhere."

There was a knot in my throat, a thick ball of anxiety stuck there like a dry crust of bread. "What—you're—wait, you're *firing* me?"

"I'm not going to let you force yourself to believe you want to manage an accounting office or you could be content with that work. That's not what you want, my love."

And this was why I couldn't put that parachute in storage yet. "But I want—"

"You want archaeology. You want to study pre-Columbian peoples and something about their deaths. You want academia and research and all of those outrageous Indiana Jones adventures."

I rubbed my temples. "You did not just bring Indiana Jones into this."

"Zelda, I *love* you. And because I love you, I can't let you waste your time working for me."

I couldn't catch up. One minute I was being fired, the next he loved me. And—and he wanted me to return to grad school. "Okay but you—you—"

"I love you," he cut in. "I love you and I need you, and all of that is too big to let you be anything but exactly who you are. Believe me, Zelda, nothing in the world would make me happier than waking up with you every morning and going to work with you every day but I'm not going to be the next selfish bastard in your life. The only place I'll be the boss is in bed and only when you want it that way."

He just didn't understand. That was it. "But I like your office. I'm good at this."

Ash nodded. "You like nurturing lost causes and you like enormous, impossible projects. You like fixing broken things and solving problems."

"Right and it serves to reason I'll be plenty fulfilled solving all the new problems you invent for yourself next week and the week after and I can't wait to see what September brings."

I didn't know why I was fighting this so hard. It just seemed, I didn't know, *unwarranted.* And Ash needed the help though there was a slightly vengeful allure to the notion of returning to grad school. I'd earned much of Denis's degree for him so it wasn't like I couldn't cut it…though after hearing it from him for years, a voice deep in my head still told me I couldn't, I'd fail, I'd never succeed anywhere.

That voice was wrong.

"You like *your* work more," Ash said. "Get real, my love. You came here with one suitcase and it's half filled with archaeology textbooks and journals. You have to run the washing machine every other day because you prioritized books over clothes. That's a statement of priorities." He drew his fingers up my leg, behind my knee. "Here's what's going to happen. You're going to find me a capable office manager. That Nobel laureate you mentioned. You're going to train that person up and then help me and my father work together on non-violent partnership. You're also going to figure out which one of the two hundred universities in the area best fits your research agenda and we'll do whatever it takes to get you a seat in the fall session. Are you with me so far?"

I bobbed my head though— "Not to haggle here but you did say you'd only be my boss in bed."

"I'm getting to that." He hit me with one of his smirks that couldn't decide whether it was sweet or salty. "In the meantime, you're going to move in with me. More than you already are. You're going to hang up your clothes in the closet and put your books on the shelves, and you're going to stay because I want it as much as you do."

All I could say was, "Okay" and then, "Do you know I love you too?"

"Yeah, I do," he said, a grin brightening his face. "But it's damn good to hear it from you."

Because I didn't know how to believe, I asked, "Is this real?"

He reached for my hand. "It's real if you want it to be."

I stared at our joined hands, my dark olive skin layered against his light golden. The face of his watch was dim but I watched the seconds ticking by in the low light.

"You don't have to say anything right now," Ash continued. "Take all the time you want to think and—"

"Yes."

I didn't want to wait any longer for my life to begin. I was here with this old stone wall of a man, all weather-worn and unyielding, and there wasn't a single reason to wait. I'd done enough of that. I hadn't hacked my way through the thicket of my childhood and the nonsense of Denis to sleep on a future I'd all but forfeited for myself. Fuck all of that and then fuck it again.

"Yes?" he echoed. "Yes to—to what? What are you agreeing to?"

"Anything," I said. "I want to do this with you. I want to try."

He squinted down at his watch before offering me a small, precious smile. "Would you like to try marrying me?"

I turned his hand over, stroked his palm. "Might as well since I've already picked out a dress and your mother will need a new project come Monday morning."

A rumbly laugh burst out of him. "We'll take this part slow."

"There's no rush," I agreed.

"No. No rush at all." He leaned in, pressed a kiss to my forehead, my cheeks, my lips. "We have all the time in the world, my love."

EPILOGUE
ASH

The next summer

Today was off to an exceptional start.

It was a fine, sunny Saturday and since I was finished with business travel for the month after arriving home around eleven last night, I had the pleasure of waking up beside Zelda—who deserved a lazy morning after cranking through a hellish two weeks of summer session finals at Boston University.

The day only improved from there. We shared a long, slippery shower that left me disordered in a very pleasant way and then we devoured Zelda's famous pancake sandwiches. Life was really fucking good.

Since I didn't understand her "system," Zelda required me to sit at the kitchen island while she washed and dried the dishes. Letting her do household chores while I watched made me feel like an ass but I'd missed her face too much to busy myself elsewhere. Instead, I wiped down the countertops and watered

Kirby the cactus and her small potted herbs on the windowsill and stole every opportunity I found to touch her.

It'd always been this way, even before I'd realized it.

I'd loved her that way too.

"What should we do today?" Zelda asked, submerged up to her wrists in the soapy water.

I stopped behind her, settling my hands on either side of the sink. "I know what I want to do."

"Again?" she asked, laughing. "But I haven't seen you all week."

"I'm pleased you understand the issue," I replied, dropping to my knees and gathering up her long skirt in my fist. I looped a finger under the band of her panties and sent them falling to her ankles. "Be a good girl for me and spread your legs."

She did as I asked but did it while saying, "We should *do* something. Go somewhere. Isn't there a baseball game today? Why not a picnic in the park? How about a visit to that used bookstore we like over in Cambridge? Better yet, one of those sunset harbor cruises we always talk about taking?"

"I'll take you on a picnic, to a bookstore, on a cruise. I'll give you anything you want, my love." I ran my knuckles between her legs. "Just as soon as I feel this pretty little pussy come on my tongue."

A shiver moved through her shoulders and she released one of those high, breathy gasps that seemed to say "*ohhhh*" with six syllables. I traced the line of her ass down to her thigh and back up again, touching only enough to make her squirm.

"I'm not finished, you know," she said, as petulant as ever. "With the dishes."

"Go ahead and finish." I leaned in, dragged my lips up the silky skin of her inner thigh. "I don't mind." I licked the crease where her ass transitioned to her leg. "You taste as good as I remember."

"It's only been a few days, Ashville."

"You're delicious," I whispered as I closed my teeth around the curve of Zelda's ass. She gave a short squeal and I heard the water splashing. I smiled, brushed my knuckles along her seam once more. "Did I tell you to stop? No. Get back to work."

She was wet and swollen, rocking her hips toward my touch. I loved her in a way that lanced pain through my chest if I thought on it too long because it was a catastrophic kind of love, which was for the best as I had no intention of ever recovering from this.

I slipped a finger through her folds and rewarded her patience with my thumb on her clit. Her gasps turned into sighs as I circled the sweetest, softest spot on her entire body and bit along the low curve of her ass while the scent of her arousal flooded me, intoxicated me. That was my punishment, of course, since I was ignoring the best part.

No, wait, that wasn't true. Pussy wasn't the best part. Teasing Zelda in the kitchen on a lazy morning when neither of us had a mountain of responsibilities to climb was the best part. Biting my girlfriend's ass and saying inarguably rude things *that turned her on* while I did it was the best part.

Although— "When are you going to marry me?"

Because it wasn't enough to merely ask the question, I pushed three fingers inside her and pressed *hard* on the spot that made her a little senseless. I dropped my other hand to the small of her back, right where that dragonfly tattoo took flight, and shifted her into an angle that would give her what she needed.

There was a splash followed by dishes clattering in the sink. Then, "*Ash.*"

"Yes, my love?" I watched my fingers disappear inside her only for them to emerge coated in her arousal and my cock was ready to burn straight through my shorts. That did it for me every time. Her responding to me, us coming together. We shouldn't have made sense, we shouldn't have even found each other yet here we were, sharing the most elemental thing of any world. "What is it? What do you have to say about making me wait?"

While it was amusing to imply Zelda was the one holding up our nuptial proceedings, that wasn't a fair portrait of reality. We simply hadn't had the time to make any progress, not with her diving head and shoulders into grad school last fall, my new business ventures keeping me on the road several nights each month, and my father scaling back to only one day a week in his office after tax season had ended. And that was on top of me and Zelda learning how to make this relationship work when we didn't get to spend every minute of every day together.

In the spirit of reality, I was the one who struggled most with my separation from Zelda during the daylight hours.

If the shortage of wedding vows spoken was anyone's fault, it was mine. As much as I'd wanted to seal this deal, there was no reason to rush. Zelda deserved time to come into her own. She'd spent far too long sitting on the shelf of her ex's design and even longer putting up with that horrendous family of hers. This was her shot at being whoever, whatever she wanted—and I had the fortune of watching from the front row.

Yeah, this was on me—but I was ready to change that.

"I'm waiting for an answer," I said, delivering an especially mean bite just an inch away from where she wanted it. "You know how I feel about waiting, Zelda."

"I—I—you know I want to," she replied, her words strained.

I slipped my fingers out and walked them along her back channel. It wasn't nearly enough pressure or friction, and the urgent rock of her hips confirmed it. "That's the best you can give me?"

"What do you want me to say?" she asked, breathless as she hooked a glance over her shoulder. "You want to set a date? Draft the vows? A promise I'll change my name? What do you want, Ash?"

"A ring on your finger to start," I said, retrieving the small box from my pocket, the one holding the sapphire and diamond ring I'd picked up in Phoenix last week. "I imagine the other pieces will fall into place after that."

Her lips parted and if I'd allowed it, this would've devolved into a precious, lovey mess of cuddles and tears on the kitchen floor. That wasn't happening. Not yet.

I set the box beside me and gestured for her to shift back into position, saying, "As you were. You'll get this when I'm through with you."

My hands filled with the globes of her ass, I leaned in and traced her seam until I found that hard pearl, all pink and eager for my attention. I gave her a long, hard suck as her hips rolled and her hands slapped against the countertop. Her legs shook as I flicked my tongue over her one last time and I knew from the throb I felt there she was primed to explode. In the end, it took only one, two thorough laps for those muscles to shiver and spasm, and all her unbelievable heat to rush over me, and then a violent pinch to her clit to make her scream.

I had my belt off, shorts unzipped, and cock out before she'd stopped twitching and somehow—*somefuckinghow*—managed to yank her down to my lap and slide inside her without anyone taking an elbow to the eye or tumbling over from the precariousness of it all. I'd mastered many things in my life but fucking my girlfriend—*fiancée*—with nothing but my arm around her waist to keep her from faceplanting on the kitchen floor wasn't one of them.

That I lasted all of two minutes was a blessing.

With Zelda still panting in my lap, I shifted back against the refrigerator. "I should tell you I'd planned to do this a bit less"—I motioned around the kitchen—"savagely."

"Why start now?" she asked.

"Fair point, Miss Besh." I kissed her temple and dropped the box into her hands. "This is for you."

She pried it open with care, as if she was concerned about the contents getting away. Then, "Wow. Just...*wow*."

"Does that mean you like it? I can take it back. I can have them make something different."

Zelda shook her head, saying, "This is quite perfect."

Since she was still clutching the box like it had the capacity to shapeshift, I plucked the ring out and slipped it on her finger. The large center sapphire gazed up at us like a bottomless lake while twin diamonds sparkled on either side. Smaller diamonds climbed down the band, twisting over and around the platinum. "I believe I deserve some acknowledgment for waiting more than a year to make it official."

Angling her hand to study the ring, she said, "Marital customs aren't my area of expertise but I thought the suitor was expected to get down on *one* knee."

"Am I being penalized for making it both knees and my face between your legs? Because I seem to recall you taking some gratification from that change."

She patted my arm. "No penalties," she said with a laugh. "It's just fun to push your buttons, Ashville."

There was a knock at the door and we frowned at each other but the sound of my sister's voice quickly answered all questions. "Ash? Zelda? I'm knocking and I need you to answer the door. I'll use my key. I swear, I will. I need to come in. Answer, answer, answer."

"Oh my god," I muttered. "What does she need at"—I shot a glimpse at my watch—"twelve thirty on a Saturday? Does she always have to barge in like this?"

Zelda scrambled off my lap and straightened her skirt, saying, "Does it matter? She's six months pregnant *with twins.* She's allowed to barge in."

My mother, for her part, had been cured of her tendency to invite herself into our apartment back in October when an eyeful of my bare ass and Zelda bent over the sofa greeted her one morning. Now, she called before she visited and called again before boarding the elevator. Just to be cautious. She was more interested with Magnolia and Rob these days anyway, always visiting to help with the nursery or something like that.

I tucked myself back into my shorts and hefted to my feet. "I don't have to like it."

Zelda paused near the door as I zipped up. "Will you like it when *I'm* six months pregnant with twins?"

"Ignoring for the moment that your question doesn't make sense, yes. When you're pregnant, I'll—" *Fuck.* I shoved my fingers through my hair because that notion was a tidal wave. It was a loud, desperate drowning in thoughts and images and emotions and *Fuuuuuuck.* "Yes, my love. You know I will."

She pressed her palm to her chest and that ring glinted back at me like a beacon. "You're right, I do know."

"I can hear you in there," Magnolia yelled. "Could you have

this conversation after I pee? Because that's the only thing that has to be resolved right this instant."

"Let her in. I'll never hear the end of it from my mother otherwise," I said.

Zelda held the door open for my sister, who bustled past us for the bathroom down the hall, calling, "Open a window. The sex hormones wafting off you two are making me woozy."

"We'll need to move." I gave the apartment an ambiguous shrug. "We'll need more space. For the twins," I added.

"And the ones we have after the twins," she offered.

"Bedrooms and…backyards," I said. "We'll need—"

"For real, dude, what is going on here?" Magnolia asked, drying both hands on her round belly. "The Very Serious Convo vibes are clashing with the Dirty, Dirty Sex vibes big time."

I blinked at her for a second. Then, "Technical question for you, Mag. Do we need to wait until after this situation"—I nodded at her belly—"is finished to get married? Does it matter to you?"

Magnolia plucked a band from her wrist and gathered up her hair as she shifted to face Zelda. "What is my brother asking me?"

Zelda held up her hand in response. Magnolia abandoned her hair to rush forward with an almighty screech. "Fucking finally," she cried, turning Zelda's hand to inspect the ring. "Am I the first to know? Please tell me I'm the first!"

"You're the first," my moonbeam bride replied.

"Yes, I love it when I'm the first! You're calling Mom and Dad right now, and Lin too. And then you have to call the girls, Zelda. They're going to die. Okay, that's the plan, you're calling *everyone* and I'll call a caterer," Magnolia went on. "An About Time Already engagement party at my house this evening. Bring your beautiful selves and I'll provide the rest." She was halfway out the door before adding, "Don't even think about getting married before these boys are born. I'm not waddling down any aisle and I'm not drinking cider instead of champagne. No autumn weddings for you two, not this year."

Suddenly, we were alone again and I said, "Spring it is, my love."

———

Thank you for reading! I hope you loved Ash and Zelda!

If you're looking for more of the Santillian triplets, check out The Belle and the Beard and The Magnolia Chronicles. Flip forward for excerpts.

Join Kate Canterbary's Office Memos mailing list for occasional news and updates, as well as new release alerts, exclusive extended epilogues and bonus scenes, and cake. There's always cake.

Visit Kate's private reader group to chat about books, get early peeks at new books, and hang out with over booklovers!

If newsletters aren't your jam, follow Kate on BookBub for preorder and new release alerts.

ALSO BY KATE CANTERBARY

In a Jam — Shay and Noah

Vital Signs

Before Girl — Cal and Stella

The Worst Guy — Sebastian Stremmel and Sara Shapiro

The Walsh Series

Underneath It All – Matt and Lauren

The Space Between – Patrick and Andy

Necessary Restorations – Sam and Tiel

The Cornerstone – Shannon and Will

Restored — Sam and Tiel

The Spire — Erin and Nick

Preservation — Riley and Alexandra

Thresholds — The Walsh Family

Foundations — Matt and Lauren

The Santillian Triplets

The Magnolia Chronicles — Magnolia

Boss in the Bedsheets — Ash and Zelda

The Belle and the Beard — Linden and Jasper-Anne

Talbott's Cove

Fresh Catch — Owen and Cole

Hard Pressed — Jackson and Annette

Far Cry — Brooke and JJ

Rough Sketch — Gus and Neera

Benchmarks Series

Professional Development — Drew and Tara

Orientation — Jory and Max

Brothers In Arms

Missing In Action — Wes and Tom

Coastal Elite — Jordan and April

Get exclusive sneak previews of upcoming releases through Kate's newsletter and private reader group, The Canterbary Tales, on Facebook.

ABOUT KATE

USA Today Bestseller Kate Canterbary writes smart, steamy contemporary romances loaded with heat, heart, and happy ever afters. Kate lives on the New England coast with her husband and daughter.

You can find Kate at www.katecanterbary.com

facebook.com/kcanterbary

instagram.com/katecanterbary

amazon.com/Kate-Canterbary

bookbub.com/authors/kate-canterbary

goodreads.com/Kate_Canterbary

pinterest.com/katecanterbary

tiktok.com/@katecanterbary

ACKNOWLEDGMENTS

The spring of 2020 was a weird time to write love stories with kissing and close proximity. So much of a weird time that I wrote two-thirds of this book in notebook on my front porch because being near a computer screen always led to doom-scrolling and low key hyperventilating.

I want to take a moment to thank all the people who helped make me to make this book a reality during a truly bizarre and harrowing time.

Sarah Hansen, who went round after round until we got the cover right...and then did it all over again.

Julia Ganis, who saw this book at its fledgling stages and helped it get its legs.

Marla and Jodi, who got me to the finish line.

Jess, who shepherded me through the "I think I need to change the title" experience and Mae, who landed the title.

My husband and child, who both put up with me, my ever-present notebook, and my occasional yelps about not being able to visit coffeeshops for "alone" time to write.

www.ingramcontent.com/pod-product-compliance
Lightning Source LLC
Chambersburg PA
CBHW061218190726
48288CB00001B/232